FAULT LINES

SHACKELFORD INVESTIGATIONS
BOOK 3

KRISTY ROLAND

To Roland and Tiffany.

Author's Notes:
If you are familiar with the Fayette and surrounding counties in Georgia, you will notice that I have taken great liberties in describing these areas. It was done in an intentional manner to fit the story as needed. All representations of police procedures may have been altered for the story.

Chapter 1

October 2016

Mitchell Shackelford walked into his house two hours later than he told his wife he'd be home. By now, the kids would have had their homework done and had supper. They were all in the living room when he walked in to say hello and he saw the scorned look on Renee's face as the boys ran to him.

"Sorry I'm late," he said, to no one in particular.

They were excited to see him, and that made a bad day much better. Seven p.m., and Renee sat on the sofa with her legs curled under her, ignoring him, so he walked over and tried to kiss her. She turned her head and his lips landed on her cheek.

Not good.

"Your supper's in the microwave."

"Thank you." Mitchell peeled his seven-year-old son, Luca, off of him, and walked into the kitchen.

Mitchell wasn't hungry. He'd eaten at Shackelford—the investigations office—also home to

Mom and Dad. Lately, he'd eaten there a lot. He took the plate out of the microwave and wrapped it in plastic, set it in the fridge.

In the mudroom off of the kitchen, Mitchell pulled his boots off, the tight boots peeling off like a skin.

Renee stood in the kitchen with her arms folded over her chest. "Are you going to eat?"

"I ate at Mom's."

Renee pulled the microwave door open, saw it was empty, then moved to the fridge where he'd set the plate. Then she threw the whole damn thing in the trash; plate and all. "You should have called."

Mitchell fished the plate out of the trash, scraped the food off, then set it in the sink. He said nothing to his wife. Didn't argue with her. Had to tread carefully. He wasn't sure where the eggshells were right now, so he watched his step. That didn't matter. Renee walked over to him and slapped him in the face. He saw it coming and didn't stop her. The sting of the slap wasn't as bad as the hurt look on her face.

For a long minute, she looked at him, daring him to say something. And he wanted to. The moment Renee got off of the sofa, all three of his kids ran into their bedrooms.

He wasn't exactly sure how they'd gotten to this point in their marriage, but the more withdrawn Mitchell became, the worse it got. Sometimes he didn't even want to come home.

He said, "I'm sorry. I'll remember to call next time."

"Your sister ate the last of the sandwich bread," Renee said.

"I used all the bread."

"Then you can go get another loaf." Renee started wiping down the counter. "I don't have anything for school lunch tomorrow."

"I got another one." He pointed to the grocery bags on the kitchen table.

"The bread wasn't here when I needed it, so you can make the kids' lunches before you go to bed. She left the back door unlocked again."

The "she" being his sister Sidra who had been kind of living with them on and off for the last four months. "I'll talk to her," Mitchell said. "What else would you like for me to help you with?"

"Nothing, Mitchell. I work a job that doesn't stop either, okay? I still manage to be home on time, and cook and clean and take care of the kids. Help them with homework, get them to practices, do all the grocery shopping. And I still have to manage my teaching plans every night. You agreed just last week you'd help more around the house."

"I'm sorry," he said. "I don't know what else to say. Private investigating isn't a nine-to-five job. I go where the work takes me."

"Maybe you should get a new job." Renee began rinsing the dish towel. "It's not like you make a fortune working for your dad."

"I like my job."

"Lucky you."

Mitchell sighed heavily. "I'm tired, Renee. I'd really like to go shower and spend a few minutes with the kids before I go to bed."

The way she looked at him, after being married to her for fourteen years, she thought it was going in one ear and out the other. It was, of course. But Mitchell didn't know what to do. Renee's patience disappeared a couple of years ago, and he had to wait for permission from his wife to leave the room.

"Go," she said.

Guilt washed over him as he walked away, and he didn't know what he was guilty about. How did they get here? Sometimes he thought about leaving, even though the house was his. It was in his name. The house he was raising his family was the same house he grew up in, a house Dad bought years ago when the area was okay. Mitchell had gotten a good deal on the three-level brick and felt good living here.

At thirty-seven years old, he'd lived at least thirty-two of those years in this house. After he and Renee got married, they'd found a little house in Fayetteville, but then when Mom and Dad wanted to sell this one, Mitchell couldn't let it go. The place had too many memories.

Not a day passed, he didn't think about his own childhood with his four siblings.

The master bedroom would always be his parents' room. Sure, everything was his and his wife's, but the laughter of his own children was the laughter of his brothers and sisters. That was too much to give up.

But sometimes he thought his wife and kids would be happier without him.

Mitchell didn't take a shower. With the way his wife dismissed him, he ended up in the basement, working out in the little room that used to be his old bedroom. He warmed up with quick stretches and noticed the scratch near his eye where Renee's fingernail caught him.

In all the years, he'd never hit his wife back.

First it was the yelling, then it was the slapping. She never hit the kids though. Yelled at them all the time, sure. But she never hit them. He was thankful for that, and if it meant taking the brunt of her frustration, he'd do it.

The two-hundred fifty pounds of weights were there from last night. Not bothering to remove any weight, he lay on the bench and worked his arms. Maybe his muscles would rip to shreds. Maybe he'd just drop the weights on his face and the anger would go away.

Mitchell needed a hit.

Something to keep him going.

When he put the weight bar back on the peg, he heard, "Jesus, Mitchell." Sidra stood in the doorway. "Why don't you just bench press the house?"

Mitchell breathed hard. "I'm thinking about it." And just throwing the house across the lake.

The way his sister looked at him—he couldn't stand it. The longer she looked at him, the more she knew about his dark secrets. She was good at figuring people out and hiding her own secrets.

"You left the back door open again."

"You and I both know I didn't leave the door open. Why do you say that?" Sidra pulled off her blue leather jacket and picked up a twenty-five-pound dumbbell, which she began curling with both hands.

"Just make sure it's shut, okay? You should warm up first."

"You should cool down," she said, narrowing her gaze at him. "I'm glad we found the boat."

The case they'd been working on was an asset recovery for a client with a stolen boat. Sidra spent two weeks pretending to be Daisy Carmichael, a boat enthusiast who wanted to buy a used Yamaha 212 jet boat. She sweet-talked the guy on a date and finally got word of who he'd sold the boat to. Where Sidra found her balls to be in the face of people, Mitchell didn't know. Not much scared him except watching his little sister walk into the hands of danger. She'd walked out of the man's house with an address, just before the police showed up to arrest the man for theft.

They'd driven all the way to Lake Lanier, back and forth, for two weeks to close this case. The boat was seventy grand, brand new. The jackass sold it for fifty. That didn't matter to Mitchell, Shackelford made a pretty penny locating the boat.

Mitchell focused on his weights, and Sidra picked up a second one. It's what he liked about her, even though she talked too much. Sidra could jump in and do anything. Change a car tire. Make a cake if she really wanted to. Last week, she helped him cut a couple of trees down.

Where was his wife? Bitching because of the noise because she had a headache. When Mitchell finished pounding away at the weights, his muscles aching with fatigue, he walked upstairs for a long, hot shower.

After his shower, he found his eleven-year-old daughter in her bedroom, working on a school project that involved a lot of fucking glitter. "Your mother's going to be upset with you."

"She already said something."

Renee walked in at that point and handed Caroline a stack of magazines. "The carpet's already ruined from the nail polish and glue and everything else. The house is going to end up looking like you sprinkled fairy dust everywhere."

Mitchell was in there for five seconds and already had hot pink glitter in his leg hair. "Do you need help?" He smiled at his daughter as he took a few steps back.

"No, Daddy. You'll try to tell me everything is crooked when I glue it on." Caroline flipped through a magazine. "Mom, I promise to be in bed by ten."

"Nine o'clock, Caroline." Renee looked at Mitchell with some kind of compassion, as if whatever

7

happened earlier never really happened. "Can you get Luca out of the tub, please?"

Mitchell quietly pushed open the kids' bathroom door. Luca was in the tub with the shower curtain pulled closed because he always got too much water on the floor. Mitchell sent one of his little toys sailing over the top of the curtain and listened as it kerplunk'd in the water. Luca feigned a scream and pulled the curtain open.

"Time to get out, buddy." Mitchell pulled the plug as Luca protested and tried to catch all of his toys, as if they were getting sucked down the drain with the water.

"What happened to your eye?" Luca said, and heat flashed through Mitchell's body.

How did Luca even notice the scratch? "Oh, I scratched it trying to get into the van this morning. No big deal." Mitchell grabbed the towel and handed it to his son. Watched him dry off.

Luca said, "I got a paper cut yesterday at school and my teacher told me to rub dirt on it. So I did. Then she sent me to the school nurse. Then the nurse asked me why I rubbed dirt on my paper cut. So I told her that Mrs. Higgins told me to and she didn't believe me."

Mitchell handed Luca his clothes. "It's just an old expression. Grandma used to tell us that all the time when we were growing up whenever we hurt ourselves."

"Why?"

8

"It just means that it's not a big deal."

"A paper cut is a very big deal, Daddy. They hurt."

Mitchell ruffled Luca's hair. "Nah, you're tough. You fell and got four stitches last year and barely cried."

This made Luca laugh because, in fact, someone would have thought when he fell off his bike, he'd have broken his neck.

In Spencer's room, as soon as Luca saw his brother using his Nintendo Switch, he said, "Hey, that's mine."

"You said I could play with it."

"I meant just yesterday."

Mitchell told Luca to put the game in his room. It was almost time for bed. When Luca came back, he jumped on Spencer's bed and so began their night time ritual of Mitchell playing the monster who tried to wrestle the boys into a blanket.

Renee yelled from their bedroom, "Someone's going to get hurt."

Luca called back, "We'll just rub some dirt on it."

"What?" Renee said, with laughter in her voice. "Don't come crying to me..."

Luca jumped on Mitchell's back.

When the boys were tucked into bed, Mitchell climbed into his own bed while Renee sat up with two stacks of papers.

"Do you need help?"

"Grading papers?"

Mitchell found his wife's bare leg under the sheet. "Or help with something else."

Renee didn't bother looking at him, kept looking at her stupid papers with that red pen in her hand. She taught fourth grade at the same school their kids attended and he didn't understand how she could handle being around all those kids all day. He could barely handle the three he had. Luca was their handful.

When Mitchell woke up in the middle of the night, his brain jazzed up in that familiar way. He quietly climbed out of bed, got dressed, then made his way downstairs to the outdoor garage.

He slipped inside and found the coke where he'd left it in an old red toolbox. Checked his back as if someone was watching him, and remembered he forgot to lock the door. But it was midnight.

Mitchell sat down in an old recliner that they'd gotten out of his grandmother's house when she passed away. The coke hit him and he sat there for a minute, pulled out his cell phone to make the call.

Thirty minutes later, Mitchell pulled off the highway in Jonesboro to the motel on Tara Boulevard. He got out of his van and knocked on door 1025.

Chapter 2

Sidra sat at her desk across from Daley, who seemed distracted. He kept adjusting the cap on his head, trying to get the fit right, but that was far from the truth. The black UGA cap was so old it had faded to gray and the fabric on the brim frayed and fit his head perfectly.

Sidra said, "Mitchell's using again."

"When did he stop?"

The hypocrite in her couldn't say anything as she finished her vodka and sweet tea concoction at noon. She'd managed to go a few days at a time without drinking, and that was good news. At least now she thought about consequences of her drinking.

"Renee's going to get fed up with him."

"Maybe he's fed up with Renee." Daley cocked his head at her. "You women have a way of—"

"Grabbing a man by the balls and squeezing?"

"If that's how you want to put it. Like we have room to psychoanalyze Mitchell."

Sidra and Daley were the two out of the five siblings who weren't married. "I'm just worried about him, that's all. He doesn't seem happy."

"I'll tell you who you should talk to about it? Mitchell. That's another problem you women have. Talk to everybody else about it except the person you have the problem with."

"I was just looking for some insight."

"I gave it to you. Simple. Either talk to Mitchell about it or stop running your trap to me." After a few minutes, Daley said, "Jorie told me you took her on a surveillance job with you."

"Yeah, I did. We had a lot of fun."

He took a deep breath and adjusted that stupid cap again. Sidra knew where this was going. "You can't take my fourteen-year-old daughter on driving expeditions while surveilling clients. You let her drive. She doesn't have a permit yet."

"She's actually an excellent driver. I think that dirt bike you bought her really helped."

"Stop being so careless with my kid. You were taking photographs from the van while she drove down Highway 85. She's fourteen."

"Working in teams makes the job much easier."

"Please," Daley said. "She's more of your accomplice than niece. I can see it now. You'll take her to get her first tattoo. Take her out drinking on her twenty-first birthday."

"You can join us if you'd like."

"You're bailing her out of jail if it ever comes to that."

Two months ago, Jorie drove her dirt bike down the main road because Sidra told her it was okay. It wasn't, but thankfully, Sidra was dating a cop. It all worked out when another police officer pulled her over.

Sidra finished with the notes she'd been putting together about the boat recovery. She was proactive about keeping up with her case notes as she gathered information. Mitchell, the paperwork slacker, would let it pile up, so she did all the work for him when they worked together.

Daley said, "Look up," and when Sidra did, he had a nerf gun aimed at her, shot the spongy bullet before she could even protest. Jesus, was he twelve or thirty-something? The dart hit her between the eyes, right on the bridge of her nose, and he laughed.

Without thinking, Sidra grabbed the empty Mason jar she'd been drinking out of and threw it at him. But that asshole ducked, and the glass hit the window right behind him where it spider-webbed the size of a dinner plate.

"Oh shit," Sidra said, pressing her hands to her face with her best Kevin from Home Alone impression.

From across the house, they heard Dad yell, "What was that?" and then pounding footsteps as he walked through the sitting room.

"Shit." Sidra stood up fast and made it to the sitting room at the same time as Dad. "I don't know," she said. "Scared the crap out of us. Maybe it was a rock?"

Shackelford Investigations was in an old renovated Victorian style home on a busy highway in Fayetteville, Georgia. The location sat between a hair salon and real estate agency, which they shared a parking lot.

She and Dad walked outside to the front porch, where he checked the window. "We heard the noise, but—"

There was no rock, and Dad carefully ran his hand over the glass. "The break's from the inside." He had that look on his face that he used to give them when they were kids, and they'd done something stupid. He walked back inside into their office. Daley sat in his chair, leaning back. The mason jar and nerf gun disappeared.

Dad inspected the window and shook his head. "What are you two doing in here?"

"Nothing," Daley said. "Just working."

"You two think I'm an idiot? I was a cop for twenty years. That window better be replaced before I go to bed tonight."

After Dad left, Daley said, "How much do you think that's going to cost you?"

"Daley, I don't even have a house. I'm living in my brother's basement. This job doesn't pay shit, and you ducked, you cheater."

"Why don't you steal Mitchell's dope and sell that?"

The only thing that brightened her day was when Dominic Getty texted her and asked her to lunch at Clemmie's. Sidra had to admit that he looked fantastic in his police uniform when he walked in the diner. He stood near the doorway, checking the place for a full minute before he walked over to her. He leaned down and kissed her before he slid into the booth where he could keep his eye on the place. Not that there was anything wrong with Clemmie's. The cop in him never stopped looking for potential danger.

Clemmie's diner was in the heart of Fayetteville, a comfortable place where familiar faces showed up every day. Dominic didn't live around here and the first day Sidra brought him to eat at Clemmie's, he thought he'd died and gone to heaven. This was the place where all the cops showed up for coffee in the morning and pie for lunch.

She'd ordered herself a burger, and had a turkey sandwich waiting for him because he didn't have long. "Hi," he said, his dimples sinking in as he smiled. Their relationship was strange, considering Sidra was homeless. They'd meet for lunch and dinner when they could, and she'd invite him to Shackelford sometimes when no one was there. When their schedules worked out, he'd go over to Mitchell's and spend the night, but Dominic thought for sure Renee hated him. "It's me she doesn't care for anymore, even though I've known her since I was fifteen," she'd told him. "Therefore, you're unlikeable by association."

15

Dominic's knuckles on his right hand were scraped. "What happened?"

"This guy tried to get away, and I scraped my hand on the concrete." Dominic looked out the window and she could tell it bothered him. He said, "The guy was complying, and everything was going right, and then he tried to run before I could cuff him. And I hate when I have to be an asshole to people, but they do it to themselves."

"I'm sorry," Sidra said.

"No, I'm sorry. I don't mean to ruin lunch." Dominic held a lot of his work in, only told her about the funny parts of his day. Sidra dug around into her bag and pulled out a tube of antibiotic ointment. She reached over and grabbed Dominic's hand, then rubbed a smidge of ointment on each of his knuckles for him.

"All better," she said.

Val, their waitress, came over. Tattoos covered both her arms in sleeves, and she had earrings down the length of both her ears. She said, "Where have you been?" as if she hadn't seen Sidra a few days ago. It was a relief that Val wasn't pissed when the apartment Sidra rented from her had burned down, which was why Sidra was homeless.

Dominic said, "They got you running around here all by yourself?" He flashed Val that smile that was always on the side of flirtatious. He even gave it to Mom sometimes.

"We're always short staffed. I'm training a new girl. Tell me how she does."

The girl wasn't a girl at all. She was a middle-aged woman who didn't seem to have a problem keeping up with the busy diner. They ate their lunch and five minutes later, Sheriff VanBuckle walked in.

Dominic rolled his eyes because he was city police, and there was always some beef between the city cops and sheriff's deputies.

Ignoring the Sheriff, Dominic said to her, "You really need to find your own place."

Yeah, she thought, because she was tired of following her brother around late at night when he was up to mischief.

***

Sidra noticed the white truck in the parking lot and thought little of it until she stepped through the back door into Shackelford. With a sense of déjà vu, she heard Casey Lincoln's voice and felt his presence before she'd seen him.

Casey and Dad stood near the front door, and Casey had a file folder in his hand. Certainly, he wasn't there to hire them. The man was an ex-criminal who could do his own investigative work. He didn't smile when Sidra walked up to them. Dad did though, and he said, "You remember Casey?"

How could she forget? Whatever job Casey had hired them to do, she wasn't going to help. Not after she almost died saving his son from drug dealers, and then he blamed her for the efforts. Brandon Lincoln, his innocent four-year-old son, was shot while they tried to escape. Now he lived in Utah with his Aunt Lexie.

Sidra noticed Daley walking across the front porch with his cell phone pressed to his ear.

"Can I talk to you a minute?" Sidra looked pointedly at Dad. They walked into his personal office and Sidra shut the door. "What the hell is he doing here? I'm not finding anyone for him again."

Dad held up his hands. "He's here for me. I lost Juan Alonso and Casey speaks Spanish. Not fluently, but it's good enough."

"A fucking translator?"

"I do a lot of work in Clayton County." The county was diverse, with a huge Hispanic population.

"Get Google translate, Dad."

He chuckled. "Can you be tolerable for maybe a few weeks? I know I'm not interested in letting outsiders work with us, but this is necessary."

"He was a drug dealer. That doesn't qualify him as a legitimate translator."

"He'll do for now. He can talk to people."

While she wanted the details of the Marquez case, she didn't have the time or the energy to concern herself with it.

"Whatever," she said, resembling a petulant child and didn't care.

She walked past Casey, ignoring him as he ignored her. In the office, she sat down, and Daley knocked on the broken window from outside. He gave her a nod to say, *let's go*. That's how it worked sometimes. Never knew what was about to happen.

Daley walked to his truck, Sidra right behind him. She jumped in and said, "What?"

"You hear what happened to Brady Ardeen?"

Sidra's heart stopped as her body froze with fear. For a second, she said a silent prayer, begging that he wasn't dead. She swallowed down the fear and told her brother, "No."

"Someone broke into his house and assaulted him."

"How?" Sidra said. Daley nearly took the turn onto 54 on two wheels.

Brady Ardeen lived in a secured neighborhood. Willow Point Estates was two-square miles of multi-million-dollar homes to some of the wealthiest people in the state. On the north side of Peachtree City, the neighborhood sat secluded inside a gate that stretched from iron to brick for nearly a mile.

The code Sidra had at the gate no longer worked. That didn't surprise her. Brady Ardeen told her he never wanted to see her again. Not after the bomb she'd dropped on him last summer. And he'd held his end of that and had not contacted her.

After showing both of their driver's licenses, the security attendant gave a quick call to the resident they wanted to visit. The gate finally opened.

"How'd someone get in?" Sidra said, an obvious question that Daley didn't have the answer to. She thought about Brady's money. He made lots designing video games, had expanded from children's games to adult games. And just this year, he'd sold the rights to one of his games to a major movie production company.

Bradford pear trees lined the entrance to the neighborhood, which was more of a community than anything. During the spring, the white trees looked like two walls of snow, but now they were bare against the gray October sky.

Brady's house was like all the other monstrosities, and Daley circled around the fountain in the middle of the driveway. Sidra expected Beverly, Brady's live-in nurse, to answer the door. Instead, it was Brady's mother, Julie, who stood there.

She wasn't shocked, just confused. She said, "Yes?" and gripped the door in place, almost as if she hadn't recognized them. Sidra hadn't seen the woman in over fourteen years. Not since Brady's car accident that left him a C6 quadriplegic. "Is Brady expecting you?"

Daley said, "Hi, Mrs. Ardeen. Do you remember—"

"I remember you," Julie said. "What do you want?"

The hair on the back of Sidra's neck stood up. Julie Ardeen's coldness wasn't natural, but expected. The woman wasn't happy when she found out that her eighteen-year-old son was in a terrible accident. What started out as a chase ended up with two stupid teenagers racing down Highway 85.

Brady Ardeen didn't win.

No one won that day, not after their lives had changed forever.

"Brady called me," Daley said. "Told me someone broke into the house."

"It's been terrible," Julie said, and opened the door so they could step inside the large foyer. The floor throughout the entire house was a light gray marble to accommodate Brady's wheelchair.

Brady's Pitbull Peaches ran to them. Sidra hadn't seen the dog in a year, and she wasn't entirely sure who was more excited. When Brady rolled in right behind the dog, Sidra caught one glimpse of him and felt everything inside of her clinch. Lost in a time when he was the complete part of her true happiness.

Sidra said, "Jesus, Brady." A black bruise started on his cheekbone and stretched up to the corner of his right eye near his nose.

Daley walked over to Brady, the two of them smiling through the past of bad friendship. "Hey, man." Daley said. People spotted the wheelchair and thought Brady was a fragile butterfly. But that was far from the truth. Of course, he couldn't defend himself if someone broke into his home, but the man would not back down, either.

"What happened?" Sidra said.

Brady glanced her way, almost as if to ask why she was there. His hands curled into loose fists that sat casually on his lap. He had minimal use of his hands and fingers, but that hadn't stopped him from trying to be active. While he had use of his shoulders and arms, the tricky injury left him with weak wrist muscles but he managed to pick up items with the sides of his hands and curled fists.

"Let's go in the living room."

They walked down a short hallway to a living room with a giant TV mounted on the wall that no one used. A red sofa sat in the middle of the room with two black winged chairs on the right side. The coffee table sat at an angle so Brady could sit in his wheelchair and see his guests on the sofa or chairs.

Daley and Sidra opted for the sofa, along with Peaches, who jumped into Sidra's lap. Brady's mother sat in a chair across from them.

Brady said, "The police looked at the security footage from the gate. No one came in that way. The houses sit far enough back that the ones with front door cams didn't catch anything."

"When did this happen?" Daley said.

"Yesterday afternoon. Marcy answered the door, and I heard her scream—"

"Who's Marcy?" Sidra said. "Where's Beverly?"

Brady wouldn't look at her. Instead, he spoke to Daley as though her brother had asked the question.

22

"Beverly is out of the state right now, so I had to hire another nurse. Her name is Marcy Floyd."

Marcy probably wasn't as pretty as Beverly. Brady probably thought so, too.

He said, "It was two men in masks. They hurt Marcy pretty badly, and one of them kicked Peaches. One of them tied Marcy up and put her there." He pointed to the chair next to his mother. "One of them got Peaches into the pantry. She tore up everything, trying to get out. She bit the guy, but Peaches is—"

A scared wimp? Abused in a previous life, it would seem instinctive for her to protect Brady. But the truth be told, Peaches was too scared to protect anyone.

Perfect companion.

Terrible guard dog.

Peaches, who rested her head on Sidra's lap and had fallen asleep, immediately picked her head up when Brady mentioned her name. Now she looked at everyone with those little honey-colored eyes as if waiting for them to tell her it was okay.

"I was in my office working," Brady said. "I came out and saw the one guy tying up Marcy and I came over here, and ran my wheelchair into him. He punched me, and by then everything happened really fast. They ransacked the office and took my computer tower, which has all my work on it."

"Is that all they took?" Daley said.

"That's enough. My whole life is on that hard drive." Brady put his curled fingers to his face and Sidra wished she could reach out to him. Touch his face. If he would just look at her.

Instead, she rubbed Peaches's ears. The only connection she had to him. Except for the baby.

"I told him he shouldn't be living alone in this big house," Julie Ardeen said, wiping her eyes. "It's bad enough he can barely care for himself because he lives alone."

"Mom," Brady said. "I'm right here."

"I'm sorry."

"I have a live-in nurse who takes care of me. I didn't think I needed a bodyguard."

Julie leaned forward. "Peachtree City may be safe. And your neighborhood may have a security fence, but you can't defend yourself."

"That's a great way to make me feel less of a man."

"It's the truth, Brady." Her voice had gone up. "I told you this was a bad idea, but you wanted your beautiful house and your expensive things when you're just one single man who needs care for the rest of your life."

Brady sat there, looking embarrassed. "I didn't ask you here for your approval."

"How can you allow them in here? You just sweep it under the rug, forgetting it ever happened." And there it was, what Julie Ardeen was really trying to say.

Brady said, "Can we talk about this another time?" He backed up his wheelchair and said to Daley, "I'll show you the office."

Sidra didn't want to be alone with Julie, so she followed them. The room had windows looking out to the front driveway and two of the walls were floor to ceiling bookcases. A gaming station sat in the corner, but Brady did most of his work at a desk on the other side of the room.

Someone tossed the entire office looking for something. Books scattered the floor, tossed from the bookcase without a heedless thought. The TV lay on the floor with Brady's most prized video games everywhere. The little prototype monsters from the first children's game Brady created were all over the floor, as though someone had swiped their arm across the shelf. Framed posters hung askew on the walls.

"All they took was the computer tower?" Daley said.

"Yes."

"What were you working on?" Sidra said.

Brady ignored her and said to Daley, "They could have taken the house and didn't. I have two gaming stations and thousands of dollars' worth of games. Plus an iPad right there on the shelf."

Sidra said, "Can you answer my question? What were you working on?"

Brady looked out the window, his back to her. "I design games. I wasn't working on any one thing in particular. Merge Weaver sold, and I've been working with multiple developers who are brainstorming other projects who are using new 3D software. Kazoo was optioned for a third trial run in the same software. It's not one thing."

"Did you keep your banking account information on that hard drive?"

Brady still wouldn't look at her. "I have a financial manager who takes care of that. But yes, I had access to bank information through the computer."

"Why'd you call me?" Daley said.

"Because I need you to find my computer."

When they were walking out of the house, Brady said, "Sidra?" and she turned to him in a hopeful way, a slight optimism that they could talk about things. But when he looked at her, those rich brown eyes were cold with a hurt that she'd put there. He said, "I told you I didn't want to see you again."

"Brady—"

"I mean it. I never want to see you again."

Chapter 3

When Sidra and Daley got back to Shackelford, Woolsey was in the office chowing down on a sandwich while he sat at a computer by the window.

"Hey," they both said to Woolsey because he'd been working from home lately. The winter beard he'd grown out over the last few years was down to his collarbone.

"You needed a break from the twins?" Daley said.

"No," Woolsey said around a bite of sandwich. "Marquette and I decided we'd put the twins in day care a few days a week. What happened to the window?"

"Don't ask," Sidra said.

Woolsey said, "So what are y'all working on? What can I help with?" Woolsey was their computer guy who knew his way around data bases like he knew his way around sandwiches.

After Daley told him about Brady, Woolsey said, "Who steals a quadriplegic's computer?"

"We're going to go talk to Marcy. Wanna go?"

"Nah," he said, and turned back to his computer. "I'm too shy for that stuff."

After spending an hour getting information on Marcy Floyd, Sidra and Daley drove to Coweta County. Newnan was a popular place to live as it was a short drive to the airport and Atlanta.

Marcy lived in an older neighborhood off of Poplar Road. The one level brick house had a couple of missing shutters. A crossover sat parked in the driveway. Next door, two kids played tag in the front yard.

Daley tossed his cap on the dash and ran his hands through his short hair, trying to smooth down the hat hair. He checked his teeth in the mirror, then worked his hair again.

Sidra said, "You want to borrow my lipstick?"

"If you have lipstick in your purse, I swear I'll give you a hundred dollars."

"Bitch face." She got out of the truck.

"Don't be mad because I'm better looking than you."

Marcy answered the door after the third knock and seemed put out because she had to get up. "Can I help you?" She looked to be in her forties, had on purple stretch pants with little pandas all over them, and a floral scrub top.

Daley made the quick introductions and Marcy let them inside. The house smelled of pine cleaner and mouthwash. She led them to a sofa in the living room and asked if she could get them something to drink. They both declined.

Marcy's wrist was in a brace. "It's not broken, but that jerk did something to it."

"Can you tell us what happened?" Daley said.

"Well, if you're here questioning me, then you already know."

Daley smiled at Marcy, and then she smiled and looked down at her feet. His lavish good looks always got him far with the ladies. He said, "I'm really sorry about what happened to you. I bet it terrified you. I don't think anyone would think something that terrible would happen in Peachtree City. Especially not to Brady Ardeen. He's such a nice guy."

"Yeah," she said. "He's a nice guy, and he pays well. He's got a ton of money. I still told him I wasn't cooking for him, that's not what I do. It's a shame he got punched in the face. I can't imagine why someone would feel compelled to do that to someone in a wheelchair."

Sidra said, "The two guys wore masks. Did you recognize their voices or anything about them? Notice anything special about their clothes or hands?"

"No." Marcy still looked at her feet. Sidra looked at Daley and he shrugged. "The one guy who put Peaches in the pantry seemed furious. I don't know if it's because she tried to bite him or just angry in general. I told the police that these guys sounded like amateurs." When Marcy finally looked up at them, she had tears in her eyes. "I was really scared they were going to kill him."

That thought crossed Sidra's mind as well. "Were you aware of who Brady Ardeen was when he hired you?"

"No. I work for a company called Happy Home Care, and that's who Brady contacted. He told them what he was looking for and I interviewed. I think the only conflict we had was that he wanted someone who would provide meals for him because he said he was so busy. I'm aware he interviewed two other nurses. Maybe they'd cook for him, I don't know. I told him he needed to look into a personal assistant. He was looking for a live-in, but I worked from 6 A to 6 P, and he was okay with that."

"Can you walk me through what the guys said when they came in?" Daley said.

Marcy nodded. "I opened the front door, and they pushed their way inside. One of them pushed me to the floor, and that's when Peaches tried to get him, so he kicked her. I told him not to do that, and he told me to shut up. He grabbed me by the arm. That's when I screamed because he twisted my wrist. I thought he broke it, but he didn't. When he shoved me in the chair, he tied my hands behind my back. Then Brady ran into him with his chair. The guy almost fell over on me. You think the police are going to find who did this?"

"Probably," Sidra said, and looked at Daley. "It's Peachtree City."

"You think Brady's going to press charges?"

"I hope so."

"What happened after that? The second guy put Peaches in the pantry and came out? Then what?"

"The one guy punched Brady in the face, and he couldn't even fight back. Then the second guy walked out and told him, 'let's go' and then they went down the hallway."

"Did they know where they were going?"

"I don't know."

Daley said. "It's okay. It's hard to remember things when you're scared, but sometimes when you think about them later, a few things may make sense."

"The cops said the same thing."

Daley smiled at Marcy again, and this time she smiled back. He said, "Did they make Brady go into the office, or did he follow them?"

Marcy nodded. "They made him. One guy was in front, the other one who'd punched him, pulled his wheelchair from behind because it doesn't push. It's electric. I told Brady he should use a different wheelchair, but he likes the electric one. Who am I to say anything?"

Fifteen minutes later, when they were driving back to Shackelford, Daley said, "We need to find out who the other interviewees were, or we're probably looking at an inside job from someone in the neighborhood."

31

"Or some rival game developer who parked outside of the neighborhood and walked in through the woods near Buckingham Street."

"True," Daley said. "I'll go to the PTC police department tomorrow and see if anyone will talk to me. The masks bother me. Brady didn't recognize their voices, but would he have recognized their faces?"

"Good question."

***

Mitchell had forgotten to make the kids' lunches last night, and he'd spent all day thinking about how pissed his wife was about it. He woke up to help her get them ready for school, and then before they walked out, all three of the kids asked about their lunch.

And Renee, who had the patience of a flea, lost it. Why was it such a big deal? Couldn't the kids eat lunch at school for once in their lives? School lunch was perfectly fine for him. The only thing he could do now was offer to make the lunches and bring them to school, right?

When Mitchell got home from doing that, he cleaned the house for almost four hours. He worked out, then sat on his back deck with a beer. When his family came home, he even had dinner ready for them. Sure, it was just four o'clock in the afternoon, but his kids were starving after eating PB & J for lunch.

But Renee said no. They could have a snack and dinner was at five. As usual, homework came first.

Because the boys sat at desks all day, they ran around the house like Neanderthals. Caroline had a bad day because she'd forgotten her school project. Why on earth hadn't she called? He could have brought it when he'd brought lunch. Oh, because Mom said life was tough and if you forgot your work at home, it's too bad. To make herself feel better, Caroline proceeded to scream at her brothers about everything under the sun.

They ate cold baked chicken and macaroni and cheese and the feeling at the dinner table was just as cold. Undermining any decisions Mitchell made was how things worked when it came to the kids. Renee knew more about how to run a household than he did, said so point blank. The kids wanted sweet tea. She said no; the choices were water or milk. Renee stared at him with those disapproving eyes throughout dinner. The boys played a little too much at the table, which only grated on his nerves.

When Mitchell thought he'd snap, Renee said, "Where'd you go last night?"

A cold fear shot through him, almost making him hesitate. "What do you mean?"

"Don't be stupid," she said.

While he looked at his wife, he was aware that all three of his kids tried not to move in fear that they would be the next targets. He hated that she called him stupid in front of the kids. When he was growing up, if his parents had an argument, it was never in front of them. And never would his parents have called one another stupid.

"I'm not stupid."

"I didn't say you were stupid," Renee said. "I said 'don't be stupid' implying that you think I'm stupid and don't know what I'm talking about."

"Can we talk about this later?" he said.

Renee stood up from the table. "I don't even care."

Mitchell closed his eyes and took a deep breath.

"Daddy, look," Luca said. "I lost my tooth at school today." Luca held out a tooth in his hand at the same time he stuck his tongue between a little gap between his teeth.

"That's great, buddy. Looks almost like a shark tooth."

Caroline said with a soft voice, "Daddy, can I go?"

"Yeah."

Caroline carried her plate into the kitchen, and he heard Renee tell her to go back and finish eating her food, and then Caroline said the chicken was dry and cold. Renee didn't care about that. His daughter came back to the table with tears in her eyes.

"It's not too bad," Spencer said.

"Shut up." Caroline took a small bite of food.

"Daddy," Luca said. "Next time cook pizza."

Mitchell waited a few minutes and when the kids had eaten at least half of the shitty food he'd made—he wasn't a cook, he had to admit, but at least he tried—

he stacked all the plates and told the kids, "You can get up now."

In the kitchen, he noticed his wife had helped herself to leftover pasta while her own plate of food had been untouched. He started scraping food into the trash.

"Why are you throwing all of that away?"

"What do you want me to do with it, Renee?"

"Make them eat it later when they say they're hungry."

Mitchell stood there for a moment. "Who are you, Mommy Dearest?"

The pot of macaroni and cheese flew towards his head. It crashed against the back door and landed on the floor in a mess. Renee stood there, so mad she was shaking.

Mitchell held up his hands. "I'll clean it up."

"I just asked you a simple question."

"I can handle you being mean to me," Mitchell said, "but you don't have to be mean to them."

"What?" And the fury began. "I'm mean to them because I don't give them what they want on a whim? Because I make them eat dinner and suffer their own consequences of their choices? I'm sorry, Mitchell. I'm trying to teach them to be independent, and not have parents who wipe their asses all day long."

"Where is all of this coming from?" Mitchell grabbed the broom. He was going to have to mop the kitchen again. "Nothing I do is good enough for you."

"Maybe you don't try hard enough."

"Maybe you're right, Renee."

Later that night, Mitchell grabbed a pillow and a blanket and lay on the sofa thinking about when he was a kid. When things were simple. He didn't know then how simple things were. Being the oldest, he was always responsible for his siblings. He had no freedom sometimes, with Daley and Sidra always following him around. Jesus, those two would fist fight so bad, Dad started calling them Rocky and Apollo. And even when his brother would be in trouble for hitting his sister, she'd antagonize him to no end. And after that, they were best friends.

Mitchell thought about Renee and wondered why his best friend—a woman who he believed to be his soul mate—had turned against him. What had he done? He could analyze it all day long and do what he thought she wanted, and in the end, it was never right.

When he couldn't sleep, he found himself in the garage, lounging in the chair for a long minute before he made another phone call. While he drove to Jonesboro, his phone started buzzing. It was Sidra, and he didn't answer it. At midnight, she'd probably watched him leave and wanted to know where he was going. She could mind her own fucking business.

Chapter 4

The rundown motel sat off of the highway with a vacancy sign flashing in neon red and blue letters. Mitchell parked at the end of the lot near the dumpsters as a guy came out of room 1025. Mitchell sent a text and when he received a response, he got out of the van and knocked on the door.

Helen Ross had on jeans and a dark blue blouse. "Hey, Mitchell," she said, and let him in. "I didn't expect to see you three times in one week."

"Me neither," he said, and took his usual spot in the armchair near the window. "Things are getting pretty bad." While Helen Ross was an attractive woman, her face was too bony, and she had a slight overbite and thin lips. Renee had a round face and beautiful eyes, and her lips were full and inviting. Renee's eyes and lips brought him to his knees, sometimes for two different reasons.

The lights in the room cast a shadow over Helen Ross as she sat in a chair five feet in front of him. She lit up a cigarette. "Tell me what's going on."

Mitchell found her through a friend of a friend. Okay, not exactly a friend. A former client who'd gone to jail for dealing drugs. A friend of an acquaintance, to be accurate. He gave him Dr. Ross's phone number and said she worked discreetly whenever and wherever a person needed to meet.

Mitchell reached into his pocket and handed Helen fifty dollars, which she put in a black zip pouch. He said, "I did all the things you suggested and nothing is working."

"Are you listening to what your wife is saying before you react?"

"Yes," he said. "And let me tell you what happened tonight." After the macaroni and cheese story, Mitchell lifted his hands. "I cleaned it up, and she acted like it was my fault."

"Mommy Dearest?" Helen said and blew out cigarette smoke. Mitchell really wished she didn't smoke. Renee would smell it and kill him if she thought he'd been smoking. "Did you tell her you were here last night?"

"No."

"You should," Helen suggested. "You need to let your wife know exactly how you feel about the way she's treating you."

"I tried reading the book you gave me," Mitchell said. The book was Love Lost and How to get your Marriage Back. "It doesn't make sense. I do the things it suggests and the things my wife wants me to do, and no matter what, it's wrong."

"Have you thought that your wife might need some counseling?"

Mitchell snorted. "Yeah, you tell her that."

"Tell me a little more about your wife." Helen crossed one leg over the other and looked at him, really looked at him. No one's looked at him like that in a long time.

"God," he said, because he didn't even know where to start. "Will you think I'm a bad person if I think my wife is a bitch? But I love her so much, I'm willing to live like that? And she's a bitch to my kids, too. And I'd never tell her this to her face, except for the Mommy Dearest thing. Which makes me a bad person because I can't tell my wife she needs to chill out."

"It doesn't make you a bad person. We deal with things in life the way we're conditioned to do so. Were things always this bad?"

"No," Mitchell said, and leaned back in his chair. "I knew she had problems, but she used to handle things better."

"What kind of problems?"

"Her parents, for one. They got divorced when she was ten, I believe. And both of them have been married two or three times. I met her when I'd gone to talk to her roommate about this case my dad was on. I was new to the job, and she was still in college."

Mitchell smiled. The smile didn't last long, the way the excitement of the relationship fizzled out around the time Luca was born. That was seven years ago.

"Are you still not sleeping?" Helen said.

"Not really."

"I can write you a prescription. Anything you want. But you have to take it to the little place on 5th and Broom Street."

He wanted to ask her if she could write one for cocaine. Could she do that? "It's okay," he said. "Talking to you helps more than you know."

By the time Mitchell was back on the boulevard, his nerves had calmed down. That was until he noticed his sister had called him again while he was in the room. He didn't call her back. Mitchell swung through the Taco Bell drive-thru and had to wait nearly five minutes in line. Why were they so busy at one o'clock in the morning? And then he had to wait even longer when a damn cop pulled a guy over right at the entrance, and Mitchell couldn't back out because the moron behind him wouldn't move.

He ate the quesadilla and thought about all those late-night surveillance gigs he'd done. Maybe his wife was right. Maybe he needed to find a new job. No, he couldn't do that. He really liked what he did. Pulling pieces apart to get to the root of a problem. He was good at that. Except he couldn't seem to figure out the root of his own marital problems.

Mitchell got home and quietly pulled off his boots. In the bedroom, he'd forgotten that his plan was to change clothes in the laundry room to get rid of the smoke smell. But Renee wasn't in bed. Or the bathroom. All three of the kids were asleep in their beds.

He opened the door to the basement and made it to the bottom of the stairs when Sidra came out of the extra room she slept in.

"I tried calling you fifteen fucking times."

"I was busy."

"Mitchell," she said, her tone getting his attention. "I followed you four nights ago to a shady motel in Jonesboro. I was trying to call you to tell you Renee followed you and if that's where you—"

"Fuck," he said.

And then Renee's SUV pulled into the driveway, and Mitchell froze. The kitchen door slammed shut and Mitchell's heart slammed into his chest. He had done nothing wrong except sneak out and lie to her about it.

"Next time, answer your phone," Sidra said.

He knew what this looked like, and now he had to face his wife. Mitchell walked back up the stairs and wished there were about fifty more steps, but when he reached the top, Renee was upstairs telling the kids to get up.

He ran upstairs. "What are you doing?"

"Leaving."

Luca started crying, and Caroline didn't want to leave. "Renee, don't do this. Let's go talk." She didn't want to talk. She wanted her kids to get up in the middle of the night and leave their home. "No," Mitchell said, blocking the doorway. He turned to the boys and told them to get back in their beds. Everything was okay.

Caroline stood in her own doorway crying. "Stop fighting," she said. "Why can't you stop fighting? If you don't stop, I'm going to run away." And then she slammed her bedroom door shut.

"Why would you wake them up?"

"I don't care if I wake up the whole fucking neighborhood."

He couldn't do this. Not when she was being this irrational. He turned to leave, and she said, "Don't walk away from me."

But he did. They'd never fought this bad. The tension between them was unbearable. He'd just gotten to the back door when Renee grabbed him by the back of his shirt. "I saw you, Mitchell. You don't have to lie to me."

"You saw me what? Go into a motel room?"

Renee slapped him.

"I'm getting really tired of that," he said, and tried to breathe to calm himself.

"Who is she?"

"Renee," he said, and shook his head. "It's not what you think."

"Tell me, Mitchell. Tell me who that fucking whore was that opened the door? Because when I knocked on the door to confront her, a man was half naked in the bed. I should have knocked when you were in there. I guess I would have my answers if I would have seen you in bed with her myself."

"What are you talking about?"

"What are you doing?" She threw her hands up and started crying. "You leave early and come home late. You sneak out in the middle of the night. You lie to me. I never know where you are sometimes. You're moody and you're quiet. You don't answer your phone when I call." She stood there in the kitchen against the light of the microwave. "You're using drugs again, Mitchell. And now you're sleeping around?"

"I just talk to her."

Renee exploded almost incoherently. Mitchell's brain shut down and all he wanted to do was get out of there. Then, when Sidra opened the basement door and tried to tell Renee to calm down, it only made things worse.

Sidra said, "I'm not trying to get into your business, but if I can hear you, the kids can hear you."

"Then why don't you get out of my house," Renee said. She turned to Mitchell. "And you too."

"This is my house."

"That's right," Renee said. "Your house. The Shackelford house. Fine, I'll go then."

***

43

Mitchell left before Renee said anything else, and Sidra knew that moving in with her brother was a bad idea. With a bird's-eye-view she was snooping in on their lives as it unraveled.

"Renee," Sidra tried. Her sister-in-law stood in the middle of the kitchen crying and she wanted to comfort her, but she was almost afraid to touch her.

"Just go," Renee said.

Downstairs, Sidra grabbed her things. She hadn't known things were this bad between her brother and his wife. The pillowcase she used as a bag filled quickly, but she had little left. That's how a person lived when they couldn't seem to settle down. Mitchell's van was in the driveway and Sidra looked for him in the outdoor garage, but he wasn't there either.

The house was on Pecan Pie Road. Such a sweet name for the angry people living inside the house. Sidra decided to walk down the street. It was one way in, one way out, with a cul-de-sac at the end. A long time ago, when Dad bought the house, there were five houses on the street. Now there were seventeen. She spent her entire childhood walking up and down Pecan Pie Road to the field. No one could build on the land because it was marsh. Behind the field was a pond. That's where she found Mitchell. Sitting on an old picnic table.

Pitch black out here. All she heard was him crying. In her entire life, hearing Dad or one of her brothers crying would be the worse sound in the world. If they fell apart, everything fell apart. Mitchell wiped his face with his hand as she walked up and sat next to him. Sidra was certain God woke up every morning and thought, *What have the Shackelfords fucked up today?* And they'd all go to church and ask for forgiveness.

"Remember when the Talberts moved in?"

"Yeah," Mitchell said with a slight laugh in his voice. "We let them know this was our pond."

"I peddled my bike all the way down the road, ran through the field, ripped my shirt off like my brothers, and started swinging."

"You'd do that now if nobody stopped you."

"I don't know about ripping my shirt off..."

She was seven when they fought the Talberts. Sidra pulled out a bottle of Jack Daniels from her pillowcase. "Five against five, and we kicked their asses and got our pond back." Sidra took a drink then handed the bottle to Mitchell.

"Donna Talbert was the first girl I ever kissed."

"I think Donna was the first girl Daley ever kissed."

"What? He never told me that."

They shared the bottle. The night was cool, and the moon played shadows on the water. Now that her eyes adjusted to the dark, she saw her brother in full view.

She said, "I had your back then, and I have your back now."

Mitchell nodded, not really able to say anything.

"She hits you because you use cocaine."

Mitchell shook his head. "I use because she hits me."

"When did this start?"

Mitchell shrugged. "She doesn't hit the kids."

"So that makes it okay?"

"No."

"Renee doesn't have to hit the kids. I saw Caroline smacking both the boys last week."

"Really?"

"Yes. You know the disdain when your life is upside down? Remember how crazy Mom and Dad were when Amy was missing?"

"That was different."

"No, it wasn't. There was so much tension in the house nobody knew what to do. You go to shady motels to make yourself feel better? How does that help?"

"I'm not sleeping with anyone," he said and looked at her. "I met this woman through a friend. A doctor. She works out of motels and offices. All I do is talk to her. She's a counselor and I only pay her fifty dollars to talk for an hour."

"Sounds shady to me."

"You're a hobo living out of a pillowcase."

Sidra couldn't argue with that. "I won't ask about details in your personal life. But what the fuck are you doing?"

"You followed me," he said. "That's not right."

"Are you listening to yourself? You're seeking counsel from a woman working out of a motel in the middle of the night. Did she propose sex?"

"No."

"Because what if she's an undercover cop or something? Did you buy drugs from her?"

"No. In fact, she'll write a prescription if someone needs it."

"And then as soon as you take the prescription, you get busted."

"It's not like that." Mitchell took another drink.

"You should go home and apologize to your wife."

"I thought you said you had my back."

"I do," Sidra said. "But Renee is my family too, and I need a place to sleep tonight."

"Always an angle with you. I can't go home until Renee cools off."

"It's her way or the highway, and you're on a road trip to hell."

***

The light from the window the next morning hit her when she woke up to the sound of a car door closing. Sidra didn't want to get up, but there was no choice. She kissed the space between Dominic's shoulder blades and pulled him to his back.

"You need to go," she said, and pressed her lips to his.

47

Guilt washed over her with his lack of sleep, but it was his choice to come over at three o'clock in the morning. "Okay," he said, and ran his hand down her naked back.

They got up and quietly threw on clothes. Dominic said, "Do you want me to go out the window?" and Sidra looked at him over her shoulder and smiled. Sneaking him out of the house would be easy as long as she could distract her parents. This was ridiculous, though. She was thirty-two years old, for crying out loud.

"Shh," she said to Dominic as she opened the bedroom door. "Did you get everything?" she whispered.

"You mean my handcuffs?"

"Stop it." She suppressed the smile and made her way down the wooden stairs. At the edge of the kitchen, she held up her hand to stop him from talking so she could make sure the coast was clear. She led him through the kitchen and out the door.

"I think your brother saw us," Dominic said. At the bottom of the stairs, she kissed him goodbye.

"He doesn't care what I do."

"You should think about getting your own place."

This was part of the reason she hadn't been serious about looking for one. She wasn't ready for Dominic to be in her life full time. He played the part well, and was around when she needed him, but she didn't want to come home to him. Or have him ask where she'd been. She wasn't ready for any of that.

"Will you call me later?" she said.

"No," he said, and Sidra kissed him again. "You call me when you have time for me. If you think about me at all."

"Funny," she said, and watched him walk away.

Back inside, she had a smile on her face as she made coffee. Dominic Getty was too sweet to make it in the Shackelford family. A guy trying to be a hard cop, but he wasn't. Not with her.

Dad said, "Who came down the stairs with you?" and Sidra turned around to look at him. His beard was growing out just as thick as Woolsey's.

"I don't—"

And then Casey Lincoln walked in from the dining room. It wasn't her brother Dominic had seen; it was Casey, and she hadn't even noticed he was in there.

"No one," Sidra said, looking back at Dad.

"Outside. Who were you talking to?"

It was Casey that spoke. "A guy. Five-ten, one-ninety. Blue eyes and big dimples."

Sidra looked at Casey and wanted to kill him.

Dad said, "Dominic was here?" He shook his head. "Don't let your mother find out."

"Find out what?" Mom said, walking into the kitchen.

"Nothing," Sidra said, giving Casey another death stare.

49

He said, "Dominic spent the night."

"He did *what*?" Mom turned toward Sidra. "Just because I invite him to Sunday dinner doesn't mean you can shack up with him in my house. You know I don't stand for that."

"Stand for what?" Mitchell said, walking into the kitchen, looking just as tired as Sidra felt.

Casey said, "Sidra shacking up with Dominic. In her mother's house."

"I was wondering what all that noise was," Mitchell said. Then he turned to Casey and shook his hand because they hadn't seen each other since last year, and Sidra wanted to kill both of them.

Mom fussed as she rummaged through the fridge and Sidra tuned her out. Mom and her, "Honest to God, Sidra," and, "This is why you can't live here." Sidra walked out of the kitchen with her coffee and Mom was still going at it.

"Yell at me later," Sidra said, walking down the hallway, and thought about ways to seek revenge on Casey Lincoln.

By the time Woolsey and Daley came in, all four of them sat at computers gathering intel on their current cases. Woolsey started doing a criminal background check on Marcy. Daley handed Mitchell a blue folder and asked him to do surveillance on an insurance fraud case he'd been working on.

Daley said, "I picked up another job. Brady Ardeen and the case of the stolen computer."

"He didn't back up his PC?" Woolsey said, chowing away on a breakfast croissant with ham and egg.

"Some of it," Sidra said, and looked at the broken window behind Daley's head. She put in a call to the glass company to see if someone would come out and look at it today. When she got off the phone, they were still talking, and Mitchell had gotten up to write on the whiteboard. He erased the Boat job from his and Sidra's names, then made notes about the surveillance case and Brady's computer. Next to Dad's name, he wrote Casey's name.

"What's that for?" Sidra asked.

"I think Dad hired him."

"That doesn't mean his name belongs on the board."

Mitchell wrote (Clerk) next to Casey's name and laughed. Sidra got up, scratched that out and wrote (Gofer). Go for this. Go for that. Casey Lincoln was about to become Dad's errand boy and he didn't even know it.

Daley handed Sidra some printouts. He said, "I got the names of the two people Brady interviewed. One of them, a female, works for Happy Home Care. The other one, a male, works independently through another contractor. I want to start with him. Brady also worked with a handful of developers on the *Shoot Fall* game. One guy who had been working on it, quit due to conflict. He still wanted to get paid per the contract, but he forfeited the pay."

"Let's go then." Sidra grabbed her jacket.

Chapter 5

Mitchell pushed the grocery cart down the aisle behind Mr. Mortensen, the old man who'd injured himself when he slipped and fell inside of the Quick Chick fast-food restaurant. Mr. Mortensen wasn't supposed to lift anything over ten pounds according to his doctor, but the insurance wasn't paying because the Quick Chick had video footage showing the old man tripped on his own feet.

Mitchell felt bad for the old man in the neck brace. Except this was the third time in the last four years Mr. Mortensen tripped and fell inside a business. He needed to get better at his scams.

Mitchell kept his cell phone angled at the man as he continued to load his cart. Opting for a dozen donuts himself, Mitchell reached inside the box and snagged one while he filmed. He grabbed a few various things off the shelves, then put them back. Walked the opposite way down the aisle, so he came up to Mr. Mortensen head on. Mitchell put the cell phone in the cart, hidden behind a bag of chips so he could focus on the donut and push the cart.

And then came that glorious money shot. Down the beverage aisle, Mr. Mortensen reached down, grabbed a case of water, lifted it to the bottom of the cart. He wanted to ask the old man if he needed help, but he didn't dare make contact with him. Mitchell pushed the cart along all the way to the beer—this couldn't be any better—and Mr. Mortensen grabbed a case of Bud and put that in the cart.

Happy with his footage, Mitchell turned off the cell phone camera and made his way to the checkout to purchase his donuts. After three hours of watching the old man's house earlier today and thinking it would be a bust...

Mitchell was so happy, he texted Daley to gloat. Told him he got another one in the bag. Easy money. But the joy didn't last long when he got to Shackelford and Renee called.

"Hey, babe," he said, thinking it would be nice to hear her voice.

"Mitchell?"

The strain in her voice gave him pause. "What's wrong?"

"You need to come home," she said. "There are some men here who want to talk to you."

He was confused. Renee should be at school today. "Why are you home?"

"They said they want to talk to you, Mitchell. Can you come home?"

Mitchell was already out the door and in the van. "Is it the police?"

"No."

"Are you okay?"

"I don't know," she said. His wife cleared her throat.

"Renee?" he said, and then the phone disconnected.

Mitchell didn't see any strange cars parked in the driveway or on the street and he wondered what was going on. With caution, he walked into the house through the kitchen and stopped dead when he got to the living room. Two men in suits. One sat on the sofa, the other looked out the window. Renee sat in the wooden rocker in the corner. Why was she home? Where were the kids?

"Who are you?" Mitchell said.

The man at the window turned around. "We're just here to talk." Their suits may have been nice, but these guys weren't government. They looked rough and trained to keep shit straight.

"Renee, are you okay?" She nodded, and then he said, "Come here," because she was sitting between the two men.

"Your wife's going to stay where she is," the man standing said.

"You're not going to come into my house and tell me what to do," Mitchell said.

"We're just here to talk. Why don't you sit down?"

"I'll stand."

55

"My name is Shane Bennett. And this is my associate, Trevor Gregory. We're looking for a woman named Helen Ross."

"Jesus," Renee said, and started to get up. Shane Bennett grabbed her shoulder and sat her back down, her eyes wide as she gripped the arms of the rocker. Trevor Gregory didn't move.

Mitchell said, "Are you with the police? The FBI? DEA?" He rattled off a few more, all while Shane Bennett shook his head.

Shane said, "Helen Ross works for one of my associates and she has money that belongs to me. I know you've seen her in the last week. Your name was in her logbook."

"I don't know where the fuck she is. I saw her, I left. You lost someone, why don't you go to the police?"

Shane looked at Trevor. "He wants us to go to the police." The man smiled with only half his mouth, then turned back to Mitchell. "I want you to call her."

"And tell her what?"

Shane held out his hands to say, *figure it out.* Mitchell pulled his cell phone out of his pocket, put it on speaker before he dialed, but the number was disconnected.

Mitchell pocketed his phone. "Not much else I can do."

"You could help us find her," Shane said. "Aren't you a private investigator?"

"Listen," Mitchell said. "I doubt you need me to locate this woman for you. I'm not in the business to locate a woman for men who show up at my house and scare my wife. So, I want you to leave before I call the police."

Shane looked at Trevor again, said, "Before he calls the police." Trevor, the silent one, nodded and stood up. When he did, an uneasiness settled in Mitchell's chest. Something niggled at the back of his mind, and he didn't know what it was about him. The guy was probably the same size, but he looked twice as mean.

Shane dropped a business card in Renee's lap. "Stay in touch."

Before Trevor Gregory made his way out, he stopped in front of Mitchell. "See you around."

"I don't think—"

Trevor punched Mitchell in the diaphragm with enough force, Mitchell bent over and gasped. Then Trevor walked out the front door without looking back.

Mitchell hunched over and dropped to one knee. "Are you okay?" Renee said, and helped him sit down. His lungs couldn't take in air. By the time Mitchell had noticed the brass knuckles on Trevor's fist, it was too late. It had been a long time since someone got the drop on him. People normally saw his size and backed off. Not this guy.

"What's going on?" Renee said.

Mitchell coughed a couple of times. "I don't know."

"This is about the woman you're screwing at the motel, you asshole." Was she ever going to stop? "How'd they find out where we live?" Renee's eyes were red from crying.

"Why aren't you at work?"

"I had to get a substitute because I didn't sleep last night and I'm pissed off right now." Renee stood up. "Do you think we need to call the police?"

Mitchell went back to his knees and finally stood up. He took a couple of deep breaths and stretched his arms up as pain ripped through his stomach. "That's probably best." The vulnerability across her face crushed him. If something happened to her?

"Renee—"

She turned around and walked up the stairs. He found her in the bedroom, packing a suitcase. "What are you doing?"

"Two strange men just came into my house. I'm not staying here with the kids if it's not safe."

"Okay," he said. "I can understand that."

"I don't want you around the kids."

"Why?"

"I'll get them from school and go stay with my sister."

"They're my kids."

Renee grabbed clothes out of the closet. "They deserve better than what you're giving them. Is that what this is about? Did you buy drugs from her? You think I wouldn't find out?" She started crying again.

"You think I don't know you?" She walked into the bathroom and when she came out, she threw a little black box at him. "Go ahead," she said. "Snort it all up your nose now and kill yourself because that's what you're doing."

He didn't want to fight with her or escalate the situation. But he had to make one thing clear. "I didn't cheat on you. Ever." He felt abandoned, like his wife was turning her back on him. That she caused a lot of grief for him, and didn't want to face the consequences. Okay, so he needed to get high sometimes. Right now, he really wanted to get high, but he fought it. The coke was in his hands. All he had to do was go into the bathroom and close the door, and for a little while, he would feel better.

"I'm going to the police to file a complaint," he said.

"A guy in a suit was there last night," Renee said. "Not the ones that were here, another one. He was walking around the parking lot on the phone when you were in the room. I watched you walk out and leave, and then another man walked in. I knocked on the door and she answered, but the man was in the bed half naked. What were you doing there?"

"Talking to her. About us. Because I don't have anyone else to talk to and I didn't want you to know. If I scheduled a regular doctor, you would find out."

Renee stood there, almost afraid to move as the awkward silence hung between them. He wanted to reach out to her, to hug her, and tell her he loved her.

But he didn't, and he wasn't sure if it would have made a difference.

***

Mitchell filed a report at the Fayetteville Police dept., and then drove to the Jonesboro Police to do the same there. Five minutes into speaking with a sergeant, they thought he could assist them with information. Were Shane Bennett and Trevor Gregory already people of interest? He wasn't sure. So when he sat down with Detective Coleman, it surprised Mitchell when he said, "We have a dead body in room 1025. If you're telling me you were in the room, I'm assuming your prints are in there as well?"

Mitchell processed all of that. The two men looking for Helen Ross said nothing about a dead body. They said Helen stole their money.

"It's a scam," Detective Coleman said. "You look smart enough to figure that out on your own. Tell me again why you were there?"

Detective Coleman was a skinny man who had on a light gray suit. The whites of his eyes looked worse than a jaundiced baby. He spread his hands as he leaned back, waiting for Mitchell to explain.

Convinced that he hadn't partaken in any illegal activity, Mitchell felt there was no reason to hide anything. "I'm having a few marital problems," Mitchell began. "This guy I met told me to call Helen Ross, so I did. I paid her fifty dollars, and she listened to my problems for an hour."

"Did she do anything else?"

"Chain smoke cigarettes."

"Okay," he said. "Tell me about the men that showed up at your house."

Mitchell told him everything that happened; the way Shane Bennett shoved his wife back down in the rocker, and how Trevor Gregory punched him with brass knuckles. "My wife—" Mitchell cleared his throat, aware of how stupid this was going to sound. "She followed me last night because I'd left in the middle of the night. She told me she went to the motel, and saw a guy in a suit walking around the parking lot. After I left, my wife knocked on the door and Helen answered it. She said she saw a man lying on the bed half naked."

"What's your wife's name?"

"Renee Shackelford." The detective wrote that down. "I'm going to need to speak with her." Then he asked Mitchell to describe his wife and asked what kind of vehicle she drove. Why did any of that matter?

"Helen Ross seemed legit enough," Mitchell said.

"It's a different type of prostitution," Coleman said. "They reel you in, you pay the money, and walk away with a written prescription. It's hard catching the pharmacies involved. This type of illegal business had been going on for a long time. I wasn't aware Dr. Helen Ross worked out of the motel until after the guy turned up dead."

"Did she do it?"

"Don't know. It's been eight hours. I was looking for Helen Ross. You may have just thrown me a bone."

***

Most graphic designers had the luxury of working from home, but Upscale Studios was in Atlanta. And while it was most important to be upfront and honest with people about why they wanted to talk to them, Kieran Knox balked at the mention of Brady Ardeen.

They had to play a different angle. Sidra called, pretending she wanted to see if he could meet with her after lunch about an urgent project. Kieran said that since she was in the area, would she be willing to stop by the Studio? Of course she would.

Driving in Atlanta was a sporting event. Thousands of cars flying through four lanes of traffic while the two right lanes were at a complete stop. At noon, this was still the morning traffic. It never ended. Eventually they'd get to the Peachtree Street exit.

"Could you live in Atlanta?" Daley said.

"If I could afford it."

Two types of people existed in Georgia. The ones who lived in the city and the ones who thought the people who lived in the city were crazy. The city had grown by millions in the last decade.

After circling the block three times, Daley found Upscale Studios tucked away in a narrow lot with parking in the back. The door buzzed after Sidra rang the bell and a receptionist told them to go down the hallway, Kieran would be waiting for them. Various artworks covered the hallway, work done in house that flowed with a city theme. The main studio opened up to a large work space with cubicles and tables along the left side.

A guy in a mustard-colored sweater vest walked toward them, little round glasses on his face. "Kieran," he said, and held out his hand. A large band-aid covered the space above his thumb.

"Sidra," she said, then introduced Daley."

Kieran gestured for them to follow him. "I pulled up some prints, but I've also got my work station setup if you want to see the digitals. What kind of work did you need? I specialize in 3D, and if I can't help you, I can find someone who can."

Sidra looked at Daley as they stopped in front of Kieran's work station. "Honestly, we're here to talk to you about Brady Ardeen."

Kieran's face tensed slightly as he looked down. "It was a contract job. I didn't finish it because Brady was difficult to work with."

A couple of people glanced their way. Others had headphones on and didn't hear his voice go up.

Sidra said, "We're not here to judge. We're just trying to get some information. If Brady was being difficult, can you tell us about that?"

"He didn't want any guidance on anything. Brady designs his own games, but he put this last one on a fast track and outsourced a few developmental areas. He'd been rendering 3D games for a few years now, but he was looking for something beyond his skills. I told him I wanted to help him all the way, but I wanted my name on it."

Sidra nodded. "What happened with that?"

Kieran shoved his hands in his pockets. "Brady has a company called Echo Quest that he's trying to build. But no one wants to work for him when he doesn't give proper credit to the people he's outsourcing. The work I did was under Echo Quest, which meant that everything I created remained with the company."

That didn't sound like Brady. In fact, Brady helped others rather than himself, and gave away a lot of money to people and projects. For as long as Sidra had known him, Brady always loved video games and the people who loved to play.

She believed Kieran's perception of Brady was off because even as a football quarterback in high school, Brady always talked about teamwork when they scored. He was an all-around nice guy who had a lot of friends. People looked up to him. His charm got him far with the students and the teachers, and he could talk Sidra into anything.

When Kieran said, "I think he only gets the deals because he's in a wheelchair. You know what I mean? He's a quadriplegic and people feel sorry for him," Sidra's temper flared.

Daley put his hand on her shoulder. "What would happen if someone took your computer, Kieran?"

His eyes grew wide with the sheer thought of it. "My work is in a cloud but..." He shook his head. "Our whole lives are on computers these days. I don't know what I'd do. It would be worse than losing your cell phone."

"How'd you meet Brady?" Daley said.

"It was at a conference about two years ago, but he didn't really give me the time of day, you know? Everybody made such a big deal about him. The success Brady's had doesn't happen to nearly enough people. I mean, there are hundreds of thousands of talented people out there—"

"You don't think he's talented?" Sidra said.

"I didn't say that." Kieran shrugged. "Many people work on a lot of projects together and when they hit it big, it's an honor to be a part of their projects."

"It sounds to me," Sidra said, "that you're not making it very far, and you were hoping to skate in on Brady's tail."

"No," Kieran said, shaking his head vehemently. "I'm the one who has better 3D skills than Brady. He just didn't want to see that. He didn't want to put the entire game in the format I suggested for the tone he was going for. And he wouldn't let us see the entire project."

Sidra wanted to push Kieran's buttons. Felt certain that if she asked him a few heated questions regarding his motives for leaving, he'd say something revealing.

But it was Daley who surprised her. "Did you steal Brady Ardeen's computer?"

"What?"

The key was to wait him out. Not say anything until Kieran did, which took a hot minute.

"Why would I steal Brady's computer?"

"You tell us."

"I didn't steal his computer." Kieran moved to his workstation and pulled out his ergonomic rolling chair. "You're barking up the wrong tree."

"What happened to your hand?" Sidra said.

He sneered at her. "I dropped a box on my hand."

"Are there teeth marks?"

"What? I think it's time for you to go."

When they were back in the truck, Sidra said, "I was fine until he took a jab at him."

"I know," Daley said. "But when you're working a job, even if it involves people you're familiar with, you have to be objective. Maybe Brady's an ass to work with. That doesn't make him a bad guy or a good guy. It just is."

Once they got through most of the traffic and were on the south side of the city, Sidra said, "Kieran doesn't seem like the type of guy who could do it. He'd piss in his pants with the thought of breaking into someone's house."

"My thoughts too," Daley said, and put his UGA cap back on. "I'm starving."

"Are you buying? Because I think I have seventy-five dollars to my name."

"Why don't you ever have any money?"

"I'm in debt. Almost two-hundred-fifty grand—"

"What?" Daley turned to her in pure shock, then he put his hand to his chest, not able to comprehend the idea.

"And my honest thoughts—"

"Too bad money management didn't come with that valedictorian diploma you received."

"I think Mom and Dad are shorting my pay checks. They're trying to ruin my life."

"I think you have that covered yourself."

"Are you going to feed me," she said, "or keep yammering?"

"Two-hundred and fifty thousand dollars?"

Chapter 6

Brady Ardeen didn't want to let her in the gate. Sidra said to the security guy, "Are you serious?"

"He said he doesn't know you."

Sidra picked up her cell phone and called him on the house phone. Julie answered, and a minute later Brady said, "What?"

"Let me in the gate or I'm walking in. Honestly, you can't hire my brother without—"

He hung up on her. *Motherfucker*. She'd have to back out of the entrance to leave. But then the security attendant said, "Okay," and the gate opened.

"Have a nice day," she said, trying to be polite.

Calm down, she thought, reminding herself that she caused Brady's anger. And he had every right to be angry with her.

Sidra knocked on the door, and Julie let her inside. Peaches came running up to her, wagging her tail with such vigor, her butt wiggled.

"He's in his office," Julie said. "He hasn't come out all day."

Sidra stepped into the office, and the room was still a mess. Books all over the floor. The TV still flipped over. Video games everywhere. Peaches came in, sniffed around, then jumped on the sofa only to curl up into a ball for a nap.

"It's not a crime scene. You can pick everything up."

Brady spun around to her. "Really? Should I crawl around on the floor like a worm and throw everything back on the shelves?" His hair was a mess, and she really wanted to walk over to him and run her fingers through it.

She went to her knees and picked up an old Monopoly board game; the pieces scattered all over.

"Leave it," he said. "You want to clean up messes, clean up your own."

"You want to do this now?" She jumped up from the floor and walked over to close the door. "How?" she said, and stood in front of him with her arms folded. "How do I clean it up?" When he tried to move away, Sidra leaned down and put her hands on his wheelchair arms so she could get in his face. "What do you want me to do? Do you honestly want me out of your life? Have you been sitting around for the last year happy that you haven't talked to me, because that's not what I've been doing."

"It's difficult to be around you."

"It's difficult to be around you, too." She moved back to the floor to pick up game pieces and books and little 3D printed prototypes. Her broken heart was overwhelming. All she ever wanted was to be with him again and she didn't understand why. Brady no longer loved her. Maybe it was the security she wanted. The feeling she had for nearly four years when it was the happiest time in her life.

Brady sat there, two feet away, looking down on her as though his anger was going to change something. What was there left to say? Even when she put herself in his shoes, he wasn't one to hold grudges, so she wondered how long it would be until he opened up and talked to her again. He watched her in silence as she stacked books and put them in their exact places. She'd spent enough time in the office looking through them.

"Daley and I talked to Kieran Knox today," she said. "He's something else. Do you think he's capable of orchestrating a break in?"

Brady didn't answer her. Barely looked at her.

"At some point, you're going to have to talk to me. You can't possibly hate me that much."

"Do you think this is easy for me?"

She walked back over to him. "And by 'this,' what do you mean? The general aspect of your life? The wheelchair? The disabilities? Your work?"

Over the last two years, Brady's health was a roller coaster. One month he looked full of life and color, and the next he was sick. She couldn't even imagine what he went through, but Brady had never looked at himself as helpless. Nor did he ever want anyone to feel sorry for him.

He said, "You. Every time I see you, it's a reminder of everything I lost out on. And you waltz in here every time without a care in the world. You could have changed everything."

She swallowed down the lump in her throat and pushed the tears away. "Okay," she said. "How does it play out? I tell you I'm pregnant, the accident never happens, and everything turns out perfectly? Or maybe you still end up in a wheelchair and we're parents at eighteen? Tell me, Brady, please. What should I have done? I've punished myself enough. This isn't easy for me either and I can't change the past."

Brady said nothing for a long minute. He dug around in a pocket velcroed to his wheelchair and, with curled fingers, handed her a photo. She recognized it right away as the picture she'd given him last year. It still had blood on it from Casey's son, Brandon.

"I can't look at it anymore," Brady said.

Sidra slid the photo into her back pocket. "We'll find your computer. And after that I'll respect your wishes and you'll never see me again." But for now, she finished putting the bookcase back together. "We talked to Marcy and the other people you interviewed. Nothing seemed to pop out. Kieran, on the other hand, is jealous of your success."

"He's over eager about everything. And his arrogance gets in his own way. He started writing code for a company that creates apps. He single-handedly deleted files by mistake and it took them two days to get everything back up and running. Three apps went down. That's not even a rookie mistake. That's a moron mistake."

"How does that even happen?"

"Those don't go there," he said, about the four Nat Geo books in her hands. She wanted to tell him that this was where they'd been, but didn't argue with him. "Put them up high. I never use them."

***

"You guys want to play a game?" Mitchell asked. The four of them sat in the office, same as this morning. A glass company had come out to fix the window that some jerk had thrown a rock at. After calling Renee to check on her and the kids at her sister's house, he needed some backup.

Woolsey said, "If your game involves me sitting on the hood of the car and you driving fifty miles an hour down Pecan Pie Road; no thank you." They all laughed at the memory.

"You fell off the car like Tweedle Dum," Mitchell said. "God, we could talk you into anything back then."

"I was eight."

More laughter. Except for Sidra, though. She sat there scowling about something on her mind. Over focused and depressed with her poor choices and no way out. For the life of him, Mitchell could never figure out what Sidra was upset about sometimes. Her life was nowhere near that difficult.

The first thing Mitchell did was clue Daley and Woolsey in on some family matters that were going on, leaving out the part about the coke. When he got to the part about the two suits and the dead man found in room 1025, Sidra nearly came out of her seat. He didn't even think she was paying attention.

"Are you shitting us?"

"If Woolsey said he lost ten pounds, that's shitting you. I'm serious as a heart attack."

Woolsey looked offended long enough to flip him off.

Mitchell said, "So, this guy, Shane Bennett—if that's his real name—left me this card. And I was wondering if we could call and see what he says."

"Like a game," Sidra said.

"Exactly."

"What do you want to do?"

They talked about it, and Sidra dug around in her purse for a burner phone. When the person answered, she pulled the phone away from her ear because of the loud music blaring through. "Hi, is Shane Bennett available?" Sidra said loudly. She wrote down Sapphire Groove Club on a piece of paper and handed it to Woolsey. "Okay... My name is Daisy Carmichael. I got this number from a friend who said I should call him..."

Sidra looked at Mitchell and shook her head. "I'd rather speak with him in person about a situation... I understand, but I'd rather speak with him... Okay, thank you." Sidra nodded and wrote a few notes. "Thank you so much."

After she hung up, she said, "Not his personal assistant."

The card Shane Bennett left was a black card with a phone number on it, and Mitchell had turned it over to Detective Coleman. Now Mitchell looked at the picture of it he'd taken. There wasn't anything else on the card.

Woolsey said, "It's located off of Old National in Riverdale."

"Who wants to go to a club tonight?" Mitchell said.

"I'm running on about four hours of sleep," Sidra said.

"Are you sure you even slept last night?"

Mitchell didn't sleep last night either. At least he knew his wife and kids were safe with Renee's sister.

"What if Brass Knuckles is there?" Daley said. "You can't just go hanging out at the club. Someone's going to notice you."

"Excellent point," Sidra said. "Let's go hang out at the pond and watch fireflies."

Speaking of the pond. He asked Daley, "Did you kiss Donna Talbert?"

"Oh, I did a heck of a lot more with Donna Talbert," Daley said, and smiled like he used to when he was a boy, and got candy and Mitchell didn't.

***

They opted out of comm links because no one could hear themselves breathe in the club, much less hear with a wireless comm. Sapphire Groove was a large club, with bright lights and the glitz and glam that screamed, *Party's Here*. The music was thumping as Mitchell split up from Daley and Sidra, and he'd chosen a sports coat so he'd look a little more businesslike.

The dance floor wrapped around the entire bar with every kind of person in the Atlanta area dancing as the lights flashed off and on. Along both sides, there were small stairways that led to tables that overlooked the dance floor and bar. Mitchell sat down on a bar stool and asked the bartender for a beer. Three bartenders worked the bar.

Thursday. Midnight.

No one here was going to work tomorrow, he assumed. Unless he'd gotten so old, he'd forgotten how little sleep young life required. No, Mitchell was never one for the club or party scene. He drank his beer from the bottle and looked around.

One bartender had blue braids down to her waist. The low-cut jeans came to her hips and exposed a bare stomach with a bellybutton ring. His sister leaned across the bar to talk to her, smiling in that way she did to get what she wanted.

All three of the bartenders resembled cartoon characters. The ones where the illustrator could put any style of hair or clothes on. Give them tattoos and big smiles. These three were living it up, and the bar was their stage.

Daley scoped out the place, looking the part of Hollywood's most eligible bachelor. They could stand him up on the bar and auction him off, and make a killing. Hell, if Mitchell had his little brother's looks, he'd be single too, and scoping out the place. But Daley wasn't going to find someone to take home. God, he hoped not.

These two fit right in, maybe because they knew how to talk to people. Mitchell learned how to watch people. That's how he noticed the couple of men in suits watching the action from a second-floor balcony above the bar.

Daley and Sidra were going to come in alone until Sidra said, "What's the plan? Are we going to describe all the men we come into contact with?" So Mitchell joined in. They would have found the suits sitting up top for sure. But these two suits weren't Shane Bennett or the ball-sac with brass knuckles.

The dipshit and his bodyguard.

Mitchell sipped his beer and made his way through the crowd, up the six steps to the tables, and sat down. The place was darker over here, but just as loud. None of the music was anything Mitchell recognized. This place was for people to come and get drunk and high and not give a shit.

Mitchell finished his beer, then walked through the tables to the bathrooms. He passed a door that read EMPLOYEES ONLY and kept going. In a bathroom stall, Mitchell pulled out his bag and took a hit of coke and waited a minute for it to kick in.

It was hot as hell in here.

When he exited the bathroom, he tried the employee door, surprised it wasn't locked. Mitchell walked up the stairs. It opened up to the seating area where the suits sat. There were two more men up here as well, and two fine young ladies in tight dresses.

As soon as they saw Mitchell, one reached for his hip. Mitchell held out his hands and smiled. "Hey," he said. "I love what you guys did to the place. It's hoppin' down there."

The men didn't relax. "Who are you?" one of them said.

"Jerry Smith." Mitchell shook all of their hands, but didn't get any introductions. "I want to open a club in Atlanta and I was told by a friend to come here. Man, this Sapphire place is amazing. What's the profit here?"

One of the guys sitting down, the one who seemed in charge of the yahoos, smiled and said, "It's lucrative."

"Lucrative. I like that. Who do I need to talk to about opening a place like this? I'm sorry, I didn't catch your name."

"Ryan Orchard."

"Like a peach orchard."

Ryan smiled at his friends, his hands palms up, *Can you believe this guy?* "Like a peach." Ryan nodded at one guy and he stepped away through a door past the sofa where the ladies sat.

Mitchell kept his eye out for anyone with brass knuckles and said, "I have this location I'm looking at. I'd love to get some tips on where to start."

"Location is perfect. How much you looking to start with?"

Mitchell shrugged. "Yeah, see, I don't know what I'm looking at. Couple hundred grand, a million? I don't know."

"You taking out a business loan?"

Mitchell put his hands on his hips. "I got money, Mr. Orchard. I'm trying to turn it into a profit."

"Try the stock market," Ryan said, and waved Mitchell away like a fly. "It's less time-consuming."

"Oh, okay," Mitchell said, trying not to sound too disappointed. "I don't think I'd be your competition or anything."

"No," Ryan said. "You're not competition at all." The man looked at him for a minute with a serious face. "Why don't you go back downstairs and have a drink on us." He gave a nod to a different guy, this one with a ruby earring in his left ear. He tried to usher Mitchell out.

Mitchell looked at Ruby's hand on his arm and said, "What the fuck are you doing?"

Chapter 7

What the fuck is he doing?" Sidra asked Daley as she leaned on a railing and looked up at the balcony.

"No idea. I hope he can sweet talk his way out."

"They're going to throw him over the balcony."

Daley said through a smile, "You watch too many mobster movies."

Whatever Mitchell said, he didn't get the vibes these guys sent out. They weren't paying attention to him. Two at the table. Two standing. Two chicks sitting on a sofa. They wouldn't break out machine guns in their own club. No, they'd take Mitchell to the back and crack his skull open.

Sidra didn't watch too many mobster movies. After shooting Edgar Burke because he broke into her house to kill her, she made the mistake of calling drug dealers to come get their guy. They bagged him up while he was still alive.

"How do we get up there?" Sidra said.

"They're taking him to the back." Sometimes he was too calm about things. His tone was flat. Slightly less excited than if he'd told her he was going for a pudding cup.

They couldn't come in here with weapons and Sidra felt naked without her Glock. She sipped her whiskey sour and thought, maybe Daley was right. Maybe there was nothing to worry about.

***

The guy escorted Mitchell down a hallway. "Okay, okay," he said, Ruby's hands still on him. He could take this guy in a second. The door down the hall was open and Shane Bennett sat behind a desk, a Boss Man in his club.

"Jerry Smith?" Shane said. "I'm glad you found the place."

"Me too," Mitchell said, and tried to shrug off Ruby and he stared down the man behind the desk, almost trying to tell him he didn't want to break the shrimp's neck.

"Leland, let the man go."

Leland let go of Mitchell's arm and took a step back into the corner. Shane came from behind his desk and sat on the corner.

"Did you find anything?"

"You got a nice club here. I was wondering if you had any rooms available for counseling sessions. Perhaps with actual doctors who didn't get their how to from YouTube."

Shane smiled. "What are you talking about?"

Mitchell looked around the office for Shane's bodyguard, but he wasn't here. Just Leland, and the guy that Ryan had dismissed earlier. The cluttered office had an organization to it. Shane Bennett took his business seriously.

Not only did Mitchell know Shane was running a scam business out of a motel, there was that little thing about the dead man.

"Are you going around and scaring all the people who Helen Ross came into contact with, or was it just me and my wife?"

"I needed to make sure you got the message."

"What message?"

"Don't be obtuse… *Mr. Smith.* If you don't know where Helen Ross is, then we have no further business. My work doesn't pertain to you. Why don't you go downstairs and have a drink on the house?" Dismissing him the same as the Peach Orchard had, and with a nod of his head, to his little buddies.

"Okay, okay," Mitchell said. "I don't want to put my nose where it doesn't belong in the fine establishment you have running here. But I think you need to be careful with your sources of income. The ones you don't report to the IRS."

Shane laughed like it was the funniest thing he'd heard. And then Mitchell felt the presence behind him. Heard the voice. Trevor Gregory said to Shane, "I heard you may have a problem?"

"Problem?" Mitchell said. "We're just having a little chat. Shane Bennett left his calling card at my house. I called, here I am. Isn't that right, Shane?"

The man said nothing and when Trevor Gregory swung his arm out to grab Mitchell, Mitchell stepped back with his hands up. "Whoa," Mitchell said. "You may have gotten me before, but not again."

Then the little shit behind him jumped on his back. Mitchell leaned over and flipped Leland to his back, stared down at the kid as he grabbed his sore back. "I mean, what is this?" Mitchell said.

Trevor took a swing at Mitchell, but he saw it coming. Punched Trevor in the nose as three guys walked into the office. Jeez, these guys thought it was bare-knuckle brawl time around here. Couldn't even ask questions about a potential business without someone feeling threatened.

Mitchell punched and blocked blows as they came at him. Got slammed backwards into a wall. Took an awful punch in the diaphragm. Got kicked in the knee.

He hoped his brother and sister were having a blast on the dance floor.

***

After a couple of guys rushed to the back, Sidra said, "What do we do?"

Daley sighed. "He engaged with the subject without a plan. Didn't even bother to let us in. Knowing Mitchell, he's probably up there telling stupid jokes."

"We need to do something."

"Do you want to go up there?"

Sidra did the next best thing. Pulled the fire alarm. The music shut off immediately, sprinklers started raining, and all the people on the dance floor screamed in the chaos. The water sprayed from the ceiling as people tried to figure out what was going on. Where was the fire? Some people didn't go anywhere. A drunk moron probably pulled the alarm and the police and fire department would come soon, but first they finished their drinks.

Sidra and Daley watched the upstairs balcony for a moment.

Where the fuck was Mitchell?

"How do we get to the balcony?"

"Come on," Daley said. "You're so worried about him."

The balcony was empty and when they made their way down the little hallway, no one was there either. They'd all gone out an EXIT door in the back. Daley pushed the door open and found metal stairs. There were black vehicles back here and Sidra made eye contact with a man in a suit who had on a red tie. That's when she noticed them pushing Mitchell into the back of an SUV.

"What is he doing?" Daley said.

Mitchell was a big guy. A fighter. Her brother could man handle a hippo into submission. Okay, not an angry hippo. Even so, why did he let them put him in the vehicle?

Sidra and Daley took off down the metal stairs as the sirens got closer. The black SUV peeled out of the parking lot to a back street between a warehouse and packing plant.

"Jesus," Sidra said, and they took off to Daley's truck. They jumped in and drove to the back of the club, through a crowd of people who stumbled around like drunk zombies. The ones who weren't drunk were trying to exit. Daley made his way down the alley.

A few more men in suits stared at them as they followed the SUV. One of them had a gun pointed in their direction but didn't shoot. They bounced through a pothole and saw tail lights to the right, hoped it was them, and turned.

"We should have gotten to him sooner."

"He's going to be fine, Sidra," Daley said, in his pudding cup voice.

***

"This has been great," Mitchell said to Shane and Trevor, "but I can drive myself home." Neither one of them said anything. "Listen, you dumb fucks. The police know about the body and your scam. I gave them your names and the card you gave me, which will tie you two to the club. If I go missing, you're going to be the first people they look at."

Shane turned around from the middle seat and said, "You're paranoid. Why would you go missing?"

"I don't know. You took me from the club? Your personal body guard seems to be attached to my hip." Mitchell looked to his right where Trevor Gregory sat next to him. He had a tissue pressed to his bloody nose.

"We're just going for a little ride, Mitchell. I can call you Mitchell, right? Or do you prefer Jerry?" When he didn't answer, Shane shrugged. "Things got a little heated in there. We'll wait for it to cool off. At least once a week, someone pulls the fire alarm. I get a bill in the mail, no big deal."

They continued south on Tara Boulevard in silence. Mitchell was familiar with his whereabouts, but he had no idea where they were taking him. This was it, he thought. They were going to shoot him in the head somewhere and he would never see his wife and kids again. At least his family would seek revenge and take justice into their own hands. At least that's what he told himself. He wanted to tell these goons, no one fucks with the Shackelfords.

His grandpa was a fire chief back in the day and he'd helped take down some Dixie Mafia guys after they'd burned a man to death inside a car. Then they came after his son. That didn't turn out too well for those guys.

They took a left on Noah's Ark Road and drove a few miles. Turned down some back roads until they came to an industrial area with a water reserve and wetlands. They stopped, and Mitchell didn't get out when everyone else did.

"Get out," Trevor said, and flicked his bloody tissue at Mitchell's chest.

"How much do you press?"

When Trevor reached for him, Mitchell punched him. That did nothing. Trevor grabbed Mitchell by the hair. They were going to kill him and dump him in the water. No one would find his body out here.

The headlights from the SUV shone in front of them. The run-down brick building had broken windows and kudzu all over it. Mitchell was on his knees in the dirt. "If you keep hitting me, you're going to be sorry."

"Is that so?" Trevor said, cracking his knuckles.

Shane whistled at Trevor. "Bring him inside."

Trevor Gregory pulled out a gun. "Phone and wallet. Hand 'em over." Mitchell thought about going for the gun—lights out for Mr. Brass Knuckles—but he thought better of it.

Cold, stale air filled his lungs as he walked into the moldy room. There was some kind of operation going on here and from the looks of it, this must be the murder room. The spacious room was dark, the dim lights broken except for a couple. Hanging from the ceiling in the middle of the room was a chain that reached down to the floor. A dried circle of blood, so old the color had turned black.

"So what are you guys doing out here? That chain looks awfully suspicious hanging like that."

"Shut up," Trevor said, and grabbed Mitchell by the back of the shirt to shove him to the left. Maybe now he should go for the gun?

"I thought we were just going for a ride. No one said anything about a secret hideout."

"Anyone ever tell you you talk too much?"

"Seems more of a one-sided conversation here," Mitchell said. "Maybe I can help y'all out. Put in an application or something. Can't be too difficult if Mr. Bennett hired you, right?" Mitchell let out a light laugh.

Trevor punched him in the kidney. Mitchell would piss blood with that one. Shane Bennett walked over with a metal chair and Mitchell sat in it.

"Are you working undercover?" Shane said.

"Undercover what?"

More headlights flashed through the broken windows and the guy who'd been driving gave out a whistle like Shane had done earlier, which prompted Shane to raise his hand. Whoever showed up wasn't a cause for alarm. Doors closed and a minute later three guys in suits walked in. They were the same guys from the balcony at the club.

"Hey, Mr. Orchard," Mitchell called out. "It's nice to see you."

When Ryan Orchard walked up, Trevor tossed him Mitchell's wallet. He took one look at it and tossed it into Mitchell's lap. Mitchell put his wallet back into his pocket and wondered why it was going to take all these guys to kill him.

"Look," Mitchell said. "We don't need to do this. Whatever you want to know, I'll tell you."

No one spoke for a long minute. Then Shane said, "You're a private investigator. Are you working with the police?"

Mitchell thought about this. His motel sessions with Helen Ross. What would he have learned if he was? That she was handing out fake prescriptions from a motel room?

"No," Mitchell said. "The police turn their nose down at private work. All I did was talk to Helen Ross and then a man ended up dead in her room. You're telling me she took your money..." Mitchell shrugged.

"Did you kill him?" Shane said. "Then take the money?"

"I didn't take any money. I don't really know what's going on Mr. Bennett, but I don't appreciate you and your muscle man coming into my house and scaring my wife."

Trevor smiled at the muscle man bit.

"You didn't come into my club because you want to start your own business?" It was Ryan Orchard who spoke.

"Your club?" Mitchell looked back and forth between Ryan and Shane, confused. Pointing at Shane, he said to Ryan, "They left me a calling card. I checked it out, that's it. Look, guys. Why don't you tell me what I can do for you? I don't know anything about Helen

Ross or the money she took. How can we make this all go away?"

"That's the best thing I've heard you say all night," Shane said.

Trevor stepped behind him and grabbed Mitchell around the neck. Mitchell pushed himself backwards in the chair hard enough to make Trevor stumble. And Mitchell wasn't even giving it his all.

***

The GPS tracker showed Mitchell's location a hundred yards away from them, which was an access road with a gate blocking them from going any further.

"How much longer?" Sidra said.

Daley looked through a pair of binoculars. "A second vehicle just showed up. Three men. All from Sapphire Groove."

"How much longer?"

Daley looked at the time on his cell phone. They were waiting for Bishop to show up with weapons. "He'll be here."

Sidra nearly bit a hole in her cheek. A little while later, a black Range Rover pulled in behind them and Bishop got out.

"You didn't give me time for shit," he said to Daley, and then to Sidra, "Hey, Hotcakes." Bishop's bald head reflected the moonlight. Old military buddies, he and Daley had one another on speed dial whenever something went down. Not that these things happened often. But Sidra was sure Daley and Bishop did illegal black ops shit together.

Logan the Rottweiler jumped out wearing a black tactical harness. Jesus, what were they going to do? Send the dog in to retrieve Mitchell?

Within two minutes, Daley gave Bishop the rundown, had comm links in their ears, and then Daley said, "Stay in the truck."

"No," Sidra said. "I'm coming with you."

Bishop pumped his hands like brakes. He told Daley, "Logan got your six. Hotcakes got mine," and then he smiled his pearly whites at her.

Daley said, "Why do you have to do that?"

"Oh," Bishop said. "You got a problem with me giving your little sister a nickname?" Then he looked at Sidra. "He don't know why I call you that, huh?"

"Don't tell him," she said.

"See, she got drunk that one time and threw up pancakes all over me. I never liked her ever since."

"That's disgusting," Daley said, and Sidra flipped off Bishop.

They'd already unpacked two black rifles that didn't look like something someone could buy at the local hunting store.

"Inspect and extract," Bishop said to her. "Do everything I say."

It was then that they heard two gunshots and Daley took off through the woods. Sidra followed Bishop as he made his way along the front. He was invisible in the

91

night and a minute later, they'd crossed over the entrance and made their way around the entire perimeter and caught back up with Daley. Logan was nowhere. A deer in the elements.

Daley and Bishop spoke and then split up again. Bishop touched Sidra's shoulder, her heart pounding in her chest as she followed him further around the building. The old Clayton County land management building was on a lake reservoir, desolate and abandoned. Margaret Mitchell probably wrote about this place in Gone With The Wind.

They hadn't posted any lookouts which meant that they weren't expecting the need for it.

"Copy that," Bishop said, then to Sidra, "Daley has eyes on Mitchell." She wished she would have thought to put in her own earpiece. "Copy that," he said again. A second later, Bishop looked through the scope attached to his weapon. She didn't know how he could see. Maybe it had night vision.

"You want to do something fun?" Bishop said.

"Define fun."

He handed her the rifle, told her to look through the scope which she did and everything had a weird green glow to it. "The broken window to the left? See if you can take out the light inside."

Sidra knew what the kickback felt like and braced herself. In one quick move, she lined up the light in the sight and shot a bullet through the window.

Chapter 8

They'd been fighting like two walruses until Ryan Orchard let out two quick shots with the gun near Mitchell's head and he froze in place.

"What?" he said, looking up at the Peach. "I'm not supposed to defend myself?"

"Get up," Ryan said. "And you—" he pointed to Trevor. "Stop taking your job so seriously."

"You know," Mitchell said, and tried to get up, but Trevor kicked him in his back, the toe of his boot connecting with a nerve in his spine. As of now, the only weapons he'd seen were on Trevor and the Peach. He was sure that if it came down to it, weapons would appear out of nowhere.

As instructed, Mitchell sat down in the chair again and still had no idea what kind of operation these guys had going on. They didn't look educated enough to take over the world, and he wondered if they were running drugs out of the club. If that was the case, how did the motel and Helen Ross play into that?

Shane and Ryan argued about what to do with Mitchell. Ryan didn't like that Shane brought him along for a ride out here. Ryan also didn't understand why Shane was so desperate to find Helen.

Shane casually put his hand on Ryan's shoulder and said calmly, "She took the money and I want it back."

"One of the customers took the money," Ryan said. "Not Helen."

And then a light above shattered with the distinct sound of a bullet.

Mitchell said, "What was that?" as the men cleared out to the front. Mitchell stood and clothes-lined Trevor before he could take another step. When the man grabbed his own throat, Mitchell threw a fist at him. First with a punch to the diaphragm, then a punch to the right kidney. When Trevor faced him, Mitchell pounded at his face until the man was down on the ground. Then he kept hitting him as blood poured from his nose and busted face.

"See," Mitchell said. "I let you get the drop on me so you'd never see me coming. On my bad days, I bench three-fifty. Imagine what I do on my good days." Then someone touched his shoulder and Mitchell spun around fast. He was relieved to see Daley. "What the fuck took y'all so long?"

"Let's go. I got Bishop charging me per hour."

Mitchell took Trevor's cell phone and wallet out of his pockets, and followed Daley to the back of the building.

Daley spoke quietly, said he had the target, and was exiting. They made it to a window, the boards across it hanging from screws on one side. Mitchell never even heard him. Neither did the guys that took him.

When they were out of the window, Bishop and Sidra stood with their backs to the wall. "Hold," Bishop said. Mitchell didn't know what that meant, but they all froze. Logan came trotting over and faced his owner. As if Bishop could read the dog's mind, he said. "We're flanked."

Bishop used his hand to tell them to go straight back. They ran fast because they were wide open now. Once they hit the woods, the darkness concealed them. The only light was from the moon above. Man, if they hadn't made it to the woods in time... A minute later, Leland came from the right and another guy from the left. They spoke for a minute, not noticing the planks of wood weren't covering the window anymore.

Daley led them through the woods, past a service road and water tower. The trek took about three minutes. The whole time, Bishop was behind them while the dog stayed to their side, watching the building and sniffing the air.

Once they circled, Daley stopped and watched the two vehicles parked in front of a gate on the service road to make sure none of the goons were in the woods watching them. Mitchell saw Bishop cross over the road, and look at things from another angle.

A minute later, Daley said, "Roger that." He told Sidra and Mitchell to stay put, he'd be back in a minute.

As soon as Daley left, Mitchell and Sidra squatted down back-to-back to keep an eye out. She said in a whisper, "Why did you let them take you?"

"I just kind of went with it."

"They could have killed you."

He knew that from the minute he stepped onto the balcony in the club. What's the point of surveillance and gathering intel if they weren't going to use it? No, it wasn't too often they did stupid shit, but it happened.

Daley came back and said, "Quiet as crickets. You want to go back in and check it out?"

"Hell yeah," Mitchell said, and Sidra's phone rang.

***

Sidra couldn't answer the phone fast enough. She thought something was wrong. The last time Brady called her was last year. She certainly wasn't expecting him to call after everything that had happened between them.

"Do you remember the trip to Washington?" he said. "Junior year?"

"Are you okay?"

"Yeah, I was just thinking about the trip."

And thought to call her? "I wouldn't forget that trip," she said, and followed her brothers through the woods.

"We had a lot of fun that week," Brady said. This is what they used to do. Phone calls in the middle of the night to reminisce about high school. She listened to Brady as he reminded her about all the things they'd seen and museums they'd visited.

The whole while, she observed her surroundings. The isolated place wasn't completely secluded. Those guys could come back at any moment. Daley disappeared around back and they met him inside.

"Have you ever been to Boston?" Brady said.

"No."

"Because I was thinking about going. Just getting away from everything. The weather is probably cold, but there're museums and the library. The historical areas must be cool."

She didn't know why he was telling her this. "That sounds fun, Brady. You've dreamed about traveling. At least you can afford to go wherever you want now."

"But I never do."

"Don't you have a private jet?"

Brady laughed. "No, I don't. Although that sounds great, how would I fly the damn thing?"

While he sounded much better, she wanted to ask him if he'd been drinking. But he wouldn't risk liver or kidney failure on liquor.

Her brothers snooped around the building; they found nothing relevant to anything. They stood in the middle of the room with their hands on their hips, talking it over. Sidra needed to get in there, but it was

Brady. And he was talking to her. And everything in the world had stopped for the last fifteen minutes just so she could hear his voice.

***

Another night with little sleep, and Sidra walked into the office the next morning only to find Casey at her desk with the bottom drawer open. When he locked eyes on hers, he slammed the desk drawer shut and stood up.

"What are you doing?" she said, stepping around him.

"I was looking for a pen."

Four pens were on the desk. Sidra held one up in front of his face.

"Thanks." Casey snatched the pen, then gripped the side of the desk and leaned in close to her. So close that if she'd have turned her head, their noses would touch. "You took my money—"

"What money?"

"Because you've been sending it to my sister."

The hair on the back of her neck stood up. Lexie swore she'd never tell him about the money. Sidra didn't look at him.

He said, "You know what happened last year to all the people who fucked me over? I'm going to need my money back."

"No idea what you're talking about. And if that's why you're buddying up with my dad, you can stop. He doesn't know a damn thing about anything."

Casey stood up straight, and Sidra looked him in the eye.

"Okay," he said, giving in to her illusion of him being an idiot. "Your dad hired me. I'm not buddying up to anything."

"Then that makes you the new guy. So stay out of my life until you clearly understand how it works around here."

The hard look on his face told her he really didn't care. He'd blame her for his son being taken away. And until he was ready to talk about that, there wouldn't be a working relationship between them.

***

While they were all concerned about repercussions of the night before, the morning was business as usual. Sidra went to see Brady Ardeen and got straight to the point.

"I need you to tell me everything that you've been doing for the last six months. Every person you've come into contact with. Anything weird on social media going on? Anyone who's pissed off at you other than Kieran Knox. Everything."

Sidra continued to rattle off more questions and concerns. They were in his office, and Sidra sat on the sofa, Brady in his chair in front of her while she took notes. At this point, he didn't have any way to track the tower because he never thought it would get stolen.

Who steals a man's computer?

"Tell me about your neighbors."

"They're rich."

"Conflict-wise, Brady."

"Sidra, you could have stolen my computer if that's the case." She understood what he meant. For the last year, he was pissed at her and if Sidra wanted to cause him ill will, stealing the computer was the best way to do it.

"What kind of information can someone get from the hard drive?"

"Personal stuff is password protected, but a smart hacker could gain access. Designing and development software is open. That's what could screw me over if someone deletes my work. And the number of contacts I have on there? I've been using that hard drive for three years."

Sidra tossed her notepad on the coffee table. "Let's go for a walk."

Hearing the word walk, Peaches jumped from the sofa and wagged her tail, almost smacking herself in the face with it. They were on the sidewalk when Brady looked up at the sun and took a deep breath.

"I can only take Peaches for a walk when I know she won't poop in someone's yard." Brady said, "I can't pick it up, and my neighbors notice the guy in the wheelchair whose dog took a shit in their yard."

Not all the homes were visible. A lot of them had driveways that stretched through the trees. And a couple of homes had gates across the front of the driveway for additional security.

This neighborhood in Peachtree City started back in the early nineties when a developer targeted the rich folks who were looking for anonymity. The first houses were on large lots, then after about ten homes, the developer put up a security fence. Later, they added the security station. The entire two square miles of Willow Point Estates were surrounded by woods. Someone would have to park in a nearby neighborhood and walk through the woods to get in.

Brady said, "I don't think anyone has ever had a break-in inside this neighborhood. We have our own Facebook group. The only time we open up the gates is during Halloween. The home owners sit at the end of their driveways handing out candy. The cars park all along the streets and kids run around all over."

"I bet y'all hand out full-sized candy bars."

Brady laughed. "Two years ago, one guy handed out iPads. One family handed out Falcon football season passes. You never know what you're going to get."

They continued walking down the sidewalk, stopping every few minutes so Peaches could sniff around. The houses were worth millions, and a variety of different professionals lived here. Sidra tried to figure it all out. Someone had to get in through a back street and walk, and she was looking for the shortest distance. Small areas of wooded land were throughout the neighborhood. A lake was on the far east side and with a huge playground near that. The sidewalk stretched for miles, which was unusual in neighborhoods because the lack of a sidewalk discouraged people from walking around. But with a gated area, the only people using the sidewalk were residents. Which worked out perfectly for Brady.

Thinking about what Brady's mom said, Sidra asked, "Why do you live here?"

"I don't know. I think it just made me feel good to buy something that cost a lot of money. Like I was important."

"You'd never been one with low self-esteem."

Brady shrugged. "I wouldn't have any self-esteem right now if my first video game hadn't sold. I guess I'd be living in my parent's basement trying to survive."

Brady was still trying to survive; he just didn't realize it.

They'd made it half-way when Sidra realized this really was a false sense of security here. It was every homeowner's responsibility to check the validity of anyone working or coming into their home. But if it was a neighbor's contract worker, that meant the person had to spend an awful lot of time researching into Brady. And that made little sense to target him for a computer tower.

It came down to who had access to Brady's home, and where to go for the tower.

"I want a list of your landscapers, your pool guy, maintenance people. Peaches's veterinarian. Your mechanic—"

"I'm never getting my computer back, am I?"

Years of hard work were on that computer. And for someone in Brady's condition, who wasn't easily mobile, he lived on his computer. It was where she'd find him any time of the day. He loved creating and designing. His whole life was online.

"It's tricky, yes. But I'm going to do everything I can to get it back."

This was what investigative work was all about. What seemed to be a boring case was Brady's lifeline. Sidra would hit the ground and interview every single person for a crumb of information.

The thing about working with her family was that there was no glory to the job. When Sidra took over the Brady Ardeen case, Daley moved to something else with no problem. He shared his notes from the police officer he'd spoken with, and also talked to her about the two other nurses Brady interviewed. As of now, Daley was still nowhere closer than Sidra had gotten.

The good news was, Brady would pay anything to get his computer back.

Chapter 9

Mitchell watched fuckhead's house. Lots of windows along the front. Two new vehicles parked out front. Being a bodyguard in a suit must be lucrative. Trevor Gregory walked from room to room, with an ice pack on his face.

That's what you get, asshole. You mess with the bull, you get the horns. Even though Mitchell wasn't so hot himself, his face wasn't broken. A bruise covered his brow bone, and his cheek was slightly swollen. Right knuckles, though? Bruised hams.

Mitchell couldn't stop texting his wife to make sure she was okay. Renee started to get annoyed with him. She was in school; she was fine. The kids were fine. They had the luxury of a school resource officer. Did he want the deputy's number? A few minutes later she texted:

I'll make sure he walks us to the car, okay?

And she'd also sent a photo of herself with the text, and it made him smile.

Earlier that morning, when Mitchell began his surveillance, he put Trevor's wallet and phone in his mailbox. Had to know Mitchell took it. Mitchell also believed that the suits thought he was an idiot the way he kept talking last night, and hopefully they believed he had nothing to do with the shot fired into the light.

As of now, he had no weird phone calls or alarms going off about anything. The police had yet to release the name of the dead guy from the motel.

A little while later, Trevor walked out of his house to the mailbox where he pulled out his wallet and cellphone. He looked around for a long minute, then looked at his house. If he noticed Mitchell's minivan down the street he wasn't alarmed.

Trevor left in a black Tahoe and Mitchell held back a minute, using the binoculars to see which way he turned. He met up with him on the main road, but held back far enough. If Trevor began making evasive maneuvers, Mitchell was burned, and he'd call it a day. They were in the Forest Park area, and Trevor made his way to Jonesboro, past the courthouse and police station, to a shady part of town across the railroad tracks.

Trevor parked at a house, molded and yellow, the color of meth teeth. He got out, knocked on the door, and Leland let him in. Before he closed the door, he looked both ways outside to check for anything out of place.

A minute later, Mitchell looked out of his side mirror and noticed a woman walk up to the van. Thin, stringy hair clung to the side of her face. Her pink cotton shirt hung off her shoulder. For a minute she stood off to the side, hoping he'd notice her, then she knocked when he didn't acknowledge her.

When she knocked again, Mitchell rolled the window down a crack.

"Lookin' for anything special, honey?"

The woman had to be in her fifties. Teeth as bad as the house Trevor visited. "I'm good," Mitchell said.

"Ten dollars'll get you real far."

"Yeah?"

"They call me Hoover." The woman laughed. "But you can call me Ducky cause I like to sucky." Then she laughed again. This woman was three sheets to the wind. When she tried to lean into his car window, Mitchell rolled it up. She slapped her hand against the window and cursed at him.

Someone from the house next door told her to come inside. She passed out in the grass instead. Thank God Trevor stepped outside. Mitchell started to follow him, but then Leland walked outside as well and got into his car.

Let's go with option two.

Leland drove like a bat out of hell, weaving in and out of traffic and pissing people off. The only place this kid was going was to his early grave. He wasn't trying to lose Mitchell. The guy was that stupid.

Leland stopped in a parking lot for a small grocery store, a pizza place, a pawnshop, and a cell phone store. He parked and waited. Leland tapped his thumbs on the steering wheel of his souped-up car, drumming to music only he could hear.

A few minutes later, a silver sedan pulled up. The guy driving wasn't a suit from the club. This guy looked homeless with a gray fuzzy beard and sunglasses. They chatted for five minutes, then Leland left.

On to Grizzly Adams. These guys were playing a game of telephone or something. Mitchell had to remind himself that he was grasping at straws and wasn't getting paid right now. How long could he keep this up before Dad noticed?

Grizzly didn't drive as fast as Leland. In fact, he drove completely opposite, didn't take a straight route anywhere, and looped through various streets back onto Tara Boulevard. There was no way this guy realized he had a tail. Was he paranoid?

Maybe he was just a lone rider. The streets were his stomping ground, and he could be anywhere at any minute when someone called. Grizzly drove towards the train tracks, then back to Tara Blvd., circled around again and drove north. Two minutes later, a black police car put its lights on behind Mitchell.

What the hell?

Mitchell pulled over and rolled down his window.

The approaching officer touched the side of the minivan as he narrowed his gaze towards the side mirror to look inside the vehicle. Probably seen too many assholes on the street today. He had a caution in his step and a scowl on his face. "You failed to use a turn signal at the stop sign."

"Are you sure?"

"Yes, I'm sure."

Too focused on Grizzly, Mitchell couldn't confirm whether he used the turn signal or not. He handed over his license and rolled his eyes. He wanted to ask the officer if he had video footage of him not using his turn signal. Thankfully, he wasn't high right now or this would be really bad.

A few minutes later the police officer came back and said, "I'm writing you a citation for failure to use your turn signal." The officer asked him if he had any questions. Mitchell wanted to ask him if he was concerned with the jackasses running around town causing problems, that maybe if he thought about that rather than people forgetting their turn signals, there would be fewer problems on the street.

"No, Officer." Mitchell gripped the steering wheel. "How much is this going to cost me?"

"You'll have to call the number on the back and they'll tell you the grand total."

The officer took a step back.

"Thank you, Robocop." But Mitchell had already rolled up his window for fear if he made further eye contact, the officer would feel threatened.

When Mitchell got back to Shackelford, he sat in the office listening to Woolsey hack away on a computer, so focused he didn't even look up as he said hello.

Outside, Dad's new assistant was pressure washing the house. Mitchell got up, scratched out (Gofer) and wrote (Sucker) next to it. Dad would have the man painting the house before too long.

Later, when Mitchell arrived at his own house, he got the phone call. It wasn't from someone he expected.

"Detective Coleman. What can I do for you?"

"I was wondering if you wouldn't mind coming back down to the station and have a chat with me. I have some information you may want."

"Of course. I can be there in thirty minutes."

He wondered if the nice detective would fix the ticket for him.

***

"Man," Coleman said. "You wake up that pretty every morning?"

"Thanks." Mitchell rubbed his swollen cheek.

"See any games this season?" Coleman gestured to Mitchell's navy-blue Braves t-shirt.

"Just on TV. Hadn't been to an actual game in years. How about you?"

Coleman shook his head. "Don't really pay much attention to baseball. Football though?"

"College or professional?"

"Depends on the team, man." Coleman let out a light laugh and Mitchell felt at ease with the detective. "Listen," he said. "I need you to back off of whatever you're doing."

"What do you mean?"

"Whatever you're doing." Coleman looked him dead in the eyes.

Mitchell leaned back in his chair. They were in a drab room with a table and chairs. A blank white board on one wall, and a cart full of various forms sat underneath it. "Just sort of looking for Helen Ross." A minute settled with Coleman glaring at him. "Okay. What have I been doing? Don't know who your dead guy is. Or Helen's whereabouts." Mitchell shrugged.

"Look," Coleman said, his tone getting stern. "I work with some mean motherfuckers. Drugs all over Clayco like it's on the border in Texas. The interstate. The gangs think they own this place. Trafficking. Prostitution. Homicides. You close your eyes and start talking about it, you're describing St. Louis. While this one thing might seem like a big deal to you, it's small in comparison, but that doesn't mean it's no big deal. Let us do our job."

"I'm not on any mission to hinder your job," Mitchell said. "I came to you with everything I had."

"You gonna make me spell this out for you, aren't you?"

This is how the police worked. Expected everything and gave nothing in return. Mitchell was used to it. He hadn't broken any laws, didn't even mention that technically Shane Bennett kidnapped him last night. So, if Coleman needed him to understand something, then he was going to have to spell it out.

"You got a clean record," Coleman said. "And I pulled the business. Your Pop was a former cop in the ATL, and the business is clean. You got siblings. They're clean too." Coleman paused and looked at Mitchell for a long minute. The air thick. "Stop following people. Stay in Fayetteville where you belong. Because you're going to end up with another traffic violation and three-square meals on a metal tray."

"So it was a bogus stop?"

"Ain't saying that." Coleman rubbed his smooth jaw for a minute.

"Who are these guys? I'm not concerned with Trevor Gregory—"

When Coleman smirked, Mitchell wondered if he knew about the ass kicking.

"What?" Mitchell said.

"Nothing."

"Shane Bennett hangs out with a guy named Ryan Orchard? One of them owns Sapphire Groove Club."

"Man," Coleman said, shaking his head. But he didn't seem surprised by what Mitchell knew. "All I'm going to tell you is this. They're not the world's baddest badasses until you piss them off. I need you to back off. You exposed yourself last night. People know you now. Back off."

Chapter 10

Sidra met Dominic at Grugan's, a little bar on the square. It was mostly a quiet place where people went to have a beer and watch a game. When she walked in, she found Dominic nursing a beer and he leaned back from the bar for a brief second to look at her.

"You dress up nice," he said, being sarcastic because she had on the same clothes she always wore. Either her black jeans or her blue jeans and one of five different tops she owned. Her wardrobe was slim. Today she had on black jeans—with a hole near the ankle from where a pig bit her this past spring—and a navy blouse. She topped it off with her favorite blue leather jacket that fit like a glove.

"You look nice yourself," she said, and kissed him. She ordered a Monday Night Drafty Kilt.

"So, um, what did you want to talk about?" Dominic said, his face full of quiet anxiety. The way he worked his jaw told her he wanted to get this over with.

"Why are you asking me like that?"

"Like what?"

"Like you're freaking out."

"I'm not freaking out. You said you wanted to talk to me, that you had something to tell me. What is it? You made it sound really important. I don't freak out." Dominic took a sip of his beer, and stretched his neck, working out the kinks of a long day. It's not like she hadn't seen his serious face before, but not mixed with this kind of nervousness.

Sidra opened her mouth to say something, then shut it. She smiled and took a sip of beer.

"Come on... Actually," he said. "Let's not talk about anything. Let's just smile at each other and drink beer." Sidra nudged his elbow as he took a sip. "That's just wrong." He laughed as he wiped at his chin.

"What I wanted to talk to you about was that I wanted to know if you'd go look at a house with me."

"Oh." He puffed out air, relieved. "Yeah, of course. Whenever you want. Just tell me where to be and I'll be there."

"Dominic," she said. "What the hell did you think I was going to tell you?"

"I don't know." He drank more beer. "Maybe you had syphilis?"

Sidra leaned her head back and laughed. A minute later she said, "You thought I was going to tell you something else."

Dominic shrugged.

They'd been sleeping together right off the bat. Met in this very bar one night, and bang, that was it. Things slowed down a bit because of Sidra's living arrangements. Dominic didn't know Sidra couldn't have children. And while he insisted on using protection, sometimes it didn't happen.

"You're not the father of my syphilis. You can relax," she said, and rubbed his back. And while it would be a fun joke to tell him she was pregnant, just to see his reaction, she didn't play around with something that serious.

***

The house was a smaller two-story with gray siding and black shutters. Nothing too special or overpriced, and the neighbors didn't sit on top of one another. Sidra and Dominic followed the real estate agent inside the house the next morning as she explained everything about the house in rapid fire to make a quick sale. The house was thirty years old, had undergone minor renovations, but the house looked great. Lots of wood trim with cream-colored walls. Book cases on each side of the fireplace. The master bedroom had a garden tub with a separate stand-in shower. Sidra had no use for a yard, but it was comfortable enough with low maintenance plants along the front.

"What do you think?" she said to Dominic.

"It's nice. The area's decent, hardly any crime over here. Only two windows on the lower level facing the front, and the garage is side entry. The doors have dead bolts and no windows near the knobs, and there's no sliding glass door. All that's great for security."

Talking like a cop.

The real estate agent said, "It won't last long. I'd put an offer in if you're interested."

Could this really be happening? Her very own house instead of a crappy rental? She could afford this house. The price was great for the location.

Dominic said, "You need to get an inspection done before you buy. The half-bath has mold that's been painted over."

Sidra saw that too.

"Is this your first home together?" the agent asked.

"Oh," Sidra said, and looked at Dominic. "We're not really together." And she smiled at him the way she did.

"I just follow her around," Dominic said.

Before long, Sidra had a home inspector scheduled and kissed Dominic goodbye in the Shackelford parking lot. "Are you sure you don't want to come to work with me today? Lots of phone calls and interviews."

Dominic held up his hand. "On the hierarchy scale, police work trumps P.I. work, so no thank you." He had a smirk on his face. "While you drive around in a soccer mom minivan, I get the cool wheels."

"Soccer mom minivan? It's practical for surveillance."

"I work late tonight." Dominic kissed her again. "Call me later?"

"If I think about you." Sidra grabbed his arm before he walked away. "I've never been to your house." Truth was, she'd never really thought about it until now. Dominic had always come to her. They both worked in Fayetteville and he lived in McDonough. Dominic shrugged and looked away. He still didn't invite her over.

Sidra tried hard to not think too much about her feelings for Dominic. She liked him a lot. He got along fine with Dad—all they did was talk police work—and a couple of times they'd gone to Daley's place to shoot guns. Not the illegal things her brother had, but the registered ones. Neither one of them got caught up in the little things. They'd had one argument, and that was when they spent four days in Savannah in July. It was over spilled alcohol. Not the spilling itself, but the half empty bottle. Dominic thought she'd drank it all. He'd woken up that morning with an accusing tone. "Did you drink all of this?" No, she hadn't, but the question upset her because he was growing aware of the problem. It was the first and only time he'd seen her cry.

Their biggest challenge was balancing their relationship when Sidra didn't have a place to live.

But she could fix that with a house.

Truthfully, she still couldn't decide how she felt about that. She wanted the house, but did she want a steady man in her life holding her down? That's what scared her the most.

Casey Lincoln was the complete opposite of Dominic Getty, and when she saw him standing near the back porch with his shirt soaking wet and his sides exposed as he reached up to pressure wash the overhang, her breath caught and she stopped in her tracks.

Casey, a former criminal. A murderer who burned bodies to get rid of evidence. A former drug-dealer who skimmed a couple million off his boss. Did the Marquez family ever figure that out? Tattoos covered both his arms, and when he looked at her, those icy blue eyes pierced hers.

"What?" he said, shouting over the machine, then he suppressed the sprayer. "Do you need to pass?" When she didn't answer him, he sprayed water at her, but he was far enough away that she only caught the mist.

Thoughts of last summer swirled in her head, and she couldn't help but wonder what the hell Casey was up to. Hanging around so he could sneak inside and snoop around for his money? She could have spent it all by now.

"What happened?" she said.

"About what?"

"Everything." She'd kept up with the case as much as she could, but nothing went to trial. "Aren't you worried someone's going to find you and do a drive-by?"

This made him laugh, but she didn't find the humor. "We came to an understanding," Casey said. "Me and Nacho. He lost his property management business and a strip club. The employees took the fall for everything else. The Griffin market's busted open. I told the Feds what I knew, but not how they operated the details. The Marquez family lives to continue business as usual until the next debacle."

The next debacle. Because kidnapping a little boy was business leverage.

"What are you doing here?"

"I needed a job. To make money." He looked at her pointedly. "Your dad offered, so I took it."

Sidra grabbed a fist around her own braid, then let it go. "I'm sorry about Brandon," she blurted out. "I should have told you everything and let you handle it."

No matter what, the outcome would have been the same. His son may not have been shot, but the police would have come for Casey, eventually.

"I'm not allowed to have contact with him. I know he's okay when my sister gives me the time of day. Do you think you could call her? When you have time?"

Sidra nodded.

Without another word, he went back to washing the house.

Dad would say that the best way to get information was to knock on doors. They had a better chance of people talking to them face-to-face. But even that started out with phone calls.

Daley sat across from her, tapping a pencil on a notepad when she sat down. Her brother spent a lot of time out of the office during the middle of the day, and she wasn't sure what he was working on. He buzzed in his chair like a bee, unable to keep still. The pencil tapping. Adjusting his cap every five seconds. She wondered if he had ADHD. Honest to God, why wasn't he ever tested?

Halfway through one of her phone calls, Sidra gave Daley an exasperated look, but he didn't get it. When she hung up, she stood up fast, pulled the cap from his head and tossed it out the office door. If she did that enough times, he'd run out of energy chasing his cap.

"Why'd you do that?"

"Are you on speed or something?"

"I think I drank too much coffee." Daley fetched his cap, and the cycle began all over again.

Thirty minutes later, Mitchell walked in and leaned against the desk and drummed his fingers. "Do you have any yoga pants?"

"They won't fit you," she said.

He asked Daley, "Do you have a business suit or bicycle shorts?"

"What?" Daley burst out laughing.

"For disguises," Mitchell said. "I found out where the Peach lives and I want y'all to come with me."

"Why do I need yoga pants to go see where a peach lives?"

"The Peach is a suit from the club. And he lives in Buckhead. You'll blend."

Sometimes Mitchell had the stupidest ideas.

Chapter 11

The idea was perfect. The Peach lived in an apartment complex smack in the middle of Buckhead. Why someone would waste their earnings on an apartment was beyond Mitchell. He had to park on the street in the thirty-minute parking spot, then move into a different space.

"When do I need to put on the yoga pants?" Sidra was in the back seat, Mitchell and Daley in the front. They'd stopped for chips and Cokes for the little road trip. Mitchell spent all morning thinking about what Detective Coleman had said, and he was going to leave it alone as he asked, but then Mitchell started looking into the Peach and couldn't help himself.

Maybe he should have come out here alone. But his sister was always the best at getting information because no one ever suspected her of anything. He felt bad using her but he and Daley did it all the time. "I don't even know if this guy is home."

"We could pay some kids to knock on his door?" Daley suggested.

"Mitchell, you wasted all of our time just to see where this guy lives? There's a reason Google maps exists." Sidra unbraided her hair and threw it up into a ponytail on top of her head. "What apartment?" she said and opened the van's side door.

"D-652."

First, she jogged down the block to a dollar store. When she came out, she had on big sunglasses, the Hollywood kind that covered her entire face. Then she headed to a coffee shop and walked out with two mega cups of coffee.

"I bet it's pumpkin spice," Mitchell said.

"She doesn't like pumpkin spice."

They both laid tens on the dashboard.

Sidra was such a crackerjack that when a guy walked out of the apartment complex, he held the door for her, her mouth moving, probably saying, *Sorry I can't get to the keypad.*

"I'm glad she didn't wear the yoga pants," Daley said. "She wouldn't have a place to put her cell phone to call us when the Peach kills her."

"Shut up," Mitchell said. "He'd give her back."

Daley opened his cell phone and tracked her, lost her for a minute in the elevators, then she appeared again at the general location.

For fifteen minutes they waited in the car. Years ago, one of the first lessons Dad taught him was never to engage with a target. Especially if it was an insurance case. They'd broken so many rules over the years, it wasn't even funny. And P.I.s were supposed to follow the laws to a tee. Mostly, they did, but it was the lying that always seemed unlawful. He'd told Coleman he'd back off, and now here he was watching Ryan Orchard's place.

Finally, Sidra walked out and turned right towards the coffee shop. Mitchell pulled out of his parking spot, circled around the block, and picked her up two blocks over. Balancing the coffees, she got in and said, "He's home."

"Is it pumpkin spice or not?" Mitchell said.

"Mocha caramel."

"Dammit. Why do you always have to be right?"

Daley grabbed the money on the dash.

"He's home?" Mitchell said, letting the lost bet roll off his shoulders.

"A woman answered the door. I asked for Barney, the guy I'd met last night on MARTA. Pretty classy, huh?"

Mitchell drove back to the front of the apartment with five different conversations going on at the same time. Sidra told them she had to be home by three because she had a home inspection she needed to attend.

"I'll co-sign for you," Mitchell said. Anything to get her out of the basement.

Daley started talking about a taco truck down the street, and Mitchell kept asking about the woman in the apartment. "Was she one of the little babes from the club?"

"What does that mean?" Sidra said, when Mitchell found a parking spot. "She looked like a wife or a sister. Short hair to her shoulders, bony face. My height. She had thin lips and an overbite."

The hair on the back of Mitchell's neck stood up. "Tell me what happened."

Sidra sipped her coffee. "The woman opened the door. I asked for Barney and she said no one by that name lived there. I looked disappointed as I told her I was sure this was the apartment number. Then I saw the guy from the club walk over. Same story to him too. Then I played dumb and said, 'Oh it's E not D', apologized and left."

"How did she talk?"

"Didn't have a Southern accent. She spoke patiently, like she was a schoolteacher—never mind, that's a terrible example. Slowly. Methodically. Someone who—"

"Like a counselor?"

"Yeah, could be."

Daley said, "Hey guys..." and pointed across the street.

Mitchell could not believe what he was seeing. Helen Ross walked down the sidewalk next to the Peach, both hidden behind hats and sunglasses. Sidra nearly spilled her coffee as she exited the van. Mitchell said, "Yoga pants, yoga pants."

Daley said, "I'm on it," and jumped out to start the tail.

Sidra hopped further in the back and changed her clothes faster than a high schooler caught in the back seat by the police. "How many times have you done that?"

"More than you, but less than Donna Talbert."

"That hurts."

Mitchell handed her two wireless comm units as she exited, and then she jogged in the same direction as Daley. The Buckhead sidewalk was busy with people bustling about, and a minute later, Mitchell heard Sidra over the comm, then finally Daley.

Mitchell said, "The woman's name is Helen Ross. Don't lose her."

For the life of him, Mitchell couldn't fathom what was going on. Helen Ross was a fake counselor, taking people's money at the motel and writing fake prescriptions. Shane Bennett came to him because Helen Ross took his money and didn't know where she was. A man was found dead in the motel—a man that Renee swore was half-naked. Ryan Orchard and Shane work together. And now they find Helen with the Peach?

What the hell was going on?

Then Mitchell tried to take into consideration everything he learned from Coleman. To leave everything alone. That he was supposed to figure things out through Coleman's clues. Before Mitchell left yesterday, he handed the detective the ticket because he said he'd fix it. Was one of the guys he'd tailed yesterday an undercover? Not Trevor Gregory. He wouldn't have hit Mitchell the way he did, even if he was undercover. Shane asked him if he was working undercover. Why was he suspicious? That left Leland and Grizzly Adams. Surely it wasn't Helen Ross, the woman who stole money and had a half-naked dead man in the room.

"I've got them at Lenox," Sidra said. "Holding hands. Definitely not his sister."

"I would hope not," Daley said.

"Don't lose them," Mitchell repeated.

***

Whether Sidra dressed in a business suit or yoga pants, she blended into the Atlanta crowd with ease. The demographics were as different as snowflakes in the sky. Walking into Lenox was no problem. They followed the couple to the food court.

Daley said, "I'm getting a hot dog."

"He's joking, right?" Mitchell said.

"That's a negative, Ghost Rider."

Daley jumped in line at the hot dog place and Helen and the Peach ordered food at a soup and salad bar. Sidra lowered the cap she put on her head and pretended to check out the mall directory. She checked the time. One o'clock. Plenty of time before the home inspection appointment.

"Eyes on targets," Sidra said. "Sitting and eating."

This was a sitting game. But gathering intel always led to something. Sidra grabbed a mall information pamphlet and moved. Her phone tucked into the waistband of her pants, the mic between her boobs. She opened up the pamphlet and casually covered her face as she made her way near the targets. Pulled out her cell phone, sat down and pretended to be engaged with the phone as she faced Helen's back. When Daley realized what she had in mind, he sat down at the table on the opposite side of them. At least he blended in with the hot dog and drink.

"When can I get out of here?" Helen said, around a bite of food. "I did everything you asked. No one said—"

The Peach held up his hand as someone walked by to sweep up trash. When the sweeper left, he said, "You'll be out of here in a week, tops. I just have to clear up a few things."

"Why can't you come with me?"

"We already discussed this. We knew it was never permanent. I have my life here. You travel with work."

"What am I going to do if he finds me?"

"He won't find you."

"You keep saying that, but what if Vince said something? To anyone?"

"Don't worry about Vince," the Peach said.

"Don't worry about Vince? He's dead, Ryan."

"Keep your voice down."

A long minute passed, and they dug into their salads.

Helen said, "Is anyone else going to die of an overdose because of this?"

"If they threaten to expose it, yes." The Peach sighed. "You'll be out of here soon. As long as Shane thinks one of your patients took the money, you're safe."

Following them back to the apartment was fairly uneventful. They found Mitchell on a street further down from where they left him. On the way to another parking spot, Sidra told him everything they said. But Daley had one better. He'd recorded their conversation.

Sidra said, "This is the woman from the motel?"

"Yep."

"What motel?" Daley said. He only had half the information. "That woman's not even your type."

"What's my type?" Mitchell said. "I'm married to a beautiful woman, thank you very much." And then he explained why he visited Helen Ross, the fake therapist who set up shop in the middle of the night in a motel room.

They watched the apartment complex for another forty-five minutes and spotted the Peach leaving in a suit. For a moment, they discussed following him, but he was most likely going to the Sapphire Groove Club.

"Maybe I should go pay Helen Ross a visit?"

Chapter 12

Mitchell went alone to keep their cover in case Daley or Sidra had to come into contact with these guys again. Helen wouldn't answer the door, but Mitchell kept knocking. When she opened the door, the chain kept it from opening all the way.

The terror on her face when she saw Mitchell was alarming. "I'm not going to hurt you," he said, as she shut the door. "But if you don't talk to me, I'm going to call the police. They're looking for you."

The door opened, and he thought she was going to run.

"No one followed me," Mitchell said. A moment passed before she finally let him in. "I'm glad you're okay."

She stood there, in need of her own counselor in the situation she'd gotten herself into. And maybe she could use a shot of vitamins. Her skin looked pale, her cheekbones protruding like Morticia Addams.

"Can you tell me what's going on? This Shane guy came to my house with his goon looking for you. I have no idea why they thought I knew anything."

Helen threw her hands up. "You shouldn't be here. The best thing for you to do is go home to your wife. I promise you, it's better for her to slap you around than Shane Bennett."

"I thought you were a real doctor," he said.

"The shitty motel didn't give me away? Cash under the table while I smoked cigarettes so you can vent about your shitty marriage?"

They stood in a little foyer and she hadn't asked him to come in. The expensive apartment had floor to ceiling windows with dark drapes hanging over them.

"I am a real doctor," Helen said. "I just choose to have my office wherever the money comes in."

"Writing fake prescriptions out of the Tara Motel? Who's the dead guy?" He thought about telling Helen that his wife followed him that night, but thought better of it. Keep Renee's name out of it.

"You're asking a lot of questions."

This was true. And in the end, Mitchell wasn't getting anything out of it. Not a paycheck or the satisfaction of closing a case. Helen Ross certainly would not bring Shackelford Investigations more clients.

Helen said, "It's not a big deal. People do it all the time. I make a tax-free income and help people out. You didn't complain about my services. In fact, I think you and I made quite a connection." Helen Ross had a way of talking to people and she got rich off of people's problems.

"How bad are these people?"

Helen looked away from him and ran her fingers through her short hair. "I just met them a few months ago. All they care about is money. I mean, who isn't when there's a ton of people out there willing to drop money for illegal substances."

Mitchell thought about himself. He wasn't addicted to anything. Sometimes he just needed something to give him a little boost. That's all.

"I'll be gone by the time you tell the police where I'm at. In fact, I'm leaving before Ryan gets home from the club tonight. No, scratch that. I'm leaving right now. Why don't you go ahead and leave?"

The woman didn't owe him anything. The danger she'd gotten herself into was her problem. Aside from the little fiasco at the club the other night, Mitchell didn't have a connection to these guys. The police wanted Helen Ross because she'd checked into the Tara Motel, and a guy ended up dead.

"Where are you going to go?" Mitchell said. "The police are going to find you."

Helen turned away from him and moved further into the apartment. She packed a suitcase in the same quick manner his wife had packed one. Thinking about Renee, he needed to check on her again.

"Do you want me to tell you what happens to people who know too much, Mitchell?"

"How much money did you take?"

Helen shook her head as she zipped the suitcase. "It's not about the money. I mean... it is about the money, but it's about the potential for more money. I'm an asset with the ability to make them money and I fucked up when I didn't report all the earnings." She dragged her suitcase to the front door.

"Wait a minute," he said. "Go to the police."

"And tell them what? I lost my license to practice psychology and I've been scamming people, and these men want me to continue doing it?"

"Whatever it is, someone can help you."

"You seem like a good man, Mitchell. Go home to your wife and forget this whole thing ever happened."

"What are you going to do if they come after you?"

She seemed to think about that for a minute. "I hope like hell they never find me. I'll be careful about who I get into business with next time." Helen did a quick sweep of the apartment, making sure she had everything.

When she finished, Mitchell said, "You're going to leave now? No concern about the consequences?"

"This is what I do, okay? I've spent two years in Georgia, it's time for me to go, and I'm never coming back."

Helen walked out of the complex ahead of him. Her plan was to take the bus out of town, and Mitchell didn't try hard to stop her.

Except, as soon as she stepped out, the Atlanta Police Department was there to apprehend her.

Helen's shock was genuine. Mitchell wasn't sure what he was supposed to do and when he stepped back inside, an officer started screaming at him to get down on the ground. Drama queen in a uniform.

And then Sidra started chirping in his ear, "Are you okay? They said nothing about taking you down. Are you okay? Answer me."

"I'm okay," Mitchell said.

"That's nice," the officer said. He had Mitchell by the arm and put him in the back of a squad car. "Mitchell Shackelford?"

A nod to confirm.

"Is the apartment still clear?"

"Yes, sir."

The officer's nameplate said Grabowski, a perfect fit the way he had Mitchell on the ground and in cuffs so fast.

Officer Grabo said, "Give me a minute." Then he spoke into his radio.

Mitchell's heart pounded in his chest. He didn't think when he told Daley and Sidra to listen over the comm and to call the police if things strayed sideways, it meant he'd end up in cuffs as an accomplice or something.

"Mitchell," Sidra said, "what's happening?"

"I don't know, Sis."

"I have to be at a home inspection by five. You think you can hurry it along?"

Four officers, two squad cars. Mitchell watched as they put Helen in another car. Grabo said, "They're going to take her in, and put in a call to Clayton." Now he took off the cuffs. "Sit tight for a minute."

A minute to Officer Grabo was more like twenty. Mitchell had plenty of time to think about the guilt he felt for turning Helen Ross in, but the truth was he couldn't walk out of there and let her go. If the police found out about that, he'd be in jail for aiding and abetting. Jesus, what would Renee say about that?

By the time Grabo finished taking Mitchell's statement, Mitchell was under strict orders to either go talk to Detective Coleman in Clayton County immediately, or they would be inclined to come get him.

***

Sidra sat down later that evening with the home inspection report in her hand. While the house had a few minor issues, there wasn't anything structural that would be a problem. When it came time to apply for the loan, she realized she was doing everything backwards after she'd spent nearly three-hundred dollars she didn't have on the inspection. It was a waste of money if the loan didn't get approved. How could she be so stupid?

Dad hadn't even looked at the house yet. Did it matter? She was an adult; she could handle buying a house. All of this finance stuff made her dizzy. As she logged off, she took a deep breath and said a quick prayer, and tried not to be too excited just yet.

Back to Brady's computer, Sidra checked the phone messages Mom left for her, and the few emails she'd gotten as well. After another hour on the phone, she wasn't anywhere closer to getting the computer back. The masks threw her off.

It had to be someone Brady would recognize, and this brought her back to Kieran Knox. The risk he'd have taken was enormous. And Brady certainly would have recognized his voice. Kieran didn't have a distinct voice. No prominent accents or drawl. His voice wasn't too high pitched or low for a guy.

As she sat there wondering about Kieran Knox, she pulled up his Facebook and Instagram and switched back and forth between the sites. People were so interesting the way they put their whole lives out in the open, a production into a story they wanted the world to see. Kieran had a lot of friends and followers. Lots of likes on everything he posted. And if he didn't have a fair number of likes, he made sure that people noticed him. He was an amazingly talented young man in his digital art and creativity. He had a website showing off his work.

Sidra spotted it after a while. The party at a big fancy house on New Year's Eve. And because social media was such an excellent resource, and half the people who tagged Kieran in photos also checked in to the location, Sidra learned that Kieran Knox spent his

New Year's Eve at 1612 Red Fox Trail in Peachtree City. Which was in Willow Point Estates.

Sidra sipped the whiskey and felt the exhaustion of the long day hit her. She needed to get some sleep, but she sat there staring at the photos on her computer screen. Trying to understand someone's motivation was tricky. Speculating was easy, but it was the facts that mattered. All she had so far was that Kieran backed out of Brady's project, and that he'd spent New Year's in the neighborhood.

The notes started with Kieran and followed with the home care nurses, including Marcy and the two that Daley interviewed. Then the lawn maintenance, the therapy pool guy, the meal preparation company, and everyone else who had been inside the home in the last six months that Brady could remember. The list had fifty plus names on it. In Sidra's mind, they were all guilty. Then there was Brady's family. Could they have done anything of this nature?

His mother said she didn't like him living alone in the big house the way he did. But Sidra knew Julie. Julie wouldn't orchestrate this. Julie hovered, but she wasn't evil. His dad, David, and sister, Erin, didn't seem likely either, and Sidra knew how much Brady's sister adored him.

The faster they found his computer; the faster Brady could get on with his life.

Mom poked her head in the door. "You're working late." That wasn't unusual.

"I'm putting in an offer on a house tomorrow morning." When she looked out of the window, she saw the sun had gone down, and it was dark outside. It would be comforting to go home to her own place again. "I'm trying."

"You skipped dinner," Mom said, when she noticed the Mason jar. She had a smile on her face that said, *You don't take care of yourself.*

"I'll warm something up. Thanks, Mom." Before Mom stepped away, Sidra said, "Wait. Did you ever talk to Julie Ardeen? I mean, after the accident? You two were friends while Brady and I were dating, but..."

They didn't talk about this because Sidra never wanted to. It meant talking about Sidra running away at eighteen, and that subject was hostile territory with Mom.

"Well, I guess if you were home, you could have seen for yourself how devastated she was, but that should be expected."

Sidra hadn't been at the accident that night. They thought he was going to die, and Sidra ran away. She fucking ran away. What kind of person did that? Brady was right, she'd abandoned him. Maybe she didn't love him.

And the baby?

Maybe she didn't love anyone.

"You're right, I wasn't home. I can't change anything but I should have been here." She drank the last of the whiskey. "For Brady. I should have been here."

And she should have kept her baby.

When Mom left, Sidra called him. She said, "What are you doing?"

"Watching Peaches chase down a grasshopper around the house. It's half the size of her."

Sidra smiled.

"Did you need something?" he said.

"No. I don't really know why I called."

"You've never needed a reason to call me."

A few minutes of silence and she closed her eyes and listened to Brady breathe into his cell phone, and for a moment she pretended she could smell him. Comforting and fresh, his sweat mixed with hers. She imagined him following Peaches as she chased down the grasshopper. Sidra thought about the past. Smiling. Happy. The summers passed too quickly, but in the end, it was worth the late nights and romps in the fields. They had nothing to worry about then when there was nothing but love in the air and an endless supply of hope for their future.

She said, "What'd you do today?"

"I won an Olympic gold medal in the pool, and then I shot down some zombies. After that I got a massage. Have you found anything?"

She told him about Kieran Knox and how he rang in the New Year down the street from him.

"I was at that party," Brady said. "The Randolphs have one every year. It's a big deal. I can ask Phil if he knows Kieran personally. He may have come with another family though."

"Are you sure he wasn't one of the masked guys?"

"I don't know. I was scared, but I didn't feel at the time that I recognized either of their voices."

Peaches barked after Sidra heard the doorbell through the phone.

"I need to go," Brady said. "I'll call you later."

"It's nine o'clock, don't answer the door."

"It's my dad, Sidra. No need to panic."

It wasn't until Brady assured her it was in fact his dad coming over that Sidra breathed. She had no idea why she was so worried about him.

Chapter 13

Late Saturday morning, Mitchell woke up to the sound of his boys running through the house. His wife didn't want him around the kids, so it surprised him that she came home even after they had a phone conversation last night.

Spencer and Luca ran to him as Mitchell came down the stairs. He scooped Luca into a hug. "I miss you guys."

But Caroline gave him the cold shoulder. "I'm going to my room," she said, and Mitchell patted her on the head as she walked away.

Renee said, "We're just here to get some things," and began packing her school supplies into a plastic crate.

Mitchell wasn't sure what to say to her that wouldn't set her off. Right now, even if he told her her hair looked nice, she'd think he was being condescending.

"Daddy," Luca said. "Can we go play baseball?"

"In a little bit."

"Why can't we just stay home?" Spencer said.

"Boys, go upstairs in your rooms for now, okay?" When they left, Mitchell looked at Renee. "When are you going to come home?"

"I don't know. Can you assure me two men in suits won't show up when you're not home?"

Renee looked vulnerable standing there in the office as she folded her arms across her chest. The chocolate-colored sweater she had on was old and thin, her favorite, and Renee would wear it from fall to spring. When he reached for her, she shook her head and picked up her crate.

"I promised the kids I'd order a pizza," she said, and Mitchell didn't pay attention as he stood there looking around the room.

Angry with himself.

Angry with his wife.

"Did you hear me?"

"I'm sorry. What?"

"You never listen." Renee walked away.

Through lunch, Caroline wouldn't talk to him, Renee wouldn't look at him. She was fine talking to him over the phone, but didn't seem interested in seeing him. Hot and cold. He was wondering about his wife's state of mind.

After lunch, he walked with the boys down Pecan Pie Road to the field to throw the baseball. The boys didn't always get along, and he remembered what Sidra told him that night at the lake. That Caroline hit them sometimes. Why hadn't they ever said anything about it?

"Stop throwing so hard," Luca said.

Spencer put his hand to his head. "That's why you have a mitt."

"Okay, okay," Mitchell said. "We'll take it easy on you."

"Daddy, why do we have to live with Aunt Vanessa? She won't let us play in the house."

"You're not living there," Mitchell said to Luca. "It's just for a little while."

"But why?"

Spencer held onto the ball. "Because you and Mom fight so much? She told Aunt Vanessa that y'all were getting a divorce."

Mitchell's throat clinched. Renee said nothing about divorce. Was she serious? And why hadn't she said anything to him. Worse, why would she have a conversation like that in front of the kids, and worry them?

"I don't want to live with Aunt Vanessa," Luca said, about to cry.

"Come here. Both of you."

The boys walked over to him, and he pulled them into a tight hug. His kids were his life. So why was he acting so carelessly? His family was falling apart, and the dope wasn't even half the problem. What was he supposed to do? Slap his wife next time she hit him? *Jesus.*

"Mom and I are not getting a divorce. We just need some time apart, okay? I need you boys to be strong and do whatever Mom tells you, okay. When I'm not around, you are the men—" Mitchell swallowed down the frustration, and took a deep breath. "Everything's going to be okay."

"Why are you crying?"

"I'm not crying. I got dirt in my eye."

"You rubbed dirt on it?" Luca said and tried to smile.

"Yeah, I did."

Just then, Caroline came running down the road, and Mitchell's heart opened up with joy, his daughter running into his arms, and everything was okay. But there was nothing on her face but fear as she cried. "Mama. They took Mama."

Mitchell ran down the road faster than all three of his kids. No one was at the house. The back of Renee's SUV was open, as she'd been loading everything in. He ran inside and started calling her name. Nothing. He realized he'd left the kids vulnerable and dashed back out, but the three of them were there. Caroline held Luca's hand, both of them crying.

"Caroline?" He grabbed his daughter's shoulders. "Tell me what happened."

Through a shaky voice, she said, "We were putting everything in the car and this van came and a man jumped out and grabbed Mama and she tried to push him away but he put her in the van and they left."

Mitchell called 911 and could barely hold the phone he shook so badly. The dispatcher asked him so many questions and he didn't have answers. "What kind of van was it?" he asked Caroline.

"I don't know."

"Like the kind I drive or bigger?"

"It didn't have windows."

"And what color?"

"Black?"

Mitchell said into the phone, "It might be a black or navy panel van... No, she didn't see the direction they drove."

A few names passed through Mitchell's mind. According to Detective Coleman, the police were going to pick up Ryan Orchard from the club last night. Helen Ross wouldn't have been able to talk to anyone about seeing Mitchell yesterday, at least not this soon. And the other guys? Why would they care about Mitchell and his family?

"I see the police officer now, thank you."

Relief washed over him at the sight of Dominic Getty. "What's going on, Mitchell?" They stepped away from the kids, but Mitchell kept his eye on them.

"Some asshole took my wife." Mitchell told him everything that had happened in the last three days. He gave them names and the addresses. And then, when he was in the middle of talking to Dominic, a call came in over his radio about a woman at the square.

"What was that? A distressed woman?"

144

Dominic's wheels spun just as fast as Mitchell's. "Unit 2-30; repeat the call about the distressed woman."

"All units, be advised. Black panel van last seen moving northbound on 85. Involved in a kidnapping..."

"Ask them if the woman was wearing a brown sweater."

But Dominic said nothing. He couldn't until dispatch finished with their BOLO.

"2-30; I'm trying to find out if these calls are related. Is the woman's name Renee Shackelford?"

Mitchell's cell phone rang, but he didn't recognize the number. He almost didn't answer, but then he thought it could be one of the suits.

"Hello."

"It's me. I'm okay." Her voice nearly knocked the wind out of him.

"What happened?"

"He threw me out of the van at the water fountain."

Mitchell tapped Dominic on the chest to get his attention, then nodded. "Get in the van," he told the kids, because he couldn't leave them alone.

The fountain in the middle of town was five minutes away and even though Dominic drove in front of him to lead the way, he certainly wasn't driving as if his family member had been kidnapped. Mitchell passed him when the highway opened to two-lanes.

He was still on the phone with Renee when he got to the fountain. Two police cars and an EMT were there. "Stay here," he told the kids.

He ran up to Renee and pulled her into a hug and pressed his face to her head.

"I'm okay. Thank God it was me and not Caroline. Is she okay?"

The thought of those words sent Mitchell into a silent rage. "Who was it?" Mitchell looked at her.

"The guy who came to the house. The one who punched you."

Okay, Trevor. I got your message loud and clear.

They dropped the kids off at Shackelford so Mitchell could take Renee to Urgent Care even though she didn't want to go. Trevor had held her down by the throat in the back of the van nearly the whole time he had her, while someone else drove. The more she'd struggled, the tighter he squeezed. The best thing to do was get it all documented properly with photos.

No matter what, Trevor Gregory was going to pay.

Trevor didn't say a single goddamn thing to her the whole time. He grabbed her, put her in the van down on her back, then threw her out on the ground like a piece of discarded trash. Aside from the bruises on her throat, bloody scrapes covered her right shoulder, her elbow was swollen, and she'd torn her favorite sweater.

She was pissed about the sweater.

"My grandma made that sweater," she said, sitting on the exam table. They'd given her one of those paper things to cover herself.

"I didn't know that."

"Yes, you did." Renee laughed. Actually laughed. "She gave it to me my first Mother's Day after Caroline was born. The poo poo brown sweater. She could have picked a better color for my first Mother's Day."

Mitchell remembered now.

They'd given Renee a brief exam, put some ointment on her shoulder and took an X-Ray of her elbow. A doctor stepped into the room and introduced himself as Dr. Trotter. "No pain in the elbow?" he said, looking a little confused.

"A little now." Renee winced when Dr. Trotter touched it.

"You have a lateral epicondyle fracture. The good news is that it doesn't require surgery, but you'll need to keep it in a sling. No problems moving your wrist and shoulder?"

"A little," Renee said, "but if there's a fracture, I don't want to push it."

A nurse came in and put Renee's arm in a sling asked her if she needed any pain medication right now. They discharged her with a prescription for pain management and told her to take it easy.

The nurse must have given her extra pain meds because when they got in the van, Renee said, "Can we get ice cream?"

"Of course," he said. "Anything you want."

They swung through the busy DQ, and Renee held her ice cream cup with the fractured hand in the sling. "Do you need help?" Mitchell said, but she shook her head. They were back on the highway and Mitchell told her how sorry he was about what happened and had to brace himself for whatever would come.

"It's always the job," she said.

"Nothing like this has ever happened. I was scared, Renee, I really was. I don't know what I would have done if something happened to you."

Silence filled the van until she said, which seemed out of the blue, "I want a divorce, Mitchell," and the words caught in her throat and she sniffled back the tears and started to cry. Everything came crashing down on him.

A divorce?

He hadn't wanted to consider what the boys had told him earlier. Actually, he hadn't had time to consider it. The plan was to talk to her about it when he thought she was calm enough to discuss it. Or if she had time away from him, maybe she'd feel better and think about what she really wanted.

He swerved through traffic because he just wanted to get back home. Except he wasn't going home, his family wasn't safe there.

"Did you hear me?"

"Yes, Renee. You spring this on me when I'm driving..." He set the cup of ice cream into the cup holder. Seemed a little pointless now. "I don't know what to say." What could he say other than no? He had to choose his words carefully. The worse thing his wife could do was take the kids away. Suddenly he envisioned his life with him waking up in a rundown trailer in the trashy part of town because he'd lost everything. Paying child support and barely making ends meet. All this work to raise a family and now he was losing it all?

"What do you want, Renee? And don't say a goddamned divorce. What do you want?"

"Things are not okay between us. We don't even talk anymore."

"And you think a divorce is going to fix that? Maybe if you'd stop yelling at me all the time, I'd be a little more inclined to talk to you. And when a man feels as though he can't do anything right, there comes a point where he stops trying."

"And lies to his wife and uses drugs?"

Mitchell sighed. He really didn't want to argue with her right now. He wasn't strung out and getting high every day. "I don't lie to you. My work day stretches out longer than it's supposed to all the time, you know that. And the other thing? Okay, it stops now."

"That's what you said before. And here we are."

"I don't want to lose you, Renee. And I don't want to lose the kids."

***

Mitchell spent Saturday parked out back at the Sapphire Groove Club. What he'd learned today was that the police never picked up the Peach because he never showed up at the club yesterday and they couldn't find him.

But that's not who Mitchell was looking for.

Trevor Gregory dumped the panel van in Clayton County and the police found it an hour after the BOLO. The stolen vehicle was from a nearby business, probably because it was missing the plate and company logo.

With two of the suits MIA, he couldn't help but watch his back. Renee and the kids were at Shackelford. At least they were safe with Dad. His parents didn't know the extent of his marital problems, but spending some time with them would help.

The Sapphire Groove was hopping with people pouring in at midnight, but the back was just as busy. The VIP section. Go through the back door, get the perks.

When Leland walked down the metal stairs to a black sedan, Mitchell held back a minute, then followed him out to the back alley, the same route they'd gone the night they took him. Leland drove in and out of traffic without a care about the speed limits.

The traffic was heavy at this time of night, but that wasn't unusual. Leland hung a left and made his way to an empty strip of closed businesses for the night. Mitchell hung back in a bank parking lot and watched him. These guys never thought they were criminals. They did what they had to do to get money. That's what it was about. Money. And the things they did to stay under police radar. Leland sat in his car for fifteen minutes, then he left again.

Did he know he had a tail?

He drove to the cemetery on Main Street. From across the street, Mitchell had a clear view of him through the binos, but then Leland got out and walked. Maybe the guy liked to talk to the dead in the middle of the night. Mitchell drove across the train tracks and past Leland's parked car, to the back of the cemetery. While the street wasn't dead quiet, it was far less busy than the main streets. After finding a place to stop, he scanned the cemetery but didn't see movement.

Mitchell was worried that if he got out, he would get jumped. Residences surrounded the cemetery, with graves dating back to 1800. And while the cemetery wasn't lit up with a full view, it was at least visible from where Mitchell parked. The gravestones wouldn't give him any cover if he started walking around to find Leland. But then Mitchell didn't have to. At the far end where two streets intersected, he spotted Leland walking to a silver sedan. The same silver sedan Mitchell spotted Grizzly driving. Leland got inside the car and they spoke for a few minutes, but instead of Leland getting out, they drove back up the street, passing right in front of him. Grizzly dropped Leland off at his car.

Last time he'd followed Grizzly, he got burned and ended up with a ticket. Rolling the scenario through his head, Mitchell wondered if Leland was a snitch and Grizzly a cop. Coleman hadn't told him as much, but it was implied.

Was this about the dead guy in the motel, or was it something else? Clayco, as they call it, had lots of gang activity in the area. Nearly everyone in the gangs around here worked inside of a theft ring. And when they weren't busy stealing, they were selling drugs. And like any city, there was a hierarchy to it—street level thugs to organized crimes.

Mitchell followed Leland back to the club, where no one seemed to miss him and everything was the same. He wondered if the police had their eyes on this place because they surely had found nothing at Trevor's house.

Chapter 14

Monday morning at 5:54 a.m., Sidra woke up to Luca poking her in the face with a toy. She opened her eyes, and he stood on her bed with no respect for sleep and told her it was time to get up.

"Luca, here." Sidra pulled the covers back for him to climb underneath. "Go to sleep."

"I gotta go to school."

"If you poke me with that thing one more time."

"Grandma wants to know if you want pancakes."

Sidra closed her eyes and smelled the pancakes and bacon. Luca poked her again. When she grabbed for him, he screamed with laughter a little too loud this early in the morning. Where did he get all of this energy?

Out of all of her nieces and nephews, Luca was the wildest. The bedroom was dark and the only thing she saw was Luca's ghostly face from the hall light. "Does Grandma need help?"

"She's burning down the kitchen."

Five minutes later... Mom was not burning down the kitchen. In fact, she had everything under control. The morning seemed to have that quiet chaos Sidra remembered growing up, when Mom got five kids ready for school and out the door on time.

"Stop playing with Spiderman, Luca, and finish your breakfast." Mom tried to get them fed and ready before it seemed to throw a monkey wrench into something, because Renee insisted yesterday that the kids could just eat cereal.

Being a teacher, Renee had to be at school earlier and Mom said she'd take the kids, but Renee argued it was a waste of gas. Mitchell didn't want his wife to go in at all, said she needed to rest with her arm in the sling.

They'd been up "talking" for hours last night. Who knew a marriage was so much work? Don't you just get married and have kids and its perfect harmony? Mom and Dad were a testament to that.

When breakfast was over, Sidra found Luca in the bathroom, standing on the counter, looking at his butt in the mirror. "Aren't you supposed to be brushing your teeth?"

"I was trying to count my teeth."

"Unless your butt has teeth, you're looking at the wrong end."

This made him laugh as she grabbed him around the waist with one arm and took him off the counter. "I got toothpaste on my butt," he said, and sure enough, he had toothpaste on his butt. How did that even happen? Sidra used a damp towel to get the toothpaste off his jeans as Luca started talking about how he had seventeen teeth and the tooth fairy still hadn't come by. It had been seven days since his last tooth fell out.

"I think the tooth fairy is a little busy right now."

Both of them. With their problems.

Renee yelled from downstairs for Luca to hurry, and it seemed to take the act of Jesus and all his saints to get Mitchell's family out of the house. Spencer couldn't find his backpack. Caroline's hair wouldn't cooperate. And then Luca couldn't find his shoes, which he'd left outside yesterday. And on top of all of that, the boys' jackets were at their Aunt Vanessa's.

There are too many people in this house, Sidra thought. *Nonsense,* Mom would say. *There are never enough people in this house when it comes to my family.*

When they were finally gone, Sidra brought her coffee in the office and turned on all the computers. The white boards needed updating, two blue books needed to be filed, and stacks of notes were spread out on her desk that needed to be typed up. Mom had a stack of invoices to file, and there was a small list of potential clients she was corresponding with.

Sidra spotted Casey's white truck pulling into the parking lot and she walked out to the front porch to watch him. Without realizing her move, she stood at the end of the front porch with her arms folded across her chest and wondered how long it was going to take him to do all the tasks Dad asked him to complete. The next thing on his list was pulling up the old shrubs around the house that never seemed to turn green anymore. When Casey got out and gave her a curt nod, Sidra blushed and left the porch.

Still waiting on the approval of the loan, she checked the email again and had nothing. When Daley and Woolsey came in, they tried to come up with a game plan about cases and moving forward. Then Mitchell walked in, closed the office door, and said, "She wants a divorce."

"Who?" Woolsey said.

"My wife," Mitchell replied as if Woolsey were stupid.

"What did you say?" Sidra asked.

"I told her fuck no."

Sidra and Daley laughed, and Sidra said, "I bet you ten bucks you did not tell your wife that."

He looked at her pointedly and said, "I did too. And I told her if that's really what she wanted, I would not give up the kids as easily as she thinks. What am I supposed to do?"

"Don't ask me for marital advice. Ask Mom, she's a fine listener."

"Don't even think about telling her anything. I mean it. What I said stays in this room."

"You make me feel better, Mitchell," Sidra said.

"Why's that?"

"Because it's nice to know I'm not the only one with a shitty life."

"Screw you," he said. "She wants me to go to counseling. Am I that bad? I mean, I do everything she asks me to do." Mitchell looked at Woolsey. "Does your wife ask you to do something and then get pissed about the way you do it?"

Woolsey said, "My wife doesn't have to ask me to do anything."

"Screw you, too," Mitchell said and threw a balled-up piece of paper at him. "You always were the Mama's Boy."

Then Sidra received two emails, one right after the other. The first one from the lender who stated that they had denied the approval for her loan and if she thought it necessary to speak with a financial advisor to call the bank. *Assholes*, she thought. She could make an appointment with one of the local branch offices, someone could help her with mortgage rates.

And then with the next one, her heart sank even further. It was from the real estate agent stating that the seller was going with another offer. She thanked Sidra for her interest and if it didn't work out, she'd be in contact.

She'd put in an offer on the house without a pre-approval on a loan, and then neither one of those things worked out. The denial of the loan bothered her. Without that, she couldn't get anything and she was back to renting.

Of course the bank wants her to come in, so they could offer her a mortgage rate with ten percent interest. Her credit was terrible. Her job was stable, even if it wasn't lucrative. Maybe she needed to get a second job. Jesus, the workload was already overwhelming. When would she have time for a second job?

Sidra groaned.

"What?" Daley said.

"Nothing."

She'd figure out something. She put her head in her hands as she listened to her brothers talk about the Peach case, and how Mitchell wanted to kill Trevor Gregory, how he was going to fuck up that guy next time he saw him. No one thought what happened to Renee was cool, even if she wanted to divorce their brother.

When Sidra went for a second cup of coffee—when what she really wanted was an early morning drink—she saw Mom at the dining room table, pulling out Halloween decorations from a box.

Shit.

She didn't want to get stuck hanging up fake spiderwebs all day. Back in the office, she set the coffee down with abandon and started grabbing her files, her notebooks, stuffed her cell phone in her bag.

"What's going on?" Daley said, nearly frozen because he wasn't sure how he should respond to Sidra's haste.

Sidra waited until she had everything together so she could be the first one out. "Mom just pulled out a box of Halloween decorations."

All three of them jumped up. "Shit," and, "I'm working from home," and, "Not me," the guys said, as Sidra threw her purse over her shoulder.

"What about the new guy?" Mitchell started writing something on the whiteboard next to Casey's name.

Sidra was halfway through the kitchen when Mom said, "What do you think about the inflatable ghost?"

"That's great, Mom. Ask them what they think. I gotta go. Love you, bye."

She was already in a bad mood about the loan and the house. The house was right for her, but she swallowed down the disappointment. Slapped a smile on her face when Brady answered the door. Felt honest to God happiness when she saw him and he smiled at her in that boyish way of his. His hair was a mess, and he was still in pajama pants.

"Brady," she said, and reached down to touch his feet. "They're popsicles." Peaches licked her face, and nearly knocked her over. "Hey, baby," Sidra said to the dog and wrapped her arms around her, the dog's tail whacking her in the face. Sidra looked at Brady. "Is your mom here?"

"Sidra," he said, sounding defensive. "I'm a grown man, fully capable of caring for myself."

It was then that a man stepped from around the corner. A home care nurse, Sidra presumed, even though he was in cotton pants and a t-shirt. "Forgot the socks, man," he said, and Sidra tilted her head at Brady.

"Don't even start," he said.

Brady introduced her to Tim, the nurse who was filling in while Marcy was out for a couple of weeks with the hurt arm. Tim was probably in his early fifties, but he certainly looked fit enough to lift Brady out of his chair if he had to.

"It's nice to meet you," Sidra said, and took the socks out of Tim's hand. He better be doing a fantastic job taking care of Brady. That he recognized Brady needed socks was a plus. Sidra set down the files and unfolded the socks.

"I can do that," Tim said.

"Ohhh," Brady said, stretching the word out with his normal silly excitement. "Please fight over who puts the socks on my feet. It's the most excitement I've had happen since the break in."

Sidra looked at Tim. "A few things to note. He's sarcastic when he's in a good mood. He's not shy, and despite what he'll want you to believe, he really likes attention. And when he gets going, he's got a pretty funny sense of humor." She lifted Brady's limp leg and slid the sock on his foot. Then, when she reached for the next leg, he patted her on the head. "It's required that you laugh at his jokes," she said to Tim, "even when they're terrible."

"Don't worry," Tim said. "I signed a contract."

"Full disclosure." Brady looked back at Sidra. "I wasn't expecting you."

"You won't even know I'm here. I just need a space to work for a little while. Do you mind if I sit in your office?"

"No, but if you need a computer, you're out of luck."

"I'm working on that."

Sidra set the files on the coffee table in the office and said to Peaches, "If our life were a TV show, you would have sniffed out the thief by now." Peaches tilted her head to listen to every word she said.

***

Mitchell didn't make it out in time and he blamed his stomach. He stopped to grab another pancake from the plate and Mom said, in that voice she uses when she's about to ask someone to do something and doesn't care if she's being an inconvenience, "What do you think about this?" He loved Mom, would do anything for her, but hanging up any type of outdoor decorations proved fatal because she was so indecisive about where to put stuff. Then he'd have to go stand out on the busy street, hope to not get run over by an idiot while he looked at the house to see if it looked perfect from the street.

But this time Casey—the poor schmuck—he got caught in the decorating too. They hung a witch from the tree out front, and cobwebs from the railings, and ghosts and goblins on the smaller trees. Nothing too scary.

Mitchell asked Casey, when he suddenly remembered the guy was a former drug dealer—Jesus, he hoped Renee didn't hear about that, he'd never hear the end of it—he asked him, "Do you know a man named Shane Bennett?"

Casey was quiet for a minute and Mitchell took it as a yes and felt a sense of victory.

"Because," Mitchell said as they walked back inside. "I'm actually looking for a guy named Trevor Gregory. Mean son of a bitch who likes to kidnap and choke women." Renee wore a scarf around her neck this morning and it nearly embarrassed him to think someone would presume he had done that to his wife. "I mean, do you know them?"

Casey followed Mitchell into the office, where he looked at his name on the whiteboard and the words next to it. "What's this?"

"Oh, it's nothing. Sidra did that. She's mean sometimes." The heat from the lie touched Mitchell's neck, and he hoped Casey didn't recognize the two different handwritings. The last thing he'd written on the board before he went for the pancake was: (minion).

If any of it bothered Casey, he didn't show it. "Shane Bennett pushes pills, been doing it for years. Heavy candy ain't his thing, but it's not off the table if he can make money. TG did some time I think, but details are lost on me."

"If I want to find the guy, where do I look? He hasn't been home in a few days and I watched the club where he works. I followed this guy I saw him talking to—little shit guy named Leland. Ring a bell?"

Casey didn't want to get involved in any drug dealing type of business and Mitchell couldn't blame him. The guy had spent years as a criminal on the streets and, according to Mom, he can't see his son right now until he gets his life together. That meant a lot of, *can't do this and can't do that*, until his sister believed Casey's son was safe. And since Casey signed over temporary custody to her, he had little to say about it.

Casey shook his head. "Lot of hustlers out there."

Mitchell agreed. "I don't expect you to know everyone. I'm just looking for this loser."

Casey looked at his shoes and Mitchell shouldn't have said that. Maybe Sidra could get info out of him. She had a way with people. Mitchell said, "Thanks for helping with the Halloween stuff."

"No problem," Casey said. "Talk to the bartenders."

"What's that?"

"At the Sapphire. No matter where you go, the bartenders have the answers. Even to the things they don't."

Chapter 15

Sidra leaned across the bar later that night at the Sapphire Groove and had the attention of the bartender with electric blue braids. She was late twenties, tall, with wide hips and a slim waist. Her midriff was showing again, exposing her rich brown skin and a belly button ring, and when she smiled at Sidra, the flecks of green in her hazel eyes lit up.

"What can I get for you?"

"Got anything special?"

"Are you picky?"

Sidra laughed over the loud music. "Not even close."

"I got you," she said, and tapped Sidra's hand. When she came back, she gave Sidra a blue concoction with a cherry in it. "This is my favorite," she said. "If you don't like it, it's on me."

The super sweet drink tasted like nectar with only a splash of alcohol. "It's perfect. What is it?"

"A blue sky, but I made it special just for you." When she said this, she let out a throaty laugh and pretended to stir the drink with her finger.

"Thanks," Sidra said. "What's your name?"

"Everybody calls me Blue."

Sidra leaned in closer. "What's your name?"

"Melinda. Do I look like a Melinda?"

Sidra shook her head with honesty and they both laughed. "I'm Sidra," she said, and held out her hand.

Blue said, "Nice to meet you," then she walked away to serve a group of people who made their way to the bar.

It was going to be a long night. The three bartenders worked together to keep the bar clear on the side without the stools. Daley worked a different bartender at the end of the bar, taking a different approach with a seriousness to his face. They couldn't risk bringing Mitchell in. Their Wild Card who was pissed off and wanted revenge.

Most people spent their time on the dance floor grinding against each other to the techno music blaring from the speakers, and the lights flashing on and off with the beats.

She recognized one suit on the balcony and wondered who the others were. How important were they to the club?

When Blue came back, Sidra said, "What's with the suits on the balcony?"

Blue didn't even turn around. "Management. They run the show from up top and make sure we all do our jobs."

Sidra took a sip of the drink. "Can you tell me anything about Trevor Gregory?"

Blue pulled back and her smile faded. "That's who you're in to?"

"Didn't say I was."

"Askin' about him."

"Where can I find him if he's not at his house?"

Blue shook her head and walked away, but she didn't seem mad. She did a few rounds, and Sidra turned back to the dance floor.

Long night with this one. Of course, she felt bad for leading people on, but Blue had to be used to it. People flirting with her all night, and she let them so she could make a few extra bucks. A tap on Sidra's shoulder.

"You a cop?"

Sidra shook her head, and Blue walked off again. When she returned, she had another blue drink in her hand but she didn't stay long, dropped it off, then worked the bar. Sidra wondered for a minute if she'd asked about Trevor too soon. The job was tricky enough to gauge people as it was, and even though she could talk to people, making it flawless was the hardest part. Play it cool, she thought as she sipped her drink.

The way Blue worked, she made the job seem effortless. The bar was home to her and the people ordering drinks were her guests. The easiness about her was inviting and the girl could sell drinks all night long. A few minutes later, Blue made eye contact with Sidra, and nodded down the bar. She followed her through the throng of dancers, down the hallway, and into the women's restroom where for a moment Sidra's heart picked up. The restroom was full, but there wasn't a line. Blue washed her hands and Sidra did the same.

Standing next to her, Blue looked like a tall Amazon goddess, her long blue braids down her back, and gold bangles on her arms. Blue said, "Why are you looking for TG?"

"Just want to talk to him."

"TG's a dick. He likes to cop a feel, and none of the girls can do anything about it. He's sick. You might not want to get your heart set on a fool like that." Blue finished washing her hands and then she walked into a stall to do her business. When she came out, she washed her hands again.

"Where can I find him?"

"Couple of places you can try." Blue pulled out her cell phone. "You can't tell him I told you though."

"Of course not," Sidra said, thankful for Blue's cooperation. She snapped a photo of the locations Blue gave her.

Then Blue surprised Sidra and grabbed her ass with both hands, their bodies smashed against one another as Blue stuck her hands into Sidra's back pockets. When she found what she was looking for, she held up the money as if to say, *This is mine now*, and Sidra nodded. It was the least she could do.

167

"Is there a way I can get in touch with you?" Sidra said. "In case I have more questions?"

"I work here every night of the week. Come see me anytime."

As Sidra walked out of the restroom, she nearly bumped into Daley, who most likely came to check on her. A few minutes later, they were both in the van where Mitchell looked to have taken a nap.

"What took so long? I finished a whole Netflix series waiting for you two."

***

The first location was a mom-and-pop pharmacy called Berry Pharmacy on 5th and Broom in Jonesboro. "This is where Helen Ross told me I could get prescriptions filled," Mitchell said. "I wonder why the police haven't shut this place down yet."

This entire area in Jonesboro was shady with the crime coming from the smaller Atlanta areas, like Riverdale and College Park. None of the surrounding areas were safe from drugs or gang activity.

The pharmacy closed hours ago. No vehicles in the parking lot except for an SUV with a busted out back window. Sidra gave up spending the evening with Brady to do this, and it was hard to pull away from him and narrow down the search for his computer, which was getting hopeless.

She wanted to tell Mitchell no when he'd called, but here she was gallivanting around town looking for

Trevor Gregory so Mitchell could beat his face in. Reminded her of Mitchell back in the day when someone would piss him off and he'd go after them without a second thought. People never grew out of that when their wives and family were in danger.

The second location was Zephyr Lanes bowling alley, and they had an hour until the place closed. Sidra and Daley scoped it out. A typical bowling alley with a food counter and arcade, thirty-six lanes and the Bee Gees on the speaker. A couple of leagues were finishing up for the night, but the place was quiet. Nobody bowled anymore.

"I'll go check out the fine dining," Daley said and took off toward the food counter, swaying a bit to the disco music as he walked. He threw a look over his shoulder just to see if she was watching him be an idiot.

If they started playing *Stayin' Alive* Sidra was running.

No wonder this place was dead empty. The smells from 1970 lived in the carpet, and the old man behind the rental counter went deaf that same year. *Hello, your star ship carpet needs updating and half the overhead lights are out.*

"I'm looking for Trevor Gregory."

"I don't have half sized shoes. You'll have to go with an 8," the old man said, and Sidra wondered if he actually had to comb those bushy white eyebrows every morning.

"No," Sidra said when he came back with the shoes. "I'm looking for a guy named TG."

"Yeah, the Bee Gees."

"Never mind." Sidra walked away.

The players in the bowling leagues brought their own shoes and balls, so none of them interacted with Grandpa, and Sidra stood there for a minute, looking around. Above the counter and arcade there was a long stretch of windows up top with offices perhaps, but all the lights were out up there.

A guy at the far end started vacuuming the carpet. He looked up when she approached him. "Have you seen Trevor Gregory today?"

The guy was middle-aged, Latino or Caribbean, and had on a brown newsboy hat. "I don't know."

"Twenty bucks if you do know." Then Sidra remembered Blue took her cash.

The guy raised his eyebrows as he pushed the vacuum in quick strokes near Sidra's feet. "Twenty bucks if I tell you whether I've seen Trevor today?"

That was a loaded way of putting it.

"Twenty bucks if you tell me if Trevor is here right now." Sidra took a step back as he hit her feet with the vacuum. One of those old metal things where the blue fabric puffed out behind it. Must have been from 1970 as well. At least they got their money's worth.

"He's not here," the guy said, and Sidra walked away. "Hey," he said and shut off the vacuum. "Where's the money?"

"Oh, you didn't think I was serious about that, did you?"

"Jeez," the guy said, and began the vacuum again.

Sidra met Daley past the shoe counter where he stood eating nachos. He had chip crumbs around his feet. So disrespectful.

"TG's not here," Sidra said.

"Yes, he is. Chick who gave me free nachos said he is."

"You know what's worse than nachos from the bowling alley? *Free* nachos from the bowling alley. You're probably going to get diarrhea."

"You're such a lady."

"What do we do?"

"He's probably hiding out."

Sidra just wanted to go back to Brady. No, she thought, surprised because suddenly she remembered she hadn't talked to Dominic since the walk-through. She hadn't even told him about the loan not going through, much less not getting the house. Then her thoughts swirled back to Brady. Sidra felt hot and bothered. What was wrong with her?

Daley licked the cheese at the bottom of the empty bowl like a barbarian. Sidra took the bowl and tossed it in the trash, then laughed because he had cheese on his nose. He wiped his face and nose and said, "We can pretend we're lost and can't find the exit."

Behind them, the old man yelled, "Are you going to get a lane or stand there all night?"

Stand here all night until we find Trevor.

"We're not getting a lane."

"We close in forty minutes."

"We're just waiting around," Sidra said. "For Trevor Gregory."

"For the what?" he said, cupping his hand around the back of his ear. Grandpa needed to go home and go to bed.

Sidra looked at her brother with her eyes wide open and he tried not to smile. He adjusted the cap on his head and walked over to the old man and introduced himself.

"Gordon," the man said and shook Daley's hand. "I own the place. Since 1970."

I must be a psychic, Sidra thought, and smiled at the man. He didn't seem to have trouble hearing Daley talk. Gordon probably thought she should be at home doing dishes.

The lights were out near the food counter. Lanes 20 and 21 had a couple of people playing at each lane and when the pins fell with a strike, a woman in a yellow league shirt fist bumped her teammate.

Daley walked over and tapped her shoulder with the back of his hand. "He's not here."

They turned for the door. "Why'd the free nacho chick say he was?"

Daley didn't answer her until they were halfway across the parking lot. "We'll come back in an hour."

They got in the van and talked to Mitchell. "And right now, they're probably warning him so he can bring in back up." He pulled the keys out of the ignition. "Hold these," he said to Daley and opened the middle console for his Glock, and Sidra looked at Daley, asking, *Are you really going to let him do this?*

Daley shrugged. "Why don't we just wait it out. If more cars show up, then we can leave and catch him off guard another day."

"Or, you two little girls sit in the van and I'll go talk to the guy. No big deal."

"This is going to turn into a Talbert brawl," Sidra said.

"This time leave your shirt on," Mitchell said and got out of the van.

Chapter 16

They looked like big shots walking across the parking lot, the three of them, side by side, with an important mission in mind. Mitchell swung the glass door open and they made their way down the carpeted entrance.

An old geezer narrowed his gaze at them, and Daley gave the man a nod, which he returned with a snarl. A group of people chatted near the right as they packed up their ball bags. Mitchell took a left and passed an abandoned vacuum cleaner, walked in front of a set of lockers, and found an EMPLOYEES ONLY door. Mitchell loved these kinds of doors. Led to great people.

The scumbags.

They took the stairs and paused only a moment to see if they'd get ambushed. When no one popped out, Mitchell kept moving. A life so dignified Trevor had to hide in a bowling alley. Upstairs was an office and a large room with a sofa and TV, with windows along one wall that looked out over the lanes. The TV was an old box set with Seinfeld on. A table sat in front of the sofa with a bowl of nachos and a fountain drink.

When a door to the right swung open, the three of them grabbed guns, robots on autopilot. A frizzy headed blonde stepped out, her head looking like a little dandelion puff, and she was buttoning up a hot pink bowling shirt. She couldn't have been over twenty, but she filled out that shirt and jeans better than a grown woman.

"Hey," Daley said, in a knowing way. "Where's Trevor?" And then there was quick movement behind her and Mitchell shoved her out of the way and stepped inside the room. It was another office, this one with a messy desk and a disgusting-looking Trevor tucking his junk back into his jeans.

"Her elbow is fractured," Mitchell said as Trevor put his shirt back on.

"Who?" His expression said he didn't give two shits who he was talking about.

"My wife, asshole. When you threw her from the van?"

"I don't know what you're talking about," Trevor said, and then stood there with his hands on his hips. The room was wood-paneling and dark, the only light coming from a lamp in the corner. "But if I did, I'd say we're even."

"You're embarrassed because I put you down in the water plant, I get that. But you're not going to go after my family. I will put you down like a dog."

Trevor had the audacity to smile as he nodded his head, absorbing the words but not really giving a shit. "Since you've got me cornered and outnumbered..."

"How about I put my gun away and they step out of the room? You really think you have a chance?" Mitchell held his hands up, his gun still in his right hand but no longer aimed at the idiot.

"Get down!" Sidra yelled.

A shotgun blast blew a hole in the wall and everyone moved so fast it didn't matter where it came from. Trevor drove himself into Mitchell like a defensive lineman and Mitchell stumbled backwards through the doorway and onto his back.

The blast came from down below, and Sidra duck walked past the windows to check it out. Mitchell punched Trevor in the head, couldn't hear anything his sister said. Mitchell got Trevor in a headlock and spun him on his back, and then they fought to get to the gun on the floor. Mitchell grabbed it and Trevor started punching again.

His brother and sister yelled for him to stop, but he didn't listen.

Someone called Mitchell's name, but he would blow this asshole's head off first. Then came the cold barrel of something on the back of his head and he froze for a moment.

"Drop the gun, shit head," a female voice said, a thick southern accent. He was expecting to turn around and see some hick-town farmer's wife, but it was the blonde with frizzy hair. "I said drop the gun."

She had her back to Daley, which was a mistake, but his brother wasn't going to take her with a shotgun pointed at him right now.

Sidra had her gun on the blonde. "How about you drop your gun?"

"Y'all ain't gonna come in here and tear up my granddaddy's bowling alley 'cause y'all are looking for money or drugs or some shit like that. Like you folks ain't got nothing else to do on a Monday night but cause problems." Then she looked at Trevor. "I told you not to bring that crooked shit here, Trevor, now I've got to fix a hole in the damn wall because I saved your ass."

"Your Granddaddy can't see shit," Trevor said.

"It looks like somebody got pissed off and threw a bowling ball through the goddamn wall, Trevor."

Mitchell waited for her to spit tobacco juice on the floor.

"Quit pointin' the gun, Roberta," Trevor said, and she stepped forward, glaring at him.

"Get up and get outta here right now before I give you an asshole through your stomach." She must have seen Daley sneaking up on her through the reflection in the glass because she said, "And you. Sweet talkin' your way to free nachos just to come in here and stir up trouble. Who are you anyway?"

"Nobody," Daley said, and Roberta smiled at him.

God, she was feisty. A little thing her size coming in here taking on four people with a shotgun? That was something. Where had Daley gone for five seconds, that she got the one-up on them?

When Roberta and Daley finished undressing each other with their eyes, Mitchell stood up and held his gun down at his side because his sister had hers aimed at Roberta.

"We're not looking for trouble," Mitchell said. "This asshole choked my wife and threw her from a moving van."

"Some ladies are into that shit," Roberta said, her face deadpan. "I don't care what he's done, y'all get out of here." When Trevor started to get up, Roberta said, "Changed my mind. You stay."

"I'm not staying here with you, you crazy bitch."

Without moving her head, she sighed and gave Daley a smile, then she turned back to Trevor and kicked him in the knee.

Mitchell told Trevor, "You stay away from my family."

"Fuck you," Trevor said.

"I'm sorry. What'd you say?"

Roberta said, "I think you have about two minutes before the police show up, so I think you need to get outta here."

"We're leaving."

As they backed out of the room, Mitchell knew this hadn't deterred Trevor one bit. In fact, he probably took it as a friendly challenge.

***

Dominic had been waiting for her when they got back at midnight. He was in the parking lot in his truck, had been waiting for thirty minutes. He met her by the tailgate, and she wrapped her arms around his neck and kissed him.

"Get a room," Mitchell said as he walked away. The whole ride home, Sidra heard nothing but Roberta's name and how she handled that situation. They were ready to hire her as a bodyguard from here on out.

"What were y'all doing?" Dominic said.

"Nothing."

"Why do I have the feeling that when the three of you are together, you're up to no good?"

Sidra smiled and kissed him again. "I don't know what you're talking about."

"You never do."

"I know a place we can go." She ran her hand down his chest. He always changed out of his uniform at the station and right now he had on sweatpants and a long sleeved-shirt that she wanted to rip off of him.

He said, "Okay."

"Is it considered breaking in if I have a key, Officer Getty?"

Twenty minutes later, Sidra pulled two beers out of Mitchell's fridge, popped the caps and handed Dominic a bottle. He leaned against the sink counter and Sidra stood there, downing the beer faster than water.

"Thirsty?"

"Long day. The bank denied the loan, which doesn't make sense—"

"You can try a different lender."

He had no idea about the debt she'd accumulated.

Sidra nodded. "But the homeowners took another offer."

"I'm sorry," he said, and sounded sincere, which is what she needed right now.

"I'm glad I didn't spend too much time being pissed about it."

Dominic took her arm and pulled her close. She leaned against his solid body, her breasts smashing into his chest. "Things'll work out the way they need to." He offered her that smile with those dimples, and everything seemed to melt away as she kissed him.

They walked downstairs to the bedroom, a room Sidra and her siblings used to play in as kids because they were so loud Mom wouldn't let them play upstairs. The crayon drawings from twenty-five-years ago, still on the wall because her brother never got around to painting over it. This room later became the golden egg for high school shenanigans that happened later at night. It wasn't unusual to find beer cans and hidden dirty magazines.

Now there was a double bed in here, and Sidra pulled her boots off and barely had enough time to get her jeans off when Dominic threw himself on top of her.

Sidra remembered a time when she was down here with Brady and Mom nearly caught them and she had to hide him under a blanket in the corner. And Mom just stood there staring at her because her shirt was on inside out, and said, "Why are you sitting down here alone in the dark?"

Brady and his boyish good looks, those arms that made her so safe, and he'd look at her and everything in the world disappeared. He could make her laugh even when she was crying. Smooth things over so easily after an argument. She thought about Brady all those times, naked on top of her and the way he'd run his fingers through her hair and pull the long strands to his face to feel her hair against his skin. And he'd smell her hair, and she'd kiss his neck and he'd laugh because they were stupid teenagers in love.

"I was so stupid."

"What?"

Dominic's voice jarred her, and he kissed her as he made love to her. And she could only think about Brady, and she hated herself so much for that because she really liked Dominic. Sidra wrapped her arms around him and ran her naked leg over his, and liked the comfort he brought. Sometimes, he was the only person who understood her craziness, the passion she had when she wanted the truth about something. He understood because he was a cop and spent so much time bringing in bad guys. He wasn't needy or possessive, and he gave her space. And she wanted to give him everything she had, she did, but that scared her because she didn't want to let anyone in. But here was Dominic, knowing more about her than anyone in the last thirteen years.

She grabbed his sweaty face in her hands and said, "I think I love you."

"Yeah?" he said. She kissed him as the first wave of warmth tightened around her body and she squeezed his hips between her thighs and she pushed him deeper inside. She held him close and thought this could be it, she could have Dominic forever and be happy, they could get a house and a dog and a boat, and she could make love to him whenever she wanted as long as he made her feel like this over and over.

Sidra's hand slipped on his sweaty back, her nails scratching across his skin, and when she cried out from the pleasure of it all, she thought she was going to melt into him.

Dominic collapsed beside her to catch his breath. "Jesus, woman," he said, and neither one of them could move. After a long day for both of them, they'd fallen asleep, Sidra's head on his chest. How long they'd been asleep, she didn't know. They both heard the noise, but it was Dominic who sat up so fast Sidra nearly fell out of the bed.

She touched Dominic's arm, silently telling him she was aware of something happening. Whatever—whoever—it was, was in the kitchen above them and their steps were very calculated. Dominic slid off the bed and put his pants on. He whispered, "Is it your brother or his wife?"

Sidra shook her head. Mitchell would definitely not be sneaking around his own house even in the middle of the night, even if Sidra was sleeping down here. The footsteps went into the dining room, then the living room. Dominic moved to the door.

"The basement steps are creaky," she said.

"I know. Stay here."

Dominic turned away before she could say anything. Sidra quickly threw on her own clothes and then grabbed a golf club from a corner in another room. The basement stairs were creaky for a person who was unfamiliar with the loose steps. Sidra had no problem stepping in the right places to make it upstairs. The door to the basement was still open because she nor Dominic bothered to shut it on the way down.

The table was to the left, twenty feet from the kitchen. Sidra listened and wondered where in the hell Dominic ran off, at the same time she heard the careful steps upstairs. Thank God Mitchell and his family weren't home. Sidra made it to her purse. She set the golf club down on the floor. Slipped the gun out, pulled the slide back to load one, and then walked past the stairs and into the living room. She saw a hand with a gun come at her fast and by the time she realized it was Dominic, he let out a breath with the same realization, and she dropped low to keep him from shooting her. Something tense passed between them and Dominic took a deep breath before he stepped away. He turned around for a brief second to compose himself, and Sidra knew she'd fucked up. He told her to stay downstairs and, even though he wasn't stupid, he wasn't expecting her to be upstairs.

Whoever had been in the house thought the house was clear because they ran downstairs without a worry in the world. Dominic bolted past her, not glancing at her, and Sidra stood up in time for Dominic to aim his gun at one of the guys she'd seen at Sapphire Groove.

"Slow down!" Dominic said. "Put your hands where I can see them. I'm a police off—"

The guy took off down the hall and Sidra moved forward, shouldered into him, and as he fell down, she jumped on top of him, felt the gun in the back of his pants. The guy wasn't big, but she was sure he'd been in a suit that night. Then Dominic was on top of her, telling the guy to stop fighting, he wasn't going to win. Sidra squeezed away so Dominic could pull the guy's hands behind his back, even though he had nothing to restrain him with. He started patting him down the best way he could while he was on top of him, removed the gun from the back of his pants and then, when he pulled the guy up, did a thorough check. No wallet, just a burner cell phone.

Dominic brought him into the living room and sat him down in a chair. Sidra grabbed a jump rope from a pile of Luca's junk in the corner.

"You can't tie him up," Dominic said.

"Why not?"

"Because it's against the law."

Sidra tied the guy's hands in front of him. "What's your name?"

"Do you really think this is going to hold?"

"Well, you're lucky I'm not tying it around your neck. Then you really wouldn't have a chance, now would you?"

"I need to call this in," Dominic said.

"No," Sidra said. "This suit wants to break into my brother's house, I'm going to let him handle it."

Dominic stood there staring at her like she'd lost her mind. "That's not how it works."

"Not in your world." When the guy tried to get up, Sidra shoved him back into the chair. "I swear to you if you try to get up again, I'm going to punch you in the balls. Would you like that? Think about all the sex you'll never have when I'm done punching you in your balls, and those jewels between your legs are the color of plums. Okay?"

"No one's going to assault you," Dominic said to the guy, "but I need you to tell me why you broke into the house."

185

"The door was wide open."

"Bullshit," Sidra said.

"Can you let me handle this?" Dominic held out his hands, almost pushing her out of the way, and she wanted to say, *Oh, here he is. The big macho cop*. Well, she'd been around plenty enough macho guys in her life to know when one felt threatened.

"I can handle him myself."

"You can't handle him. You have no idea what you're doing. Can you back off and stop talking so I can deal with this guy?"

"I know what this is about," she said. "I said I love you and now you think you're trapped, and you need to act like an alpha male in charge. You're not trapped. It's fine, I don't really know how I feel about you. But what I can tell you is that this guy is going to get his ass kicked, and you don't need to feel bad for him."

"I don't feel trapped."

"Can I go home?" the guy said. "I feel trapped."

Dominic stood in front of him so he wouldn't go anywhere. "Sidra, go get me a cell phone, please."

She wanted to tell him no, she'd watch the guy and he could go get the cell phone, but since hers was in her back pocket...

After Dominic made his call, Sidra called Mitchell. At three o'clock in the morning, he didn't seem too happy to be woken up.

"Caught you a fish," she said, and then snapped a picture of the guy.

Took Mitchell a few minutes to wake up. Dominic looked like his head was about to explode. Mitchell said, "That's Leland."

And then Sidra explained what the hell just happened, and that Dominic insisted on calling the police and they'd get there before he did.

"So who sent you?" Sidra said. "Because you're a small dick in this operation and someone put you up to it. Was it Trevor or Ryan Orchard? Or the main man Shane?"

"I want my lawyer."

"I'm not a cop, so I don't give a fuck what you want."

"I got a lot of money coming my way so you need to let me go."

"I don't think so."

Leland stood up fast and head-butted Sidra before she realized he'd even left the chair. Dominic grabbed him by the front of the shirt and slammed him to the floor. He said, "I'm trying to be really fucking nice to you here, but that was uncalled for." Dominic looked at Sidra. "Are you okay?"

"Yeah," she said, her ears ringing. He'd gotten her, and she'd have a shitty headache, but it could have been a lot worse.

By the time the police showed up, Dominic was giving her the cold shoulder. Maybe this wasn't going to work out. She walked into the kitchen and wrapped ice in a towel for her forehead, as she listened to Dominic explain to four cops what happened, and they laughed about the jump rope, but only because they thought it was clever. "Whatever it takes," one officer said. "We'll keep it as a backup for next time. Whole lot cheaper than the silver bracelets."

They found his car down the street and searched it. Mitchell showed up to tell the cops he knew where the guy lived and everything that happened in the last week, and Clayco was already on it. He asked Sidra what she was doing there, and she shrugged, because he was dumb if he couldn't figure it out. Of course, he figured it out. He rolled his eyes and said, "Maybe it's time you got your own house," but he wasn't mad about it. At least someone was here to stop the shithead from whatever he was doing.

Dominic cornered her in the kitchen, literally trapped her between his arms so she couldn't go anywhere. He looked at her for a long minute, his face inches from hers, and his eyes skimmed over her forehead where the asshole head butted her. He said, "I'm pissed that I pointed my gun at you. That's what I'm pissed about the most. I can't even begin to explain what that felt like. And I'm pissed that you didn't listen to me."

Definitely not going to work out.

Sidra calmed her breathing, but said nothing. Was it even worth it?

"And I'm particularly pissed that you jumped on a guy who had a concealed weapon on him."

Particularly pissed.

Would he be *particularly pissed* if he found out that she killed a man?

"You trust me because I'm a cop, and I want you to trust me. You can put your life in my hands and I'll make the right decisions. But I don't know what you're capable of and I can't make decisions for both of us in situations like that when you're not trained for it."

Jesus, her brothers came from the same mold.

Listen to me. Do as I say.

She stood there clenching her fists and wanted to scream, knew damn well she didn't need a lecture. Okay, so it wasn't going to work out. She should have known this when she found out he was a cop. He's bossy. He's controlling. He wants things his way. *I understand.*

"But I don't feel trapped. I think I love you too."

She stood there conflicted, her heart and head not quite getting along right now, and the emotional roller coaster wasn't helping. She needed a drink, but she didn't dare move. There were a couple of cops still mulling around, filling out notes and talking to Mitchell in the living room.

Keeping her voice down, she said, "I know what I'm doing. I won't sit by and watch anybody jump into a fire. I assumed the guy had a gun, even if I didn't see it. The guy breaks in and I'm supposed to sit by and wait for justice to come into play?"

"Even if I'm off duty, anything I do wrong can get me into trouble. They're joking about the rope, but I'm going to get a reprimand for it just because I'm a cop. My ass is on the line when things go south. Not yours, you're a civilian."

A civilian.

"Right," she said, "because you're in a cop world where you're better than everyone else. And let's not forget that you don't trust me."

His face showed pain with the words, and she shouldn't have said that to him. "Don't twist my words."

This wasn't going to work.

He touched her face and kissed her gently on the head where the guy got her. "For the record," he said. "I would have let you punch him in the balls."

Chapter 17

"This guy?" Mitchell said the next morning in the office. "Leland Marple. I think he was a CI for Clayco. 'Was' because he just became a rat in a cage. He said he was looking for info on Ryan Orchard because Shane paid him a lot of money to break in. They think I had something to do with Ryan disappearing after the whole Helen thing. They're going to put a hit out on me or something."

Sidra looked bored as he said this. Probably because she already heard some of it. Secret information from her cop boyfriend.

The only thing that stood out was that if Leland was a CI, then Grizzly was definitely his handler. Mitchell chowed down on his second plate of eggs and biscuits after he'd helped Renee get the kids off to school. "After last night, we can't go home anytime soon. Renee wants to go back to her sister's but I don't think that's a good idea." He was talking to himself here because Sidra was off in La-La Land somewhere. "Are you even listening to me?"

"I'm listening. Because unlike you, I have the ability to focus on what you're saying and concentrate on the facts and emotions flooding my brain right now. Would you like for me to repeat everything you just said back to you?"

"No," he said, around a bit of biscuit and egg, and wondered why she was so bitchy. "I really want to let the police do their work, but I want to know what the fuck these guys are up to? And the dead guy in 1025 was some loser looking for pills. Now that Clayco doesn't have their eyes and ears in Sapphire Groove, what are they going to do?"

"Shane Bennett sends Leland. Why would he think you had anything to do with Ryan? You said that Helen was afraid of Shane, so I don't think she would have spoken to him directly about seeing you, and if she did, what information would you have that Shane didn't?"

"Exactly," Mitchell said. "It's a conspiracy and they're trying to frame me for something."

"That's a stretch."

When Daley walked in, Mitchell laughed, said, "Do I have a story to tell you." And then watched with amusement as he told Daley about Leland, the little rat-faced bitch who broke into his house.

"And Sidra was there making out with her boyfriend who caught the guy."

"Excuse me," Sidra said. "But technically, I caught the guy. Dominic wanted to talk him into compliance.

Until I got head-butted, then he wanted action. Long story short, watch your back."

When Woolsey walked in with his brown leather messenger bag, Mitchell said, "Hey, Chewbacca. Long time no see."

And this made Woolsey smile because he always took the cruel jokes. He slapped Mitchell on the back before he sat down and said, "How's your marriage coming along?"

"Screw you," Mitchell said as his little brother settled in. "Just wait. Ten years from now, we'll revisit this conversation."

"No," Woolsey said, a slick smile on his face. "Because I took notes from you of what not to do."

Mitchell shook his head. "I think I'm going to drive to Berry Pharmacy today and see what's going on."

"I think," Daley said, his face serious, "I'm going to go check on Roberta and make sure she's okay."

"Roberta?" Sidra said. "What happened to Faith?"

"Faith no more," Daley said.

"But *Roberta*?" Sidra said.

"Did you see the way she held that shotgun?"

Show Daley a woman who could handle herself with a gun and he was a goner.

Sidra said, "I'm sure Roberta will make a fine step-mother for Jorie," and Daley rolled his eyes.

***

A lot of places in Jonesboro were old, it's what gave the city its historical appeal. But when places like Berry's were filling bad scripts, it's those things that brought the city down. They had a bunch of medical crap in their windows, a sale on candy, and they also rented out medical equipment, such as wheelchairs and nebulizers.

They were a small compounding pharmacy and busy at nine o'clock in the morning, mostly with elderly people looking to get their medications so they could stay alive one more day in this great world they lived in. The place smelled of disinfectant and gum drops. Reminded Mitchell of his grandma's house.

He looked around and saw nothing too out of the ordinary. Two women worked the counter, and then a pharmacist and a tech. No one was going to the back for anything special and the place certainly didn't scream, *Buy Your Illegal Drugs Here.*

Mitchell felt the itch, like a buzzing under his skin, but he told himself no. He hadn't had anything in days. That was okay. He could usually go weeks and he wondered how he was going to make out in a couple of weeks when he was really needing something.

At the counter, Mitchell told the woman—her nametag read Anita—that he needed to get a prescription filled. "But I forgot my prescription at home."

"We can't fill it without the prescription," she insisted and pushed her thick glasses up her nose.

"It's from Helen Ross. A doctor. Have you heard of her?"

The woman didn't flinch if she recognized the name. "I have to have the prescription in hand to fill it."

"You think I could talk to the pharmacist?"

Anita sighed heavily. "We're real busy here, sir. If you don't have a prescription, we can't help you."

"It'll only take a minute to speak with the pharmacist."

When Mitchell didn't move, Anita turned around to get the pharmacist, which took a hot minute. His name was William Waltz, and he seemed friendly enough with his white hair coming out of his ears. Surely this man would understand what Mitchell needed.

"How are you, sir?" Mitchell asked as they stepped further down the counter, out of the way. "Are you filling prescriptions? Because I got one from Helen Ross but I left it at home."

William let out a hefty sigh, blowing out the air in his lungs in a long, exaggerated way. "Sorry, can't help."

"I've gotten a prescription filled here before," Mitchell lied. "Can I give you my name?"

"You can have your doctor call us." He raised his eyebrows, asking if that would work.

"I mean, I hate to bother them. They're so busy. Do you know a man named Ryan Orchard? He can vouch for me."

William Waltz's sour expression said he did, but he shook his head instead.

195

"Okay," Mitchell said. "Thank you for your time."

He wasn't going to get anywhere and wondered what would have happened if he really had a Helen Ross prescription. He wasn't doing anything but kicking up a hornet's nest, and that wasn't very productive.

Then, when he sat back in the van and really thought about it, he didn't know what he was doing anymore. What was he trying to learn? There was no client paying for all this running around. With Helen Ross in custody, what was the point?

Besides wanting to beat the life out of Trevor Gregory, there was no skin in this. He'd been sitting there for five minutes when he noticed a green sedan pull to the back of the building. To get a better view, he moved the van to the adjacent building and watched as the pharmacist came out the back door after the gentleman rang a bell. So that's how it's done. Not from the front door.

Mitchell wondered what would happen if he created a fake prescription online and brought it in. How would that work? Go to jail, dumbass, that's how that works. Then what would Renee say?

The man in the green sedan got his little white bag and drove away as William Waltz looked around for a minute, then closed the back door. Something was definitely going on here. Mitchell wasn't one for paperwork and online researching. Loathed it. He'd rather be sitting in his vehicle watching people than sitting at a desk. But right now, he didn't have a choice because he needed some information about Berry Pharmacy.

In the office, he sat down at the desk he usually used and asked Woolsey to pull up some information on Shane Bennett. Sidra walked in drinking out of her favorite Mason jar, and Mitchell said, "It's ten o'clock in the morning."

"You and Mom. Two peas in a pod who know how to tell time," she said, flipping that long braid over her shoulder with an attitude.

Woolsey said, "Shane Bennett owned a bar in Atlanta that was shut down for financial reasons. There was also a bar in Savannah that burned down, but he was co-owner on that one. Ryan Orchard was the second owner. Their history in Georgia goes back only fifteen years. Trevor Gregory spent five years in the Army, then worked for a security company in Atlanta called AP Security. Has a criminal record for battery, spent two years in the slammer. I'll keep digging."

Sidra paced the front porch as she smoked a cigarette and smiled at whoever she was on the phone with. He liked Sidra whenever she was in a good mood. When they were younger, she was the breezy one out of the bunch. Go with the flow and never got her feelings hurt. Something changed her, though. Brady's accident and when she ran away. She didn't come back the same.

Now she drank all day and hid her problems.

Renee had been quiet these past few days, and he wasn't sure what was going on. They talked, and she wanted to go to her sister's house, but she hadn't actually left. It was only a matter of time before living at Shackelford would be too much for the both of them, with Mom hovering all the time. They'd have to go back home at some point. But they couldn't until he eliminated the threat. Three times these assholes have shown up at his house. First, with Shane and Trevor asking about Helen Ross. Then Trevor snatched Renee. And last night Leland broke in.

When Sidra came back inside, she drank the last of whatever was in her glass. Her phone rang, she answered and shook her head. When she ended the call, she put on her blue leather jacket and grabbed her purse. "I'm going to Atlanta."

"You need help?"

"I hope not." And then she flashed him a smile, suddenly the world at ease in her life. She walked up to Woolsey and patted him on the back. "I don't spend enough time with you," she said. "We should hang out sometime."

Mitchell said, "Don't do it, Wools. It's a trap."

Chapter 18

Kieran Knox practically bounced on his toes as he stood in front of Sidra telling her about this incident that happened when he was working on The *Shoot Fall* project. "We'd only gotten together a handful of times, but Brady didn't seem to get along with this guy named Nate. I never got his last name. He's a game writer."

She didn't understand why he couldn't tell her this over the phone after trying to get in touch with him for three days. And now he miraculously remembered a guy named Nate? Sidra was sure she'd heard the name before.

Kieran stood in front of her, smiling, his hands in his pockets. He looked suave in his burgundy shirt and avocado green sweater vest, topped off with a bowtie in a similar shade of green. While he looked quite trendy, he looked like his mother dressed him for fall photos. The only thing missing was the little red wagon and staged pumpkins.

"Do you want to see some projects I'm working on?" Before Sidra could say no, Kieran turned around to his computer station. "Digital interactive children's books. It's not a totally new idea, but once the reader gets started, they can choose the outcome of the story. Cool, right?"

Kieran scrolled through beautiful illustrations of a strange fuzzy spider in the forest, and it looked as though part of the story would be animated. "How does it work?"

"I'm glad you asked." Kieran pushed one of his computer monitors over for a better view. "You can read a passage and choose what happens. So, let's say we want Truffles—that's this guy—to go into the cabin. Click here, and then we continue the story. Let's say we want him to climb the tree." Kieran clicked back a few screens and changed the command for Truffles, and then the story changed to match that command.

What he was working on was bare bones of the digital animation, with only a sample of the idea.

"It's going to take me months to finish this," Kieran said, turning to judge her expression. "It's a hobby project. I'm going to have to get help with some things though."

"Why do you say Brady and Nate didn't get along? What happened?" If Kieran started talking, she could probably pull something important out of the details.

"They argued a lot, and I didn't think they'd ever get anything done. We spent almost all our conversations with the two of them talking over one another, and we accomplished nothing. Then an hour later we'd get an email with bullet points from Brady about what to work on next."

"Where'd you meet up?"

"Mostly we video chatted online every week or had conference calls."

"And how long did you work on that project?"

"Four months, but it was too much work for the little pay I was getting. I should have asked for a hell of a lot more money up front in the contract. And he was keeping too much hush-hush." Kieran rolled his eyes as he leaned back in his chair. "You want to see something else I'm working on?" His eyes widened, full of hope.

"I see you have two towers here. Do they both belong to Upscale Studios?"

He tapped one of them with his foot. "This is my personal tower. I lug it to work with me every day so I can work on my stuff when I have time." He shrugged. "They don't care what I do here as long as I finish my work."

Sidra wondered if he lugged Brady's computer to work every day and couldn't help but check out the nearby cubicles. Brady's tower had stickers on it. She'd spot it in a heartbeat.

She promised Brady she'd find it, but the daunting task was becoming hopeless. She looked at Kieran and cast judgement on him, even though that wasn't the right thing to do. She didn't know what it was about him, but something was off. An uncomfortableness settled around him in his effort for acceptance, and his eyes had something behind them that would set him off in the blink of an eye.

Too smiley, and too eager. While Kieran had skills, he wasn't arrogant. But he wanted to be noticed.

"Kieran," Sidra said. "Did you steal Brady's computer tower?"

He looked at her, truly hurt. "Why would I steal Brady's computer when I have my own?" then he rolled his eyes and looked away from her. "Forget I ever called you," he said. "You can leave now."

***

Sidra found Brady in his office playing a sci-fi video game. The main female character had big boobs and a big gun. This would be the woman of Daley's dreams, if that wasn't sexist to say, and she wondered how he was doing with Roberta.

"Hey," Brady said, not taking his eyes off the TV. "You want to play? I can put it in two player mode. I finally made it to Sugar Jewel's final battle."

"Sugar Jewel?"

"The guy who created her did an amazing job."

"I got off the phone with you hours ago and you were playing that game."

"I told you. I've been playing since six this morning. If I don't get my computer back, I'm going to go nuts. Do you want to play?" A pad with a joystick and buttons sat on his lap, and the intense expression on Brady's face said that he was so into the game he couldn't be distracted right now. She really wanted to go over there and turn off the TV, but that would be cruel. So she sat on the sofa behind him with Peaches.

She reached up and ran her fingernail down the back of his neck and he flinched with the distraction and tried to shrug her off. "I'm almost done," he said.

She pulled Peaches—the forty-pound sack of potatoes—into her lap. The dog's tongue flipped out of her mouth and nearly touched her eye. She was in heaven with the belly rubs. "You're the best dog ever. And if Brady doesn't stop playing video games, I'm going to dump a cup of cold water on his head." Peaches wagged her tail.

"Okay, jeez, I'm done," Brady said, and spun around. He put the control pad down on the coffee table. "Do you remember what you used to do to get me to stop playing?"

Sidra blushed and couldn't believe he mentioned that. She set Peaches on her feet, stood up and said, "Who's Nate? I remember you talking about a Nate before."

"Nate's a friend who I work with on almost everything. Why?"

"Kieran Knox implied that you and Nate didn't get along when you were working together. Could this Nate guy have anything to do with it?"

Brady almost laughed. "No. Not even close."

"How can you be so sure?"

"Because I've known him for eight years and he's a brother to me. He lives—Hold on." Brady fished his cell phone out of a pocket.

He dialed, and then a voice said, "Yo."

In thirty seconds, Sidra deducted they had a close working relationship because they spoke in half sentences and knew what each other was talking about. Nate was aware that Brady's computer was missing and told him he needed to start looking under rocks for that thing.

Brady said, "You remember Kieran Knox? I got my P.I. lady—"

His P.I. lady?

"—on it, and he's implying that we don't get along and you took my computer."

"Yeah," Nate said. "We don't get along at all. In fact, you can come walk your ass to Kentucky right now and get your computer back if you want it." And then he let out a deep, maniacal laugh. Sidra gave Brady a look that said, *Who is this guy?*

Brady turned his phone around, balancing it between the palms of his hands and on his knuckles. He'd been video chatting with a guy whose smile took up the whole screen. Nate pulled the phone back and said, "Oh, hey P.I. lady."

"Hi," Sidra said. Then she noticed he sat in a wheelchair, too. Kieran didn't mention that.

But then Nate said, "Oh, I see you looking at my wheels. Listen, the extent of my injuries aren't as bad as Brady's, okay." And then he stood up and both the guys laughed.

"Dude," Brady said, but he was smiling the way he always smiled when he was with people who cared about him.

Nate sat back down and said, his voice serious now. "For real. What do we need to do to finish this? You don't have your shit in a cloud?"

Then they started "arguing" as Kieran put it, loudly and talking over one another. Nate didn't steal Brady's computer. This guy cared about his friend.

When he hung up the phone, Brady said, "I don't know what kind of shit Kieran's trying to pull, but I should have known something was wrong with him from the start. He's got a silent fury in him when he doesn't get his way."

That explained a lot. The way Kieran had looked at her when he'd told her to go, he was trying to contain his silent rage.

"He's working on some kind of interactive book thing. A children's book where they choose what happens next. It's got a little fuzzy spider named Truffles—"

"A fuzzy spider named Truffles?" Brady said, his eyes wide and sounding surprised.

"I guess it's kind of silly—"

"Was it this spider?" Brady turned towards his desk, then stopped. "Oh, that's right. I can't show you because my computer is missing. Okay, hold on." Then he moved to grab a laptop off of a shelf. What would have taken her ten seconds to do took him longer. When he finally had the laptop up and running, he said, "Was it similar to this?"

"Possibly," Sidra said. The spider Brady showed her was cartoonish with buck teeth, and it used one of its own missing legs as a cane.

"Because this is Truffles. A tour guide for a game I worked on."

"What's the point of stealing someone else's work?"

"To screw them up." Brady slammed the laptop shut and then turned his neck to stretch it out. Without hesitating, Sidra walked over and massaged his neck the way she used to.

His skin was warm, and she worked her thumbs in circles around the dark freckle on his neck and then worked his shoulders. The tight muscles loosened under her hands.

"This is what happens when you don't move enough all day."

"You really want to be the one to tell me how to better myself?"

"I guess so, since we've always had a no bullshit relationship."

"Remember that," he said, "when I start in on you because I know damn well you don't like hearing about it."

He leaned his head back and they held eye contact for a long minute, and she thought of a thousand things she wanted to say to him, but couldn't muster up the courage to say a single one of them.

***

She jumped on I-85 through Tyrone, turned up Green Day on the radio, and noticed him following her right away. Which meant he followed her to Brady's neighborhood. He couldn't get in, so he must have waited for her at the nearby gas station.

She called Mitchell. "Your boyfriend is tailing me."

"Where are you?"

"Interstate near the airport. I'm going to Atlanta to watch a guy."

Trevor stayed a few cars behind and Sidra tried to figure out if he was tag-teaming her the way she and her brothers did when they needed multiple eyes on a target.

Mitchell said, "I can get to you in thirty minutes."

"I'm okay for now unless he starts a highway shoot out. Let me see what he's going to do and I'll call you back."

"Call me in ten minutes."

She kept an easy speed through the early afternoon traffic. Driving to Atlanta twice in one day wasn't her idea of fun, but her instinct guided her in this direction, and she listened. Losing Trevor may be easier once she got on I-75, but for now she drove as though she didn't have a tail. He was in a black SUV and she reminded herself of what happened to Renee.

Why would Trevor follow her when he was lying low from the police? Bad guys made such dumb moves when their brains were in mission mode. Atlanta south zipped by, then she hit traffic again. With the traffic this thick, she couldn't lose him, but she stayed near the exits to confuse him.

While she wasn't triumphant when she didn't see him at the exit, she circled around the block once near Upscale Studios. She wanted to follow Kieran, but with Trevor on her tail, she had to get creative. She pulled her hair out of the braid, and threw it into a loose bun, changed into a different blouse, and then put on a pair of fake purple eye glasses.

Walking into Upscale Studios, she pretended to be part of the crew and didn't stop to check in at the front. The young lady behind the desk barely noticed her. The middle of the floor had a row of computer modules, and Sidra sat at an unoccupied monitor. She didn't have a clear view of Kieran, but she also didn't see him at his own desk. Sidra wiggled the mouse on the computer and it came to life. Unfortunately, the system was password protected. She grabbed a binder off the desk and began flipping pages, hoping no one would notice her.

When Sidra spotted Kieran coming from a door in the back, he had a smile on his face and tried talking to a couple of people who weren't interested in what he had to say. Then he moved to a guy who shook his head and turned away. As Kieran spoke to multiple people,

Sidra heard him telling them he got the Coca-Cola project. No one showed interest. "I got the Coke project," he said again, and she almost felt sorry for him.

Now that she confirmed Kieran was at work, Sidra left the building and headed over to the little Chinese place next door, ordered orange chicken and fried rice, and kept her eye on Upscale Studios parking lot the whole time.

She didn't see Trevor and considered she'd lost him. A couple of hours later, Kieran Knox left in a blue Prius. Sidra followed him to a game bar where he had a quick drink and chatted with the bartender. Then a quick stop for pizza. Before Kieran drove home, he stopped at a computer store barely noticeable with the non-existent store front. It was in a small business strip off of one of the Peachtree streets a mile away from his work. Computer World was one of those low-income places that somehow thrived. Kieran ran inside and then came out with a box that he struggled to hold while he opened the hatch on the Prius. Next, he made another stop at a different computer store called High Tech, but there wasn't anything high tech about it at all. It was the twin to Computer World. Then Kieran hit a bar in Little Five Points, this time sitting there for an hour with a couple of techy guys, and laughed about the CGI effects in the latest action flicks. Sidra sat down and had a drink, and Kieran didn't even notice her.

Kieran lived in a small house on DeKalb Ave. He didn't take the box out of the back of the car. Instead, he grabbed a backpack and a water thermos and went inside through the front door. These narrow residential streets in Atlanta were busy, so when she parked the van a few houses down and walked to the Prius, she didn't worry about walking into Kieran's driveway. Get a fence, she wanted to say. As if that would keep people out.

The Prius had a glass back, the box clearly visible, and loaded to the top with a bunch of computer parts. Kieran didn't even lock his car door. Sidra shook her head. All these break-ins in Atlanta. *Yes, I'd like to report a robbery. Um, no, I forgot to lock my car.*

She checked the box of computer parts, hoping that the disassembled pieces weren't Brady's computer. With a careful eye on the house, she crept around to the passenger side of the car. Kieran kept the car clean. But in the glove compartment she found a credit card receipt for gas in Peachtree City, dated the same day someone broke into Brady's house.

Chapter 19

Sidra snapped a photo of the receipt and thought about what she needed to do. Breaking into someone's car was illegal, so the way she found the receipt was illegal. Cops needed warrants, but she didn't. She could go to the gas station and ask about video footage on that day, see if there was anything there. She'd think about the legality of everything later. Right now, this was the first hint of Kieran's responsibility for the theft. And Brady needed his computer back before he fried his brain playing video games all day.

She'd been driving down the highway in Riverdale when she spotted Trevor again. God, he was good. And when things couldn't be any shittier, her right passenger tire blew right in the middle of a bad area that screamed crime was up a thousand percent. She gripped the steering wheel as the van swerved, and she'd just passed the Krispy Kreme, and managed to get the van in the parking lot next door.

The black SUV passed her, then Trevor put on his left blinker, indicating he planned to loop around and continue to watch her. The Glock comforted her, and she stuck it in the back of her pants as she got out to check the tire situation. She must have run over something because the tire popped in the middle. Groaning, she didn't want to deal with this right now. Not right here. She'd been inside her vehicle for the last few hours, she knew no one tampered with the tire.

Now she lost sight of Trevor, and that sent her nerves on edge.

"You all right?"

Sidra spun around to a guy standing ten feet away from her. His t-shirt had brown stains, and he smelled of motor oil. He had a brown paper bag clutched under his arm and she recognized the shape of a bottle right away.

"I'm fine. Thank you."

"You need help? I can change a tire."

"I can do it. Thanks."

The guy said, "Okay," gave a friendly shrug and walked away.

"Hold on," Sidra said, and scanned her eyes across the highway to locate Trevor's black SUV. "I can change the tire myself. Will you watch my back?"

The guy sauntered over and leaned his head in. "Watch your back for what?"

"I'm feeling a little vulnerable out here. It's getting dark and my back's gonna be exposed."

"This ain't the Bronx, you know? I come from the Bronx. This? This ain't shit. This high-class livin' out here." That didn't make her feel any better. She should probably call one of her brothers.

The man in front of her said, "Yeah, I keep an eye out. I spent two years in prison for a crime I didn't commit. I wish somebody had my back that day, but now I'm out and I'm blessed to be alive."

"Amen to that," she said, and put the gun back in the van. There was no way she could squat down to change a tire without it exposed. And even with a warning, she may not have enough time to go for the gun if Trevor showed up.

Sidra stepped to the back of the van to get the spare and the tools. She had the busted tire off while Earl told her all about his life story, all the way back to when he was a little kid and wanted to be a fireman. By the time Sidra tightened the tire bolts, she shook Earl's hand, gave him ten bucks, and told him it was the least she could do, and saw Trevor leave the parking lot across the busy highway. Sidra got in the van and tried to lose him again. Then she slowed down and called Mitchell. "I'm heading back with a tail. You want to come check him out?"

"Oh, yeah," he said. "I'll be in the Taurus."

***

Tailing someone at night was damn near impossible. Ahead was nothing but tail lights. Behind, nothing but head lights. Why Trevor followed his sister was beyond his comprehension. He wasn't going to discover any kind of information by following her. Unless this asshole was going to stalk her to get to him. First his wife, now his sister.

Trevor passed Shackelford as Sidra pulled into the parking lot. Her plan was to hop in a different vehicle they used for two-team surveillance. They followed Trevor—each taking turns being the lead car—to Stockbridge and Mitchell kept telling Sidra, "You're going to lose him."

"I've got two interstate ramps here, Mitchell, with a shit ton of traffic."

"Don't lose him."

Congested traffic blocked the I-75 ramp and one of them had to stay close to Trevor in the dark to keep the tail. "He's still heading east," Sidra said, and Mitchell pulled forward.

"Don't lose him," Sidra said, on Highway 138 between the two Interstates, and Mitchell saw all the police lights because the ramp was a clusterfuck because of an accident.

"Shit," Mitchell said. "Last minute south. Can you follow?"

"Negative, Ghost Rider. This accident is blocking everything. I can turn around and try to catch him up ahead."

If Mitchell didn't get out of this traffic, he was going to scream. "Come on," he yelled at some moron who pulled in front of him and blocked both lanes of traffic. "It's a bust. Shit. You want to go bowling or dancing."

214

"Ah, what the hell. Let's go bowling."

Zephyr Lanes was dead. If not for the leagues practicing, no one would be in here. Mitchell paid for a lane and the old man didn't seem to remember them.

"Fifty bucks if I win," Sidra said, and Mitchell couldn't be tempted. She won at everything.

"Why don't you just take my money now?"

They got their lane set up, and Sidra bowled first. She lined up her shot far enough back that she had enough space to throw the ball hard and knock six pins down. Five minutes later, he heard, "What the hell are y'all doing here?" and they turned to see Roberta standing there in her hot pink bowling shirt, her little frizzy blonde hair not moving on her head. "Your free nacho brother stopped by today and I told him I didn't want any of you in here ever again. Either he didn't give you the message or you two are really stupid."

Even without the shotgun, she was threatening.

"We're just bowling," Sidra said. "Why don't you sit down and chat for a bit."

"I don't have time to chat. I got a bowling alley to run."

Mitchell let out a light laugh. "What do you mean? Seems to run itself. That's what I'd call an established business." When Mitchell took his turn, he threw the ball hard but only knocked down one pin.

Roberta said, "The pins are in front of you, not in Texas. You want me to get the bumpers up?" and Sidra leaned over and laughed, the funniest thing she'd ever heard. Roberta sat down and lit up a cigarette.

"Are you supposed to be smoking in here?" Mitchell asked and turned his back for his second throw. Not much better this time, either. He should be bowling with his kids, not his sister. Then he'd have a better chance at winning.

"My granddaddy owns this place. What's he gonna do, kick me out?"

Sidra said, "We followed Trevor tonight. Would you care to know why?"

Roberta shook her head. "Not really. He's a good for nothin' piece of dog shit."

"Yeah, we figured that." Sidra took her turn.

Mitchell told Roberta about his wife and she said, "Well I can understand the hostility but I told him he couldn't hide out here anymore."

It would be nice if the police would hurry and catch this guy. Mitchell should have called the police right away instead of following Trevor. But he wanted Trevor to fully understand who he was messing with before the bastard went to jail. It was wrong, but people like Trevor Gregory did the same bad things over and over, and didn't seem to lose their appeal with the crime life.

Mitchell traded places with Sidra for the lane.

"She's kickin' your ass," Roberta said, when he flopped the throw. Then she stood up. "Watching you bowl is worse than watching someone play shot put in a padded room." She grabbed a ball and told Mitchell to move, threw the ball fast and hard and knocked all the pins down. All that with a cigarette dangling out of her mouth, a trailer park princess standing in front of him. Please someone, get her a tiara.

Forgetting the game, Sidra said to Roberta when she sat back down, "You came out of the office last night buttoning your shirt."

"Well, I certainly couldn't walk around with my boobs hanging out, could I?"

Mitchell said, "You could," and the scorn on Roberta's face told him not to mess with her that way, so he backed off. Sidra gave him a look that said, *Not you too.* Roberta finished the rest of her cigarette, put it out in the fountain cup she'd picked up.

"As much as I despise him," Roberta said, "I can't stay away from him."

"Been there, done that." Sidra said. "He followed me tonight all the way to Atlanta, and I don't know why. Have you talked to him at all today?"

"I did," she said, and it surprised Mitchell after what happened last night. "He thinks you're an undercover cop or something."

"He's a fucking idiot," Sidra said.

"No, I'm not."

"I meant Trevor."

Roberta said, "Trevor's not an idiot either. He might be Shane's shadow, but he's very calculated. If he was following you, there's a reason."

"Why are you telling us this?" Sidra said.

"I sit in this bowling alley all day. I get bored."

***

"Where did you go? You left out of here like something was on fire." Renee said when Mitchell walked into the spare bedroom at his mother's house. "Have you been smoking?" Renee took a deeper sniff. "Where the fuck have you been?" She sat up straighter in bed, the papers falling to the side, and God, even in all her craziness, he thought his wife was the most beautiful woman he'd ever laid eyes on.

"I was out looking for the guy that choked you and fractured your elbow. I was with Sidra—"

"There's your problem."

He didn't want to argue with her or have to defend his sister. Right now, if it made her get off his back, he'd let her say whatever she wanted about anything under the sun.

"I'm going crazy here," Renee said, in a way that meant she wasn't already there. "Your mother is driving me crazy."

"Because she helps with the kids and makes sure they're fed and ready for school and their homework is done?" He made sure he was out of arm's reach when he said this, and the only thing she had to throw at him was a purple felt-tipped pen, which Mitchell caught with no problem.

He stared her down for a long minute and then Renee said, "I want to go home."

"With me or without me?" Mitchell grabbed clothes and headed for the shower. "You can tell me the state of our future by the time I get out of the shower."

None of his kids were asleep in the big room with all the beds for the grandkids. He opened the door to the boys giggling, and Caroline telling them they were disgusting.

"Who farted?" Mitchell said, and the boys fell into hysterics.

"Daddy," Caroline said. "Can I please go sleep in another room?" She sat up in the bed. "Mom said I had to sleep in here but Grandma said I didn't have to." The house had four extra bedrooms down the hall. "I never have to sleep in here when I spend the night."

"Okay," Mitchell said, and sat down on her bed. In the last few days, Caroline hadn't spoken to him, and now she looked at him with pleading eyes, and he couldn't say no to her. "Come here." He pulled her into a hug and his daughter sent a flood of emotions through him. Mitchell couldn't lose his kids. And oddly enough, being here at Shackelford, he'd seen his kids more in the last four days than he had in a month. "Go sleep in another room if that's what you want."

"Thank you." Caroline hopped out of bed and stuck her tongue out at her brothers.

Spencer and Luca were in a double bed, laughing with that last bit of energy before they crashed for the night. It was nine-thirty. Way past their bedtime. "Okay, boys. Time to go to sleep, or I'm going to separate you two."

"Can we live here forever?" Luca asked. "Grandma gives us ice cream every night before bed."

"And Grandpa put the TV in here for us."

Mitchell turned around to see the small flat screen TV on the dresser. Dad would have never done that for them when they were kids. In fact, they didn't watch much TV as kids. Mom kicked them out of the house and told them to go play.

Mitchell spent fifteen minutes saying goodnight to the boys before he finally made it to the shower. When he went back into the bedroom, Renee hadn't moved from her papers. He climbed into bed next to her and looked at one of the papers. History. So boring. Top notch boring for fourth graders. Renee marked one paper up with question marks and a note that said, *Did you read pg. 62?* The kid wrote random junk for answers because, according to him, George Washington marched with Martin Luther King Jr. in Alabama.

Mitchell rolled to his side to get closer to Renee's face. She leaned away from him. "What are you doing?" she said, her voice flat.

He held her chin so she couldn't pull away from him, and he kissed her. She opened her mouth to him, and she held everything that was meaningful in his life. And then she said, "My arm," through the kiss and tried to move away, but Mitchell didn't budge. He knew her too well. Her arm wasn't bothering her. It was an excuse to push him away.

"Renee," he said, looking into her eyes as he brushed his thumb across her cheek. "Just let me love you." He brushed his thumb over her soft lips and she closed her eyes for a moment as he waited for her to give him something, anything. There had to be something left. Renee pressed her hand to his and gently kissed his open palm. He tossed the papers down to the floor, kissed her neck, her mouth, and slowly made his way down the length of her familiar body.

Chapter 20

Sidra curled up on the sofa in Mitchell's living room, watching TV and waiting for Dominic to get off of work. The fog that lived in her mind was a living thing she'd grown so accustomed to she didn't know what to do without it. The fog bit into her with sharp teeth and the headaches became part of her life. The only way to keep them at bay was the alcohol. The alcohol was the one thing that kept her going, otherwise; she walked around with incapacitating guilt because it was the only way her brain knew how to function.

She wasn't a drunk, but she drank enough to dull the pain, just enough to take the edge off. And her whole fucking family knew it and they'd look at her as such a fuckup. But they had no idea. She wasn't drinking right now, at this very moment, and that gave her a sense of accomplishment. But her mind flooded with all the things she needed to feel in order to move through the day.

The headlights shining through the window as Dominic pulled into the driveway put a smile on her face. A driveway that didn't belong to either of them, but at this moment, him coming home to her, felt like bliss. It hit her now how much she wanted this. Wanted someone in her life that she could settle down with.

This is what I want, she thought, and got up to unlock the front door for him. He had a box of donuts in his hand and he smiled as he kissed.

"Cops and their donuts," she said, and Dominic walked inside. The bright side of a bad day who could pull the toxic thoughts right out of her mind. Their tension from nights ago discussed and settled.

They sat down on the sofa and Dominic said, "Speaking of a donut. Why is there one on your van?"

"I got a flat earlier today."

"Why didn't you call me?"

Sidra bit into a chocolate-covered donut and said, "I know how to change a tire. I worked at a mechanic shop for a year. I can change your oil if you want me to."

Dominic smiled. She really needed to see him smile. "You know you can call me if you need something, right?"

"You were on duty, and I was in Riverdale not—"

"Riverdale? That's even worse." Dominic shoved a half a donut in his mouth. "You could have been jumped."

"It's not like it's the Bronx," she said, then watched Dominic's face as she told him about Earl watching her back.

When she told him about following Trevor, he said, "I don't want to hear it."

"It's not illegal to follow someone." Sidra pulled her legs up and curled into him.

"Excuse me, but if you know someone's location and he's wanted by the police for kidnapping, assault and battery, I'd say it's failure to report and that's illegal. Especially if you know this."

He was getting all serious. Dominic's phone vibrated on the coffee table. Even with the phone face down, Sidra knew the number that popped up. The calls started about two months ago. She didn't know who it was. There wasn't a contact name attached.

"Are you going to get that?"

Dominic tensed for a moment. "It'll go to voicemail."

He always sent it to voicemail. Sidra had the number memorized. Wondered what would happen if she called it one day. Wondered what kind of person would answer the phone, because they called so much and the call went straight to voicemail. Would they be angry? Impassive? Would the voice be female?

Ignoring her thoughts about that, she said, "How about we make a deal that we don't talk about our work. Just don't bring it home."

"That might be a good idea," he said, and pulled her close. "That way I'm not an accomplice in your criminal activity."

Dominic thought he was joking, but he didn't know the half of it.

***

The next morning, Sidra rolled over in bed and didn't want to get up. Not when she was lying next to all his warmth. She lay her head on Dominic's chest and he woke with a slight groan.

"What time do you start your shift today?" Sidra asked.

"Two."

"Instead of you going all the way home, let's just stay in bed all day and not do anything."

"That sounds perfect but I need a clean uniform."

"I'll wash your uniform. And your dirty undies."

She pulled herself on top of him, her hair falling loose from the braid. He said, "Do you ever take this out?"

"Not really. My hair is always in the way."

"Then why don't you cut it."

Sidra kissed him. "I wouldn't cut my leg off because it was in the way."

"You're a strange woman, but I think I love you anyway."

That sounded nice. "I think I love you too," she said and kissed him until he was fully awake.

When they'd finally rolled out of bed, they ate breakfast, which consisted of scrambled eggs and the kids' lunchables she'd found in the fridge. She threw his dirty clothes in the washer and Dominic insisted he take her to get the tire replaced.

She climbed into his truck and listened to his stupid country music, but it was okay, she could deal with it because it was Dominic. Sidra spotted a bracelet in the cupholder, picked it up and said, "What's this?"

Dominic looked at it as if he didn't know how it got there, but he took the slim gold bracelet out of her hand and palmed it. "I found it in the squad lot yesterday. I forgot to turn it in to lost and found."

"I'm going to find a house," she said. "So I can wake up with you every day."

"Sounds nice." Dominic reached over and took her hand, the bracelet gone now, and then he started belting out along with Alan Jackson, sounding cheesy because he thought he knew how to sing.

***

"Was wondering if you could help me out," Sidra said later that day to the manager at the gas station. She held up a printout of the receipt from Kieran's car. She introduced herself and gave the whole P.I. spiel, hoping this guy would give her what she needed and too dumb to know the law.

His name was Andrew, and he said, "Do you have a warrant?"

"If you cooperate, no one needs a warrant," she said, throwing on the charm.

Andrew eyed her carefully. He was in his fifties and resembled the kind of man who worked his entire life only to make ends meet. "I don't know."

"Come on, Andrew. What if it was your computer? Wouldn't you want me to do everything I could to get it back?"

"Well, yeah," he said, leaning against the chip rack, and Sidra hoped the thing was bolted to the floor. "I just don't really know what you're going to do with it."

"Actually, all I need you to do is look at the time stamp on the video. Tell me if the vehicle was a Prius and give me a description of the person who pumped gas. This would just mean that he was one-hundred percent in the area at the time."

Because Kieran could say that someone stole his car and his credit card to get gas. Then Sidra thought about something.

"And if it's not a Prius though—"

"I don't have time for this," Andrew said, and Sidra felt deflated, but then he said, "Come on," and waved her to follow him. He brought her into a tiny office with ten years' worth of paperwork sitting on the desk. "Gimme the paper."

"Thank you, Andrew. I can't even express how much this means to my client. He creates video games and someone stole his computer—"

"Brady Ardeen?" Andrew turned around to look at her.

Sidra hesitated slightly because she couldn't read Andrew's face. "Yes."

"Well, shit, why didn't you say it was Brady in the first place? My son, he's got Down syndrome, and he met Brady last summer at this camp. He thinks Brady's a superhero. My son's not a boy anymore. He's thirty-five and was working at the summer camp with disabled kids. It means the world to him when Brady takes time to talk to him when we see him."

Brady is a superhero, Sidra thought and asked, "What's your son's name?"

"Ollie."

"I'll let Brady know how helpful you've been."

A minute later, Andrew pointed to the computer monitor. "This is what I've got."

The video on pump five showed Kieran Knox, clear as day—well, grainy, but she knew it was him—pumping gas into his Prius. Someone was in the passenger seat. "Can you look at the other camera to see who this guy is?"

Andrew pressed a few keys and a minute later there was a better shot of the passenger, a grainy image that offered her nothing.

"Would you be willing to save those clips to a thumb drive?"

"Absolutely. You tell Mr. Ardeen if he ever needs anything to let us know."

***

Sidra still didn't have entry access into Willow Point Estates and sat at the security gate for a few minutes while security called Brady. The home owners paid their salaries to sit in a booth all day, but really, the man had been watching TV on his phone. Sidra could still hear laughter coming from whatever comedy he was watching.

The gate opened, and he nodded at her. Halloween decorations covered the Bradford Pear trees, along with all the houses in preparation for their open trick-or-treating festivities later this month.

Brady's driveway wasn't long, but it sat further from the street and small crape myrtles stretched down the drive. A fountain with a dragon sat in the center of the circular driveway and Brady sat out front, throwing a tennis ball for Peaches.

The dog ran up to Sidra for only a moment because she was so focused on her ball. "Hey," Sidra said, when she stood next to him and he smiled up at her with that boyish grin. A cool breeze blew by, balanced out with the sun pressing down with its last hope of heat before the winter. "Can I have a code to get in?"

"All you have to do is call me. It's no big deal."

It was a big deal to her. Brady was locking her out. "I had a code for years."

"They upped the security." The way he looked at her, she knew he was lying. He'd cancelled her access code last year after he'd told her he didn't want to see her again.

Sidra sighed. "Kieran Knox got gas at the station on the corner the day of the break-in. This was thirty minutes later, and he had another guy with him. I needed to see if you recognized the guy." She had her laptop ready. "Do you want to go inside?"

"It's nice out here."

Sidra stood in front of her van and opened the laptop, inserted the thumb drive and waited for it to load. Brady threw the ball for Peaches and the dog knew to bring it back and drop it in his lap.

The file loaded, and Sidra opened it. Before Brady rolled his wheelchair over, he looked at his house, almost confused, longing for something inside of the house. She lowered the laptop so he could see the screen. "Do you recognize that guy?"

"No." Brady used the side of his limp pinky to slide over the mouse pad, right clicked the mouse with his other pinky, then clicked enter. The video showed the Prius pulling up to the pump, Kieran getting out, looking around while he pumped gas. The other guy sat in the passenger seat, half asleep.

"Both of the men that broke in had on black sweatshirts with hoodies," Brady said. "Kieran's wearing a t-shirt."

"He probably took the hoodie off."

"Are you going to give this to the police?"

"This doesn't really tell me anything except that Kieran was in The Bubble the same day as the break-in."

"And if you don't live in Peachtree City, you're not in The Bubble. An outsider using our gas stations."

"If the police were to question him about this, it's a free country and I'm sure he'd have a ton of reasons he was in the area. I may have to knock on all the nearby doors and ask if they have front door cameras and see if I spot the Prius in any of the neighborhoods. That would be worth a try, but it's a lot of work." Because this was the only lead she had, she was going to have to be very thorough to get the results. Even if it seemed a waste of time.

"Or he didn't do it," Brady said, his voice full of disappointment. "And this is a big waste of time."

"What do you want me to do?" Sidra closed the laptop. "Daley spoke with the police the day after the break-in and a few cops knocked on doors in the neighborhood behind Willow Point, but they got nothing. I can go back to look around for cameras and see what I can get. After that, if I don't get anything you can pull it."

"I just don't want to waste your time with you looking all over the state for my computer tower."

"This is my job. It's what I do. You're the one paying Shackelford." Although she felt certain now that she didn't want him to have to pay a dime for this, a friend helping a friend, but she knew Mom had spoken with him over the phone about expenses.

"Sounds like you have your work cut out for you."

Peaches brought the ball back, but this time she shoved it to Sidra's thigh. "Hey, girl." The ball was slobbery, but Sidra threw it down the driveway, where it rolled into the grass.

"She's a great dog," Brady said, and they watched her as she picked up the tennis ball and threw it in the air, playing ball with herself.

Just then the front door swung open and Beverly stepped out, and Sidra said, "Oh," because she hadn't expected her to be here. "I thought you were out of town?"

"I was taking care of my sick grandmother in Virginia. But I miss this guy too much to stay away," Beverly said, and put her hand on Brady's shoulder. She'd been his live-in nurse for over a year and did more than what her job expected, but Brady paid her lucratively for her help. "Brady told me what happened, and I had to come back."

Brady said. "I told you I was fine."

Beverly was more of a comfort for Brady than anything. When Peaches came over, she had poop on her back from rolling around in the grass. Beverly and Sidra stepped away from her, but poor Brady got it on his cotton pants. Sidra grabbed Peaches by the collar. "She's going to need a bath."

"Peaches," Beverly said. "Why? I have so much stuff to do right now."

"I can call the groomer," Brady said, and Sidra thought that was absurd.

"If you're going to pay a dog groomer," Sidra said, "then pay me. Drying is extra though."

While Brady changed his pants, Sidra had Peaches in the tub in an extra bathroom downstairs. This one had a shower sprayer that really made it easy.

"Are you sure you don't mind," Brady said, making his way into the bathroom.

"You know, I worked at animal control for six months *and* a vet hospital part-time. I had plenty of dog washing days."

Peaches didn't enjoy taking a bath, but she wasn't trying to run away. Once the poop was off her back, Sidra got to work with the dog shampoo. While she leaned over the tub on one side, Brady looked in right next to her, rubbing Peaches's face.

"Do you know someone named Ollie? Helped at a camp last year?"

"Good ol' Ollie. Super nice guy who loves video games."

"Well, his dad is the manager at the gas station, and that's who I got the footage from. He said that Ollie adores you and it really means a lot to him when you talk to him. He said that Ollie thinks you're a superhero."

"I'm not a superhero," Brady said.

"To some people you are. I mean, you've overcome a lot and made a success out of yourself and people like you. You're an inspiration to people."

233

"Superhero," Brady said, and when Sidra faced him, he had his curled fists on his hips and his chest puffed out to resemble a superhero.

"I think the fact that you try to help so many people is humbling."

"I have a ton of social media followers." Because that was the thing these days to stay connected to people. And Brady wasn't shy about his disability, even though it was an inconvenience. He let people know how he felt when he opened up about things.

Sidra made quick progress washing the dog, and when her braid fell in the way, Brady pulled it back over her shoulder. She turned to look at him as he had the tail end of her hair in the palm of his hand, and it was almost as if she felt his touch through her hair.

Peaches shook off the suds and jolted Sidra out of whatever she'd just felt, and she paused a minute to gain her composure. By the time she got the dog dried off and smelling decent again, Sidra's black jeans were wet and full of dog hair, but it was okay because it was Brady's dog.

Chapter 21

Mitchell couldn't take the smile off his face all morning. Then he got a phone call. "Mr. Shackelford," Coleman said. "Was wondering if I could have a chat with you."

So now he was Mr. Shackelford. "Yeah, what's going on?"

"You think you can meet me down at the station? Same place as last time?"

Mitchell groaned and wondered what the hell this was about. Even though he'd thought about the fake prescription and going to Berry Pharmacy with it, he decided that was a bad idea.

"Sure," Mitchell said.

And same as last time, he met Coleman in a little office inside the Jonesboro Detective Bureau, they made small talk about the weather and college football. "Love those dawgs," Mitchell said, and he could tell Coleman was only half interested. Maybe he was a Yellow Jackets fan. If he was, that said a hell of a lot about him as a person.

"We found Ryan Orchard," Coleman said.

One less suit to worry about. "Did he tell you what they're doing?"

"He's dead. Homicide," Coleman said, and adjusted his suit jacket as he got a read on Mitchell's response. Coleman sat there, eyes wide, because of the homicide part.

"What happened?"

"You tell me." Coleman held his hands out as though he wanted Mitchell to produce pertinent information that would solve the case.

"No idea. Last I saw Ryan Orchard, he left his apartment before the APD nabbed Helen. I was under the impression he'd go to work. But then no one could find him."

Coleman opened a file folder in front of him and turned it so Mitchell could see the 8x10 photo. "Tagged your van when we looked through local video footage."

Mitchell recognized his van in front of the white building, but he didn't remember where it was. "Okay. What are you getting at?"

"I asked you once to leave this alone." Coleman tapped his finger on the photo. "This was at the gas station on Main Street, across from the cemetery. What were you doing?"

"I followed Leland Marple from the Sapphire Groove to the cemetery. He met a scuzzy guy who drives a silver Altima, and they drove away. Look, when I saw Grizzly Adams—"

"Grizzly Adams?"

"The bearded guy," Mitchell said, and Coleman gave one slow nod. "I left it alone after I saw him the second time. You insinuated things and I put it together. I think he's an undercover and I'm certain Leland was a CI?"

"CI? Where'd you hear that?"

"I'm guessing. Am I wrong?" he wasn't exactly guessing. He'd gotten word about it from Dominic, who didn't actually say that, but he didn't have to.

Coleman shrugged. "Who are you talking about?" He sounded as if he really didn't know, but Coleman was a perfect liar. That was part of his job. Probably gave Deception 101 classes in detective school.

"While I know you're in the whole open investigation phase, is there anything you can tell me?"

Coleman didn't hesitate. "Two in the chest, one in the head. Dumped in the cemetery. A woman found him early Monday morning when she put flowers on her husband's grave."

"The cemetery, huh? At least he didn't have to go far for a burial," Mitchell said, and laughed at his own joke. Coleman didn't find the humor. "Did Leland ever say anything else about my house?"

"Thought you were an undercover."

"Trevor Gregory thinks the same thing. Do I look like a cop?"

"No," Coleman said, and Mitchell was glad. Not that there was anything wrong with being a cop.

"What do you need me to do?"

Coleman leaned close. "Nothing," the detective said. "And Mr. Shackelford, consider this your final warning."

"Okay, okay." Mitchell held up his hand. "But Berry Pharmacy is handing out prescriptions from their back door. If you can get me a fake prescription, I'll prove it to you. But you can't arrest me when I'm done."

"*What?*" Coleman said.

***

Driving back to Shackelford, the phone rang with an unknown number. He answered with his usual greeting. "Mitchell Shackelford."

"We need to meet."

"I'm sorry. Who is this?"

He was well aware of who called him, but he wasn't going to say so.

"How about you meet me at my office around five p.m." While Shane Bennett could have found Mitchell easily and said what he needed to, that's not how he approached the situation.

"You want to tell me what this is about?"

"We'll meet."

"No," Mitchell said. "You want to talk to me? We can meet at the park on Jonesboro Road. That's as far as I go."

"I'll see you then," Shane said without hesitation.

The park on Jonesboro Road wasn't that spectacular, but it was open enough so that if Shane

Bennett wanted Mitchell dead, at least there would be witnesses. Then Mitchell looked around at the couple of kids playing with their moms and thought the idea was terrible. If Shane wanted him dead, it was going to ruin these kids' lives. But he couldn't call and change the location.

When Shane parked and got out of a black sedan, he was alone, so if he felt threatened, his demeanor was nothing but confidence. Maybe he had guys the same way Mitchell had guys.

"Approaching from the west," Daley said in his ear through a wireless comm.

Mitchell stretched his arms high above his head and rolled his neck as Shane walked over in his expensive gray suit and tie. He nodded a silent hello and sat down on the bench with a foot of space between them.

"Beautiful day," Shane said, not a care in the world. "You still interested in running a club in Atlanta?"

Mitchell looked over at him. "You're the one who left me a business card. I was just following a lead."

"I set up Leland Marple," Shane said.

"What do you mean?"

"After the Helen Ross thing. I mean, I don't know if you took the money or not."

"Believe me," Mitchell said, wanting to show the man his bank account. "I don't have any money, much less yours. And really, how much money could she have taken from scamming people about being a doctor?" Mitchell did some quick math. "She charged fifty to a hundred dollars an hour to listen to people complain about life, and then extra if she wrote a prescription. What's that? A couple thousand in one night?"

Shane looked over at him, and Mitchell stared back at him. Shane said, "Ryan took something that belonged to me and I'm assuming he and Helen sold the stolen goods out of the motel and kept the money. The profits were beyond a couple grand."

"And why do you think I had anything to do with that?"

"You were the only one that never asked for a prescription. You're not the average bear. I got the feeling you were in on something after Ryan dropped your name. That's why I came to you that day."

That would mean Ryan Orchard set Mitchell up and he'd never even met the guy. "Ryan's dead," Mitchell said, and he watched Shane feign surprise. He nodded, said, "I guess you would know that." Why didn't they get rid of the body, though? Why dump him in the cemetery?

A minute passed, the wind blowing the sounds of the kid's laughter in the wind. The warm sun on his face, as he thought about their innocence. He could take his own boys fishing this weekend. Or out to a park where they could run around, instead of being cooped up inside.

Mitchell said, "Why'd you set up Leland? That doesn't make sense."

"I heard I had a rat," Shane said. "Took me a few days to figure out who. When I did, I told him you had the money, and if he found it, half of it was his."

"I don't have your money. He could have hurt someone, you sending Leland to my house for kicks. I don't want to have a problem with you, but Trevor Gregory is being a pain in my ass and you need to call him off or he's going to get hurt."

"Let me ask you something, Mitchell. How much do you separate your business life from your personal life?"

"What do you mean?" Because Mitchell worked for a family business, the lines became foggy.

"You can't. There is a problem when we make choices that put the ones we love in jeopardy. And there will always be the Trevors of the world who want to settle a score. Trevor's not acting on my behalf, but he does a job for me and he's paid well. I think the two of you could work well together if you're looking for another source of income."

Mitchell looked over at Shane Bennett as though he'd lost his mind. "You're offering me a job?"

"If you're interested. Trevor could also use a babysitter. He gets in my hair sometimes."

"I'm not interested. In fact, after this little chat, I don't want you or your friends to come near me or my family. I want to go live back in my house and not worry about you showing up or someone breaking in. Can you make that happen?"

"You have three children, correct?"

Mitchell took a deep breath and gripped his hands together. While he gathered his thoughts, Daley said into his ear, "I can put one through his left eye." But after Daley's shot, someone would do the same to Mitchell.

"Don't threaten my family. I've done nothing to you to screw you over in any kind of way. I got twisted up in something that had nothing to do with me."

"And yet here you are," he said, as calm as he was when he'd first sat down.

"Trevor kidnapped my wife. He choked her and threw her out of a moving van. And now he's following my sister. I have a problem with that."

"I think Trevor knows too much. And sometimes he's too passionate about showing people who's the boss," Shane said and stood up, blocking out the sun as he loomed over him. "If you need protection, I have people who could help you out. Wouldn't cost you much."

Now, he wanted to tell Daley. Just kill him now. But he didn't, and Shane Bennett tipped his invisible hat to Mitchell and walked away.

***

Fifteen homes later, and the lady with the bright red shutters was the biggest break Sidra had in a week.

"Yeah, I saw that car. They parked out there for an hour and I wondered why in the hell they'd park in front of my house, but I wasn't going to ask them that."

Her name was Louisa, and she stood in her doorway with a white kitten on her shoulder, a furry parrot happy to be off the floor. The little kitten played with a dangling gold earring. Louisa would regret this when the cat weighed fifteen pounds.

"I was going to report the car because they parked it on my side of the street in the wrong direction. But I said, 'Louisa, mind your own damn business for once,' and I let it go."

"Did you see anyone get in or out of the car?"

"I saw two *boys*," she said, stressing the word because that's what they were to her, considering Louisa had to be in her sixties. "I thought they were visiting Joan across the street. She has a couple of grandkids, you know, that come and see her sometimes."

"You didn't get the plate, did you?"

"No." The woman turned to the kitten. "Stop that, Rocky." But he kept swatting at the earring.

"What did they look like?"

"Oh, I don't know. They came running from that way and went to the car. I asked Mr. Hobbs if he knew anything about it, but he saw nothing and it's no wonder, he's eighty-five. He can't see his mailbox from his house. Rocky." Louisa put the kitten on the opposite shoulder as if that was better.

"Were they carrying anything?"

"A box," she said. "One of those metal computer boxes. Whatever they're called."

Louisa was saving her life right now. "Do you remember what time it was that you saw the car?"

"Oh, it was one o'clock for sure. I'd just gotten back from taking Rocky to the vet. He had worms. I got him from this lady whose cat had a litter of ten kittens. You believe that? I think I got the best one." She scratched the kitten on his head.

"Thank you," Sidra said. Louisa told her it was fine if she walked through the backyard. The walk to Willow Point Estates took five minutes, and she ended up near the playground. So that's how they got in. Why have gated security when people could walk right in?

Because it was *The Bubble*. The place where crime was low and money flowed, and break-ins were rare in Peachtree City. What Sidra really wanted to do was bust down Kieran Knox's front door and search his place for Brady's computer tower. But the asshole most likely sold it by now. Instead, she had to play it safe. Armed with her information, she drove over to the PTC police department, told the desk Sergeant everything she'd uncovered so far.

"This is important," she said to Sergeant Perez.

"I agree," he said. "We didn't take this lightly. I'll get in touch with Atlanta and we'll get someone on it."

"I'm going to call you twice a day until I hear from you."

Sergeant Perez chuckled. "I wouldn't expect anything less."

While she was certain Kieran Knox broke into Brady's house, if the police didn't do anything, she was going to do far worse than bust down Kieran's door.

Chapter 22

"**Don't touch my** plate," Spencer said to Luca later that night at the dinner table. When the family sat down to eat, it was never a quiet meal. Everyone talked over one another, laughter erupted, arguments broke out. Someone always had something to say.

Too many people in this house, Sidra thought.

The huge dining room table sat twelve, three seats at each side, and nothing made the kids happier than when there was enough space for them at the big table instead of the kitchen table where the little ears were out of mind.

As they sat eating lasagna, the voices in the room were almost deafening. Mitchell and Dad argued about football. Big surprise there. Even though they were both Bulldog fans, Dad wasn't happy the way they played this season. Mom and Renee discussed Halloween plans, and Caroline, Spenser, and Luca were interrupting because they wanted to go shopping for costumes. Daley and Jorie argued about a sleepover Jorie wanted to go to, but Daley told her not on a school night.

And Sidra sat there drinking her whiskey so she could get through it. Mom stopped mid-conversation to tell Dad, "You need to call your sister Doreen," and Dad ignored his wife, but he nodded in her direction.

Jorie said, "Dad, I've spent the night out on school nights before. Chloe's dad doesn't let us stay up late and we get to school on time. We have this project we have to work on."

And then Caroline, who idolized her older cousin, began telling Jorie about her own school project.

Too many people.

Daley asked Sidra, "Anything new on the computer?"

Mom stopped mid-conversation again. "Not right now," Mom said, only because once they started about business, it's all they talked about.

Sidra said, "I think I got something. Hopefully, the police can handle it from here."

Dad said, "Can you make sure you do your paperwork correctly? I just had to track down notes on the Fieldman DD."

Sidra and Daley both pointed at Mitchell. It was his case. Dad shook his head.

"What's a DD?" Spencer said, lasagna falling out of his mouth.

"Nothing," Dad said.

"I know what it is," Jorie said, and Caroline wanted to know, and no one wanted to explain to the kids it stood for Dirty Dessert. A cheating spouse.

"We have ice cream for dessert," Mom said, distracting the boys.

"Is it a dirty dessert, Grandma?" Jorie said, with a smile, proud she could take part in the adult conversation.

"Sorry I mentioned it," Dad said, and stabbed at his lasagna so he didn't have to see his wife's disapproving stare.

"When can we go home?" Luca said. "I want to play my video game. Aunt Sidra, can you ask that man for another code to my game so I can update the players?"

"His name's Brady, and yes I can."

Renee said to Luca, "It's Mr. Brady."

"He has a wheelchair, Mom," Luca said, flashing a gummy smile with all his missing teeth.

"He's still Mr. Brady," Renee said.

Jorie climbed out of her chair and squeezed herself in Sidra's lap as if Sidra weren't trying to eat dinner. "What are you doing?"

Jorie wrapped her arms around Sidra's neck, and she said desperately, "Please talk my dad into letting me spend the night at Chloe's."

"No," Daley said, shoving a half of a dinner roll in his mouth, and then he looked over at them with a serious face. "I have rules." Jorie was a good kid, but she did some things that were questionable, and Daley thought Chloe was a bad influence.

"I can't wait to get my license," Jorie said. "Then I can do what I want."

"That's what you think," Daley said.

Mitchell said, "Who's going to pay for your car? And insurance? Your Dad who you won't listen to?" and Jorie glared at her uncle. It took a village...

"If you want to do what you want," Dad said, "then you need to be honest and do the right thing."

And then Jorie snapped her attention back to Daley. "What did you say?" she said to him, and Sidra felt her niece tense.

Daley tossed his fork down on his plate. "I think that's enough."

A long moment passed where she defiantly stared him down, and Daley wouldn't budge. "Fine," Jorie said, and she spun around to get off of Sidra's lap. When Jorie started to leave, Mom and Dad told her to come back, to finish her dinner, but she didn't.

And then, as though nothing happened, everyone fell back into their conversations, except for Daley, who sat there looking defeated.

After dinner, Sidra walked into the kitchen and heard Mom say her name as she spoke to Renee while they cleaned up. They stopped talking as Sidra brought over the last of the plates from the table. "Don't stop talking about me just because I'm here," Sidra said.

"We weren't talking *about* you," Mom said. "I just mentioned your name. No need to be hostile about it."

Sidra leaned against the counter and said to Renee, "What are you going to do?"

"We're trying to figure it out," Renee said.

Mom wiped her eye with her shoulder. "Life's not easy. We'll just take one day at a time. We'll get through it." The way she said this implied that Renee had spoken to her about a divorce, and maybe what was going on with Mitchell's drug use.

"Whatever you decide to do, Renee, it's not just about you."

"What's that supposed to mean?" Renee shut off the water and faced her. "That you think I'm selfish and I haven't thought about my kids and everyone else in this family?"

"That's exactly what I want you to consider. Because you've been a part of this family for a long time and you're one of us, and if you're not here on Sundays and if the kids aren't here on Sundays... It puts a big hole in the family."

Renee wiped away her own tears. "So I'm supposed to endure a shitty marriage so you can be happy?"

"That's not what I'm saying."

"Then what do you suggest I do, since you know so much about being married."

"Girls," Mom said, and Renee and Sidra took a deep breath.

"He loves you."

"I know that. But sometimes it's not enough."

"Then fix it."

"What do you suggest I do?"

"Fuck, Renee. I don't know." Sidra moved to the other side of the counter and poured sweet tea into her glass, followed it up with too much whiskey. Sidra turned to look Renee in the face. "The way you're handling things needs to change."

"Be an example of your own advice, then you can talk to me about change." Renee gave her a pitiful look because what started out as a conversation about not wanting this woman to separate the family ended up with it turned back on Sidra. Maybe Sidra didn't know how to express her feelings. *Fuck feelings*, she thought and shook her head then walked out the back door.

She nearly tripped over Daley who sat on the back steps looking out into the back yard. "Everyone in this family has fucking problems," she said. "It's like, there's this list. And the day we're born God starts checking off the list of all the problems assigned to us. And our entire existence is us just getting through our lives trying to uncheck those boxes."

Sidra sat down next to Daley. He snatched the glass out of her hand, took a sip and shook his head. "Maybe we're born with a clean slate and our decisions puts the checked boxes."

"Shut up." They sat there for a few minutes, then Sidra said, "What's going on with you and Jorie?"

"Nothing."

"We used to do a lot of stupid things when we were her age."

"No, you used to do a lot of stupid things. And you're everything she wants to be."

"You were far from perfect."

"Okay, you're right. And that's why she can't do what she wants. All that shit with Amy when she was missing? That's all I think about sometimes with Jorie."

That made sense. Sidra hadn't thought about it in that context. Fear and concerns from an actual parent.

"I found a condom in her purse. And I'm aware it's wrong to dig through her stuff, but I found it. She's fourteen."

"Did you talk to her about it?" His silence said he hadn't, but there was nothing worse for him than being a single dad to a teenaged girl and having to talk to her about sex. Even if Jorie didn't have a mom raising her, she had plenty of women in her life who have taken care of her over the years.

"I just haven't had time yet." Meanwhile, he'd keep his daughter locked away so he could protect her. "She's never going to trust me when she finds out that I dug through her stuff."

"True," Sidra said, and Daley looked at her.

"She scares me sometimes," he said. "She's growing up so fast and I can't keep up. She's not a little girl anymore." When he took a deep breath, Sidra felt bad for him.

"She hasn't said anything to me about this." Which bothered her because she'd been so open with her niece over the years. Sidra was sure Jorie would come to her if she had questions or opinions about something. "I'll talk to her, okay? You should have told me about this sooner. And you're not a failure because your daughter doesn't want to talk to you about personal stuff. Trust me, you don't want to know what's going through a teenaged girl's mind."

"That's even scarier. I mean, where does she even learn about any of that stuff?"

"How old were you when you kissed Donna Talbert?"

"Oh, God."

"You stick to teaching her how to survive, and I'll teach her everything else."

"Defcon-2," he said, and Sidra laughed.

***

Mitchell kissed his wife goodbye and helped her get the kids in the car for school. They should probably go home. The kids thought they were on vacation, but he could tell his wife would explode soon if they didn't go home. It had been a week and they could only live out of suitcases for so long.

He walked into the office the next morning; surprised Sidra wasn't there yet. That's two mornings in a row she came in late. Good thing they weren't a normal business with normal hours. It would be fun if he and Renee could get away for the weekend. He could plan something and then be back Sunday night. A weekend getaway in Savannah. Or the quiet mountains in north Georgia. Just him and Renee, and nothing but free time for a few days. Thinking about that made him giddy. He could already feel himself relaxing in a hot

253

tub on a cool fall night. Could he do it? Plan something and then tell Renee to pack a bag? He could bring her breakfast in bed and they could stay there all day holding each other. And sex. Lots of sex. He could chase her around the room the way he used to.

Everything used to be so easy.

Even when his kids were in diapers, things used to be easier. Now? Mitchell's life was falling out of his grasp. But he could fix it. He had to save his marriage. Renee still loved him; he was certain. She still looked at him with a sparkle in her eye. Sometimes that sparkle turned to a hint of something deadly, but it was something.

An hour later, Sidra showed up after Woolsey and Daley, and Mitchell had been trying to book a lodge in the Blue Ridge Mountains. Mitchell said to her, "Are you enjoying playing girlfriend and boyfriend in my house?"

"Actually, I am. Your shower is amazing."

Mitchell groaned. "You're sick, and I despise you."

Mitchell focused back on the lodge and checked out photos of the shower. Sidra handed him a piece of paper over her head and said, "Can you start this skip trace?"

"Why can't you do it?"

"Because I'm days behind after partying at the Sapphire Groove for you."

"You could have been working last night instead of, you know, shacking up in my house." Maybe Mitchell didn't need to go home. That way, if Shane Bennett came for him, he'd get Sidra instead.

He found himself looking up news reports on Ryan Orchard found dead in the cemetery. Shane didn't kill him personally. No, he made one of his goons do that for him. Mitchell kept replaying the conversation he'd had with Shane yesterday over and over, listening to the subtleties of his threats. Those were the people he had to watch out for. Mitchell had clarified that he had nothing Shane wanted. He hoped the man got the point.

***

Sidra didn't see Dominic last night because he said he needed to go home after work and take care of something early in the morning. Which was fine because he met her for lunch at Clemmie's the next afternoon. He was in jeans and a baby blue shirt that matched his eyes. Dominic sat with his back to the wall with a clear view of the diner, and he'd eaten here enough times now that he'd learned everyone's names.

Dad sat in a booth talking to Archie Glencoe, the owner of Clemmie's, and they could have passed for brothers, both of them sitting there relaxed with an arm thrown over their respective booths.

I could get used to this, she thought. Her family and her hometown were so much a part of her, she'd never be able to move out of Fayetteville. And having Dominic here seemed right, almost too right. He was easygoing and he fit in nicely with her family when he came to eat dinner with them sometimes on Sundays when he wasn't working. Or even if he was and had to go in later, he made it work.

And he sat there laughing with Val, who told him the Shackelfords were a bad influence, and then she playfully pushed Sidra's shoulder because they'd been friends a long time. Mom showed up and told everyone hello because she knew nearly every single person inside the diner, and then she sat down with Dad and Archie.

Even when they didn't come here to eat, Mom and Dad stopped by sometimes just to chat with people because that's the type of people they were.

The Shackelfords, the Glencoes, the Attwells; they were all old Fayetteville families that had been here for well over a hundred years. And now the city had grown so much, but still had that small-town feel to it where people knew everyone.

And that's how it felt sitting here with Dominic, the cop who'd become a familiar face and Sidra felt herself at peace for once, and she thought again, *I can get used to this.*

Sidra's phone rang, and it was Brady. "Sorry," she said, but Dominic didn't seem bothered about the call.

Brady said, "I need to see you." She couldn't tell by his tone what was going on.

"Are you okay?"

"Yes, but can you come here?"

"Of course."

Sidra hung up the phone and looked at Dominic. "I need to go."

"Is everything okay?"

"Yes," she said, and slid out of the booth. She dug around in her purse for money.

Dominic squeezed her side, and said, "I got it."

Sidra leaned over and kissed him. "I love you," she said. "Please be careful at work tonight."

"I will," he said. "I love you, too. Call me later."

"I will if I think about you."

Dominic smiled because it was their little joke. She grabbed the rest of her burger and walked out the door to find out what the heck was going on with Brady.

He opened the door with a huge smile on his face, backed up the wheelchair so she could come in and Peaches nearly knocked her over.

"What's going on?" she said, almost nervous but praying that he was happy about what she was hoping for.

Brady moved out of the way and gestured behind him, and there, sitting on the tiled floor, was his computer tower decorated with all kinds of gaming stickers. "The police just dropped it off."

She was so happy she wanted to hug him. "What happened?"

Brady laughed. "The police talked to Kieran, and the computer was sitting right by his front door."

"Did they arrest him?"

"I have no idea what's happening. They asked me if I wanted to press charges."

"You better."

Brady didn't answer her. He should press charges; it was total bullshit.

"Can you help me get the computer hooked up?"

"Of course." Sidra picked up the computer tower and followed Brady into his office, where he practically bounced in his chair, waiting for a new present.

He said, "If he screwed up any of my game designs, I'm going to kill him. Hurry up. Put that on the desk behind the monitor."

God, he was bossy. Sidra grabbed the cable and connected them, and within a couple of minutes, the monitor was up and running. And the moment of truth...

Brady used the joystick and mouse pad to scroll through files and engines and whatever else he was looking for to make sure Kieran hadn't messed up anything. And then he let out a big victory air-punch and said, "Yes!" Opened up another file and said, "Please, please, let her be there." He opened up an art portfolio, scrolled through pages of drawings, then let out a sigh of relief. "She's still here."

The female character on screen had long, braided hair, an updated Lara Croft. She looked a lot like—

"Brady, is that me?"

"Nooo," he said, then he looked at her. "Possibly. Don't be mad. I just needed some inspiration."

"I'm not mad. I'm surprised, that's all. I thought you'd never want to look at me again."

Brady touched his computer screen with the back of his hand. "This is why I needed my hard drive back so bad. When I'm done with the story, she's going to be a hero and save the world."

"Why did he steal your computer?"

"I don't know. I'm going to comb through everything meticulously and make sure he didn't put any bugs or anything on it. It's a jerk thing to do considering most of the developers I know are really cool people."

"Well, I'm glad you got your baby back," she said, and those words hung in the air between them.

"I can't wait to get back to work," he said, and it made her laugh because no one ever said that.

"I guess this is it." She held her hands open, not sure what else to say, but not really wanting to leave.

"You know I'm a night owl," he said. "You can always come over and watch me play video games if you want."

"So what are you saying?"

"Thank you for finding my computer?"

Sidra sighed. "You're welcome."

"5423," he said, and she knew it was a gate code.

***

Sidra walked into Shackelford with Mitchell asking Daley, "Come on, how much do you press? It's not a difficult question."

"Even if it's not as much as you," Daley said, "I can still take you down."

She stepped through the kill zone and looked at Daley. "Brady has his computer back." She erased his name from the board, and hated to do it because she really enjoyed looking at his name.

"Two-fifty?" Mitchell said.

Daley said around Mitchell's head, "Who? That little shit, Kieran Knox?" and Sidra nodded. "I knew it had to be him. Something wasn't right with that kid. I bet if you looked into his medical history, he's been in the psych ward a time or two."

They didn't have access to medical information, but Kieran gave off that vibe. And knowing what he's capable of, it made him seem ridiculously dangerous. "Two people broke into Brady's house. Who's the second guy?"

"Woolsey, you work out lately?" Woolsey turned to Mitchell and flipped him off.

"If we dog pile him," Sidra said, "he'll shut up."

And then Mitchell wheeled his chair closer to Daley, put his arm on the desk and said, "Come on. If you win, I'll buy you a beer."

"Dude," Daley said. "Why don't you go play Tetris with the cars in the parking lot and leave me alone." But he didn't back off either. He put his arm on the desk and got into position to arm wrestle Mitchell. After a minute of this, both of them struggled in the rolling chairs. Daley's papers slid across the desk, and something was going to get broken. Most likely Daley. Mitchell slammed his arm down and gave out a big whoop when he won, because something as simple as that seemed to stroke his ego.

"Can I work now?" Daley said, massaging his shoulder.

"You owe me a beer." Mitchell looked at Woolsey. "You want to try?"

That was the thing about working in an office with these guys. They were distracting and talked about stupid guy stuff half the time. If she had her own place, she could work from home.

But where was the fun in that?

Chapter 23

Mitchell picked up the skip trace and headed out to talk to the guy's mother. He had to get a feel on the guy's timeline. That was the easy part about a local case. Sometimes they'd have to drive all over when a simple phone call wouldn't do. But Mitchell didn't make it that far. He spotted Roberta and that frizzy head of hair walking out of a little pawn shop north of town. Town folks spent a lot of time trying to get the shady place shut down. They bought whatever people brought in, sometimes stolen goods, and resold them. Roberta hopped into an old Ford pickup with her shotgun in a rack across the back window.

Mitchell followed her from the pawnshop in Fayetteville to another place in Lovejoy, this one a small electronics repair shop specializing in vacuum cleaners. Next, an herb shop a mile up the road from that. They were having a sale on vitamin C.

Roberta drove all the way back to Fayetteville, up the highway to a small hardware store in Riverdale that went out of business a long time ago. Roberta came out a few minutes later with her big purse slung over her shoulder, looking every which way—cautious but not nervous—before she got back into her truck.

When Roberta stopped at Berry Pharmacy, Mitchell scratched his head. What was she doing? Not just in here, but at all these places? And not only that, but Mitchell told Coleman about this pharmacy selling prescriptions out the back door. Have they done anything about that yet?

Okay, that kind of stuff took time. When he thought about it further, he knew the police—the narcotics unit—would have to build a case, and that was a slow process. Clayton County had a strong gang and drug task force, it was just a matter of getting everything lined up for a bust with charges that would stick.

When Roberta parked at Zephyr Lanes, Mitchell got out a minute later. He walked inside the bowling alley and caught up with her at the end of the big carpeted hallway.

"Hey," he said, his voice casual and light. "Roberta. Just the person I was looking for."

When Roberta turned around, she was pissed. "What do you want?" The long jacket she wore was the color of army green, but it wasn't an army jacket. It was something trendy and girly, with big buttons down the front.

"You know, I thought I would stop by and see if I could get some bowling lessons."

"I don't know what makes you think I give bowling lessons, but I got shit to do."

"What if I help you out? I could polish the bowling balls? Work for some free lessons?" Mitchell held out his hands with his proposal, but Roberta stood there with her hands on her hips, wanting to shoot him, instead of teaching him how to bowl.

"I don't know what planet you're from, numb nuts, and I certainly don't know what you're trying to imply by 'polishing the bowling balls' for 'bowling lessons' but you can turn yourself around and get out of here."

When Roberta reached into her big purse without taking her eyes off of him, Mitchell held up his hands, "Okay, Jesus," he said, and took a step back, but she came out with a pack of cigarettes and a lighter.

Roberta laughed. "What? You thought I was going to shoot you?" She lit up a cigarette. "Why do I have the feeling you're not here for bowling lessons?"

"You're pretty perceptive."

"I don't know what that means, but it better not be an insult."

"I wouldn't insult you." Mitchell smiled. "Nice girl like you."

"Girl? I'm thirty years old."

"So, what do you do for fun?"

Besides blow holes in walls with shotguns.

Roberta blew out cigarette smoke and stepped over to a trash can to flick the ash inside. Hope the damn thing doesn't catch on fire.

"I don't have time for fun. And I don't have time for your games. Now I mean it. Get the hell out of here or

264

the next time I get something out of my purse it's gonna light your ass up."

**

"That's what she said. She was gonna light my ass up," Mitchell said to Daley and Sidra when he got back later that evening. "Do you believe that? So I have another project for us."

Daley put his hands behind his head and leaned back in his chair. "How much are we getting paid for this project?"

"Did you go talk to the skip trace's mother?" Sidra asked him.

"Yeah." Jesus, why couldn't they just listen? He handed her a page of notes, which she took and began putting into the computer. "How can we find out what Roberta was doing in those businesses?"

"Let me guess," Sidra said. "You want me to go in there and ask them?"

"Since you're offering."

"I'll do it, but you're going to have to pick up some of my workload so we can get these jobs done."

The little things piled up if they didn't stay on top of them. But they never had to worry about that because Mom sent them daily emails reminding them of incomplete tasks.

"I've been working on stuff. I even have notes."

Sidra tilted her head sideways, trying to find the truth in his words. She didn't have room to talk, little miss late two days in a row, using his shower.

"So tomorrow," Mitchell said. "And I'll keep my eyes on Roberta to see what else she's up to." Then he scrolled through the mountain resort website for weekend getaways instead of working.

***

The guy behind the glass counter at the pawnshop wore a black bandana with weed leaves on it. Counters lined the walls, with one glass counter in the center. Sidra browsed for a few minutes, checking out cell phones and old car radios, and catching her reflection with her disguise in the mirror. Everything in the store was in a glass case or bolted down. Robberies happened here at least once a month.

When she was finally alone in the pawnshop, she made a comment about how quickly cell phones became outdated, which got the guy talking about technology. Tony thought it was all a big government scam, and they watched everyone, anyway. Talking to people was easy when you found that sweet spot that got them going.

"I have a stack of laptops if you're looking for a computer. A couple of brand-new HPs, barely a year old."

Sidra walked over and leaned against the counter. "You know I can get you some product that would sell a hell of a lot quicker than any technology."

"What kind?" he said, and Sidra wondered how this guy protected himself from robbers. And not really with weapons. He could hide behind a toothpick, he was so skinny.

"I'm talking about something that starts with green and rhymes with business arrangement." Sidra held her hands palms up. Maybe Mitchell needed to get down here and do this himself. She didn't know the street talk for, *Hey, I'm part of the in crowd*. Or Roberta may have made her rounds just to say hi to all of her friends. But she couldn't ask about Roberta because the first thing Tony would do was call her. Tell her that some chick had been there asking about her.

It wasn't a secret that the pawnshop pushed drugs. From the way Tony acted, valued customers got the goods. And while she had cash in her pocket, buying illegal drugs that she didn't want to use wasn't a top priority in the case. Going to jail was at the very, very bottom of the list of things she wanted to do for her job.

With all of that, she had to take her chances. "Roberta stop by yesterday?"

"So?" Tony opened the glass case closest to him to add jewelry to it.

"I can get you twice what she's bringing you at a lower cost."

"Who are you?"

"For now, I'm a ghost. What you need to know is that I've got connections coming straight out of Atlanta that can give you half of your sales. Let's face it," Sidra said, holding out her hands. "This place isn't that lucrative." She thought about the Marquez family, a local cartel in the southeast. Sidra pretended to be a business associate. Everyone wanted money. "You can cut out the middleman and get what you want straight from a known dealer."

"I don't know," Tony said. "I don't get traffic for that."

"All depends on how much you're willing to put in. Come on, man, the money's there. I can put you in touch with some people, give you something to think about. Tell me this. What kind of percentage have you been making?"

"Depends on the sales. On what product they're bringing."

Sidra shook her head. "I can get whatever sells in this area."

"Pills," Tony said. "I don't know where they come from, but I make a decent cash on any kind of Opi I can get. I just raise my price, but these people around here will pay for what they want."

That's all it took to bring a town down. These drug dealers came in, made their money, and brought down businesses quick. All it took was one bad turn and Tony would lose his business. But if that's the kind of business they wanted to get into...

"I'm talking half the sales would be yours, but you have to put in the work."

"I kept telling Roberta that," Tony said. "If I hired on another guy, we could do a lot more."

"How often are you getting restocked?"

"Once a week, give or take. She'll kill me if she finds out I'm getting product from someone else."

"Well, when I make a deal with her, she'll be happy as a clam. But you're going to have to give me a couple of weeks on this. I have to set it up. You'll be hearing from a woman named Dani Cameo, so make sure you're here during operating hours." Sidra felt the heat creep through her veins when she said Cameo's name. Tony wouldn't be hearing from Cameo. She was dead.

"Are these people cool?" Tony asked.

"Tony, they're drug dealers. How cool can they be? You piss them off, they kill you. But it's not going to be that way, right? We bring you the goods, and you'll get your cut."

When Sidra walked out of the pawnshop, she knew for sure she was going to jail. She got behind the wheel of the extra sedan she'd parked at the far end of the parking lot, and when she drove away, she pulled the blonde wig off her head. At least that would slow things down if Tony talked to Roberta.

She didn't bother going to the other little shops. If the pawnshop sold opioids that Roberta supplied, then the chances were high that the other places were doing the same thing.

"She's supplying the pawn shop with pills," Sidra said later that afternoon to Mitchell when he returned from whatever he was working on. "I also implied that I worked for a cartel and I could get him more money than Roberta was offering."

"Nice," Mitchell said. "Shane implied Ryan stole something from him and Helen Ross sold it out of the motel. I wonder if it was pills."

"They're all getting the pills from the pharmacy and backstabbing one another."

"I think it's sad that Helen Ross is actually safe where she's at right now."

"I think she's where she belongs. People who make money off of scamming other criminals are brave. A guy ended up dead in the motel room. Let's not forget how far she was willing to go to save her skin."

"Ryan killed the guy in the motel and now he's dead himself. I'd say justice was served."

"No, because the person who killed Ryan is still out there running around."

"That's the circle of the criminal lifestyle. Don't worry, you'll see that when you supply the pawnshop with opioids from a cartel." Mitchell leaned forward and looked around. "It's been nice being here for the last week. I'm going to miss starting my work day in my pajamas."

"The job does have its perks."

"There's a couple of houses for sale behind the BBQ place."

Nothing felt worse than being an adult and living with family. It appeared her only option was renting. "I guess you're kicking me out of the basement?" Mitchell looked conflicted. Maybe it was Renee that didn't want Sidra there, but Mitchell wasn't going to do anything to cause more conflict with his wife. "It's okay. I'll check out the houses. Thanks."

"Great work today," Mitchell said and stood up.

Later that night, Sidra sat on the bed in the spare bedroom at Shackelford. Floral wallpaper covered the walls, and it always seemed as though she could smell the flowers when she walked in here. The white gardenias reminded her of her grandmother's garden, and on a warm day, the scent would drift all the way to the backyard where they played as kids. That was a long time ago. Grandma was long gone and surely her garden was dead now, too.

In the closet, Sidra moved a stack of clothes and blankets on top of a cardboard box inside. The hidden safe contained nearly two million dollars she'd stolen from Casey Lincoln.

There was no doubt she was going to use the money to pay off her own debt. The problem was that she couldn't do it all at one time. Her meager income didn't touch the money she owed from her medical bills. She'd had an emergency cesarean section because of a placenta accreta, and later a hysterectomy. The IRS would come after her if suddenly she no longer had the debt.

271

The money inside wasn't crisp bills from a bank. Hundreds and twenties were wrapped in homemade wrappers the drug dealers used to keep their money accounted for. Sidra pulled off a handful of twenties, then closed the safe and put everything back in place to conceal it.

Chapter 24

On Sunday afternoon, Dominic was back on day shift for a thirty-day rotation and he'd stopped by for twenty minutes to have a quick lunch. Cops needed food too, but he would be ready to run when he had to. The kids, always relentless when Dominic was in uniform, asked him more questions than the adults.

"I'm exhausted," he said before he left. "I hate the first days of rotation."

It didn't help that they'd spent two hours on the phone last night. *I'm going to find a place to live and fix this.*

Sidra kissed him goodbye and then the little kids surrounded them again. "Grandma said these are for you." Luca handed Dominic a napkin full of chocolate chip cookies.

"Tell your grandma thank you."

"Be careful," Sidra said, and he looked at her with a smile for a long minute before he climbed into his squad car. For fun, he turned on the sirens and made the kids scream with delight before he drove away.

The long Sunday afternoon turned deadly when they all sat around the big table for a mean game of UNO. There aren't any dirtier UNO players than the Shackelfords. By the end of the first round, Dad threw cookies at people when he got two draw fours in a row.

When everyone left, and the house was quiet, Dominic came back after his shift. Sidra sat curled into him on the sofa in the sitting room, talking about all sorts of things because there wasn't a TV in here to watch, which was perfectly fine with both of them. As the bright sun began to set, Dominic leaned his head back and fell asleep. She watched him for a long time, as all the stress of his day escaped him and his eyelids twitched as he began to settle into a deeper sleep. Sidra took comfort in the sound of his heart beating, and she closed her eyes and fell asleep tucked underneath his arm.

***

There was no such thing as a weekend around here. Not by the true definition of a weekend, and by late Monday morning, the four of them hacked away at computers trying to get as much work done as possible.

Dad came in and asked Sidra, "Can you go down to Kama Electric and get this lady's statement about a policy violation and then the manager is going to give you their handbook because it didn't come through the email. Make sure you get the handbook."

And without a question, Sidra drove to Peachtree City to Kama Electric to interview a woman who'd gotten into an altercation with another employee a few days ago. The problem was that the company tried to fire the woman, yet; it didn't state in their handbook that altercations were grounds for termination. That's why it was so important to have correct verbiage in the handbooks. It's like saying, *I'm not going to get fired for fighting at work because it's not written in the handbook.* This was the third policy case they'd taken this year.

When Sidra pulled into the parking lot, a silver BMW convertible was in her spot. As Sidra got out, so did the tall blonde, who walked right over to her and looked her up and down.

"Can I help you?" Sidra said.

Tight jeans, boots, long white sweater. Her blonde hair pulled back with pins, and half of it flowed down her back in waves. Manicured pink nails with matching lipstick, and earth toned makeup. She had diamonds in her ears and a rock on her finger the size of Texas. The light vanilla scented perfume she wore filled the air, and reminded Sidra of Christmas cookies.

"I'm Taylor Getty," she said, and the last name rang a bell.

"Hi." Sidra offered a smile.

"I want you to stay away from my husband," she said, and for a confused moment, Sidra stared at her.

The surrounding air disappeared as she tried to remain impassive.

"I'm sorry. What?"

"Dominic," she said, and folded her arms across her chest, making sure Sidra noticed the ring on her finger. She couldn't miss it. What the fuck was this woman talking about? "I've asked him to stop seeing you, and he obviously hasn't, being that he comes home with scratches down his back, so I'm asking you to stay away from him. He didn't come home again last night."

The wave of emotions started in her chest as her heart pounded and her hands shook. This wasn't happening. She was with Dominic. He was her boyfriend. There was no way he was married. No, he wouldn't lie to her like that. He was sweet and funny. This woman was confused.

Then Beautiful Taylor dug around in her purse and handed Sidra a wedding photo, and there he was, in a light gray tux, standing next to his bride in a field with the sun playing shadows on them.

"I um…"

"I take it you didn't know. That's fine. I don't have any problems with you but I want it to stop now."

Dominic's married.

Sidra tried handing her the photo back.

"Keep it," Taylor said.

"I don't want it."

Taylor took the photo and tucked it underneath the van's windshield wiper like one last nail in a coffin.

Sidra cleared her throat to keep from taking it out on this woman. What "it" was, Sidra didn't know yet.

"I'm begging you," Taylor said, her voice surprisingly calm. "He won't listen, so I'm asking you to do the right thing. The next time he doesn't come home at night, there's going to be a problem. He's my husband and I'm trying to make things work here."

Sidra held up her hand, but couldn't look at the woman. The embarrassment was too much. "I get it. I'm sorry. It'll never happen again."

Taylor turned. "Nice boots," she said, then walked away. Sidra didn't know if she was being facetious or not.

God, she was going to be sick.

This wasn't real.

Her chest shook with a rage she'd never felt before. No, Dominic can't be married. How could she be so stupid?

Sidra grabbed the wedding photo off of the van and looked at it again. A few deep breaths later, and she could move her numb body out of the parking lot. Casey was there on the sidewalk, blocking her and she ignored him when he said hello. She rolled up the photo and grabbed a drink, then she began pacing in the sitting room.

Call him.

She dug out her phone and then stopped. This wasn't a conversation to have over the phone while he was on duty. Why should she care about whether he was on duty? Because, unlike him, she thought about people's feelings.

Think.

When Dad asked about the interview at Kama Electric, Sidra tried to act normal. Nothing was wrong, *act normal*, but she couldn't focus on what he said. Her father, the man who was her entire life, sat at his desk right next to her and she wanted him to tell her it wasn't true. That everything was okay.

Sidra, back in the office, her brothers cutting up because they were useless, and really distracting her. She sat down hard in her chair and did the one thing she should have done the day she met Dominic Getty. Investigate him.

The truth was that they'd met on the presumption it would be a one-night stand, but then he showed up the next day in a uniform. And because she was so busy working on a case, she didn't think further into it. What started out as nothing more than sex turned into feelings. She would have never pegged Dominic as a liar.

Fuck, did he have kids?

Dominic didn't have a strong social media presence, but Taylor sure as hell did. Photos after photos of that beautiful bitch and her adorable dimple faced husband.

Sidra was going to kill him.

Murder him.

She poured herself another drink.

When she went back to the computer to obsess over Dominic and his wife, she saw that two weeks ago, when he was too busy to stay with her, he was somewhere with *her*. At a family member's birthday party. A niece. She was seven. And his whole family, the beautiful magazine models that they were, seemed happy and normal. Sidra wanted to throw up.

She looked behind her to make sure Mitchell wasn't paying attention to what she was doing. Sidra bit her lip to keep from screaming.

And then a photo of Taylor sitting on Dominic's lap, both of them smiling, and his hand—his left hand with a wedding ring—on her leg. The rust-colored seasonal long sleeved cotton dress she wore was short, and she had on brown cowboy boots. Sidra couldn't take her eyes off his hand on her leg.

Nice boots.

Taylor was a beautiful sunset over an ocean, and Sidra was a dirty bucket of water.

That photo did her in, and the tears fell. She clicked off of social media and had to get out of there fast. She grabbed her glass and took a walk to think about this. Walked down to the square and back twice. She pulled out her phone to call Dominic, now that she knew the truth. She was calm. She could talk to him. No problem. But she didn't call him. She stood in front of the old courthouse and screamed, "Fuck!"

She walked back to Shackelford, squeezing the empty glass in her hand and wanting it to break so she would feel something besides the pain in her chest.

Call him.

But instead, she engrossed herself with stalking the man who told her he loved her, who just so happened to be married.

Seven months of lies.

Lies.

They were supposed to meet tonight at Grugan's. How long was he going to keep up this charade? Wasn't he crazy with lying to her? No, because she was the fantasy. The excitement. No wonder he never invited her over and was so private sometimes. Juggling two lives did that to a person.

She ignored his text: Grugan's later? The mental responses she had were endless. Starting with: *Will Taylor be joining us?* and, *You lying, cheating bastard, why?*

In her mind, she had it all planned out how she was going to handle the situation. But proper planning never worked out the way she wanted. She was going to calmly sit next to Dominic and ask him calmly about his wife. Or keep it simple and say, *Why'd you lie to me?*

Dominic had proven to her he was a very calm and rational person, so in her mind he'd admit the lie and apologize and beg for her forgiveness.

But that's not what happened.

Not able to shake the anger, she walked in and saw him sitting in the middle of the bar, and he looked at her, his smile fading as she walked to him. Then she took the wedding photo and slammed it into his chest so hard he had to catch his balance before he fell over.

Sidra took a deep breath, looked at him as he picked the photo up from his chest, and then she turned and walked out of the bar, not bothering to see his reaction. Very proud of herself for not punching him in his face.

She'd made it all the way across the street to the fountain parking lot when she heard him call her name. She didn't turn and had plenty of time to make it to her van. But as she opened the door, he slammed it closed again.

He gathered his thoughts—*his lies*—and he looked at her for a minute, almost shaking as much as she was. You don't spend seven months sleeping with someone and pretend it didn't hurt. She loved him.

"It's not what you think." He sounded wounded with his chosen words, and his face full of despair, on the brink of losing something that he never really wanted.

"Are you or are you not married?" He looked away for a moment. "Answer the question."

"I am, but—"

"I swear to God, Dominic—" A wave of anger surged through her like a tornado, and she didn't know what to say as she fought the hot tears that were betraying her. She really wanted to hit him. Pound her fists on his chest and let it all out.

"Can you give me a minute to explain?"

"There's nothing left to say." She tried to open the van door again, but he pushed it. "Dominic, take your hand off the fucking door or I'm going to call the police. That won't look good for you."

"Will you listen to me?"

Sidra got in his face. "I'm trying really fucking hard right now to keep it together. When your fucking wife has to tell me you're married, what do you expect me to do? So, no, I don't want to listen to you. I don't want to see you again. Ever." This time, he let her open the door. "You told me to trust you, and I did. I trusted you, Dominic. Stay the fuck away from me, you lying piece of shit."

As she drove away, Dominic stood there with his wedding photo in his hand.

Sidra sat in the Shackelford parking lot and drank from a flask she kept in her jacket pocket. Breathing, she let the liquor work its way through her veins, and looked to the left as the sun disappeared. It was the same sunset she'd watched last night with Dominic when they'd fallen asleep on the sofa together.

She took another deep breath.

This isn't the worse thing she'd ever had to deal with. Life wasn't over and she was going to be okay. She knew that. But damn, she was pissed. When she finally had enough sense, she walked into the kitchen and found Mom and Dad sitting at the table eating ice cream out of the container. All these years and they were still in love.

"Hey," they'd both said without really looking at her and then Mom said, "Have you been crying?"

"I'm fine," Sidra said, and walked into the hallway. Then she stopped for a minute and put her head down. She turned around, and then sat with them at the table. "Dominic's married."

"Why would you want to date a married man?" Dad said, his voice accusing, and Sidra froze with her hand mid-air to wipe her eyes.

"Harvey," Mom said. "Could you be any more oblivious? She's crying and trying to tell us."

"Oh," Dad said, nodding as he looked at her. "I was confused. What do you mean, married?"

"You know. You and Mom are married. Mitchell and Renee are married. Amy and Ian. Woolsey and Marquette. Dominic and Taylor are married." Those two names didn't taste good coming out of her mouth.

"What an asshole," Dad said. "I never liked that guy."

"Yes you did," Sidra said. "You loved talking cop shit with him, it was your favorite pastime."

"Well, there was something about him."

"No, there wasn't," Sidra said. "Everyone liked him. It's my fault. I trusted him too easily."

"Sweetie, are you sure?" Mom said.

"I'm sure, Mom. He's married, and I was his mistress slut."

"I'm sorry," Mom said, apologizing in that way she did when one of her kids were upset.

"I guess you were right. We were just shacking up together."

"I'll take him off the Christmas list," Mom said.

"I'm okay. I feel embarrassed and stupid, and I wanted to let you know he won't be coming around anymore."

"He better not," Dad said. "And if he gives you any trouble, I'll call Chief McCall"

***

Sidra put Brady's case file in a blue folder, along with a few files that needed documentation, and set it on a shelf in the office. Her desk was a mess with a couple of empty glasses and food crumbs, a half-eaten apple that was now brown. Stacks of papers and folders sat on the desk in no particular order, yet she knew what everything was and where to find it when she needed it.

The office had little toys they'd collected over the years. A nerf gun, a basketball hoop above the door, a Dick Tracy action figure on a shelf next to Ripley from Alien, the four Ghostbusters characters, and little characters tossed up there for fun. The grandkids' toys also found their way into the office, and no one bothered to walk them back upstairs. A poster hung on the wall that read: DON'T GIVE UP, and surrounding that were stickers with silly sayings. *Don't ask me, I just work here.* And, *I hate my coworkers.* And, *In case of an emergency, bang head here.*

The trash overflowed. One of the rolling chairs was falling apart. Stacks of books and files needed storing. For the past ten years, Mom tried to keep the office organized, but at this point, she'd given up. Especially when the stickers started going on the walls.

"This doesn't look professional," she said, and no one bothered to stop adding them to the wall.

Sidra looked around the spacious office. The only one missing this past week was their sister Amy. But otherwise, the entire clan was working.

She was about to call it a night when her cell phone rang.

"Hey, Brady."

"I want to show you what I made. Are you busy?"

Sidra put her face in her hands. "Um... Not really, but—"

"Because it's really cool."

She knew he wanted to show her video game art, and she wasn't in the mood for that. But she said, "Okay, I'll be right over."

When she got to Brady's house, he looked terrible. He hadn't slept in days. But it was Brady who asked her, "Are you okay?"

"I'm fine. You don't look so hot yourself."

"You're not fine. You've been crying."

"You've been up for two days straight crunching to get your project completed."

He looked over at his computer screen. "I have been, but it's so amazing." He'd colored in the character and she looked so lifelike it was uncanny. Almost as vivid as a photograph. But that wasn't all. She ran across roof tops, jumped, rolled, and fired her weapon at an alien who was amazingly detailed. "This is Shoot Fall and I hope to have it completed next summer."

"That's really awesome. I'm sure it'll all work out for you. Where's Beverly?"

"She was watching TV," Brady said. "Are you going to tell me what's bothering you?"

"I'm worried about you."

Brady slowly shook his head. "You can't lie to me. Something's wrong. And… you keep looking at me like I did something wrong, or you want to tell me something." Then his eyes went wide. "I hope there's not a second kid you didn't—"

"Brady," she snapped, and he smiled. "It's not funny, and it's not something to joke about."

"If you can't joke about stuff, then what's the point. It's just between you and me, anyway. If you can't find the good in a bad situation, then it's that much harder to deal with. Now, tell me what's wrong with you."

"I thought you had work to do."

"I'm waiting for this engine to update my changes."

Sidra sat down on the arm of the sofa. "I was seeing this guy and found out he's married."

"I didn't know you were seeing someone."

"That's because you hadn't talked to me in over a year."

"And the final points go to Sidra." He circled his arm, whooping like a sports fan. "I think she stated the same thing in three consecutive conversations. I've never seen play this well before." He was being so dramatic, but he accomplished what he wanted and made her laugh. Then he became serious. "I don't want to talk about any of that anymore. None of it. So tell me about this guy, and how I need to kick his ass."

"He's married, and I was an idiot. I don't think there's anything left to say."

She pulled the coffee table to the side of the room, then shoved the arm chair in front of the TV.

"What are you doing?" Brady said as she grabbed a video game controller.

"You want to play or listen to me talk my way out of a bad mood?"

"I won't turn down a video game, but I can think of other ways to get you out of a bad mood."

Sidra snapped her head towards him as he sat there smiling.

"What I mean," he said, "is that I know you don't like playing. We can go for a late-night walk or sit out on the patio."

"Come on, Hotshot. Unless you're afraid to play me." Sidra turned on the TV.

"I'm not afraid at all," Brady said and grabbed his controller pad.

The next morning, Sidra woke up curled in a ball at the bottom of Brady's queen-sized bed. He was flat on his stomach with his head turned to the left facing the window, his right arm bent at an odd angle. Even though Brady's expensive bed was comfortable, Sidra stretched her back and felt the tightness in her muscles. She got up and went around to his side of the bed and carefully moved his arm.

His eyes popped open. "What time is it?"

"Seven."

"Don't go yet."

"What am I going to do? Watch you sleep until noon."

"Yes," he said and smiled, and then closed his eyes again. "I need supervision. I might fall out of my bed."

"That's why you have a bed rail."

Sidra pulled her boots back on, then set out to the back of the house to let Peaches outside. The cold morning air nipped her arms as she stepped outside on the spacious back porch, and Peaches ran off to do her business. It was peaceful in the mornings. The next place she lived was going to have a back porch and a place to look out into the woods or a field. A quiet place so she could clear her mind when the fog disappeared. Because that's how she felt right now. Clear mind. No fog.

Still pissed at Dominic, though. But she couldn't dwell on him anymore. He was probably at home with his pretty wife, waking up next to her, Sidra total history in his life, and she couldn't help but wonder honestly what he was doing right now.

Stop it, she told herself. *Just stop.*

In the kitchen, she had to search for coffee and found it hidden in the pantry. Then she had to remember how to use the single serve machine. While she drank her cup of coffee, Peaches looked at her and then spun around in a circle. "Are you hungry? What time do you normally eat?"

Peaches spun around again, and Sidra filled her bowl full of kibble, which she finished in a snap. Sidra sat in this enormous house and thought, *This house is too quiet,* and wondered how many people could fit in here.

Later that morning when Brady and Beverly woke up, it took an hour to get his cold muscles stretched out, then he wanted to use his indoor therapy pool, then he needed his ostomy bag changed, and finally when he found Sidra sitting in the office reading a book about Spain, he said, "You want to take me to the Halloween store? I'll drive."

The minivan had a ramp, and the driver's seat had been removed so Brady's wheelchair could be locked down for driving. Everything was touch screen, and he had a joystick he used to control the van, and it took him a hot minute to get the chair locked in place and his seatbelt buckled. He'd turned off the voice control while they were talking, and the whole time Sidra kept glancing behind them for a Prius or a black SUV. She never knew when the danger was around and she couldn't be too careful.

They made it to the Halloween store in ten minutes. When they entered, he said, "I'm looking for something for Peaches."

"You came all the way over here to buy the dog a Halloween costume?"

"Yeah," he said. "We have the big Halloween bash next week and she looks so cute dressed up. You should come. Maybe we can find you a costume." They made their way through the store.

Sidra's Halloween costume was a cat headband and drawn whiskers. "I don't think so."

Brady was all over the place looking for dog costumes. When he found them, he wanted to dress Peaches up as a taco, then he saw the Wonder Woman costume and could hardly contain his joy. "She's going to be so excited."

A couple of teenaged boys followed Brady and whispered behind him out of earshot. She didn't know what these two kids were up to, but Sidra was ready to grab both of them by their ears. Brady either didn't notice, or he did and wasn't paying attention. After a couple of minutes, the boys pressured each other. "Do it," one of them said. "No, you go." Sidra put herself in a position near Brady and scowled at the boys.

Brady said, "How about that?" and pointed to a picture of a costume on the wall.

"A sexy nurse? No—"

"Is the cop costume with the fishnets out of the question?"

"Absolutely out of the question."

"You can match Peaches." Sidra didn't tag along with him to get harassed about sexy costumes, and when she gave him a look, he said, "If you dress up and come out to play, you'll forget all your troubles for one night."

That's what liquor was for.

"I'll think about it, but I'm not wearing anything foolish. What are you going to wear?"

"I have to dress up as Merge Weaver. All the kids love it."

When she turned around, the two teenaged boys stood there looking at Brady, both shy or curious, she couldn't exactly tell. Then finally, one of them held out his cell phone. "Is this you?"

Brady said, "No, I look way better than that guy," and he flashed the boys a grin.

"I told you." Both of the boys started arguing and then asked Brady a hundred questions about video games. Sidra stepped away. She felt bad that her immediate thoughts were that these boys were up to no good.

"They said they were my biggest fans," Brady said when he found her a few minutes later.

They ate lunch at a Mexican restaurant where the staff seemed to know Brady and his diet issues. He ordered shredded beef enchiladas without red sauce, and the waitress joked with him about making sure it was right so he wouldn't return it five times.

"You're that guy?" Sidra said, but she knew he stayed away from certain foods.

"I leave a big tip."

Their conversation was casual, last year never happening. They talked about whatever came to mind and high school memories. When their conversation circled back to Kieran Knox, Sidra suggested he talk to the police and find out what was going on.

It ached for her to watch him struggle, but everything he did came with years of practice and it became Brady's normal everyday life. He wasn't shy about asking for help, but he also didn't want to be a burden to anyone.

Which was why Brady had this big house and had a live-in nurse that did more personal assistance for him than medical assistance. Beverly was out grocery shopping when they got back, and then he spent an hour in the bathroom.

Sidra held up the Wonder Woman costume to Peaches. "He's going to make you wear this." And Peaches jumped around full of excitement about being a superhero for the night.

Chapter 25

Mitchell took his family home a couple of nights ago and it was nice to sleep in his own bed. Not letting his guard down for a second, he told the kids they couldn't play outside alone, and definitely not go to the pond without him. Even though he was in his own bed, he slept restlessly, getting up every few hours to check around. Jonesboro police would soon catch Trevor Gregory and figure out what the hell kind of illegal activity Shane Bennett was running out of the Sapphire Groove Club, and it wouldn't be long before they figured out who killed Ryan Orchard.

Mitchell was staying out of it. It didn't involve him, even though something nagged at him. A puzzle that needed solving. Take down Shane Bennett and the whole shindig falls apart.

At work today, Mitchell focused on the paying assignments, but once back at home, the relentless desire to hurt Trevor crept back into his mind, and he couldn't leave it alone. Shane asked him at the park if he needed protection. *No, asshole, I want you to leave me alone.* But Trevor was the problem. The one that had something to prove since that night Mitchell played dumb and let Trevor knock him around. Then, Mitchell kicked his ass. He'd do it again if he had to, but he was sure Trevor wasn't going to come at him with brass knuckles next time.

The silence between him and Renee was worrisome. Not only that, but she was being quiet in general, and trying really hard not to yell at the boys when she wanted to.

"Knock it off," Mitchell told them three times at the dinner table when they kept playing around, and Luca nearly spilled his water. Later, they started fighting over the TV and Renee left the living room.

He found her sitting on the bed, staring at the wall near the window. "Are you okay?" he said.

"I'm tired. I'm going to go to sleep." Her voice, above a whisper, sounded a million miles away, as though she was trapped in a glass house and if she spoke louder her voice would break the walls.

"Renee, it's seven o'clock."

She kept staring at the damn wall.

"I was wondering," he said, "if we should go somewhere. Just me and you. We can get away for a weekend in the mountains. I looked into cabins and it wouldn't cost too much. I mean, Mom can watch the kids. We can leave on a Friday evening and—"

Renee dropped her head, and her shoulders shook. He didn't hear her crying, but that's what she did. This scared him. Her silently crying. Mitchell walked over and knelt down in front of her. "Renee, what's wrong? What did I do?" She said nothing, sat there silently crying. He put his head in her lap because he didn't know what to do.

After a minute, she said, "I'm okay."

"No," he said, catching her eyes through the tears. "You're not okay. You need to go see a doctor."

She wiped her nose with the back of her hand. "I guess that's what I need." She sounded defensive, but something was going on and she needed help. The kind of help that Mitchell wasn't able to provide. He could only be her punching bag for so long.

"What do you need?"

"I don't know."

"Are you still contemplating what you told me after the hospital?"

Mitchell's heart pounded. A quiet talk teetered the verge of her exploding, and he knew better not to follow her in here, but he was a little screwed either way.

"Are *you*?"

"I don't want my family broken up."

Before Renee said anything, Caroline stood in the doorway, crying and said, "Mama, I cut my pants."

"What?" Renee said and turned to her daughter.

Caroline walked over and lifted her leg to show her. "I was cutting people out of a magazine and I accidentally cut my pants."

"Those are your brand-new jeans," Renee said.

"I know."

"It's no big deal, I'll sew it up later." Renee reached up and touched Caroline's face.

"Mama?"

Renee pulled Caroline next to her on the bed and put her arm around her daughter, and squeezed Mitchell's hand. He wondered for a minute if Caroline accidentally cut her jeans or if she'd done it on purpose to stop an argument. While Renee had no problem shoving Mitchell out of the way, she was a bear when it came to her children.

Later that night, Mitchell climbed back into bed after doing a perimeter check. He'd fallen asleep, and woke up to the back door closing, noticed right away that Renee wasn't in bed. She stood out on the back porch, smoking a cigarette. He threw on shoes and grabbed a coat. When he opened the door, she turned around to look at him, then turned back to the backyard.

"When did you start smoking?"

"I guess the same time you started doing cocaine."

Mitchell pulled the coat tighter and looked up at the bright stars in the night sky. They were so close together this time of year, but he tried to imagine how far apart they really were. "So you have some understanding, I don't use every day. That doesn't make a difference to you, but I don't consider myself a drug head, okay? And also, I can't really deal with you sometimes. A lot of times. So I use the coke to get me through. I go months without doing it. Doesn't that mean something?"

"It means that you *occasionally* use drugs."

"Drug," he said, because he needed her to get it right. "Only one. But it's gone now, and I won't buy it, I promise I won't use again. You need to believe me."

"You don't need to convince me," she said, blowing out smoke into the night air. "You need to convince your kids."

***

Sidra walked into Brady's bedroom and found him sitting up in his bed with the mattress in a position to accommodate him. She'd gone back to Shackelford to take a shower and grab her laptop.

"I thought for sure you'd still be working," she said, and walked over to his bed.

"You wore me out today," he said and flashed her a smile. It was because she wouldn't let him take a nap earlier and kept talking to him. He'd even dozed off in his chair at one point, but she woke him up.

When Brady's leg began to spasm, he tried to press his hand to his leg. "This guy won't cooperate today," he said about his left leg. "Come sit next to me." She did, and he said, "Throw your leg over mine. The weight helps."

"Oh," she said, and took her boots off to do what he said. "This isn't weird at all."

"The pool a couple of times a day really helps work the muscles."

When his leg began to spasm again, she said, "When is this going to work?"

"It's not. I wanted you to sit next to me."

"You think you're slick," she said, and laughed. Sidra moved into a position to stretch his leg out for him, bending it at the knee, moving it straight up and back down.

"I was faking the spasms too so you would stretch me out."

"Well, you're really good at faking it," she said, keeping her voice light as she looked at him, knowing he couldn't fake the spasms if he tried. Sidra carefully picked up his right leg and started working that one out.

She put his leg down and he said, "Can you take off my socks, please?"

Next, he was going to ask her to take off his pants. She pulled his socks off and inspected his toenails. Beverly did a great job of taking care of Brady, and how could she not? Brady paid well for being such a demanding patient. Sidra sat next to him on the bed, curled up on her side to look at him.

"I've completely wrecked your life."

"I don't believe you have. But you are a pain in the ass. After you left that day, I wanted to call you back, but what would I say? And every day I wanted to call you, but then I remembered how you wrecked my life."

He smiled when he said that. "I know you and I kept waiting for you to show up, but you never did. You never came back. And then there you were walking through the door and I was mad at you all over again."

"For what it's worth, I'm sorry. About everything."

"I'm sorry, too."

"His birthday's tomorrow."

"Oh?"

"I always buy a cupcake and wish him a happy birthday." Sidra took a deep breath. "It gives me this sense of connection, even though he has no idea I exist."

"Do you ever think about looking for him?"

"No," she said, and sat up straight. "There's not a day that goes by that I don't think about him, but I would never do that to him. I keep imagining that he's perfectly happy, and he's surrounded by people that love him. The couple that adopted him were very nice people."

"You know who they are?"

"Yes." Sidra had their names, had met them twice, and signed a contract stating she wouldn't contact them. Ever. The people at the adoption agency were so helpful and walked her through everything every step of the way. And when she handed the baby to his new mother, she was certain she made the right decision. Didn't once regret what she'd done until nearly a year later. That's when the drinking started.

Brady said, "Can you imagine us now if things would have been different? Having a baby in college, getting married too soon. We'd probably be divorced by now with three kids, bankrupt, and I'd be paying child support, and we'd both be alcoholics."

"I'm not an alcoholic." Sidra playfully shoved his arm. "I imagine that life went according to our plans, and we both made it through college, and I became a famous soccer player and you became a big football star. And we live a very lavish life with three kids and three dogs in a mansion on the beach, and fly first class."

"Where do we fly to?"

Sidra thought about that. "New Zealand and Spain because that's where our vacation homes are. Actually, we own a private jet and fly all over the country whenever we want."

"What are the dogs' names?"

"Peaches, of course. And the golden retriever named Charlie that we always talked about. And, let's see..." Sidra thought a little more. "Your hero, Stan Lee."

"I'm surprised you remember that."

"Of course I remember."

"Can I have a motorcycle in this fantasy?"

"As long as you let me ride with you. And you have to wear leather pants."

Brady cracked up laughing, and it was the best sound she'd heard in a long time.

"Come here," he said.

"Come here where?"

"Right here." He gestured to his lap, a flagman bringing in a plane, and the moment his face turned serious, her heart pounded in her chest.

She stared at him for a long moment, not processing what he wanted.

"Come here," he said. "I can't physically pull you to me."

Sidra swallowed hard and got to her knees, then she threw her leg over his and straddled him. With the bed angled high, his face was inches from hers. He reached for her, his hands soft as silk because the muscle tone was gone, and she slid her palm across his. She leaned in and kissed him, his mouth opening to let her in, a magical moment she'd been yearning for. His mouth pulled at hers and his hands, the sides of them, glided down her sides and then her hair. She pulled back, breathless, and Brady found what he was looking for. The end of her braid. He pulled the holder out, then ran his hands through her hair the way he used to. The way he loved to. And when her long hair flowed around her front, he lifted as much as he could in his hands and smelled her hair, as though it was the first time. He pressed his cheek to her hair and ran it across his lips.

Sidra never took her long hair for granted, never cut it. Brady loved her hair.

"Smells just as I remember," he said, and she kissed him again. She could stay here all night, kissing him

301

until she was dizzy. He pushed her back to break the kiss and said, "Take off your clothes," and she looked at him with a confused look. "Or you don't have to. I don't want you to do anything you don't want to."

What was there to do other than kiss? Her look betrayed her and gave her thoughts away. "Trust me," he said, and she did.

Sidra got up and closed the bedroom door, then locked it just in case. She stood at the side of his bed and untucked the silky blouse from the front of her jeans. Brady said, "Slowly. Like that Valentine's Day. Remember?"

She tempted him with a strip tease back then, and now she slowly unbuttoned her blouse and watched him as he watched her undress. Before she climbed back on top of him, he removed his own t-shirt. "Just ignore that, but be careful," he said, talking about his ostomy bag. She did carefully ignore it. His chest, while he spent a lot of time in a therapy pool and lifted light weights with help, was not what it used to be, but it was Brady and nothing compared to his touch. He reached for her breasts and she opened his left hand and placed it over her breast so he could feel the whole of it, then did the same with the right. Holding his hands there, she watched his face as he touched her, and her life and her love was always him, and Brady was the difference between life and death for her, a lifeline that kept her fog away, and for a moment, tears filled her eyes and then she kissed him again until she was dizzy.

Chapter 26

Sidra sat in Brady's office on the floor with her laptop on the coffee table, with Peaches snoring softly in her ear behind her as she lay on the sofa. Brady called her from the kitchen, his voice casual as he asked for help. She walked into the kitchen and he had cake supplies scattered around the island.

"The mixer's not cooperating," he said.

She knew what he was doing and moved in and began mixing the batter. She hoped he had all the ingredients properly measured inside because he'd made a big mess.

"It's lemon," Brady said. "Lemon cake is one of my favorites."

Sidra knew that. "This is perfect." The gesture was sweet, and she didn't know why she was surprised he remembered what she'd told him last night, but he had.

"Remember that Christmas at my grandma's?" Brady said.

"Oh, God. Please don't talk about that." Christmas from hell. She'd eaten too much fudge and shit in her pants. The problem was that she had on a dress with tights.

"You came out of the bathroom ready to hit the road, and when I told my mom we needed to leave, she wouldn't let me go. You had to call your mom to come get you."

"I was mortified. I've never been so embarrassed in my life."

"I can think of a few other times."

"Like when?"

"Like when my dad caught us in my bedroom."

She laughed with embarrassment. "I don't think he saw anything."

"Oh, yes, he did. We talked about that years later."

"He just—" She laughed hysterically. "He walked in and then walked right back out. We were so stupid."

"Was last night stupid?"

"No," she said, her voice serious now. "Do you need me to pour this, or you got it from here?"

"I don't got it."

Sidra smiled at him and poured the batter between the two circle pans he'd set out, and then she set the two pans in the oven. "How long?"

"I got that." Brady set a timer on the microwave. "I don't regret a thing."

What happened last night was hours of kissing and touching, no penetration, of course, but that didn't seem to matter. The body was capable of achieving great things when the mind allowed it to travel to the right places. Last night was everything she'd wanted for a very long time.

"I can talk to my doctor," he said. "I can't take Viagra because my heart races like I just drank fifteen Redbulls. But I can get a shot, you know. In my..." He gestured to his crotch and mouthed the word *dick*.

"You don't need to do that."

"I want to. It could be even better."

"We don't need to talk about this."

"We need to talk about it. It works, I just need some advance notice."

Her mind was racing, and she didn't know what to say. She stood there frozen, not sure how to respond to him.

"Okay," he said. "I see you're appalled."

"Not appalled at all, Brady. I'm just surprised."

"Because you assumed I was a dead piece of meat?"

She snorted with laughter. "You've never talked about what you can and can't do. This is all new to me."

"The first thing I did when I woke up after the accident was ask the doctor if it worked, and he said no and I thought, well, my life is over. But, he said with some help, it was a possibility. And I do work. Just fine with some help. Do you know how much medicine has changed our lives?"

"We need to slow down and not get too ahead of ourselves."

"Are you kidding me?"

"I mean." Why did she want to take things slow? This was what she wanted. She didn't want to screw it up, that's why. "I just got out of a relationship and—"

"Stop. Just stop. You can take as much time as you want to get through that. You can talk about it if that helps, and I'll listen, you know I will. But I don't give a shit about some guy who didn't respect you enough to at least tell you he was married. Sidra, I'm not a rebound. I have feelings too. You and I have enough history together to figure it out." He tilted his head back with exasperation.

She started to say something but stopped.

He looked her in the eyes now. "I want to feel you on me again. I want you to lie with me and be with me."

Tears caught, and she looked away. "Why now, Brady? You've pushed me away for years."

"And you kept coming back. I understand now why you wouldn't go away. Now I know. But when you didn't come back, I really thought I'd lost you. You were always around and I took you for granted. We're connected by something bigger than us, and I can't ignore that anymore. And I just want to get laid again," he said, and she laughed and wiped her eyes with the back of her hand. He came over to her. "Kiss me," he said, and Sidra leaned down to kiss him, deepening the kiss as he touched her face. "I don't want to be a burden to anyone."

"You're not a burden."

"I know you'd do anything for me, no questions asked. Everything about you that drives me crazy is the same reasons I love you. But if we're going to make it work, then we need to talk about it. I just need you to be patient."

"And I might need some time."

"Okay."

The timer beeped on the oven a little while later, and while they waited for the cakes to cool, they took Peaches for a walk. The sun was out but didn't seem to warm up the chilly breeze that passed. Everyone had decorated their mailboxes to prepare for the big Halloween bash. They made their way around half the neighborhood and turned down another street to head back.

"Did you decide if you're going to come or not?" Brady said about the big night and he sounded so hopeful. "It's a lot of fun."

How could she say no to him? "Alright, I'll come but I'm not wearing some stupid costume."

"I'll talk you into it," he said, moving ahead of her so he could have the last word.

By the time they returned, the cakes had cooled and Brady insisted on frosting it himself. He did a great job, but he had frosting everywhere. She couldn't help but laugh when she said, "You have frosting on your face."

"Lick it off."

"I'm not licking your face."

"I said, 'get it off'. God, what's wrong with you. Why would I want you to lick my face?"

"No," she said. "You said, 'lick it off'. I heard you."

"Get the candles."

She grabbed a towel instead and wiped his face before he washed his hands, and then Sidra put a single white candle on the cake.

"Put fourteen," Brady said, and she did. "Grab the lighter."

When the candles on the little yellow cake were lit, Sidra sat down and looked at all those little fires. One candle for every year. Sharing this moment with Brady came with a sense of reckoning, a reassessment of when their lives were intertwined and they were too young to understand the decisions they made had a lasting effect on their lives forever.

"Sidra," he said, his voice gentle, and he put his hand on hers. "This is the last cake, okay? You have to let go."

But he'd never understand how for her, the baby boy lived in her heart, kindred of a living breathing thing, and there would never be a last cake. She thought about the boy every day, but his birthday was different. It was the one day that she let go of the guilt and allowed the connection to be real.

She looked at this man sitting next to her, his mind open to the world around him, and maybe Brady knew better than she did about life, and love, and loss. He surrendered himself to his own trust, and maybe he was right, she needed to let go. A person didn't go through what he had and take anything for granted. If he could forgive her, then she could forgive herself.

Brady blew out the candles and the smoke filled the space between them for a moment until it finally disappeared.

Chapter 27

Sidra spent the rest of the week at Brady's house and showed up on Halloween night in leather pants and a gold button-up shirt tight enough to pop the buttons. Eyes wide, he said, "Wow. I knew you'd come out to play at some point." She'd left her hair down because he liked it.

Brady had on jeans and a white t-shirt, his hair sprayed green to match the character, Merge Weaver. Peaches ran around in her little Wonder Woman costume, bouncing around because she knew what fun she was about to have and attention she'd get. Brady's parents were there, along with his sister Erin, her husband, and their three-year-old son. The nurse scrubs Beverly wore were splattered with fake blood, which seemed fitting with the vampire fangs in her mouth.

For the last seven years, Willow Point Estates opened the gates for Halloween night and promptly at five p.m. cars began parking along the streets. They had set up the pavilion near the playground with all sorts of fun games. Hotdogs, cotton candy, and popcorn were all free. They'd gone all out to make it a fun night.

By five-thirty, the sidewalks were full of trick-or-treaters. And while Brady himself wasn't famous, Merge Weaver was, and he was a big hit with the kids. They were at the end of his driveway handing out candy, and Sidra had to admit she was having fun.

By six-thirty, the cauldron needed refilling, and the crowd was thick, and the kids were so cute in their costumes. Then she spotted a man staring at her in a ski mask, his eyes baring into hers for a long minute and an alarm flashed, and a chill went down her spine.

"I'll be right back," Brady said, and Sidra looked at him as he wheeled himself inside. When she looked back, the guy in the mask was gone.

She found Brady in the kitchen drinking water out of a thermos. "Are you okay?"

"I think I ate too much candy."

"I think you're right."

"Thanks for being here," he said.

Sidra walked over to him, put her hands on the sides of his chair to get closer to his face. "I'm happy when I'm with you."

"I know," he said, and Sidra kissed him.

Back outside, they found Beverly and Peaches where they left them, and Sidra refilled the caldron of candy. "These kids have stopped by three times," Beverly said.

"Isn't that what you're supposed to do?"

Then she spotted the guy in the mask again, this time leaning against the light post, watching them.

"Brady," Sidra said, and tried to get his attention. "Does the guy in the mask across the street look familiar? Like Kieran?"

Brady couldn't see anything over the kids walking past them, and he pointed out, "If he's in a mask, how am I supposed to recognize him?"

"Because he had on that same kind of mask the day he broke in." And if he was here, then where was his number two? But then he was gone again. "I'll be right back." Sidra walked through the throng of kids and out into the street where she looked both ways but didn't see anything. How could she? Hundreds of people walked along the sidewalk, all dressed up. Too many costumes, she thought.

Maybe she was being paranoid.

When she turned back to Brady, he said, "I need to go inside," and he turned around fast towards the house. Sidra followed him back inside, where he filled his water bottle and drank too quickly, his hands slightly shaking.

"What's wrong?"

Suddenly pale, Brady took a deep breath and looked weak. "Can you get Beverly?"

Without another word, Sidra ran back outside for his nurse. "Something's wrong with Brady," she said, and a panic set in.

Beverly set down the bowl of candy, called Peaches to follow, and ran inside to find Brady. The nurse in her kicked in, asking him questions to assess his symptoms. In his bedroom, she took his blood pressure, which was slightly low. Then she pricked his finger to check his blood sugar, which was slightly elevated. But Brady didn't have blood sugar problems that Sidra knew of.

Beverly said, "How much candy did you eat?" her voice of a concerned mother.

"Too much." There was no tinge of silliness in Brady's voice right now. He may have eaten too much candy even though he knew better, but with his health, illness scared him because it always triggered something further.

"Let's sit here a minute," Beverly said. "I'll check your blood sugar again to see if it's spiking."

"Can I do anything?" Sidra said, feeling useless.

"You can hold my hand."

She moved to sit on the bed and took his hand in hers, and watched him as he tried to keep his breathing normal.

Beverly said, "He gets hyperglycemic sometimes, but it's not anything too alarming. The doctor changed his thyroid medicine last week, and it's too high of a dose in my opinion."

Brady let go of Sidra's hand. "I'm gonna—" and before Sidra knew what was happening, Beverly reached for a bag, flicked it open with one hand and held it up to Brady so he could throw up.

Beverly grabbed a tissue and wiped his mouth, tossed the tissue in the bag. When he said, "Okay," Beverly gently touched his face before she stepped away. His mom and dad walked in concerned, but he and Beverly assured everyone that he was okay. When his sister came back from trick-or-treating with her son, Brady came out of his bedroom to say goodbye.

When they left, Julie told David, Brady's dad, that she was going to collect their things. In the kitchen she screamed a high-pitched shriek, and by the time David and Sidra stepped away to investigate, Julie walked from the kitchen with the man in the mask right behind her.

Chapter 28

"Who are you?" David said.

"Shut up."

"He has a gun," Julie said.

Kieran Knox pulled the mask off of his face. Jittery eyes looked around the room as his hand shook with the gun, and the sounds of happy kids outside reached the house.

David didn't make any fast moves, but when Sidra stepped closer, Kieran shoved Julie into her husband and pointed the gun at Sidra.

"Put the gun down, Kieran, before you hurt someone."

"You think I don't know how to use a gun?" He took a shot to the left of Sidra's head, and it sent Peaches into a barking frenzy. Sidra grabbed the dog by the collar as Kieran said, "Stay back." They stood near the foyer, past the kitchen. Brady and Beverly weren't far behind them. "Go," Kieran said, gesturing with the weapon he had in his hand.

Brady was right about one thing. Kieran didn't sound like himself. A higher pitched, wavering voice came out of his mouth, an imposter holding something back the times she'd spoken with him.

"Kieran—"

"Shut up," he said to her. "Before I let it loose on everybody in this room."

When he had them corralled into the living room, Sidra noticed Julie had her phone in her hand. Kieran focused his attention on Brady.

Sidra said, "Where's your friend? The one who helped you last time?"

"My brother?" Kieran looked indignant. "I don't need him anymore. I can take care of myself."

"Let's talk about this," Brady said.

"I tried talking to you, but you want to do everything your way. Well, I'm doing things my way now. You think you're some big shot who doesn't need anyone's help. You don't want to talk to anyone. You use people to get what you want." Whatever kind of person Kieran tried to make himself out to be, this was the real guy. A guy about to snap. An idiot who would stop at nothing to get what he wanted.

"What do you want, Kieran?" Sidra said.

When someone tried to come in the front door, Kieran turned and shot the gun towards the entrance. Peaches started barking. David tried to move towards Kieran. Kieran elbowed David, he fired the gun—on

317

purpose or accidental, Sidra wasn't sure—the bullet hitting the chair between Brady and Beverly.

Three shots fired so far.

The guy was a loose cannon and someone was going to get hurt. At first Sidra thought it was the police trying to get in, but she didn't see any blue lights.

"You," Kieran said to Beverly. "Go close the curtains and if you do anything stupid, he's going to get shot." Kieran pointed the gun towards Brady. Sidra left her purse and her gun locked in the van. Why didn't she think to bring it with her? Why didn't she go get it as soon as she spotted him in the mask?

She'd throw herself in front of Brady if she had to. She would die, not him. But it would not come to that. Kieran needed to calm down. Her heart pounded in her chest with the million thoughts clouding her judgment. There was nothing worse than a guy waving a gun around, and not knowing what he was thinking.

As soon as Kieran saw the blue lights flashing through the blinds, the panic set in. "Move! Get up!" Then he looked at Brady. "You stay there."

"You don't need to do this," Brady said.

Kieran told everyone to move down the hallway. He grabbed Brady by the shirt and looked at Sidra. "Don't do anything that will get him shot," he said to her. When they were all inside Brady's bedroom, Kieran said, "Close the curtains." Beverly moved toward the windows and pulled the blackout curtains.

Peaches set her focus on Kieran and barked at him, tried to snap at his leg and Kieran failed at kicking her. The dog backed up and David scooped her up, struggling to contain the forty-pound dog.

Sidra started looking around for something useful. If she moved too quickly, Kieran would shoot, but he had to know that this wasn't going to end well for him.

They hadn't been in the room two minutes when the main phone line rang. A shrill in the silence, and Kieran screamed, "Hang it up," and Julie pressed a button to make it stop.

Sidra looked at Brady, his eyes trying to tell her he was so sorry. But he had nothing to apologize for. Everything was going to be okay. Between the low blood pressure, high blood sugar, and the surge of adrenaline, Brady leaned over, not looking good at all.

Sidra said, "Kieran, Brady's not feeling well. We may need to get him to the hospital—"

"I don't give a fuck. I'm not feeling well, okay? I haven't taken my meds in two weeks. He's the reason I don't feel well," he said, and tapped his head with the gun. "You want to know why I can't get anything right in life? Because—" The phone started ringing again, and Kieran said through his teeth, "Somebody answer the phone and tell them not to call back."

Julie grabbed the phone and listened for a moment, then said, "Yes... Yes." With a shaking hand, she held the phone out to Kieran. "Someone wants to speak with you."

"Who?"

Julie hesitated a moment. "The police."

"I don't want to talk to the police," he said, his voice suddenly calm, and Julie relayed the message. "Hang up the phone." Julie continued to answer a few questions as Kieran told her again to hang it up, and when she didn't, he started shouting, "Hang up the fucking phone," not moving the gun from Brady's direction. Julie pressed the disconnect button, and then Kieran told her to turn on the phone and set it down. Now no one could call again.

Kieran began pacing but didn't take his eyes off of Brady. "All you had to do was treat me with respect, but instead you thought I was a nobody. A pathetic loser and you were better than me. I worked so hard for you, and all you did was say, No, No, No!" Kieran started crying. "I just wanted you to accept me."

"We can work this out," Brady said.

"It's a little too late for that."

"Why don't you let everyone else leave and we'll talk. Just you and me. That's what this is about, right? You and me. Let's talk and you can let my family go."

Julie's cell phone rang, and she answered it before Kieran said anything. Then she said again, "The police want to talk to you."

From outside the house, someone said Fayette County SWAT and Sidra couldn't exactly make out the rest, but the house was surrounded. Twenty minutes had passed since Julie contacted someone. Even with

SWAT outside, she didn't feel relieved. They were making Kieran nervous.

Kieran stood there arguing with Julie about the phone. The front door was unlocked, and Sidra tried to think about what the police would try to do. Certainly, they would not do anything that would put them— hostages—in danger.

"Put the phone on the bed where I can get it," Kieran said, and Julie slowly did what he said. Then Kieran dropped the phone on the floor and stomped on it. He walked over to the bedroom door and slammed it shut.

"You should talk to the police," David said. "We can get this all sorted out."

"Shut up. Sit," Kieran told him, using the gun to get his point across and David squatted down to the floor with Peaches. "If you say one more thing..."

"Leave my family alone," Brady said. "Just let them go."

"No."

"What do you want? Money? Is that it?"

"Don't mock me," Kieran said, his voice even higher than before. That's why Brady hadn't recognized him. He was off his meds, which helped him control the demon that lived deep inside of him. The longer time ticked away, the fear built up inside of her. Kieran paced and rambled, and he cried, said he was going to kill himself.

"It's okay," Brady said.

321

"It's not okay."

"You're upset. We can work this out."

"Shut up. Just *shut up*."

How was she supposed to protect these people?

They all looked silly standing around in their Halloween costumes in such a hostile situation. She heard Dominic's voice in her head, *You didn't train for this.* And right now, no one could talk their way out with Kieran so hot. He didn't want to listen, and he couldn't focus his eyes on one thing long enough to have a plan. She could rush him, but then she risked getting shot. No one knew how to handle these kinds of things when their lives were on the line. Do what Kieran said right now, and no one would get hurt.

"I'm not going to jail," Kieran said. "I'm going to kill all of you and then I'm going to kill myself. Then I'll be famous for something. I'll be famous for killing you. Wouldn't that be irony? The guy who thought he was better than me, wanted to give me all his money, 'Please don't kill me,' and then he dies, anyway. What kind of fucking superhero are you, Brady Ardeen?"

Surely, the SWAT team would come through the window any minute. They were still on the loud speaker trying to get Kieran to come out. The look on Brady's face was of nothing but defeat. He couldn't do anything to fix this, nor could he physically do anything about it.

Something moved underneath the door. A black tubular thing. A camera. They were right outside the door, trying to figure out what was going on in the room.

"I need to go to the bathroom," Beverly said, and walked to the end of the bed. Kieran blocked the path to the bathroom, and that's when Sidra saw the hypodermic needle in her hand, and she thought, *Oh, God*, what is she doing? Whatever the hell was in that needle had to be something that worked quick. What kind of medicine did Brady use that would do that?

Kieran had his back to the bathroom while Beverly was inside. He couldn't point the gun at everyone at the same time, but he sure in the hell kept it aimed at Brady. Sidra stood in front of him again, and Kieran said, "Move out of the way."

"Kieran, he's sick."

From behind her, she felt Brady push her hip towards the bed and when she turned to look at him; he was pissed off. "If you're going to be a coward and shoot me, then get it over with."

"Too bad you're not Merge Weaver."

Then Beverly stepped behind Kieran, and maybe Peaches thought Beverly was in danger because she was too close to the man causing so much stress, but the dog pulled away from David and went at Kieran. Behind Sidra, Brady threw up again, and she turned at the retching sound. The door busted open, booming voices shouted. The sound of a single gunshot, then multiple gunshots, so loud in the small space. Sounds and voices behind her she didn't recognize; lost in a wave of repercussions she couldn't piece together. Her eyes locked on Brady as a searing hot pain ripped through her back.

And Sidra's whole world fell apart.

Chapter 29

She lost focus and the sound disappeared around her. Sidra opened her mouth to scream, but nothing came out. She couldn't focus on anything but the blood coming out of Brady's chest as he gasped for air. And he looked at her with his half-grin on his face, but it was nothing but pain. It all happened so fast, and yet a slow disconnection separated her reality and there was all this blood and it wouldn't stop. There was no sound, yet the world around her was a deafening wave of shouts and movement behind her she did not see.

"Oh God, Brady," Sidra said, and tried to keep his head up. Julie screamed beside her as she looked at her son, and David pushed Sidra out of the way. No, he pushed her to the bed and shoved something to her shoulder.

Immense pain rushed through her entire body.

A wave of paramedics rushed in, and this was all wrong. What was happening? Please don't let him die. *I'll go. Take me.* They took him out of his chair and onto a stretcher, trying to work on him, but everyone was in the way and she couldn't see what was happening.

Someone stood in front of her, his mouth moving, and she looked up and couldn't make out the words.

She was suddenly cold, a shiver running down her spine, a cold finger pressing into her flesh and bone, and she tried to see Brady through the wall of people, and then two paramedics stood in front of her trying to look at her arm.

Her heart pounded in her chest. She wanted to throw up, her entire world was falling apart. *Take my strength and be with me.*

With every breath she took, pain surged through her body, a freight train heading straight for her. Her breathing slowed down and everything that happened ran through her mind over and over, and Brady's brown eyes etched in her mind like a painting.

She kept thinking, *What could I have done differently?* The words circling around in her head over and over.

Sidra woke up in a dark hospital room. Mom sat in a chair in the corner, crying. Dad looked out the window, his reflection showing a worried old man. They wrapped her shoulder up so tight, it was immobile. An IV line ran into her left arm, and she felt tired and drugged, and wanted to go back to sleep.

"Mom?"

She jumped up at the same time Dad turned around.

"Is he okay?" she asked, and a sob escaped Mom's mouth.

It was Dad who spoke. "He's not okay, baby. He didn't make it."

Something dark reached into the depths of her and squeezed, because the sound that came out of her didn't sound human even to her own ears.

***

The next days were a blur. The hours, in fact, she couldn't even remember hours ago. Nothing seemed real and no matter how many times she told herself he was gone, her mind couldn't wrap around it. She loved him. And her heart was a raw open hole ready to give up on everything.

The bullet ripped through her shoulder and into Brady's chest. She couldn't stop it. Not that she tried, she just stood there and did nothing. She didn't move or fight. Stood there afraid to do anything that would make things worse. Dad said to her that day in the hospital, "It's different when someone you love is in danger. People think they know how they're going to respond, but that's never what happens. Your heart's pounding a million miles a minute when someone's got a gun and threatening to shoot someone you love."

She should have had her gun to protect him. But she wasn't a superhero. She couldn't save anyone. Mom told her, "You're going to have to find something to wear to the funeral."

The funeral.

Sidra didn't want to hear it. She shouldn't be picking out clothes to wear to Brady's funeral at all. "We can go shopping." She didn't want to go shopping.

Nor did she want to do anything. What she wanted was to get away from everyone. Her entire family. From life. Instead, she took three pain pills and crawled back into bed.

They didn't work.

Twelve stitches across the back of her shoulder. Eight along the front. All that pain and only twenty stitches. They had to go in and stop the bleeding, repair damage to the tissue and muscle and bone. She was lucky. The doctor told her the bullet missed the axillary artery, and that was good news. Was it really?

Six inches to the left and the bullet would have hit her spine.

She didn't have enough time with him. She wanted him back.

When she woke up, she took a shower, careful to keep the bandage dry. She couldn't move her right arm without pain and she would need physical therapy to get back full use of it.

Sidra found a black dress in the closet and struggled to put it on without the use of her right arm. When she looked at herself in the mirror, she was angry that she didn't take time to find a better dress for today. She pulled the damn thing off and threw it.

Slowly, like Valentine's Day, she heard his voice say. Sidra looked at herself in the mirror and pressed her hands to her breasts, imagined they were Brady's hands, and felt herself let go and finally break down.

***

328

A thousand people must have shown up at the funeral. Plus media coverage because the hostage situation was such a hot topic right now. It flooded local social media with every topic, from how the police handled it to the victim's mental illness. The victim being Kieran Knox. Kieran could have easily shot Brady the day of the break-in, but he stole his computer instead.

The police shot him when they came into the room.

Kieran Knox died before he hit the floor. There would probably be an internal investigation, considering they had the whole thing on camera from under the door.

The day turned out to be warm and Sidra stood with her family as Brady's casket was lowered into the ground in a cemetery in Fayetteville where his grandparents were buried. The atmosphere was quiet and calm, people trying to get through it to pay their last respects to a life lost too young. There was nothing worse than hearing a mother cry over the loss of her son.

When everything was over, Sidra watched Ollie make his way to everyone, and he walked up to Sidra and said, "Sorry for your loss," his tongue sticking further out of his mouth because of the down syndrome.

"Brady thought a lot about you," she said to Ollie.

"He did?"

"Yeah, he thought you were a really cool guy."

"I think he was a really cool guy too." Ollie moved on with his condolences.

There was a gathering at the church hall afterwards, but Sidra didn't want to go. She couldn't stand anymore of this. Instead, she drove to Beverly's house because she wasn't there. Didn't even make it to his funeral. Sidra knocked on the door, then banged on it with her left hand until Beverly finally swung the door open. Red puffy eyes stared back at her.

"You didn't go," Sidra said.

"I couldn't."

Sidra stepped inside and threw her good arm around the nurse that blamed herself for everything that went wrong that night.

***

Later that afternoon, when Sidra got back to Shackelford, she stood in front of the hutch in the dining room, loaded with liquor bottles. Each one of them called her name. The voices swirled through her mind with its liquid vile voice. *I'll warm you and dull the pain, take you to the place where there are no windows and the world is dark and you don't have to see anything.*

Nine days.

She hadn't had a drink in nine days.

Let me take your hand. Walk with me to a warm place where nothing else will see your pain. Take me. Hold me. I'm yours.

"Fuck you," she told the bottles. "You're the devil."

Before she made it out of the dining room, there was a knock on the back door and through the curtain over the window, she saw it was Dominic. She had a moment where she thought about going the other way down the hall. He'd called her, but she didn't answer the phone, not one single time in the last week.

She let the calls go to voice mail, and didn't bother to listen to a single one.

Sidra swung the back door open with a little more force than intended because of her right arm. She said, "You can't come in here." Because this home meant family, and he didn't belong here.

"I've been trying to call you."

"I told you not to."

"I heard about what happened and that's really fucked up. I'm sorry to hear about your friend."

It's your fault I was there in the first place.

"It's a really bad time right now." She reached for the door.

"Sidra, I need to talk to you," he said, his voice almost desperate.

"Can you just go away?"

"Not until you hear me out."

She sighed heavily and waited while he took his sweet time gathering his thoughts that he should have already put together.

"Can I come inside so we can talk?"

"No." Because she was going to make this as uncomfortable as possible for him. The cute guy who knew he was cute and wanted to get away with whatever he wanted. Have his cake and eat it too. That was such a stupid saying.

"I don't know what to do."

Sidra almost laughed. "Whatever you decide, it won't involve me, so maybe that'll make things easier for you."

"She left me," he said, the she implied.

"Serves you right."

"I mean before. Before I met you, she left me. She was living with someone else, so when I met you—"

"You were still married."

"Yes. She came back a few months ago and wanted to work things out—"

"So go work things out."

"I don't want to."

"Then don't. But don't talk to me anymore."

Dominic stood there with his hands at his sides and he closed his eyes for a second before he looked at her again. She wanted to ask him if he'd been sleeping with his wife these last few months while he was sleeping with her, but it didn't matter.

The truth was that if Brady had called her at any time to be with him, she would have gone to him in a heartbeat. What kind of person did that make her? She wasn't any different from Dominic, was she? How many times did she think about Brady when she was with him?

She was just as much of a liar as he was.

She can admit that now.

"You want to know where I went right after I learned the truth about you? To someone else. I went to someone else because I'm a train wreck." No, she went to Brady because he called her and she loved him. Because she'd always loved him, and for the rest of her life she'd never be able to love anyone the way she loved him. "Neither one of us needs each other in our lives. We're no good for one another. You have a lot of things to work out, and I just want to be alone right now."

"I never meant to hurt you."

She'd let him wrap his arms around her if he tried. It took a lot for her to not need him right now. But Sidra shut the door and watched as he walked away.

The next day, Sidra drove around just to get out of the office because she needed to breathe. Her head pounded and her skin crawled. Her hand itched to have a glass in it because her body said, *This jittering you keep feeling? You can fix it really fast.* And she told her body to shut the fuck up. If she started convulsing because she needed alcohol to get through this, then she'd know for sure she was an alcoholic. It was almost a game she played with herself.

How many days can I go until my brain finally explodes?

The police car behind her made her nervous, and she wanted to laugh. She'd swerved a minute ago because of her arm, and thought she drove better with alcohol in her system than she did sober.

She wasn't sure if it was Dominic behind her, but he kept his distance, and then when she turned down a side street, so did the police car. A minute later, when a second police car came into view, the first car sped up and put his lights and sirens on. Sidra went to the right side of the road to let him pass, but he pulled up behind her and got out of the car. She thought this was some stupid move on Dominic's part.

You won't talk to me, so I'll get my buddy to mess with you.

Sidra made the mistake of opening the door to step out of the van. The officer pulled his gun and started yelling at her to stay where she was.

"Put your hands where I can see them!"

"What's going—"

"Hands up!"

Seconds later, two more patrol cars showed up and officers jumped out. It all turned into an intense situation really fast. Four officers yelled at her to do something. *Put your hands where we could see them. Stay where you are. Don't move. Don't fucking move.* Panic set in and she almost thought about running. What in the hell was going on? One of them told her to show him her hands, but he didn't realize her arm was in a sling as she was halfway out of her van. She tried to tell him she couldn't, and he yelled at her, told her to cooperate.

Then one of them grabbed her by the left arm and pulled her out of the van. "Do you have any weapons?"

"What?"

He patted her down and repeated himself, then asked for her name.

"Sidra Shackelford and don't touch my arm."

"Do you own this vehicle?"

"Yes. Why?"

The officer had a tight grip on her left wrist because he couldn't put her in cuffs. If Dominic Getty had anything to do with this, she was going to kill him. That cop code and brotherhood and all that? Dad knew the chief of police personally; he wouldn't tolerate this.

"Can you tell me what the fuck is going on?"

The police officers checked her van, looking for something in particular. "We just got a BOLO on this vehicle—"

"Found them," an officer said from the other side.

"Why didn't you tell me you had guns in the vehicle?"

"I have a Glock in my purse, but don't worry, I don't know how to use it."

"Are you trying to be funny?"

The other officer came from around the van and set two guns down on the hood. Two guns that Sidra had never seen before in her life.

Was that fucker trying to set her up?

335

Chapter 30

Mitchell sat outside on his back deck talking to Dominic. He finally found someone to talk to about his marital problems. Someone who understood firsthand. And even though Mitchell wasn't pleased that Dominic lied to his sister, who was he to judge? Mitchell was just happy that anything he said wasn't going to turn into family gossip. Dominic didn't stand a chance with Sidra, and if the guy so much as looked at her funny, he'd knock his lights out. No, really, he would.

They sat in lounge chairs, a cool breeze blowing while they drank a beer in the middle of the afternoon, almost comparing notes on their wives. Well, Dominic's soon to be ex-wife. Mitchell wasn't getting divorced, no matter what. He hadn't told Renee that yet.

Mitchell's phone rang, and he looked down at the unknown number on his screen.

"Mitchell Shackelford."

"It's me," Sidra said. "I tried calling Dad and he didn't answer. I got arrested, and I need someone to call Lindell Fulton."

Mitchell sat up straight in his chair. "You got what?"

"They were looking for guns and they found them exactly where they thought they'd be."

Mitchell pressed the speaker button, then put his finger to his mouth so Dominic wouldn't say anything as Sidra's voice rose a thousand decibels.

"They pointed their fucking guns at me. I've been through hell in the last week and I have no idea what the hell Dominic thinks he's doing—"

"What are you talking about?" Mitchell said, and looked over at the guy, well aware he could hear everything his sister said. He'd only put the phone on speaker because he thought Dominic would know what was going on.

"I think he planted the guns. He probably stole them out of evidence or something. I need you to find Dad and tell him to call our attorney."

"Hold on, Sidra. Hold on." Mitchell pressed the phone to his chest. "You plant guns in her car?"

"No, I didn't plant guns. Gimme the damn phone." When Mitchell handed him the phone, Dominic said, "Sidra, it's me—"

"What the hell are you doing, Dominic? I swear to God you're going to wish you never met me. I'm going to get a lawyer and sue you, and every cop in the entire state is going to see how dirty you are. But I guess that doesn't matter because they're just as dirty, following along with your stupid plan."

"Will you calm down," Dominic said. "If you hyperventilate at the phones, they're just going to step over you."

"Very funny—"

"I did not plant guns in your car. What's going on?"

"You tell me. They got a call from a man who said I tried to rob him at gunpoint and then I drove away—"

Mitchell said, "Sidra, it had to be Trevor Gregory. Those guns? I bet you a hundred dollars they're connected to the dead man in the motel or Ryan Orchard."

"Get me out of here," she said.

Mitchell found Dad inside Clemmie's yacking away with Archie Glencoe. The smell of grilled food reminded him he was hungry. "Why aren't you answering your phone?"

"What's wrong?" Dad said, sitting up straight with alarm.

"Your daughter's in jail."

"What the hell did she do?" Dad climbed out of the booth. "See ya later, Archie. I gotta go bail my kid out of jail."

On their way out, Mitchell said, "Call Lindell Fulton."

"Shit," Dad said.

***

"I don't know anything about that," Roberta said and blew cigarette smoke in Mitchell's face.

"Here's what it comes down to," Mitchell said. "You're distributing drugs to local businesses and all it takes is a phone call to shut it down."

"You can go to hell."

"Roberta." Daley leaned forward to get her attention. "Either you do what you do because you make a lot of money, or someone's got the squeeze on you. What's going on?"

"I have four kids to take care of—"

"Four kids?" Roberta didn't seem the motherly type.

"And we ain't makin' shit at this bowling alley."

Mitchell circled his finger around in the air. "How's it work?"

Roberta hesitated for a minute as she shook her little blonde dandelion puff of hair and thought about what she wanted to say. "Not here," she said, and turned from the bowling alley entrance. They followed her upstairs where the hole in the wall looked patched up by Ray Charles. She plopped down on the torn leather love seat. Mitchell and Daley opted to stand.

"This pharmacy down the street—"

"Berry's, yeah?"

"They file fake prescriptions with the insurance to get the money. They take their cut and give the profits to Shane Bennett. He turns around and buys lower quality pills—stuff from Puerto Rico—and sells that at the club. But there are suppliers from various outlets. It's a whole goddamn system and once you're involved, you're stuck."

"How'd you get involved?"

"I met Trevor about a year ago and he asked me if I wanted to make some extra money. Not only do I deliver for him, but I've also brought in business. If I had enough money, I could run the whole damned operation and make a shit ton of money. More money than them morons who wear their stupid suits all day long acting important."

"Where can we find Trevor?" Mitchell said, getting to his point.

"You're not going to come in here and fuck things up for me. I need this money so I can get me and my kids the hell out of here. Trevor keeps taking more and more of my cut, and Shane didn't do a damn thing about it."

"Maybe you can call him and get him to come over. Bait him with some free nachos," Mitchell said.

"I can tell you two are related," Roberta said.

***

"Am I going to lose my license?" Sidra asked Dad the next morning when she found him and Mom sitting in the dining room.

"Did you just walk home from the police station?"

"It's around the corner, Dad."

340

Even with their attorney involved, they wouldn't release her because of the guns. Sidra moved towards the liquor hutch, then stopped.

Bad habits.

"You could have called me."

"I needed to air out all the germs I accumulated in jail. They took my gun and I have to apply for a release before I can get it back."

"They shouldn't have come at you like that. Lindell's filing a complaint."

"It won't go far. Not that I'm trying to defend them, but it happened really fast. Someone called 911, accurately giving my description, my license plate and location of my vehicle. Said I tried to rob them and I was armed and dangerous. Said I claimed to have murdered a man in Clayton County. Two minutes later, I'm spotted driving down 85."

"That's still ridiculous."

"No," she said, the whole situation pissing her off. "I started to get out of the van because I thought it was Dominic. As soon as I did, I hit their ape-shit button. Trevor Gregory probably watched the whole thing."

"I'm glad you're okay," Mom said. "Do you want something to eat?"

Nothing seemed to interest her right now. "I'm going to go take a shower. Maybe go back to sleep. I'll pick up my work load this afternoon."

"You need to take some time off," Mom said.

In the bathroom, Sidra took off the arm sling, then her shirt, careful not to move her right arm as pain continued to shoot to the elbow. The bandage was old, and the wound started to ooze. Maybe she shouldn't have denied the medical attention the police offered her. Trying to straighten her arm, she ground her teeth, but once she got past the initial shock of the pain, she moved her arm.

She stepped under the hot spray of the shower and didn't care if she got the stitches wet. She could take Casey's money and run, but that wasn't going to make anything right. She thought about Peaches and wondered if she was okay with Brady's parents. *Go get the dog.* Peaches was her dog to begin with.

Sidra got dressed, braided her hair and tossed her hair over her shoulder. With a new purpose, she got in touch with Julie, who was at Brady's house, but she didn't tell her what she wanted.

Everything hit her at once when she stepped through the front door. The entire house gave off a somber vibe. Not just because of what happened, but they were clearing everything out, taking away the belongings that meant so much to someone.

"You're packing everything up already?" Sidra asked Julie when they stood in the middle of the large foyer.

"We can't afford the mortgage on the house. We have to sell it."

Would anyone even want to live here after what happened?

"I was going to call you," Julie said. "I have some things for you."

The door to Brady's bedroom was shut, and Peaches sat in front of it waiting for someone to let her in. When the dog noticed Sidra, she finally got up and walked over, but not in her usual cheerful way. Peaches had her tail tucked between her legs and her head down.

"Hey, girl," Sidra said, and pulled the dog into a hug.

Julie said, "I have the box in here."

They stepped into Brady's office, and she tried not to burst into tears. She thought this would be easier, but it wasn't. The house was Brady's home. The place that brought him comfort and joy. A home where he laughed, and probably cried sometimes when he was alone.

"There are old letters, a photo album, some old high school stuff."

"He kept all this?" Sidra looked into the box and found CDs they'd burned with their favorite music, her bright yellow soccer socks, a hair ribbon, an old notebook she recognized that had doodles on it from science class sophomore year. While she dug around in the box, Julie reached inside and pulled out a photo tucked away in the photo album. She held it out so Sidra could see.

It was a copy of the photo she'd given Brady last year. The one of her in the hospital holding the baby. Sidra looked up at Julie and swallowed the lump in her throat.

Julie said, "He told me about this last Christmas."

"I don't know what to say." She couldn't judge whether Julie was about to scream or cry.

"He said he didn't want the baby and the two of you decided it was for the best. I wish you would have said something to me. Or your mother would have said something. I wish someone would have told me what was going on."

"I never told my mom." Sidra was confused about what Julie said to her. "What did Brady tell you?"

Julie tucked the photo back into the box. "That the two of you decided to give the baby up for adoption. You broke up before the accident and thought it was best."

Even when he was pissed at her about what she'd done, he protected her. Recognized his part and took responsibility. *Thank you, Brady*, she thought, and closed her eyes for a moment.

"You didn't even tell your own mother?"

"No."

"Well, you better. Because if you don't, I will. The two of you shouldn't have taken this lightly."

Sidra hadn't taken it lightly at all.

"I want to take Peaches," Sidra said. "She was my dog before—"

"I know." Julie held up her hand. "I understand. Just promise me you'll take care of her."

And not give her away?

"I will."

Surprisingly, Peaches's belongings took up the entire back of Sidra's van. She had a custom-made wooden dog bed, two Serta dog beds, a variety of leashes and harnesses. Dog bowls and food. Two bags full of toys. A beach ball, and her favorite rubber chicken. Four blankets, a duck hat, her Wonder Woman costume, and bath supplies.

"You're not spoiled at all, Peaches," Sidra said to the dog as she rode shotgun on the way back to Shackelford. "I don't really have a place to live but it'll all work out."

She found Mom and Dad in the same position as this morning in the dining room, except file papers covered the table because they had to organize everything for an end of the month review and yearly taxes.

Mom said, "Don't tell me you got a dog." Peaches smelled around the dining room, then walked out.

"Don't you remember her? I found her years ago and gave her to Brady because my landlord wouldn't let me have pets. She's going to live with us now."

"What's this 'us' business?"

Peaches trotted into the kitchen, her toenails clacking on the hardwood floor, and Sidra said, "I need to talk to you about something before Julie Ardeen does."

"What did you do now?"

"Dad, I'm getting tired of your accusing tone. How about you listen, or maybe just say, *poor baby*, because that would be better than the tone."

Dad didn't say anything.

"I want to tell you why I drink so much." Because honestly, even though she hadn't had anything, the urge to drink was too strong to say she quit. She put the copy of the photo in front of Mom. "When I ran away, I had a baby and gave him up for adoption."

"Oh, Sidra." Mom said, with that same disappointed tone Dad had. She took one glimpse at the photo and the sob caught in her throat. "Why didn't you tell me?"

"I didn't tell anyone. Not even Brady."

Mom got up and walked into the kitchen and came back with a dish towel. With all the crying she was already doing she was going to need a beach towel.

"You were gone for months," Dad said. "We were worried sick about you that whole time. We told you to come home that—" He paused a moment and put his hand to his mouth. "We thought you ran away because of Brady's accident."

"I let you believe that because I couldn't tell you the truth. Julie Ardeen knows, I don't know who else."

"You mean to tell me," Dad said, "there's a baby— our grandchild—out there somewhere?"

"A boy. He weighed five pounds, two ounces, and he looked just like Brady. But no, he's not out there somewhere. He's with a family that loves him. It wasn't some shady adoption; an agency was involved, and I met the couple and they were nice people."

"Do you know where he is?"

"No, I don't and I'm not going to fuck up his life and go find him."

"Oh, Sidra," Mom said, and cried. "You should have told me."

"I thought I could handle the decision." Sidra sighed as the weight lifted off her shoulders. "Now you know why I drink so much."

She stood up and Dad said, "Sit down." And because she had nothing left to hide but her shame, she did.

"This is really hard for me, okay?" Sidra said. "I thought I made the right decision, that it wasn't going to haunt me for the rest of my life, but I was wrong. And I think about him every day and what might have been. But the truth is that deep down inside, I wasn't ready to be a mom. My life is so screwed up—"

"You do this on purpose," Mom said, her voice with clear understanding. "To justify what you did. You screw it up so you don't feel guilty about it. You don't take care of yourself, so how would you have ever been able to take care of a baby? And it makes sense now. When you came home, you were so sick."

"I came home to you taking care of Daley's three-month-old daughter, and it didn't seem fair. But in some strange way, holding her made everything easier."

"That's why you bonded with her the way you did."

"I know she's not mine, but she's the world to me. And if her mother showed up right now, none of us would let her go. Which is why we're going to leave the boy alone and let him live the life that I chose for him." Even if it's been the hardest thing she'd ever done.

"Well," Mom said, looking at the picture she hadn't put down. "He's beautiful. And he does look like Brady. And look at all that hair." Mom's words made her proud.

Dad got up. "Come with me," he said. "Bring the dog." She followed him out to the Highlander, and he didn't tell her where they were going. But as soon as they got to the south side of Fayetteville and turned down Rest Road, Sidra knew.

Peaches sat in the back seat trying to look through the window.

It was her grandmother's house. The house where Dad grew up. The grass was recently cut, the overgrown shrubs pulled. No one has lived here for eight years since Grandma Shackelford passed away.

"I thought you sold the place?"

"I sold it to your cousin Martin, who did nothing with it. When he passed away, I got it back."

"Why are we here?"

"Because I was going to surprise you after I got the place dusted. It's furnished. You can live here unless you shouldn't be alone right now."

"The house is haunted."

Sidra looked at the two-story farmhouse. Years of neglect that would take a long time to restore. The place wasn't falling apart, but it wasn't pretty. A black wrought-iron fence enclosed part of the property. Not only that, the last she heard, bats had taken residence in the attic. And Grandpa Shackelford walked around at night, opening and closing doors. Grandpa Shackelford was dead. While she wanted to be thankful Dad would let her live here, she didn't know how she felt about the spooky house.

"It has its own cemetery," Sidra said.

"It's my family."

That didn't make her feel any better. This house was fun when they were kids, but as they got older, no one ever wanted to spend the night at Grandma's anymore.

"Casey got the grass cut, and the shrubs cleared out, and next spring he's going to repaint the house."

Sidra said. "I'm also two-hundred fifty grand in debt."

Dad gave her a side-glance. He cleared his throat, and said, "Poor baby."

Chapter 31

Car doors slammed outside of Shackelford and Mitchell looked out the window. A black unmarked SUV and a Fayetteville police car sat parked in the driveway. Detective Coleman walked to the front porch, accompanied by two Fayetteville police officers.

"They're coming for me," Mitchell said, not sure why, but he had a bad feeling after Sidra's arrest from the bogus gun call. Daley stood up and turned around as they knocked on the door. Mitchell gave one look at his younger brother, and thought, See ya later.

He opened the door, and Coleman didn't smile. "Just the man I'm looking for."

"What now?" he said.

"May I come in?"

Mitchell let Detective Coleman inside and the two police officers stepped in as well and looked around. Daley leaned against the office door frame and folded his arms across his chest. Mom walked into the sitting room and introduced herself to everyone. Even offered them coffee, which they declined. She sat down on the leather sofa, nosy about what was going on.

"Unfortunately, I have some bad news," Coleman said. "I'll get right to the point because of the nature of why I'm here. Are you familiar with a Roberta Dodson from Jonesboro?"

"Yes."

"Can you tell me how you know her?"

"From the bowling alley." Mitchell looked over at Daley, wondering if his brother figured out what was going on yet.

"How long have you known her?"

"A week or so. I got word from someone at Sapphire Groove that Trevor was hiding out at the bowling alley. I checked it out and met Roberta. Why?" Mitchell let out a chuckle. "She giving you a hard time about something?"

"She's in the hospital."

Daley hadn't moved a muscle. Cool as a cucumber. Mitchell started sweating bullets and knew it made him look guilty about something.

"What happened?" Mitchell said.

"Her grandfather found her this morning in the bowling alley. Trevor Gregory put something ugly on her, and left a message for you." Coleman pulled out his cell phone and showed Mitchell the note.

Keep your friends close and your family closer. Who's next?

Daley moved to look at the photo on the phone. "We can't find this guy," he said to Coleman.

"We'll find him this time," Coleman said. "I'm holding Shane Bennett for as long as I can until we can get to the bottom of this."

"Is Roberta okay?" Mitchell said.

"No, she's in critical condition with a fractured skull."

"I need to make a phone call." He tried Renee's cell phone and knew she wasn't going to answer if she was in the middle of class, but he tried three times, anyway. Then he called the main school line and asked to speak to the principal, Mrs. Jackson, said it was an emergency.

While Mitchell was on the phone, Daley asked the officers if someone could go to the elementary school. The officer nodded and started talking on his radio.

"I'll call Dad," Mom said, and went into the office.

A minute later, Renee picked up the phone out of breath. "Mitchell?"

"Are you okay? I need you to go check on the kids and make sure they're in their classrooms."

"What's going on? You're scaring me."

"I'm a little scared myself," he said, imagining Roberta in the bowling alley. "Can you get eyes on the kids?"

"Yeah, but I've got to put the phone down."

Mitchell said, "She's checking to make sure the kids are okay," and he felt a tremor in his hand as he waited.

352

They were the longest minutes of his life while he imagined Trevor sneaking into the school and taking one of the kids. No, there were safety precautions in place. That wasn't going to happen.

"All three of them are fine," Renee said, and Mitchell let out a breath and nodded to Coleman.

"Don't leave the school by yourself with the kids. I'll pick you up later, okay?"

"Okay," she said, and hung up.

"What am I supposed to do here?" Mitchell asked Coleman. "Because if that maniac hurts one person in my family, I'm going to—"

Coleman put his hands up. "Stop, you're going to get yourself in a lot of trouble. Keep your eyes open and don't go looking for Trevor Gregory."

One officer said, "I need the names and addresses of your family members."

Mom said from the office. "I can't get in touch with Dad."

***

Dad said, "What's this maniac doing?" at the same time, Sidra told him to watch out. A white van sat in the middle of the narrow road, blocking them. Rest Road was a half a mile long with no traffic because there were only two old houses and a ton of land.

"Back up," Sidra said as the maniac started rolling.

As soon as Dad threw the Highlander in reverse, the white van sped up, and they were doing fifty miles an hour backwards down a dead-end road. "Hold on," he said, and Sidra was concerned about the dog in the back seat rather than herself. They were nose to nose with the white van, and she could see Trevor Gregory in the driver's seat.

"That's the guy who planted the guns in my van."

"Hold on." Dad looked for an opening near a ditch, and he spun the wheel to the left to back up into the field. Peaches slid across the back seat. Dad put his old patrol officer driving skills to use and weaved them far enough away from the van. Both drivers sat there trying to figure out who was going to move first.

"He wants to ram us," Sidra said, knowing that once Trevor put them in an immobile position, he would probably start shooting at them. She pulled out her phone to call 911. She'd missed fifteen calls from everyone in her family. Because this was Mitchell's problem, she called him first.

"Your psycho friend has us cornered on Rest Road."

"We're not cornered," Dad said.

Mitchell said, "What's happening?" and Sidra explained. Then Mitchell said, "Roberta's in the hospital. Trevor nearly beat her to death."

Dad started to move forward.

"What are you doing?" she asked Dad, and hung up on Mitchell because she couldn't concentrate, but she trusted him to call the police. Dad moved forward a few feet. Trevor revved the engine of his van. As Dad continued to go forward, Trevor gunned the engine, heading straight for Sidra's door.

The open field had knee-high grass and they couldn't see shit on the ground as Dad sped up. As soon as Trevor got close enough, Dad spun the wheel to the right in a donut, and floored it back the way they came. This carried on for a few minutes after Trevor blocked the exit of the field.

"Do you want to make a run for it to the old house?"

"I'm not leaving you," Sidra said. "Why isn't he shooting at us?"

"Why don't you get in the back," Dad said. Trevor was hot on their bumper.

"Don't flip us."

"We won't flip." Dad braked and turned the wheel toward the opening again.

Sidra grabbed hold of the passenger handle. "Shit, Dad," she said, as Trevor clipped their rear. Peaches started barking. Dad corrected the Highlander and lined up the nose with the opening. Rest Road was so narrow that when he flew out of the field, they were about to land in the ditch on the other side. The tires hit the shoulder and Dad corrected the vehicle as it spun dirt and grass behind them.

Sidra turned around. Trevor smiled. With the Highlander back on the road, Dad picked up speed. "He's going to push us onto the highway."

There wasn't enough time. Sidra threw her seatbelt off and jumped into the back seat over Peaches. A sharp pain ripped through her shoulder, and she felt too constricted with the sling on her arm, so she pulled it off. With no place to go but straight, they were going to end up in the crossway traffic if Dad didn't slow down.

"Hold on."

"We're getting Mom a shotgun for Christmas."

Dad slowed down. Trevor kept the nose of the van on their bumper. So close she could see the whites of his eyes. The deranged look told her he wasn't going to give up. Trevor was so focused on hurting them he couldn't see through what was happening.

Dad tried to make the turn on the highway, but Trevor rammed them, pushing the front into oncoming traffic. The driver of a car swerved to avoid hitting them, but the second time Trevor pushed, they weren't so lucky.

The oncoming truck hit them head on, and Dad let out a yelp when the airbag hit him. Sidra's neck snapped back as she held on to the dog. Peaches was okay. Dad not so much. Sidra didn't have time to think. Trevor walked past the Highlander, tried to open the driver's door but it was locked and with one quick hit he'd cracked the window with a tool, kept hitting until he'd made a hole. When he got the door unlocked and opened, he reached over to unbuckle Dad's seatbelt.

"You're coming with me, asshole," Trevor said. Peaches kept barking at him and tried to lunge over the driver's seat.

Dad fought Trevor off. Sidra didn't know what she was thinking. She threw the back door open and jumped on Trevor as every nerve in her body screamed in pain. Trevor took his hands off of Dad and stepped back.

Trevor abandoned whatever mission he had in mind. He changed gears and grabbed Sidra off of his back. When he did, he grabbed her bad arm, and she screamed. People gathered, and she heard sirens in the background. The sweetest sound she'd ever heard.

But Trevor dragged Sidra to his van and threw her inside the side door hard enough she almost threw up. The back was empty. Trevor climbed inside through the side door, shut it and then climbed into the driver's seat.

She'd rather die than let this fucker take her.

Dad, his mouth bleeding from the airbag, stood outside the Highlander with two people, but Trevor was going to run them over if they didn't move. Barreled the vehicle through them until they jumped. Sidra threw herself at Trevor as he sped out between the throng of people and the edge of the highway. He didn't feel the punches Sidra threw at him.

"What's wrong with you?" she said, as he straightened out the van and sped away.

"Shane said if I brought him one of Mitchell's family members, everything would work out." Trevor looked into the rearview mirror.

"Shane set up Leland, you idiot, so that he'd get caught because he was a rat. He most likely set you up too."

"All I want is your brother." Trevor looked in his rearview mirror, said, "We got company," and floored it.

Sidra turned around and saw Daley's truck gaining on them. She tried to think fast about what her brother would do. She stepped to the back of the van and slid the door open.

Jump, she told herself.

"Do it," Trevor said, but then he slammed on the brakes. Sidra flew sideways into the back of the passenger seat, hit her head, and landed on her shoulder. Trevor was on a suicide mission. The guy had nothing going for him except revenge and rage, and he loved every minute of this.

Trevor grabbed her with one hand, a pistol in his right, and pulled her out of the van at the same time Mitchell and Daley jumped out. Sidra tried to kick him, but she was no match for this guy. He outweighed her by at least one-fifty. The traffic stopped behind them. Car horns honked. Drivers tried to get by on the opposite side. Trevor walked to the front of the van, pulled her along sideways with his back to the woods. She heard the sirens, saw the blue lights at least a mile down the two-lane highway.

She silently told her brothers, *Don't do anything stupid to save me. I'm not worth it.* Daley had a gun drawn and told Trevor to let her go.

"I don't think so," Trevor said with the gun to Sidra's head.

Sidra was so tired, and after the last week with Brady and Kieran, she didn't have any fight left in her. She didn't want to die, but she sure as hell didn't have any strength left.

Trevor egged Mitchell on. "Why don't you come get her, tough guy? You want to trade places with your sister?"

her shoulder, tapped her right leg twice, and made a spinning motion with her finger.

Daley stepped back to one of the police officers. Within minutes, the police had the situation contained with one officer talking to Trevor, the others in position. Every cop in Fayetteville showed up. Someone was probably in the woods right now, ready to put a bullet in Trevor as soon as Sidra was clear.

"Turn around and walk towards me," Trevor said.

The officer in charge shouted, "No one's coming to you, sir. Let the woman go, and put down your weapon. Do it now."

They'd gained some distance on him, but Trevor started moving sideways down the street again. Traffic backed up for miles. This would not be good if a gunfight broke out.

Trevor said, "If you shoot me, you'll shoot her too. I know you don't want that."

"Sir, you have nowhere to go," the officer said. "You are surrounded. Put your weapon down."

Whatever the police had planned, they'd done it quickly because more of them showed up and were

Chapter 32

Trevor had his arm tight around Sidra's neck and she could barely breathe as he slowly walked them down the highway.

"Yeah," Mitchell said. "Take me and let her go. She has nothing to do with this."

"You had nothing to do with this either until you tried to play tough guy. But that's okay, I think your sister can pay the price for that."

"Nobody has to get hurt, Trevor. Put down the gun and I'll come to you."

A man exited his vehicle and approached. Trevor started shouting at the man to get back, which he did. Having to walk on her tippy-toes to keep him from pulling on her neck, she thought about dropping her

scattered throughout the vehicles. A couple of them had shotguns with bright orange handles aimed at him. Mitchell was the one that was wide open if Trevor started shooting.

"What do you want, Trevor?"

"I don't know. Maybe we could work it out, you and me. Man to man right here in the street."

Sidra waited. Ready. Her heart pounded in her chest. Waited for Daley's signal. Daley turned around, nodded to the police officer, and readied himself for a sprint.

Gave her the nod.

Sidra wrapped her right leg around Trevor's, pulled his leg up with hers, and with the slightest stumble, she dropped to the ground. As soon as she'd moved her leg around his, police hit him with the bean bag rounds and Trevor stumbled down as well.

Sidra rolled and grabbed Trevor's pistol. She stood up and aimed it at his head, the gun steady in her left hand. This piece of shit lying on the street would get the brunt of every bad emotion in her right now. She saw Kieran Knox's face and all it took was one bullet for her world to fall apart. She wanted to put a bullet in something and end the torment she knew she'd live with for the rest of her life. She zeroed in on Trevor's head. One little squeeze...

She couldn't save Brady.

"Sidra," she heard Brady's voice, and felt warm tears spill down her cheeks. *Sidra, it's okay. I forgive you. Just let go.*

"Sidra!"

Someone grabbed her hand and forced the gun down. Dominic stood there with his hand on hers, and suddenly she realized the police surrounded her with their guns drawn and her brothers shouted at her to get her attention.

With the gun down, two officers grabbed Trevor to arrest him.

"Let go of the gun," Dominic said, his voice calm, and she let it slip into his hands.

***

After all that, the police were telling one another, "Good job," after the whole incident happened without a shot fired or a fatality. They had to be feeling the same adrenaline rush as Mitchell. He spotted Dominic with one of those orange shotguns in his hands.

"Hey," Mitchell said.

"I thought she was going to kill that guy."

"Nah," Mitchell said. "She had the whole thing under control."

Dominic's expression on his face said he didn't agree. He held up the beanbag shotgun. "I got that asshole in the kidney. I hope it ruptured."

"You want to have a beer later?"

Dominic turned and looked at Sidra.

Mitchell said, "She's never going to talk to you again. But I'm the best Shackelford there is, so what do you say? Beer at Grugan's later?" and he clapped Dominic on the back.

"Sure," he said. "But you're paying."

At three o'clock sharp, Mitchell met Renee in her classroom and had never been so happy to see his wife. "You'll never believe what happened," he said, and pulled her into a hug. "I don't want a divorce, Renee." He grabbed her by the shoulders so she'd focus on him. "Things are going to change. A lot of things. The first thing we're going to do is find a counselor who can help us. The second thing we'll do is find you a doctor, because I don't know what the fuck is going on with you."

Renee's brows narrowed.

"Then after that, we're going to enroll you in a kick-boxing class so you can take your frustration out on someone else."

She looked away and bit her lips between her teeth to stop herself from whatever she was going to say. Mitchell wasn't trying to make light of the situation and Renee didn't laugh about it. But then she finally smiled at him and pressed her head to his chest.

"I love you," she said.

"I know," he said. "I love you, too."

A few minutes later, his kids walked into the classroom, surprised he was there. The three of them swarmed around them into a big hug.

"Daddy," Luca said, "I lost another tooth."

Chapter 33

On Sunday, Sidra sat outside the Haunted House on the swing in the backyard, wrapped in a blanket in the cold late morning. The morning fog had disappeared, and the sun left a warm glow on everything it touched, but it didn't do anything to warm the air. Peaches sat on the swing next to her, keeping an eye on the few squirrels that dared come in the yard.

Sidra had only been in Grandma's house a few days, and she felt at home in a safe place to lay her head at night. As long as she ignored Grandpa Shackelford.

For the last thirty minutes, Sidra had been texting Mom because she hadn't planned to visit today for family lunch. The alone time to clear her head left her less guilty about things that were out of her control. Plus, she felt grumpy. That's what happened when your body screamed for alcohol it wasn't going to get.

A car door slammed shut and Sidra didn't bother to get up. Probably Mom coming to check on her. Mom would find her out back and they'd sit and talk about everything. But mostly—probably—just talk about Brady. But nothing was going to bring him back. Grief was a tricky bastard. And she didn't want her family to watch her go through it.

But it was Jorie who swung the back door open and ran to her. Jorie's arms wide open, her blonde hair blowing in the wind, the sunshine hitting her face with a kiss of the afternoon. Her niece threw herself in Sidra's lap.

"Hold me," Jorie said, and threw her legs on the swing as she wrapped her arms around Sidra's neck. Peaches climbed on top of her.

"Don't you think you're a little old for this?"

"Never," she said, and smiled brightly.

"How'd you get here?"

"Everyone's here," she said, and then Sidra saw them.

Her whole family. Some of them coming through the house, Mom and Dad walking around the yard. Her brothers, and her sister Amy. All of her nieces and nephews. Ian and her two sisters-in-law. The whole family walking to her, a Superhero Squad, coming to save her from herself.

She didn't go to them for Sunday lunch, so they came to her. Her family. The ones who were there for her when she never even knew it.

Sidra swallowed hard, and Jorie looked at her and wiped away Sidra's tears like a mother would do for her child. "I love you, Aunt Sidra."

Keep in touch at:

http://www.kristyroland.com

facebook.com/Kristy-roland

Thank you for reading!

Made in the USA
Columbia, SC
12 February 2022

55680950R00224

essential careers™

A CAREER AS A
COSMETOLOGIST

SALLY GANCHY

ROSEN
PUBLISHING®
NEW YORK

Published in 2013 by The Rosen Publishing Group, Inc.
29 East 21st Street, New York, NY 10010

Library of Congress Cataloging-in-Publication Data

Ganchy, Sally.
A career as a cosmetologist/Sally Ganchy.—1st ed.
    p. cm.—(Essential careers)
Includes bibliographical references and index.
ISBN 978-1-4488-8240-3 (lib. bdg.)
1. Beauty operators—Juvenile literature. 2. Beauty culture—Vocational guidance—Juvenile literature. I. Title.
TT958.G345 2013
646.7'2—dc23
                                        2012011682

Manufactured in the United States of America

CPSIA Compliance Information: Batch #W13YA: For further information, contact Rosen Publishing, New York, New York, at 1-800-237-9932.

contents

INTRODUCTION   4

CHAPTER 1: BECOMING A COSMETOLOGIST   7

CHAPTER 2: A FLAIR FOR HAIR   16

CHAPTER 3: SPECTACULAR SKIN   25

CHAPTER 4: MASTERING MANICURES   36

CHAPTER 5: CAREERS IN COSMETOLOGY   43

CHAPTER 6: GETTING A FIRST JOB AS A

               COSMETOLOGIST   56

GLOSSARY   67

FOR MORE INFORMATION   69

FOR FURTHER READING   72

BIBLIOGRAPHY   74

INDEX   77

INTRO

Hairdressing can be a great career for people who enjoy helping others feel their best.

DUCTION

Almost from the dawn of history, we have records of people using cosmetics and hairstyles to beautify themselves. Ancient Egyptians used cosmetics to line their eyes and redden their cheeks and lips. During ancient China's Chou Dynasty, royalty painted their fingernails gold and silver. The eighteenth century in France was a hairdresser's dream. Among the nobility, powdered wigs piled high with white hair, bows, ribbons, and even small sculptures of birds and ships were all the rage.

During the twentieth century in America, hair and makeup styles reflected the movements transforming society. Each decade there was a reaction against the styles and ideas of the past. In the 1920s, newly liberated women expressed their independence by chopping off their long hair and wearing sleek, Jazz Age bobs. In the 1950s, women celebrated the return to normality after a long war by creating elaborate hairdos that looked natural but were actually held in place with intense styling. The hippies of the 1960s and 1970s expressed their longing for a more free and natural lifestyle by growing their hair long.

Today, how we choose to wear our hair, nails, and makeup continues to reflect our values, aspirations, and preoccupations. Style can make a statement about who you are. Looking good can help you project an aura of confidence, competence, and control. Beautiful hair, skin, and nails can make a special day like a wedding or prom even more perfect. They can make an average-looking actor into a star. And who has the power to radically transform appearances? Cosmetologists.

Cosmetologists are professionals trained in the art of cutting and styling hair, manicuring nails, performing skin treatments, and applying makeup. Cosmetologists may be employed by a salon or spa, or they may go into business for themselves. They may work part-time to earn a little extra cash, or they may become fashion moguls who open up chains of salons in all of the world's great cities.

Cosmetology is a growing field that offers many different job opportunities. Cosmetologists are able to work with their hands and use their creativity to help people. They face new challenges every day. Are you up for it?

chapter 1

BECOMING A COSMETOLOGIST

Working in cosmetology—whether it's as a nail technician, makeup artist, hairdresser, or aesthetician (skin care professional)—doesn't just demand certain skills. It also requires specific personal qualities. Before you start to train as a cosmetologist, consider whether you've got the right stuff to become a first-rate beauty professional.

DO YOU HAVE WHAT IT TAKES?

As a cosmetologist, you'll be working with people all day, listening to them, talking to them, and learning about them. In fact, building relationships with clients is an important part of growing your business. If your clients enjoy your company, they'll be more likely to use your services again. You must be enthusiastic, outgoing, friendly, compassionate, diplomatic, and energetic.

Cosmetologists are creative, and they work with their hands. If you excel at sculpture, painting, design, or other arts, you'll find that those skills will serve you well as a cosmetologist. For instance, hairdressers need the eye of a sculptor as they cut and shape hair. Colorists and makeup artists need a painter's understanding of color.

It's also important to have an interest in fashion. Clients often rely on their hairstylists to keep their look updated.

Makeup artists are asked to provide fresh makeup ideas for special events.

A cosmetologist must be clean and organized. You must be willing to work quickly and efficiently so that you don't waste time during an appointment. You should be a self-starter, especially if you hope to start your own business.

OPTIONS FOR TRAINING

The journey toward becoming a cosmetologist begins with finding the right training. There are a number of different options, depending on your interests and goals.

There are vocational high schools across the country where students can start their cosmetology training before they get their high school diploma. However, these students will still need to complete some training after high school and earn a cosmetology license before going to work as a cosmetologist.

It is also possible to train as a cosmetologist at a college or university. At a college or university, you can learn cosmetology while taking advantage of a wider variety of educational opportunities. Colleges and universities may also offer more options for financial aid.

The most common route to becoming a cosmetologist is to enroll in cosmetology school, which is also known as beauty school. In many states, you must have graduated from high school or earned a GED to go to cosmetology school. Check the requirements in your state.

Some students opt to go to a school that only covers their specific area of interest. Therefore, you may hear aspiring beauty professionals talk about going to nail school, aesthetician school, hair school, barbering school, electrolysis school, or makeup school.

COSMETOLOGY SCHOOLS AND BEAUTY SCHOOLS

Cosmetology schools and beauty schools teach students the science and theory behind cosmetology and the basic techniques for beautifying and caring for hair, nails, and skin. At any cosmetology school, you'll have a textbook to introduce basic concepts and skills. You'll take tests, just like in high school. Many beauty schools have an in-school salon for students to practice their new skills.

It might be surprising, but good cosmetologists need to know the science behind their craft. It's helpful to know the biology of how nails, skin, and hair grow and how they become damaged or diseased. Cosmetology programs also teach a bit about chemistry so that you understand how the products you use will work on your clients. It is also important to know the hazards of some of the chemicals that you will be working with as a cosmetologist.

In cosmetology school, you'll learn how to style hair like a professional, from salon shampooing techniques to strategies for sculpting every type of hair. You'll practice executing all of the classic haircuts. You'll also learn the art of hairdressing, executing hairstyles like updos and French braids. Then there are hair treatments meant to change the texture or color of hair. You'll color and dye hair, create highlights, perform permanent waves, and straighten curly hair.

In cosmetology school, you will also learn about nails. You'll give manicures and pedicures and discuss how to choose proper nail treatments. You might opt to receive some advanced training in preparing and applying acrylic nails.

And no comprehensive cosmetology education would be complete without an introduction to aesthetics. In this area, you'll learn about the proper care of the skin. You'll learn how to give facials and how to safely remove unwanted body and facial hair. You'll also master makeup, from the basics to advanced techniques such as applying fake eyelashes.

Many cosmetology schools allow students to pick an area of focus. While it's important to get a strong overall education in cosmetology, it's also important to know your strengths and pursue a specialty.

Every aspiring cosmetologist needs plenty of practice. At the in-school salon at the Minnesota School of Beauty in Lakeville, Minnesota, instructor Angela Ericson (right) teaches hair coloring techniques to student Kellie Meier (left).

HOW LONG WILL IT TAKE, AND HOW MUCH WILL IT COST?

There is no hard-and-fast answer as to how long your education will take and how much it will cost. First of all, what do you want to do? If you live in Arizona and want to become an aesthetician, you will need to complete 600 hours of training and practice. You can get your license in that area alone. However, if you want to be licensed as a full cosmetologist, you will need 1,600 hours of experience in order to get your license.

Where you live is also a consideration. In New York, a cosmetologist needs 1,000 hours of training; in Idaho, 2,000 hours of training or 4,000 hours of apprenticeship are required for a cosmetology license. Of course, the process of going through cosmetology school will be longer in a state where the licensing rules require more practice hours. And if the schooling is longer, it will likely be more expensive. The average cosmetology program in the United States takes less than 2,000 hours to complete.

CHOOSING THE RIGHT SCHOOL

So you've decided to take the plunge and go to cosmetology school. How do you know if you're choosing the right school?

First, consider location. Where do you want to study cosmetology? If you want to stay close to home, it makes sense to look for a beauty school nearby. However, many aspiring cosmetologists are willing to travel far from home in order to attend a quality school or study in an area of the country with lots of job opportunities.

Of course, finding a school in the right place isn't enough. You'll need to do more research, asking many questions about each program. What classes does the school offer? Do the students practice on mannequin heads, or can they practice on

real clients in an in-school salon? Do students have the opportunity to take advanced courses in your preferred field of study?

What are the school's hours? If the school offers night and
weekend classes, it may make it easier to practice with real, live
clients or work while you go to school. How long is the program? Do students have to attend full-time, or can they go to
school part-time?

It is also a good idea to find out how successful the school
is at transitioning students into the working world. Does the
school offer assistance with job placement after school? What
percentage of the school's graduates find work in their fields?

Many students feel that it is important to go to an accredited beauty school. If a cosmetology school is accredited, it can
give government financial aid to its students.

To answer these questions, read the school's materials and
ask questions of school representatives. Visiting the campus
can help you decide whether the school is right for you. When
you're on campus, you can see the teaching style of the instructors and watch how the students interact with each other. Do
you feel comfortable at the school? Do you feel inspired? Try
talking to current students. What do they see as the school's
strong and weak points? Contacting graduates of the program
for information is a good idea, too.

FINANCING YOUR EDUCATION

Beauty school, while generally less expensive than many colleges
and universities, still costs money. Before you apply to beauty
school, consider whether you can actually afford it. Will the
school be able to help you with grants or loans? If not, can you
go to school part-time so that you can put yourself through
school by working? Does the school offer work-study programs?

Many students hope to spend as little time and money as
possible on their education. But remember, you can't fake skill

THE COSMETOLOGIST'S TOOLKIT

As a cosmetology student, you'll need to start assembling your professional toolkit. Here are just a few of the items you'll need:

Hair: Hairstyling tools, including combs, various styling brushes, smocks, shampoo cape, sectioning clips, styling shears, thinning shears, cutting shears, blow-dryer, rollers, curling iron, permanent wave rods, shaving razor, rubber gloves, and a mannequin head with real hair (for practice).

Nails: Manicure kit, including nail clippers, cuticle nippers, cuticle pushers, files, buffers, nail brush, and a bowl.

Makeup: Full makeup kit, including tweezers, eyelash curlers, applicator wedges, and a wide array of cosmetics.

This beginner's hairdressing kit includes various combs, shears, curling irons, curlers, brushes, a blow-dryer, and two mannequin heads for practicing styling skills.

and confidence in the salon. If you have a solid education, it will show in your work. Well-educated cosmetologists can work more efficiently and produce better results for their clients. As a result, cosmetologists who train at top schools have better job opportunities.

On the other hand, students who start their careers deep in debt face a big challenge. In the first few years of your career, when you're still building a client base, you will probably struggle to make ends meet. This will be even more difficult if you have to make big student loan payments. You will need to decide the right balance between the cost of your education and its quality.

BEYOND SCHOOL

Your journey to becoming a cosmetologist does not end when you finish school. Before you become a professional, you must obtain your license. You will take a written test and demonstrate your skills by carrying out a number of common beauty procedures while an examiner watches you work. Your beauty school should help you prepare for your state licensing exam.

chapter 2

A FLAIR FOR HAIR

Many cosmetology students make the decision to go to beauty school because they want to become hairdressers, also known as hairstylists. As a hairdresser, you can make a career cutting hair for children in your hometown salon or styling hair for models during Paris Fashion Week. It all begins with a solid education in hairdressing.

Hairdressing is perhaps the most demanding and difficult of the subjects in cosmetology school. Here is a taste of what a professional hairdresser is expected to know.

THE SCIENCE OF HAIR

Good hairdressers need to understand the science of hair. During your cosmetology training, you will learn all about the anatomy of the hair. You'll study the natural life cycle of hair—how hair grows and how it stops growing, falls out, and is replaced by new hair. You will discover what makes straight hair lay flat and curly hair curl. This might sound academic—until you consider that as a hairdresser, you will often be asked to put volume and curl into straight, fine hair or to make curly locks sit perfectly flat. You will likely get a basic grounding in chemistry so that you can recognize which commonly used hairdressing chemicals are useful for treating hair problems or achieving certain styling results. You will also be trained to spot medical conditions, such as dandruff and psoriasis, as well as infectious diseases and pests, such as head lice and scabies.

Your new scientific knowledge will help you answer clients' questions. It will help you plan your haircuts to look better even as they "grow out." And it will allow you to design cuts to cover bald patches, disguise thinning hair, or avoid strange growth patterns like cowlicks.

Since you'll be touching clients' scalps all day, cutting their hair, and perhaps sometimes even nicking their skin, you will learn to maintain a professional standard of hygiene. Your beauty school should teach you to disinfect your tools (scissors, brushes, combs, clips, etc.) and your work area after each client. It should emphasize the importance of keeping capes and towels freshly laundered. If you fail to maintain a high standard of cleanliness, you will run the risk of spreading infectious diseases.

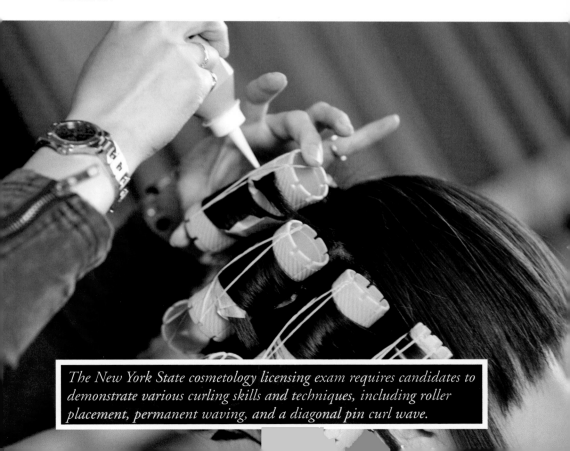

The New York State cosmetology licensing exam requires candidates to demonstrate various curling skills and techniques, including roller placement, permanent waving, and a diagonal pin curl wave.

HAIR CARE

Cosmetology school will introduce you to the basics of hair care for different hair types, from fine to thick, from straight to curly, from oily to dry. You'll learn which products can balance out an oily scalp, moisturize dry hair, and strengthen damaged hair.

Cosmetologists perform hair care tasks differently than untrained people do at home. There's a professional way to perform a shampoo in order to relax the hair, get rid of any tangles, massage the scalp, and prepare the entire head for a cut. There's a professional way to comb, brush, blow-dry, curl, and flat iron. These professional techniques all have one aim: to make hair look great without damaging it.

Speaking of damage, you will also learn how to spot hair that's been damaged by too much sun, clumsy or hasty styling, or excessive treatment. It's very important that you recognize damaged hair so that you can treat

Some high-end salons employ special shampoo technicians, who shampoo and rinse clients' heads, often in combination with relaxing scalp and neck massages.

COMMUNICATING WITH YOUR CLIENT

One very important part of designing a haircut is speaking with the client. After all, the goal is not necessarily to give the client the haircut you think would look best on him or her. You want to give the client a great new look that will fit the person's lifestyle, career, and personality. For example, you shouldn't give a wild, punky cut to a client who works at a conservative law firm. And you don't want to give a high-maintenance cut that requires a lot of styling to someone who doesn't even own a hair dryer!

Client communication goes beyond making sure that the cut fits the client. Sometimes a client may want to make a change that is impossible, considering his or her hair thickness, movement, or texture. Sometimes a client may request a change of texture that you believe will not be flattering. In cases like these, you need to be able to explain your concerns tactfully. In addition, it is important that you learn to recognize damaged hair. If a client with seriously fried hair asks you to perform a chemical treatment like a perm or relaxing, you will need to refuse and explain why. Knowing how to communicate with a client in an honest yet positive way is one of the cosmetologist's most important skills.

Communicating with your client is one of the most important steps in creating a hair design.

it gently as you cut and style it and teach the client to prevent further damage.

Hair Design

All great haircuts start with a great design. Studying hair design can help you plan your haircuts to complement different facial shapes, balance facial features, and help clients mask imperfections. For instance, oblong faces can be softened with short haircuts that kick out, or with layered looks. If a client has a round face, you can lengthen it with long hair. You'll learn what types of cuts work best for thick hair, fine hair, limp hair, tightly curled hair, and everything in between.

Once you know the theory behind which cuts look great on which faces, you can customize your cuts for the lucky person sitting in your salon chair. You can start to approach your work not just as a hairdresser, but also as an artist.

Hair Cutting and Styling

Taking a full head of hair and cutting it into a new shape may sound like a daunting task. That's why you'll learn how to use facial features as guides to keep your haircut symmetrical and balanced. You'll practice sectioning the hair before you cut it. And you will discover strategies for dealing with surprising hair growth patterns such as bald spots and cowlicks.

After you're trained to execute simple hairstyles like classic bobs, you'll learn advanced cutting techniques like notching, slicing, thinning, and chunking to create trendy and complicated, sometimes asymmetrical, styles. Your finishing touches are the key to creating sleek, sharp cuts; soft, feathery looks; and even chunky and funky styles.

No visit to the hairdresser would be complete without styling. Clients need the personalized attention of the stylist so

Good hairdressers know how to cut and style every type of hair, from thick and curly to fine and straight.

that they can see the full potential of their new look. You'll become a master stylist, using a hair dryer and brush to create volume or tame unruly and wild hair. You'll use irons to create curls or erase them. You'll be able to confidently pick styling products to recommend to customers so that they can recreate their new look at home.

Also covered in the curriculum of most beauty schools are braiding and adding extensions to your clients' hair. You may also learn how to care for wigs—a useful skill if you'd like to work in movies, television, or theater.

AFRICAN AMERICAN HAIR

As you probably know, African American hair comes with its own unique set of needs and rewards. African American hair is typically tightly coiled, which makes certain styles (such as Afros and dreadlocks) easier and other styles (such as long, straight hair) more challenging to achieve. There is a whole range of beautiful, culturally specific hairstyles, from braids to twists to fades to relaxed hair, that requires in-depth knowledge to create and care for. If you think that caring for African American hair will be a significant part of your career, you may want to consider going to a hairstyling school that focuses specifically on African American hair in addition to, or instead of, a wider cosmetology program that includes aesthetics and nail care.

Caring for and styling African American hair calls for special techniques, and often, special products.

HAIR COLORING

Many clients visit a salon because they want to change their hair color. They might want to cover up gray hair. They might want to correct for color changes that happened after a salon

A hairdresser helps her client choose a new hair color. Hairdressers need to know which hair colors complement various skin tones.

disaster, overtreatment, or other damage. Or perhaps they simply want to experiment with a new look.

You'll learn about how to recognize clients' true hair color and respect and work with the natural coloring of their skin. You'll understand the differences among various hair shades and hair tones. You'll study how to mix colors and identify how long each color takes to "develop" once it's applied to the hair. You will practice a variety of methods for applying color to a client's hair. By the end of beauty school, you should know how to tint hair, highlight it, lowlight it, or change its color completely.

Hair Texturing

Many clients book a salon appointment because they're dissatisfied with the texture of their hair. Changing a client's hair texture is one of the more difficult tasks that a hairdresser has to face.

Cosmetology school will teach you how to perform a permanent wave, or "perm," to change a client's hair from straight to curly. The process includes treating the client's hair with chemicals and heat. You'll also be initiated into the secrets of relaxing curly hair and making it straight. You may even study specialized treatments, learning to give your clients Brazilian blowouts or Japanese thermal hair straightening. Finally, you will practice instructing clients on how to care for their new style so that it will last a long time.

chapter 3

SPECTACULAR SKIN

Aesthetics, or the maintenance and beautification of the skin, is one of the fastest-growing subfields of cosmetology. There's so much to learn. Scientists and cosmetologists are constantly working together to create new cutting-edge techniques to rejuvenate and beautify the skin. Before studying these exciting new procedures, you need to learn the basics.

THE SCIENCE OF SKIN

You may have heard of collagen, pores, and UV rays. You probably know that each of these terms is related in some way to the skin. But could you define them all? If you choose a career as an aesthetician, you must be able to understand and use these terms, and hundreds of others, at a moment's notice.

The aesthetics curriculum begins with the study of the anatomy of skin. The skin is the body's largest organ. It covers the muscles, internal organs, and bones, and it protects us from pollution, injury, and infection.

The hair and nails are outgrowths of the skin. Hair and nails, however, consist of dead cells. Skin, in contrast, is living. Therefore, the skin can give us an important overall indication of a person's health. When people drink enough water, eat a balanced diet, exercise, and generally take care of themselves, their skin usually looks good. If they don't get enough sleep, are

This aesthetician works at a beauty supply store, helping clients find beauty products that will best suit their skin.

constantly dehydrated, or over-indulge in alcohol, cigarettes, or drugs, this tends to take a toll on their skin. Unhealthy living ages the skin prematurely.

SKIN CARE

Even the healthiest people need to take good care of their skin to keep it young and fresh looking. Many people don't realize just how seriously the sun's UV (ultraviolet) rays can damage their skin. Others have never given much thought to keeping their skin moisturized or hydrated.

An aesthetician is able to identify whether a client's skin is oily or dry, sun damaged or dehydrated. After making an assessment, the aesthetician recommends how the client might best improve his or her skin. Should the client get a facial treatment? Or perhaps change his or her diet or vitamin regimen? The aesthetician can help craft a plan of action to help clients improve their skin.

Aestheticians must educate their clients about how to use diet and lifestyle to keep their

Creating facial treatments can be one of the most satisfying and creative parts of an aesthetician's job.

skin looking good. They share tips with clients about how to use sunscreen, moisturizer, and other products to protect and preserve the skin. And they can plan and perform a course of facial treatments.

HYGIENE

A good aesthetician also learns to recognize various skin disorders. If you treat someone with a serious skin condition inappropriately, you may harm him or her. Moreover, if you treat a client with an infectious skin disease, you could spread that disease to other clients—or even catch it yourself.

However, not every disease is visible to the eye. That's why it's important that every aesthetician maintain a sanitary, sterile work environment. The people who give the aesthetics licensing exam observe carefully to make sure that candidates use sterilized equipment and that they know how to keep their work areas pleasant, clean, and safe.

FACIALS AND OTHER SKIN TREATMENTS

One of the most satisfying and creative parts of being an aesthetician is giving facial treatments. A facial typically includes removing the client's makeup, cleansing and toning the skin, and perhaps applying eye cream, massage cream, or other products. The aesthetician might also massage the face, scalp, and shoulders to stimulate blood circulation.

Other parts of a facial will vary from client to client. Exfoliating scrubs help clear away the very top layer of the skin, which is generally made up of dead cells, and reveal the healthy, vital cells beneath. This is also the goal of facial treatments such as microdermabrasion. In microdermabrasion, the aesthetician uses a special machine to blast dead cells off the surface of the face and reveal the younger, glowing skin underneath.

The aesthetician may also add a facial steam, pack, or mask. In your cosmetology program, you'll learn how to choose a prepared mask or design and create your own facial mask out of pure ingredients. The point of a facial mask—whether it is made from cucumbers, yogurt, honey, or mud—is to replenish and balance the skin. The same is true for packs, cream masks, and gel masks.

There are so many treatments, techniques, and options for people hoping to improve their skin. The choices are positively dizzying. That's why clients are willing to pay to consult with a skin care professional who can help them craft a personalized skin care plan.

WAXING AND OTHER HAIR REMOVAL TECHNIQUES

Skin care is not the only area that aestheticians handle. Aestheticians are often tasked with hair removal through waxing, plucking, or more specialized techniques.

Any hair removal process starts with a client consultation. Some clients should not undergo hair removal. If they have certain allergies, skin disorders, or are taking certain medications, having hair professionally removed may be dangerous to their health.

Aestheticians learn how to remove body and facial hair from both men and women. This might be a simple procedure, such as an eyebrow wax. It could involve using tweezers to pluck and shape certain areas or using a depilatory to weaken the hair and make it easier to remove. Whatever the method, you will have to learn to perform the hair removal procedure in the cleanest, most efficient, and least painful way possible. A waxer or other

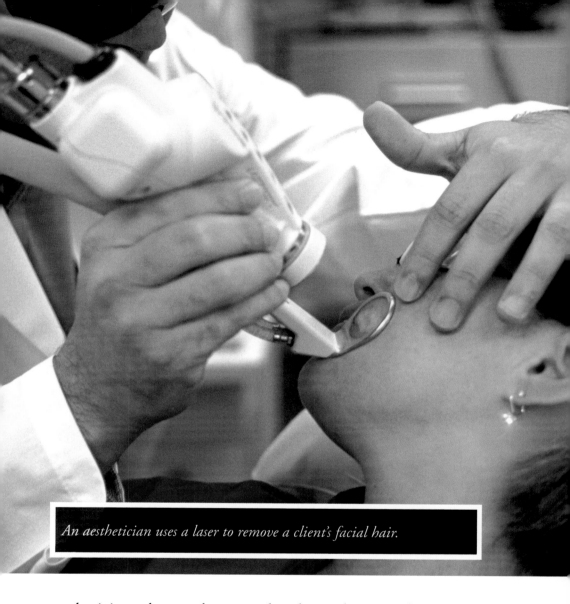

*An **aesthetician** uses a laser to remove a client's facial hair.*

aesthetician who can be trusted to keep clean conditions and treat clients with compassion will likely win a lot of return business.

Aestheticians may also learn more advanced forms of hair removal. These tend to be more expensive than waxing and tweezing, but they last longer, are cleaner, and in some cases, lead

OTHER AESTHETIC METHODS AND TREATMENTS

Aesthetics professionals are constantly at work inventing new ways to rejuvenate and beautify skin. Here are a few of the advanced methods that you may offer your clients as an aesthetician:

- **Desincrustation** uses a weak but steady electrical current to increase the amount of fluid that the skin can absorb and then flushes the skin with fluid. It is good for making oily skin less greasy and hydrating dry skin.
- **Manual lymphatic draining** is a type of massage that keeps lymph flowing through the body's lymphatic system, which helps immunize the body against disease. This massage is supposed to help the lymphatic system purge excess bacteria and waste.
- **Microcurrent** uses low doses of electrical current to imitate the electrical signals that cells send when the body is healing. This electricity is supposed to jump-start the body's healing process. Aestheticians use it to fight the effects of aging on the skin.
- **Acupressure** is a type of massage that stimulates pressure points (similar to those used in acupuncture) to relieve pain and stimulate healing.
- **Aromatherapy** uses fragrant oils and other fragranced products to reduce stress and promote a better mood. Some aromatherapists claim that aromatherapy can also be used to treat illness.
- **Hydrotherapy** uses water to relieve pain, relax patients, and sometimes treat specific medical problems. Hydrotherapy

is practiced in many spas and can take many different forms, including mineral baths, underwater massage, or even a simple soak in a hot tub.

- **LED light therapy** uses light waves that can pass through the skin to encourage damaged cells to heal. Aestheticians use this therapy to treat acne and reduce wrinkles.

A woman enjoys a water massage. Hydrotherapy is a popular treatment at many spas.

to permanent hair removal. These other methods of hair removal require advanced training and sometimes a separate license.

Electrolysis is a popular method of permanent hair removal. This method may sound somewhat strange. The aesthetician slides an extremely thin metal probe into a hair follicle and zaps it with electricity. The hair is destroyed, and the hope is that after several treatments, the hair follicle will be permanently damaged and will no longer produce hairs. There are many methods of electrolysis, all using different equipment. As an advanced procedure, electrolysis requires its own training. In many states, electrologists must obtain their own special licenses.

Laser hair removal works along the same lines as electrolysis. Instead of inserting metal rods into the hair follicle, the hair follicle is damaged with a laser. Another related hair removal process is photoepilation, which involves intense pulsed light.

Scientists and cosmetologists are always trying to find less painful and more permanent forms of hair removal. Perhaps by the time you study cosmetology, there will be a brand-new "hot" form of hair removal for you to master and offer to your clients!

MAKEUP

Part of your comprehensive cosmetology education will be learning about makeup. You'll begin by learning cosmetic color theory—what colors pair well with various skin tones and hair colors. You'll be trained to use all the major forms of cosmetics, from everyday items like lipstick and lipgloss to complicated cosmetics like individual fake eyelashes. Above all, cosmetology school will teach you how to use makeup to emphasize striking features, while downplaying features the client dislikes. This is called corrective makeup.

Makeup artists use makeup to create a wide variety of looks, from subtle to dramatic, demure to glamorous, conservative to outrageous.

Learning about makeup is typically a small part of cosmetology school, but there are people who make a living solely as makeup artists. There are even makeup academies where you can focus on specialty makeup, such as fashion makeup, bridal makeup, and special effects makeup. Going to cosmetology school may be useful for some of these career choices but irrelevant for others. If you have a clear vision of your future life as a makeup artist, do your research. Look up people who have the career you want, and find out how they got there. Follow in their footsteps.

chapter 4

MASTERING MANICURES

W e've already taken stock of the hair and skin secrets that you'll learn in cosmetology school. But your education won't stop there. Every beauty school student has to spend some time learning about nails. In fact, some students with a real passion for nails may choose to focus their careers in that direction, becoming manicurists, sometimes called nail technicians. Nail technicians are trained to clean, trim, and polish fingernails and toenails. Some skilled nail techs create nail extensions and fake nails. Many enhance their clients' experiences by providing hand, arm, foot, and leg massages.

A comprehensive cosmetology education will definitely come in handy as a nail technician because at some salons, manicurists are also expected to provide hair removal services.

THE SCIENCE OF NAILS

Before you beautify a person's body, you must understand it from the inside out. Manicurists or nail technicians must understand the anatomy of nails. They need to know how nails grow, what makes them weak, what makes them break, and what strengthens them. They should understand the chemistry of the nail so that they will know why certain substances adhere to the nails. This is especially important for nail technicians, since they spend so much time painting nails, coating them, or stripping them.

SAFETY AND HYGIENE

Just as in other areas of cosmetology, it's important to learn about safety and hygiene when working with nails. Some clients may be allergic to your materials, from nail primers and polishes to gel or acrylic tips. Nail techs work with a wide array of chemicals and processes that need to be treated with care. It is important, for instance, to the health of nail technicians and clients that manicures and pedicures be performed in well-ventilated areas.

Nail technicians should also know how to spot and deal with common problems, such as the fungal infections that can sometimes develop in the space between a natural nail and the false nail laid down on top of it.

MANICURES AND PEDICURES

As a nail tech, you'll become an old hand at performing manicures and pedicures. Typically, the nail technician follows a number of steps, including exfoliation and moisturizing; trimming or pushing back the cuticles; shaping, buffing, and cleaning the nails; and finally, polishing and drying. The manicure may also include extra services, such as a paraffin wax dip or a massage. Nail technicians also learn to do specialized manicures, such as men's manicures.

Pedicures follow the same basic procedure as manicures but come with their own set of challenges and rewards. If you're a person who hates looking at and touching feet, becoming a nail tech is definitely not for you! Not only will you have to clean and shape toenails, you will also have to file off calluses and deal with corns and blisters.

Figuring out ways to help clients grow strong natural nails while maintaining their preferred manicure schedule is part of an accomplished nail tech's bag of tricks.

During cosmetology training, you'll learn how to create different edges on nails using files, emery boards, cuticle knives, electric files, and other tools. You'll learn about how different shapes may complement or detract from various hand shapes—and what kinds of manicures will work best for different clients. Just as a wild haircut will detract from a conservative client's life, an easily broken manicure will be totally inappropriate for a client who works with her hands.

NAIL ART AND DESIGN

The fun part of giving manicures and pedicures is the ability to transform a client's nails through polish or nail art. Some of the nail designs covered in cosmetology programs include full coverage, half moon, hairline, and free edge. In cosmetology school, you will practice giving manicures that are designed to

Nail techs sometimes have the opportunity to create unusual, playful designs. These Hello Kitty nail art appliques were created by Japanese nail artist Yoko Matsuda.

simply augment and perfect the natural look of a hand, as well as manicures that involve acrylic tips and outlandish colors.

Today, there are so many ways for clients to make a fashion statement with their nails. Many manicurists enjoy creating fun nail designs or using nail wraps that allow them to apply complex pictures and patterns to nails, much like pasting over a billboard.

ARTIFICIAL NAILS AND NAIL ENHANCEMENTS

Many people go to cosmetology school to learn how to do the demanding work of creating nail tips and extensions. These "fake nails" are much more complicated and demanding than press-ons. As a nail technician, your clients will look to you to create strong, natural-looking, and fashionable nails. Some of the nail extension technologies that you might be called upon to use include silk, fiberglass, or linen wraps; acrylic tips; and gel nails.

Wraps are used to add strength and length to the nail. This can be done with silk, which is flexible, lightweight, and natural; linen, which is strong and thick and can be more noticeable than silk; and fiberglass, which can be both strong and flexible. These wraps are especially useful if the natural nail underneath a tip or extension has been damaged and must be protected.

Nail technicians also use acrylic nails to add length. First, artificial tips are added onto the nail. Next, the nail and tip together are covered with a layer of acrylic. A perfect shape is achieved by fitting a form over the nail and tip. After about fifteen minutes, the nails harden. These nails are formed chemically, so they must be removed with solvents.

Gel nails are similar in many ways to acrylic nails. Gel nails can look very natural, and they do not need to be polished to look great. They harden under a UV light. Plus, while acrylic

BRIDAL COSMETOLOGY

One of the most exciting and fast-growing segments of the cosmetology world is bridal cosmetology. Many women who normally wouldn't splurge on expensive beauty treatments are happy to spend a little extra money to look their best on their big day. Brides are big business for spas, hairdressers, aestheticians, and manicurists. Many brides even provide their bridesmaids with beauty treatments like facials, manicures, or hair styling as a thank-you gift for participating in the wedding.

Some hairdressers and makeup artists specialize in bridal hair and makeup. Many women decide that on their wedding day, they want a more elaborate hairstyle or a special look that will complement their dress. Those who specialize in bridal hair and makeup need to know how to execute elaborate hairstyles, especially those that can accommodate a veil, flowers, or other hair ornaments. Bridal makeup artists should be able to work quickly but meticulously under pressure. Promptness and responsibility are absolute musts! Anyone working with brides should be diplomatic, calming, and kind. Many cosmetologists who choose this field enjoy working with clients during one of life's happiest events.

Brides can be demanding clients, but helping a woman look gorgeous on her wedding day can be incredibly rewarding, both financially and emotionally.

nails have a strong odor, gel nails have the advantage of being almost odorless. However, gel nails are very difficult to remove; basically, the client must grow her nails out and cut the gel off a bit at a time.

Both acrylic and gel nails need to be filled regularly. As the natural nail grows out, it pushes the artificial nail away from the cuticle, leaving a gap between the skin and the artificial nail. A nail technician can "fill in" the gap with more gel or acrylic. This will also keep the nail strong. Nail techs also need to educate clients about how to care for their artificial nails.

NAIL TECHNOLOGY SCHOOL

Many students who know that they want to focus exclusively on nail technology may decide to skip cosmetology or beauty school and go straight to nail tech school. It is possible to obtain a license to do nails only, and the amount of time required to get this license is much shorter than the overall cosmetologist degree or license sequence. However, nail techs who exclusively give manicures and pedicures tend to make less money than cosmetologists who are able to offer their clients services in several different areas.

chapter 5

CAREERS IN COSMETOLOGY

S o you've graduated from cosmetology school and gotten your license. Now it's time to get down to work. Your license will open the door to a variety of wonderful cosmetology careers. Although there are some salons where you may be able to work in multiple fields of cosmetology, it's more likely that you will need to specialize.

HAIRDRESSERS AND BARBERS

The classic cosmetology career is hairdressing. You already know a hairdresser's basic duties: consulting with clients, cutting hair, styling it, and educating clients about how to care for their new cuts. As a hairdresser, you might work in a small-town Supercuts salon giving basic cuts to local families or in a high-fashion urban salon where stylists make big money working with demanding, wealthy clients.

Not all men feel comfortable going to a hairdresser. Some men prefer to go to a barbershop. A barber is a professional trained to cut and trim men's hair and care for their facial hair through shaves, trims, and grooming. In fact, many barbers go to special barbering schools.

School founder and senior instructor Augustine Souza (second from right) *oversees students at the Real Barbers College in Anaheim, California.*

MANICURISTS AND NAIL TECHS

Manicurists and nail technicians perform manicures and pedicures. At more advanced levels, they may lengthen clients' nails using acrylic or gel nails.

Some nail techs work in special nail salons that concentrate exclusively on giving manicures and pedicures. Others work in salons and spas that offer a wider array of services. In some salons, the manicurist may offer hair removal services or double as an aesthetician. Still other manicurists work toward opening their own nail shop.

AESTHETICIANS

Aestheticians are often employed by spas or salons to give clients facials, perform body wraps, and design skin care regimens. Aestheticians may also remove unwanted facial and body hair for clients. Some are trained in high-tech hair removal techniques, such as electrolysis, laser hair removal, or exotic and lesser-known techniques such as sugaring and threading. A firm grounding in cosmetology is recommended, as the aestheticians at some spas and salons are asked to give manicures and pedicures as well.

Aestheticians may also receive special training that qualifies them to offer their clients special services, such as aromatherapy, reflexology, acupuncture, LED light therapy, hydrotherapy, and acupressure. As an aesthetician, there will always be something new to learn to offer more value to your clients.

HAIR REMOVAL PROFESSIONALS

Some aestheticians specialize in hair removal. Electrologists specialize in permanent hair removal through electrolysis. Others focus on laser hair removal. These professionals are sometimes entrepreneurs who run their own businesses and build their own loyal clientele. They may work out of their own establishment or visit the salons and spas of others in order to practice their trade. Check your local laws to find out what the electrolysis licensing regulations in your state are.

PARAMEDICAL AESTHETICIANS

Paramedical aestheticians work in doctors' offices, helping to prepare clients for cosmetic surgery and other medical procedures. Paramedical aestheticians might offer other services like Botox injections, chemical peels, skin care after surgery, and hair removal for clients whose medical situation disqualifies them from seeing a regular aesthetician. Paramedical aestheticians also offer clients pre- and post-operative care for face-lifts. They might also use makeup to help clients conceal healing skin while recovering from surgery. In many states, paramedical aestheticians need a special license.

MASSAGE THERAPISTS

Massage therapists are often employed by a salon or spa to give clients relaxing and rejuvenating massages as part of a luxurious spa experience. But massage therapists can also alleviate serious physical pain. Using touch, physical pressure, and manipulations of the muscles through the skin, massage therapists can significantly improve a client's life.

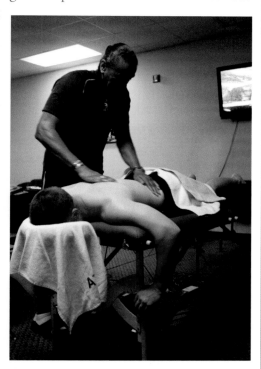

If you're interested in a career as a massage therapist, forgo cosmetology school and proceed directly to massage school. You'll learn many different techniques, including deep tissue massage, Swedish massage, Japanese shiatsu massage, and sports massage. Massage therapists may find employment with a salon, spa, hotel, resort, retirement home, or even a sports team. Others are self-employed, traveling with portable massage tables and making their own schedules.

Massage therapist Ozzie Lyles works for the Oakland Athletics, helping baseball players stay in prime condition. Here, he massages relief pitcher Joey Devine before a game.

MAKEUP ARTISTS

Some makeup artists make a living simply by working in cosmetic stores, beauty supply stores, or at cosmetic counters in department stores. There is no special training needed for these jobs. In fact, some beauty professionals recommend that if you are considering a career as a makeup artist, you might want to first get a job at a makeup counter or makeup store. That way, you can see whether the job is truly to your liking before investing in beauty school or makeup school.

As technology makes it easier to document our lives, makeup artists are more in demand than ever to prepare ordinary people for special events like weddings and proms. Bridal makeup is a lucrative and growing field. Even funeral homes employ makeup artists for mortuary makeup.

At higher levels, skilled makeup artists are in demand to prepare models for fashion shoots and runway shows. You must be extremely well respected and lucky to land these jobs.

Some makeup artists and hairstylists land glamorous jobs preparing models for photo shoots or fashion shows.

And of course, theater, film, and television productions always need makeup artists. The work in these industries can range from simply making a great-looking star look even better to artificially aging a young person, changing a person's gender, or even creating an outlandish character like an orc, werewolf, dwarf, or alien. Special effects makeup is extremely specialized and uses all sorts of advanced techniques like airbrushing and latex application. So anybody who is serious about going into this field had better be trained. Some special effects makeup artists attend special schools, while others apprentice with an established special effects makeup artist.

PERMANENT MAKEUP

"Permanent makeup" refers to the practice of tattooing designs that imitate makeup onto a client—for instance, applying lines on the eyelids that look like eyeliner or eye shadow. This field combines the skills of the makeup artist and the tattoo artist. The job is high stakes, and there is very little room for error. It requires special training and licensing. The demand for these services varies greatly from region to region. Research the demand for permanent makeup artists in your area before you commit to a course of study.

COLOR OR TEXTURE SPECIALIST

A salon might have a hair texture specialist who is responsible for taking on challenging texture jobs and staying informed about the latest hair texture procedures, techniques, and products. This specialist may also train other hairdressers in the salon to use new texture processes and products. Salons sometimes employ a hair color specialist, whose job is to perform expert highlights, lowlights, tints, and dye jobs. This colorist might also train fellow hairdressers in color application.

SALON MANAGERS

A busy salon needs a manager to keep the establishment running in an efficient and professional manner. The manager's job is to hire, train, and schedule employees. He or she also hires receptionists, janitors, and other staff. Managers order beauty supplies and ensure that the salon's equipment is in working order. Above all, the salon manager sees that the salon is running smoothly and that customers are happy.

Managing a salon isn't a job that you get straight out of beauty school. In general, managers start out as hair stylists or aestheticians. They learn about the creative side of the trade, get a little experience, and see how the salon works. After that, they may be able to take on more managerial responsibility.

SALON OR SPA OWNERS

Ambitious individuals with a passion for beauty often dream of owning their own salon or spa. The routes to this career are numerous. You might buy an existing salon so that you don't need to choose a location, buy fixtures, or build a clientele. Or you might build an entirely new salon from the ground up.

As the owner of a salon or spa, you must be aware of every detail of the business. Before attempting to be an owner, you should have already mastered all of the skills of the salon manager. Besides this, you must also deal with paying rent, paying employees, marketing the salon, attracting customers, and a thousand other day-to-day details of running a business. You must have a vision for your business so that you can create a plan of action that will make your dream a reality. This is a difficult career path, but the rewards can be tremendous.

Because there is so much involved in starting a successful business (or even buying an existing business and keeping it

Owner Nadine Debrowski (right) *and manager Meredith Mazak* (left) *show off their beauty business, About You salon in Bayonne, New Jersey.*

successful), many salon owners decide to study business at the college or graduate level.

BEAUTY SUPPLY STORE OWNERS

There are so many aspects of the beauty industry that take place outside of the salon. One important place is the beauty supply store, where professional cosmetologists—and some nonprofessionals—go to purchase shampoos, conditioners, cosmetics, styling tools, extensions, hair colors, and other supplies. If you've gone to beauty school, you, as the owner of a beauty supply store, will be able to apply your knowledge of basic anatomy and chemistry, your familiarity with the best brands and products, and your awareness of what tools beauty professionals need.

If your ambition is to own a beauty supply store, you may want to invest in business education. A solid business education will help you run your business in a professional manner and allow you to avoid unnecessary mistakes that could cost you your dream.

COSMETOLOGY INSTRUCTORS

It takes a special sort of person to become an instructor in a cosmetology school. A good teacher is organized, confident, patient, compassionate, perceptive, and passionate. And he or she can

FASHION INDUSTRY JOBS

Stylists who work in prestigious salons are sometimes given the opportunity to create hairstyles for fashion magazines and runway fashion shows. While this work can be exciting, fulfilling, and creative, it can also be difficult and fast-paced. In fashion shows, most stylists will work under a main stylist who creates the overall look; other stylists must learn the hairstyles and be ready to work quickly under pressure. In this industry, you need to know how to deal with difficult personalities, plus how to keep cool under pressure by troubleshooting small problems quickly and creatively.

Other fashion industry jobs include writers and editors for beauty and lifestyle magazines, trade show directors, and beauty product marketers.

communicate ideas clearly and succinctly. Of course, instructors should have several years of real-world experience under their belts and have a good reputation in the industry. The more respected you are in your field, the more attractive you will be to schools that might want to hire you.

Some beauty schools offer teacher training. Ask your favorite teachers at your beauty school how they got to where they are today. Perhaps you will be able to emulate their career paths.

SALON TRAINER AND MANUFACTURER EDUCATOR

Being a cosmetology instructor is just one way of working as an educator in the beauty industry. Many larger salons employ salon trainers. Salon trainers are responsible for training new employees to perform advanced techniques, such as hot new haircuts or new aesthetics techniques. As a salon trainer, you will help experienced cosmetology professionals improve their skills so that they can make their clients' lives better.

Many beauty supply manufacturers also employ cosmetologists as manufacturer educators. Manufacturer educators travel to salons and train cosmetologists to properly use their products. For instance, a manufacturer educator might travel throughout the northeastern United States introducing hairdressers to a new styling gel.

chapter 6

GETTING A FIRST JOB AS A COSMETOLOGIST

The personal appearance industry is growing all the time. According to the U.S. Bureau of Labor Statistics *Occupational Outlook Handbook* for 2010–2011, the number of people employed as personal appearance workers in the United States is projected to grow by 20 percent from 2008 to 2018. This growth rate is faster than the national average for other industries.

However, beauty, like many other competitive and exciting industries, can be hard to break into. The employer wants to hire someone with experience. But if nobody hires you, how will you gain experience?

APPRENTICESHIPS

Luckily, many well-respected salons run apprenticeship programs. As an apprentice hairstylist, you will observe master hairstylists at work and assist them. You may also shampoo clients, sweep up hair, and help keep clients comfortable. The salon is not only concerned that you learn how to cut, color, and texture according to their methods. It also wants to know that you will fit into the salon's culture—that you can be friendly and professional with clients and a good team member with your salon colleagues.

The pay for these jobs varies from place to place. In many salons, the apprentices earn minimum wage, plus any tips. You may be given the opportunity to give your own haircuts for a lower fee than senior stylists.

At this cosmetology training center in Cologne, Germany, trainees learn to style hair on mannequin heads.

Although apprenticeships are often associated with hairdressing, aestheticians have assistants and apprentices, too. Research the apprenticeship and internship opportunities in your area.

Some savvy students become apprentices while they are still going through cosmetology school. That way, they are more likely to be ready to earn their license and go straight to work when they graduate.

Some students go on to work at the same salon where they apprentice. However, this depends on a variety of factors. Before you take an apprentice job at a salon, it's worth asking yourself how well you fit in there. Do you feel comfortable? Have friends? Could you see yourself spending the next few years working there?

If you play your cards right, you may earn work experience and get your foot in the door at a great salon—before you even graduate from cosmetology school!

CAREER SERVICES AT COSMETOLOGY SCHOOL

Many cosmetology schools offer their graduates assistance with career planning and job placement. This means that the school guides you in your search and, in some cases, actively helps you find a job. In fact, this is one of the main factors you should consider when you are deciding where to go to school. Ask the schools to which you are applying for details on their job placement programs and other career services. Don't be afraid to ask to see job placement statistics or lists of graduates who have found work in prestigious salons.

JOB HUNTING

Although you may dream that after beauty school glamorous salons and spas will be immediately fighting over your services, the reality is that you will probably join many other new graduates as a job hunter.

One well-known job-hunting technique is to check the classified ads in your local paper, on job listing Web sites, and on message boards for open positions. To reply to these kinds of ads, you'll need an updated, neat, and professional-looking résumé. You'll also need an impressive portfolio, or "book," with photographs of your best work to date. Choose just a few exceptional looks to showcase. The styles you include in your portfolio should give the viewer a taste of your personal style while demonstrating that you can adapt your artistic vision to meet a client's needs.

In addition to applying for advertised positions, there are other job-hunting strategies you can try. Networking is important. Let your friends know that you're in the market for a new job! Ask your friends to tell you if they know about any salons that are looking for employees. Poll your friends and family about their favorite salons and spas. Then contact those places and let them know you are looking for work. Your classmates can be another good source of information—especially any who graduated before you. Consider creating a blog or a Web site highlighting your work, inspirations, and personal style. This can help you sell yourself to future employers.

If you are bold, try stopping by a salon or spa that you admire to show your résumé and book. Even if it's not hiring, it might be able to tell you about an establishment that is. Or perhaps it'll just keep your résumé on file. Either way, introducing yourself in a friendly and professional manner can't hurt! Always keep a positive attitude.

If all else fails, you can consider getting your foot in the door at a great salon or spa by starting out in a noncreative position, such as receptionist. In the meantime, keep making yourself more attractive to employers by staying on top of the latest techniques and learning how to do the hottest new procedures.

HAZARDOUS CHEMICALS AND SUBSTANCES

If you're contemplating a career in cosmetology, you should know that the work may pose risks to your health. Many potentially harmful chemicals are used in hairdressing. Hairstylists who color hair and do hair-straightening treatments may be exposed to fumes that can be hazardous to the lungs, eyes, and skin. Some develop asthma or skin conditions if they are exposed for too long. Nail technicians who work with acrylic nails run the risk of inhaling acrylic dust, plus fumes from polish and polish removers.

That's why it's important for cosmetologists to arm themselves with information. It's your responsibility to keep yourself educated about the health risks in your workplace. Read the labels of the products you work with, and always follow the safety instructions. If you are working with strong chemicals, wear plastic gloves. Whether you are a hairdresser performing a chemical treatment or a nail tech filing off acrylic nails, make sure that you work in a well-ventilated area and, if necessary, wear a mask. If you spill a chemical, make sure that you clean it up right away to minimize exposure to your lungs, skin, and eyes. If you are worried about the chemicals used in your workplace, contact your supervisor and ask if you can switch to a safer substance.

Of course, cosmetologists should also use commonsense safety precautions in the salon. Keep your work area and tools sterilized to minimize infections and pests. When hairdryers, curling irons, and other electric equipment are not in use, keep them unplugged. And finally, be careful while walking in the salon! Many a beauty professional has broken a bone after slipping on spilled water or hair trimmings.

Some hair salons employ colorists, who perform expert highlights, lowlights, tints, and other color changes. This colorist uses gloves to protect her hands from stains and chemical exposure.

PLANNING YOUR CAREER

Most of all, it's important to develop a clear image of what you want your career to be like. If you don't know what you want

Backstage at the Katie Gallagher 2012 fall fashion show in New York, lead hairstylist Cesar Ramirez prepares a model for the runway.

out of a career in cosmetology, it's easy to drift, unsure of the best route to take. Working in a salon seems just as good as working for yourself; staying in rural Alaska seems as good as moving to New York. But if you can articulate exactly what

you'd like your life to be like, you can plan backwards and craft a series of action steps for yourself.

Perhaps you dream of working backstage at fashion shows as a hairstylist. This may seem like an impossible goal to reach, but the journey of a thousand miles begins with a single step. Brainstorm a series of action steps that will move you closer to your goal, bit by bit. For instance, the most important fashion shows take place during fashion weeks: periods of time when designers show their collections in cities like New York, Los Angeles, and Miami. If you want to work backstage at a fashion show, you'll need to live and work in a city that has a fashion week. The stylists backstage at fashion shows are often hairdressers who work at prestigious salons. So you'll need to get a job at a respected salon in the city.

Next, break each action step down into even smaller action steps. For instance, before you can get a job at a prestigious salon, you need to know which salons are prestigious. Research the hottest salons in your city, and try to meet people who work in them. (Your school's career services can be helpful in making these kinds of contacts.) Then ask your contacts at those salons what they look for in employees. Where did most of their hairstylists go to beauty school? What qualities do these salons look for in an employee?

If you can't even imagine what action steps might lead you toward your goal, get on the Web and find some people who have already achieved your career goal. Contact them politely and respectfully, and ask them if they would be willing to talk to you about how they got where they are. If you find people who are willing to answer some of your questions, you might ask: did they go to an excellent beauty school? Which one? Did they gain some valuable experience in high school? Do they have any advice for aspiring cosmetologists? Ask yourself how you might follow the career path that they forged.

You can learn more about how to fulfill your beauty industry goals by reading trade magazines such as *American Salon* and *Modern Salon*. Consider attending beauty conventions and trade shows. Talk with any professionals you meet.

Connect with cosmetologists in your area, and ask them to share their thoughts about how you might build a career.

If you find yourself knocked off course, working in a job you don't love or a place you wish you could escape, don't give

Attending beauty trade shows is a great way to meet other professionals and pick up new skills. Here, stylists demonstrate haircutting techniques onstage at the 2007 International Beauty Show in New York.

up. Everyone experiences career setbacks. Keep trying to figure out how to get to where you want to be. In the meantime, keep educating yourself and improving your skills. Be prepared so that when an opportunity presents itself, you will be ready to seize it.

Launching a career may seem daunting now—and no one will tell you that it's going to be easy. But if you have a passion for beauty and you have determination, vision, and grit, eventually you will build a career. As Vidal Sassoon once said, "The only place where success comes before work is in the dictionary."

glossary

accredited Officially recognized as meeting the quality standards of an accrediting agency for curriculum, instruction, facilities, etc.

apprentice A junior artisan or craftsperson who learns from a more experienced colleague, while working for low wages in exchange for hands-on training in a trade.

barber A personal appearance worker who specializes in cutting men's hair and shaving facial hair.

callus A part of the skin that has become harder and thicker than the skin surrounding it.

chemical peel A beauty treatment that uses chemicals to peel a layer of dead skin away from the face, leaving younger and smoother skin behind.

corrective makeup Makeup meant to camouflage certain facial features or blemishes. Corrective makeup can be used to slim a face, mask a scar, and make features look more balanced.

cowlick A section of hair that grows in a different direction or pattern than the hair surrounding it.

cuticle The thick skin lining the sides and bases of the fingernails and toenails.

dandruff Flakes of dead skin that are sometimes found in hair.

diplomatic Able to deal with sensitive people and situations without causing offense.

exfoliation The process of washing or treating the surface of the skin with a cosmetic preparation in order to remove dead skin cells, revealing the healthy skin beneath.

financial aid Grants, scholarships, or loans intended to help a student pay for his or her education. Financial aid may be provided by a school, an outside organization, or the government.

hair follicle A small cavity in the skin where an individual hair is rooted. Each hair grows from a follicle.

hazardous Risky, dangerous, or potentially harmful.

head lice Tiny parasitic insects that live in hair and feed on blood through the scalp.

mannequin head A fake head with hair that is used by cosmetology students to practice techniques for cutting, styling, curling, and perming hair.

solvent A liquid substance that is used to dissolve another substance.

sterilization The process of killing any microscopic organisms such as bacteria, fungi, or viruses. Cosmetologists sterilize their equipment so that they will not unwittingly pass infectious diseases and pests between clients.

updo A hairstyle that sweeps the hair up, away from the face and neck, instead of letting it hang loose. Updos are often used for formal occasions like weddings.

vocational high school A high school that aims to give its graduates a firm grounding in a vocation, or trade, so that they will be ready to go to work soon after graduating.

for more information

Allied Beauty Association (ABA)
145 Traders Boulevard, East
Units 26 and 27
Mississauga, ON L4Z 3L3
Canada
(800) 268-6644
Web site: http://www.abacanada.com
The ABA is an association of manufacturers and distributors
of professional beauty products and equipment for use in
beauty salons and spas. It upholds industry standards and
organizes beauty trade shows in Canada.

American Association of Cosmetology Schools (AACS)
9927 E. Bell Road, Suite 110
Scottsdale, AZ 85260
(800) 831-1086
Web site: http://www.beautyschools.org
This association connects cosmetology educators with each
other and with potential students by publishing *Beautylink*
magazine, hosting conventions and conferences, and
maintaining the Web site BeautySchools.org, an excellent
resource for prospective cosmetology school students.

International Nail Technicians Association (INTA)
401 N. Michigan Avenue
Chicago, IL 60611
(312) 321-5161
Web site: http://www.americasbeautyshow.com
The INTA helps nail technicians grow professionally by
providing expert education; networking opportunities;

valuable information about fashion, trends, and techniques; and standards and ethics guidelines.

National Beauty Culturists' League (NBCL)
25 Logan Circle NW
Washington, DC 20005-3725
(202) 332-2695
Web site: http://www.nbcl.org
The NBCL is a trade organization for cosmetologists and
    allied industries, supporting the professionalism, excel-
    lence, and growth of the beauty industry. It has a special
    focus on multicultural beauty, making sure that cosme-
    tologists provide safe and professional care to African
    American, Asian, and Hispanic clients. It offers conven-
    tions, continuing education classes, and more.

National Black Cosmetology Association (NBCA)
P.O. Box 91
Somerdale, NJ 08083
(856) 873-6003
Web site: http://www.nationalblackcosmetologyassociation.com
This professional association focuses on providing commu-
    nity, networking, and advocacy for beauty professionals
    working with African Americans, particularly hairdressers
    and barbers.

Professional Beauty Association (PBA)
15825 N. 71st Street, Suite 100
Scottsdale, AZ 85254
(800) 468-2274
Web site: http://www.probeauty.org
The PBA is a nonprofit trade association that represents
    the interests of the professional beauty industry from

manufacturers and distributors to salons, spas, and beauty professionals. It offers a host of activities, including competitions, networking events, industry shows, professional development opportunities, and advocacy in Washington.

WEB SITES

Due to the changing nature of Internet links, Rosen Publishing has developed an online list of Web sites related to the subject of this book. This site is updated regularly. Please use this link to access the list:

http://www.rosenlinks.com/ECAR/Cosme

for further reading

Brown, Bobbi. *Bobbi Brown Makeup Manual: For Everyone from Beginner to Pro.* New York, NY: Springboard Press, 2008.

Davis, Gretchen, and Mindy Hall. *The Makeup Artist Handbook: Techniques for Film, Television, Photography, and Theatre.* Waltham, MA: Focal, 2012.

Ferguson Publishing. *Careers in Focus: Cosmetology.* 4th ed. New York, NY: Ferguson, 2008.

Gearhart, Susan Wood. *Opportunities in Beauty and Modeling Careers.* New York, NY: VGM Career Books, 2008.

Gelb, Adam, and Karen Levine. *Getting It Right: Milady's Survival Guide for Cosmetology Students.* Clifton Park, NY: Thomson/Delmar Learning, 2004.

Halal, John. *Hair Structure and Chemistry Simplified.* 5th ed. New York, NY: Milady/Cengage Learning, 2009.

Institute for Career Research. *Careers in Cosmetology: Hair Stylists, Makeup Artists, Skin Care Experts: Opportunities Nationwide in Beauty Salons, Barber Shops, Day Spas* (Careers, no. 54). Chicago, IL: Institute for Career Research, 2007.

Jefford, Jacqui, and Anne Swain. *The Encyclopedia of Nails.* Florence, KY: Cengage Learning, 2006.

Lees, Mark. *Skin Care: Beyond the Basics.* 4th ed. Clifton Park, NY: Milady, 2011.

O'Connor, Siobhan, and Alexandra Spunt. *No More Dirty Looks: The Truth About Your Beauty Products—and the Ultimate Guide to Safe and Clean Cosmetics.* New York, NY: Da Capo Lifelong, 2010.

Pope, Nicky, and David Goldman. *The Professional's Illustrated Guide to Haircare & Hairstyles: With 280 Style Ideas and Step-by-Step Techniques.* London, England: Lorenz, 2009.

Sandlin, Eileen Figure. *Start Your Own Hair Salon and Day Spa: Your Step-by-Step Guide to Success.* 2nd ed. Irvine, CA: Entrepreneur Press, 2010.

Sassoon, Vidal. *Vidal: The Autobiography.* London, England: Macmillan, 2010.

Stalder, Erika. *The Look Book: 50 Iconic Beauties and How to Achieve Their Signature Styles.* San Francisco, CA: Zest Books, 2011.

Tezak, Edward J., and Terry Folawn. *Successful Salon & Spa Management.* 6th ed. Clifton Park, NY: Milady/Cengage Learning 2012.

Toselli, Leigh. *Pro Nail Care: Salon Secrets of the Professionals.* Richmond Hill, ON, Canada: Firefly Books, 2009.

Wright, Crystal A., and Andrew Matusik. *Crystal Wright's Hair, Makeup, & Fashion Styling Career Guide.* 5th ed. Los Angeles, CA: Set the Pace Publishing, 2009.

bibliography

American Board of Certified Haircolorists. "ABCH Study Portfolio Full Edition." Retrieved February 27, 2012 (http://issuu.com/haircolorist/docs/abch_portfolio_complete_compiled/179).

Bailly, Jenny. "O Investigation: Hair-Straightening Treatments." *O, The Oprah Magazine*, October 2008. Retrieved February 27, 2012 (http://www.oprah.com/style/The-Truth-About-Hair-Straightening-Treatments).

BeautySchoolAdvisor.com. "Beauty School FAQ." Retrieved February 27, 2012 (http://www.beautyschooladvisor.com/beauty-school-faq).

Brain, Marshall. "How Hair Coloring Works." HowStuffWorks.com. Retrieved February 27, 2012 (http://science.howstuffworks.com/innovation/everyday-innovations/hair-coloring.htm).

Bureau of Labor Statistics. "Barbers, Cosmetologists, and Other Personal Appearance Workers." *Occupational Outlook Handbook*. 2010–11 ed. Retrieved February 27, 2011 (http://www.bls.gov/oco/ocos332.htm).

Cison, Kelly. "A–Z: What to Expect After Beauty School." FirstChair.com, June 9, 2010. Retrieved February 27, 2012 (http://www.firstchair.com/features/advice-for-new-stylists/a-z_what_to_expect_after_beauty_school_125292573.html).

Cormier, Colette. "How to Become a Makeup Artist." Squidoo.com. Retrieved February 27, 2012 (http://www.squidoo.com/becomeamakeupartist).

DeVellis, Michael. "Bridging the Gap: Elle." BehindtheChair.com. Retrieved February 27, 2012 (http://www.behindthechair.com/displayarticle.aspx?ID=979).

Fornecker, Amanda. "Here Comes the Bride...and a Lucrative Beauty Career." SpaBeautySchools.com. Retrieved February 27, 2012 (http://www.spabeautyschools.com/article/v/8426/here-comes-the-bride--and-a-lucrative-beauty-career).

Frangie, Catherine M. *Milady Standard Cosmetology*. Clifton Park, NY: Cengage Learning, 2012.

Gerson, Joel, Janet D'Angelo, Sallie S. Deitz, and Shelley Lotz. *Milady's Standard Esthetics: Fundamentals: Step-by-Step Procedures*. Clifton Park, NY: Milady/Cengage Learning, 2010.

HairdressingWorld.com. "Hairdressing Design." Retrieved February 27, 2012 (http://www.hairdressingworld.com/Hairdressing-Design).

HairdressingWorld.com. "Texure—Basic Hairdressing Design." Retrieved February 27, 2012 (http://www.hairdressingworld.com/Hairdressing-Design/Basic-Hairdressing-Design/texture.html).

Helmenstine, Anne Marie. "Hair Color Chemistry." About.com. Retrieved February 27, 2012 (http://chemistry.about.com/cs/howthingswork/a/aa101203a.htm).

Hudgins, Catherine. "Cosmetology Hazards." eHow Money, April 25, 2011. Retrieved February 27, 2012 (http://www.ehow.com/info_8293371_cosmetology-hazards.html).

Milady Publishing Company. *Milady's Art & Science of Nail Technology*. 2nd ed. Albany, NY: Milady Publishing Company, 1997.

Noelliste, Leila. "Beauty Schools Ignore Natural Hair at Their Own Peril." *Clutch*, July 13, 2010. Retrieved February 27, 2012 (http://www.thegrio.com/opinion/why-are-beauty-schools-ignoring-natural-hair.php).

OneSkin.com. "Features—Basic Skincare." Retrieved February 27, 2012 (http://dermatology.netfirms.com/oneskin.com/Features/skincare.html).

OneSkin.com. "Skin Anatomy." Retrieved February 27, 2012 (http://dermatology.netfirms.com/oneskin.com/skin Anatomy/skin%20anatomy.html).

Purifoy, Jennifer. "History of Fashion—History of Cosmetics." Digital History. Retrieved February 27, 2012 (http://www.digitalhistory.uh.edu/do_history/fashion/ Cosmetics/cosmetics.html).

Purifoy, Jennifer. "History of Fashion—History of Hair." Digital History. Retrieved February 27, 2012 (http://www .digitalhistory.uh.edu/do_history/fashion/Hair/hair.html).

Rosevear, Paul D. "Keeping It Healthy at Esthetics Schools." Retrieved February 27, 2012 (http://www.spabeautyschools .com/article/v/837/keeping-it-healthy-at-esthetics-schools).

Spear, J. Elaine. *Haircutting for Dummies*. Hoboken, NJ: Wiley, 2002.

Warfield, Susanne S. "Planning Your Esthetician Career." BeautySchool.com, June 1, 2010. Retrieved February 27, 2012 (http://www.beautyschool.com/blog/beauty-jobs/ esthetics-career-planning).

index

A

acne, 33
acrylic nails, 40, 42, 45, 60
acupressure, 32, 46
acupuncture, 32, 46
aestheticians, overview of job,
    25–35, 45–46
  paramedical, 46
American Salon, 64
apprenticeships, 56–58
aromatherapy, 32, 46
asthma, 60

B

baldness, 17
barbers, 43
beauty school, 9–11, 54, 58
  career services, 13, 54, 58, 64
  cost, 12
  duration, 12
  financing, 13, 15
  how to choose, 12–13
beauty supply store owner, 53
blisters, 38
Botox, 46
bridal cosmetology, 41, 48

C

calluses, 38
chemical peels, 46

chemistry, 9, 16
clients, communicating with, 7, 19
college or university education, 9, 53
color specialist, 7, 50
corns, 38
corrective makeup, 34
cosmetologists, characteristics of,
    7–8
cosmetology, history of, 5
cosmetology instructors, 54
cowlicks, 17

D

damaged hair, 18, 19, 20, 24
dandruff, 17
desincrustation, 32
depilatory, 30

E

electrolysis, 34, 45, 46
entertainment industry, careers in,
    35, 50
exfoliation, 29, 38

F

face-lifts, 46
fashion industry, careers in the, 16,
    35, 48, 54, 63
financial aid, 9, 13
fungal infections, 37

G

gel nails, 40, 42, 45
general equivalency diploma
    (GED), 9

H

hair
    African American, 22
    care, 18, 20
    coloring, 10, 22–24
    cutting and styling, 10, 20
    design, 20
    science of, 9, 16–17
    texturing, 10, 24
hairdressers, overview of, 16–24, 43
hair removers, 30–31, 34, 36, 45, 46
hazardous chemicals, 10, 37, 60
hydrotherapy, 32–33, 46

J

jobs
    planning a career, 62–66
    searching for, 58–59

L

laser hair removal, 34, 45, 46
LED light therapy, 33, 46
lice, 17
licensing, 9, 12, 15, 29, 34, 46, 50

M

makeup artists, overview of career,
    35, 48–50
manicurists and nail techs, overview
    of career, 7, 36, 45

manual lymphatic draining, 32
manufacturer educator, 55
masks, 30
massage therapists, 47
microcurrent, 32
microdermabrasion, 29–30
Modern Salon, 64
mortuary makeup, 48

N

nails
    art and design, 39–40
    artificial and enhancements, 10,
        40, 42
    manicures and pedicures, 10, 38–39
    safety and hygiene, 37
    science of, 9, 36
nail technology school, 42
nail wraps, 40
networking, 59

P

permanent makeup, 50
permanent wave, 19, 24
photoepilation, 34
plucking, 30, 31
portfolio, 59
psoriasis, 17

R

reflexology, 46
relaxers, 24
résumé, 59

S

salon manager, 51
salon owner, 51–53

salon trainer, 55
scabies, 17
skin
   care, 10, 27–29
   hair removal, 10, 30–34
   hygiene, 29
   makeup, 10, 34–35
   science of, 9, 25–27
   treatments, 10, 27, 29–30
spa owner, 51–53
student debt, 15
stylists, 54
sugaring, 46

T

texture specialist, 50
thinning hair, 17

threading, 46
tools, 14
training, 8–9

U

ultraviolet (UV) rays,
   25, 27

V

vocational high schools,
   8–9

W

waxing, 30, 31
wigs, 21
work-study programs, 13

ABOUT THE AUTHOR

Sally Ganchy is an educator and author living in Brooklyn, New York. She has worked with at-risk youth on study skills and career counseling. She has also written books for Rosen about how to use your interests, hobbies, and skills to build a career.

PHOTO CREDITS

Cover (model) © iStockphoto.com/Nikola Miljkovic (head and hands); cover (background), p. 1 © iStockphoto.com/Nicholas; p. 4 Wavebreak Media/Thinkstock; p. 8 Zoonar/Thinkstock; pp. 10–11 © Joel Koyama/Star Tribune/Zuma Press; p. 14 © Marianna Industries; pp. 17, 23 Imagemore Co, Ltd./Getty Images; p. 18 Jupiterimages/Comstock/Thinkstock; pp. 19, 28, 48–49 iStockphoto/Thinkstock; p. 21 rolfo/Flickr/Getty Images; p. 22 George Doyle/Stockbyte/Thinkstock; pp. 26–27 Dave and Les Jacobs/Blend Images/Getty Images; p. 31 Michelle Del Guercio/Photo Researchers/Getty Images; p. 33 Ray Kachatorian/Taxi/Getty Images; p. 35 MartiniDry/ Shutterstock.com; p. 37 © Bost Anne-Sophie/Oredia Eurl/ SuperStock; p. 38 Christopher Elwell/Shutterstock.com; p. 39 Yoshikazu Tsuno/AFP/Getty Images; p. 41 Mel Yates/Digital Vision/Getty Images; pp. 44–45 © Paul Rodriguez/The Orange County Register/Zuma Press; p. 47 Michael Zagaris/ Getty Images; pp. 52–53 Reena Rose Sibayan/The Jersey Journal/Landov; p. 57 © vario images GmbH & Co. KG/Alamy; p. 61 Hutch Axilrod/Photodisc/Getty Images; pp. 62–63 Amy Sussman/Getty Images; pp. 64– 65 © AP Images; back cover © iStockphoto.com/blackred.

Designer: Matt Cauli; Editor: Andrea Sclarow Paskoff; Photo Researcher: Marty Levick